A MEETING OF MINDS

Dr. Harris reached out and grabbed the cheery yellow CAN I READ YOUR MIND? button pinned to the young professor's jacket long enough to read it. Then he tapped the button sharply with a forefinger, twice. "The answer is no. Not mine, not anyone's. Did you hear my address just now?"

"Yes," Jonathan managed.

"Then I can only assume you did not understand it," Harris said. "This prattle of yours about 'directly observing consciousness as a property of living systems'—ludicrous."

Sucker-punched, Jonathan gaped, staggered. The quote was not from the sheet he had handed Harris, but from his submission to the symposium's review committee.

Harris was not finished. He leaned closer, crowding Jonathan and looming over him at the same time. "You might as well be trying to photograph fairies or phlogiston. Listen carefully, and you might rescue your career: Mind does not exist. Only brain exists. You are wasting your time, Dr. Briggs—and mine."

Also By Michael Kube-McDowell

The Trigon Disunity Future History:

Emprise (1985)

Enigma (1986)

Empery (1987)

Alternities (1988)

The Quiet Pools (1990)

Exile (1992)

Star Wars:
The Black Fleet Crisis Trilogy:

Before the Storm (1996)

Shield of Lies (1996)

Tyrant's Test (1997)

With Sir Arthur C. Clarke:

The Trigger (1999)

MICHAEL
KUBE-MCDOWELL

VECTORS

BANTAM BOOKS

VECTORS

A Bantam Spectra Book / November 2002

SPECTRA and the portrayal of a boxed "s"
are trademarks of Bantam Books, a division
of Random House, Inc.

ISBN 0-553-29824-0

Published simultaneously in the United States and Canada

Bantam Books are published by Bantam Books, a division
of Random House, Inc. Its trademark, consisting of the
words "Bantam Books" and the portrayal of a rooster,
is Registered in U.S. Patent and Trademark Office and
in other countries. Marca Registrada. Bantam Books,
New York, New York.

PRINTED IN THE UNITED STATES OF AMERICA

OPM 10 9 8 7 6 5 4 3 2 1

In memory of Marion Zak
and John McDowell

who now know
the answer
to the question

ACKNOWLEDGMENTS

The song *Circles* is copyright © 1977 by Gwendolyn Lee Zak, and is used by permission.

Many friends have been part of a long-running exploration of the themes of this novel. To preserve their privacy, I would like to thank them obliquely by place rather than by name: Starwood, Otter Creek Park, Heartstone, Windshadow, Hotel California.

The following people graciously answered questions in their areas of expertise or previewed portions of the work in progress:

Arlene E. Bradford, *University of Michigan Office of Continuing Medical Education*

Cindee Hayes, *Briarcliffe Apartments*

Colleen, *Village Green of Ann Arbor*

Dr. Rob Allen, *USAF*

Eve Madsen, *University of Michigan Department of Biology*

Greg Cronau

Michael J. Tines, *Assistant Manager, Huron Towers*

Dr. Michael A. Kron, *Associate Professor of Medicine, Michigan State University*

Brian Proctor
Villy Somthida, *California Alumni Association*
Susan Carpenter, *University of Michigan
    Department of Neuroscience*
Arlyn Wilson
and the GEnie gang, R.I.P.

The following allies made other invaluable contributions to the writing of this book:

Russell Galen, *Scovil Chichak Galen
    Literary Agency*
Betsy Mitchell, Tom Dupree, Michael Shohl,
    and Juliet Ulman, *Bantam Spectra*

Special thanks to my wife, Gwen, for her unwavering love and support, and to my children, Matt, Amanda, and Gavin, for helping make the future something to look forward to.

CONTENTS

1 The Dance of the Electrons   1

2 The Intersection of Purposes   15

3 A Discontinuity in the Continuum   74

4 The Fine Thread of Reason   112

5 The Inchoate Incarnate   157

6 A Spark Flies Upward   219

7 The Ghost in the Machine   256

VECTORS

1

The Dance of the Electrons

Dr. Jonathan Briggs's train from Toronto was stopped and boarded by armed men twice before it reached Ann Arbor. It was almost enough to give him second thoughts about his journey.

In Windsor, the VIA New International was halted on the main line, in a right-of-way corridor flanked by walls of green trees. Customs & Revenue agents swept the train with bomb-sniffing dogs and chemical-sniffing wands. The agents were polite and quietly professional, and their sidearms remained invisibly holstered. In less than thirty minutes, they had satisfied themselves that it was safe to send the train on through the tunnel below the Detroit River.

In Detroit, what had become the Amtrak New International was diverted to the edge of a deteriorating concrete sprawl in front of a towering ruin of a train station. Looking out his window, Jonathan could hardly believe it was the same season—everything was a depressing bombed-out brown.

But it was clearly not the same country. Homeland

Security officers carrying unslung automatic weapons herded the passengers off the train and into the shabby structure for processing. More men with assault rifles looked on from the rooftops, and a three-meter-high fence topped with razor wire steered them in the right direction. After two hours, their keepers had still not satisfied themselves that it was safe to allow the passengers into the country.

"Is it always like this?" he asked a fellow passenger as they waited together in a plywood-walled cubicle to be called to their interviews.

"Since the trouble at the Ambassador Bridge," the man said with a bob of his head. "But it's worse trying to cross the border in a car. You Canadian?"

"Mostly."

The stranger grunted. "Aren't you headed the wrong way, then?"

It wasn't the first time he'd been asked that question. His mentor at the University of Toronto, Dr. Bernard Hoffman, had tried to talk him out of applying for the neuroscience post at the University of Michigan.

"You should be catching an elevator going up, Jonathan—not an elevator going down," Hoffman had said. "I can think of ten schools where you'd be better off, and at least half of them would be happy to have you. Hell, there're probably a half dozen research labs that'd be interested, and you'd get paid twice as much and not have to teach."

But Jonathan had his reasons, and he had prepared for his interview with Dr. Elizabeth Froelich as diligently as a presidential candidate preparing for a debate he could not afford to lose.

The train finally reached Ann Arbor in late afternoon, giving him time to walk through the campus and spot some of the blemishes that the official tour would bypass. The obvious blemish was hard to miss: the red brick and wrought-iron "castle wall" going up all around the main campus, turning it into an island fortress in the middle of the city.

Though he was curious to see it, the wall was not a surprise. The *Observer* and the *Michigan Daily* had thoroughly documented the violent year on campus, the worst in a decade-long deterioration of the atmosphere on and near campus. There had been shootings on the Diag and in the Law Quad, two dozen rapes in the dorms, and four murders.

The perpetrators were nearly all outsiders, many from Ypsilanti and points east. But the victims were nearly all students. Even so, it had taken a student strike, a donor revolt, the exodus of several key professors, and—finally—the glare of national publicity to break through the denial and force the decision to create a closed campus.

It was clear to Jonathan that the "Harvard of the Midwest" reputation of the university and the cosmopolitan cachet Ann Arbor had once enjoyed were both on the wane—victims of the general economic blight and the violence that had crept westward from Detroit until it engulfed both. The new wall was a symbol of the new realities: Ann Arbor was no longer a place where graduates strove to linger, and the university no longer quite the magnet for top talent it had once been.

But that was not enough to keep him away. In fact, as he wandered, he counted it as a reason to hope.

Card scanners kept him locked out of the Medical Science Research buildings, but he roamed through the University Hospital and most of the Kresge labs unmolested. At the Taubman Medical Library, he took over a terminal and spent half an hour sizing up the collection and the connections. Along the way, he struck up conversations with anyone who seemed receptive—

half a dozen students, a cheerful clerk in Research Administration, and a pair of facilities engineers on their dinner breaks.

As night was falling, he wandered out into the city, scouting the storefronts, browsing at Borders and Ulrich's. When hunger seized him, he indulged himself with a massive deli sandwich, a Vernors, and a poisonously rich dessert at Zingerman's. He took his time eating, eavesdropping on the students and townies at the other tables and scrolling through the free papers he'd downloaded at the counter—an arts calendar, a sex-classifieds rag, and an eccentric alternative paper called the *Iconoclast*.

By the time he returned to his hotel room, he was already starting to feel that he was where he belonged. The only obstacle left was to persuade Dr. Froelich of that.

Though barely five feet tall and elfin in face and build, Dr. Elizabeth Froelich had a sharp, sure mind and a quick tongue that earned her all the authority her appearance tended to deny her. She was friendly but focused during the tour of the medical center, and even her casual questions seemed meaningful. In the privacy of her sun-bright office, her questions were pointed, probing, and hard to answer with interview glibness. More than an hour spun by before she showed any interest in the details of his vita.

"You worked for Dr. Hoffman at the University of Toronto?" she asked, lifting one corner of a paper on her desk, then letting it drop.

"Yes."

"And did your masters' work with James Anderson, at MIT."

"Yes," Jonathan said, shifting in his seat. "He retired the spring I graduated, or I would have stayed there."

"Fine letters of recommendation. They were both obviously impressed with you. As I am, to be honest. Jonathan, can I be blunt?"

"Of course."

"Why do you want to come here?"

He cocked his head at her. "What do you mean?"

"Your credentials are excellent. Your recommendations are glowing. Your thesis is interesting and probably publishable. The field is healthy enough that someone like you has lots of options," Froelich said. "I'd like to have you here, but I don't want to bring in someone who thinks hanging out for a year or two at Michigan would be a great way to cozy up to a biomedical company."

"Dr. Froelich, it's probably a character flaw, but I hate the idea of letting some MBA or marketing guru tell me what I'm supposed to be interested in," said Jonathan. "If I wanted that, I could have gone into making widgets, or politics."

She laughed, startled. "I've lost a senior professor and three associates in the last eighteen months. I don't want to bring in someone who sees this as a steppingstone to what they really want. So I need to know what you really want."

"I want to see your other triaxial SQUID," Jonathan said, sitting forward. "After I've seen it, I'll be able to tell you the rest."

"The other one? You already saw the one that's available."

"I saw the one that already has a date for the prom. I want to see the one that's been sitting home alone."

Shaking her head, Froelich flashed a quizzical smile. "You know, I've had candidates try to hold me up for university cars, free housing, and the department secretary's phone number, but this is the first time I've ever had someone ask me to fix them up with a dead SQUID," she said, her smile broadening at the punch line. "But, all right—let's go get the key from Charlie. We've been keeping your date locked up in the basement."

The BioImaging SuperSQUID superconducting quantum interference device was a triaxial 3-D scanner design based on the 2005 New York University prototype. By using compact fast-response "warm" superconductors licensed from IBM, BioImaging had cut the size and cost of the system in half.

Even so, the guts of the machine occupied four gray cabinets the size of dormitory refrigerators and required a control station worthy of a small research reactor. The cabinets, the crates of cabling and auxiliary equipment, and the several file boxes of manuals nearly filled the little windowless storeroom.

Froelich stood by the door and looked on silently as Jonathan removed plastic dust tarps and peered through the slatting of the crates. "Is it all here?" he asked finally. .

"As far as I know. Are you going to tell me why you're so interested in it?"

Jonathan straightened up and looked back at her. "There are nineteen SuperSQUIDs in Canada, and they're all still front-line diagnostic machines with three-month waiting lists," he said, brushing at a smear of greasy dust on the sleeve of his dark blue suit coat. "But there're more than 160 of these beasts in the United States, and most of them are considered two generations behind the technology curve. This is one of three that aren't being used at all—the other two are at NIMH and Cambridge Neuroscience."

She nodded uncertainly. "The University Hospital replaced this one with a META scanner a year ago. They tried to sell it, but the offers were so pathetic that the U decided to keep it. I offered it to the department, but no one had any use for it. So it's waiting here to be cannibalized for parts—we'll probably end up selling it a piece at a time."

"I have use for it," he said, and started making his way back toward her. "You asked me what I want. What I want is for you to take this thing off the market and have it moved into a lab with my name on it. I can't take the work I want to do any farther without this equipment, or the freedom to modify it in ways that'll probably make it useless to anyone else."

His boldness took her by surprise. "What problem do you intend to work on?"

"The same one you addressed in your master's thesis. The problem of consciousness. Is consciousness a metaphor? An illusion? Or a process? How does the brain experience itself? What is it that thinks, and even thinks about thinking?"

Despite herself, Froelich smiled, pleased and surprised. "That's another interviewing first for you. They've always read my last paper, but my master's thesis—well, you are thorough. Go on."

"Everyone's interested in disease, because that's where the money is. Neuropsychiatric disorders and neurotherapy. Alzheimer's and alcoholism. Learning disabilities." He was gesturing animatedly with his hands. "Well, I already told you I'm not interested in going into business. I'm interested in the healthy mind. I want to reopen some of the questions the Dennett school closed—individuality, personality, personal identity."

"Metaphors," she said. "Not neurologically meaningful."

"You didn't believe that eighteen years ago."

"Eighteen years ago I was—younger."

He pounced on her answer. "But there's something inside you providing continuity between then and now, something that connects yesterday and today— the I, the ego, the self. Something endures. That's what I want to look for—that something."

"I see now where your doctoral work fits into that. But—"

"Dr. Froelich, I want a chance to show that personality isn't just a psychological metaphor. I want to look for the neural signature of human individuality, the DNA code of our uniqueness. I think it exists. I think I can find it. I think Anderson vector matrices are the key. And this machine is the key to mapping them."

She nodded slowly and pursed her lips. "This is a serious question, Jonathan—if such a signature exists, why is it still waiting for you to be its discoverer?"

"Maybe because no two people think alike—"

"You're assuming your conclusion," she said with a hint of a smile. "Not a good start."

"Maybe because no one else has looked for it. Everyone's written off consciousness in favor of neurochemistry. And, yes, they've made wonderful discoveries—but what they've discovered doesn't cover all the bases. A program needs more than code. It needs structure."

"So—you want to use my department as a base from which to declare war on Clement Harris and the materialists?"

"That sounds like a jazz band," Jonathan said, wrinkling his brow. "Dr. Froelich, I am a materialist. But I'm not satisfied with the answers we have to the paradox of consciousness. Are you? Don't you feel like a 'you' exists? Don't you speak and act and think of yourself as though there were something more to experiencing than some complicated set of electrochemical levers inside the skull?"

She frowned and crossed her arms. "Yes."

"Even what we're doing right now—is this a conversation between two minds, or two neurochemistries? The Dennett disciples would say there's no distinction. Dr. Froelich, what do you say?"

She was looking at him oddly. "Two minds," she said. "I would vote for two minds. We share the same universal neurochemistry and we still think differently."

"Exactly," Jonathan said. "Because there's something sitting on top of consciousness, mediating experience."

"*Cogito ergo sum.*"

"Yes! Nothing enters the mind without first being translated by the consciousness. So that's where I have to look to see what a human being really is."

"Then you're looking for nothing less than the soul—the ghost in the machine. Do you believe in souls, Jonathan?"

"No," he said firmly. "Do you believe in ghosts?"

She thought for a moment. "Yes," she said. "I have no choice. If I say no, I deny myself. Tell me, do you have any idea what it is you're chasing?"

Words had been pouring out of him, but that question stopped the torrent for a moment. "I really don't know," Jonathan said slowly. "I imagine it as some kind of dynamic synthesis—thought, experience, hormonal cravings, sensory responses, all captured in the vector matrix. I could see it being an elegant organic program that starts with biology alone and then overtakes it, becomes self-modifying and starts grabbing the biological interrupts. But, the reality—"

He raised his hands in surrender. "If I knew, I wouldn't need this job, or this machine. Dr. Froelich, how many candidates are you interviewing?"

"Seven."

"How many of us have you already seen?"

"As it happens, you're the last of them."

"Do you have a timetable for making a decision?"

Dr. Froelich pursed her lips and sighed. "Jonathan, I don't think you even realize that this conversation would have blown your chance to get hired at ninety-nine out of a hundred labs."

"I only need one position—this one. Dr. Froelich, you said you wanted stability," he said earnestly. "I'm looking at two years' work just getting the system up. I only have fifty-one vector maps, all of them just three-axis—I need better maps and I'm going to have to collect tens of thousands of them, do longitudinal case studies. For better or worse, if you want me here, I'll likely still be here when you retire."

"I want to make something very clear," she said, frowning. "I'm not just hiring a researcher. Our budget doesn't allow us that luxury. You're going to have to teach—everyone has to teach here, even me. One grad, one undergrad, and you'll supervise a GA who's teaching two more."

"I do understand that."

"You also need to understand that the department doesn't have much money. You're going to need to hustle grants, and you're probably going to have a hell of a time doing it."

"I know. Excuse me, did I miss a job offer somewhere in here?"

"No. This is it." She held out her hand. A slightly dazed smile spread across his face as he shook hands with her.

"Jonathan, welcome to the University of Michigan. It's not official until we turn some paperwork, but you can go home and start packing while you wait for the letter."

His smile widened to a grin. "Thank you, Dr. Froelich—"

"Elizabeth," she said. "I prefer names to titles."

"Elizabeth. Would you have any idea where I might start looking for a town house? Money was tight, so I took a chance and bought a one-way ticket," he said. "As far as I'm concerned, I am home."

It was the last dream of a restless night in a strange bed.

Jonathan Briggs stood on the grass, watching as a gusty wind curtained the evening sky with a quilted blanket of churning steel-gray clouds. The wind and the clouds carried all the turbulent energy of a summer thunderstorm, but none of it touched Jonathan. The air on the lawn was almost still, no more than a dry breath on his face. The light filtering through from above was a cool, pale yellow, draining the color from the world—

It was a familiar dream. He remembered the storm, and knew what was to come. Sometimes there were others with him, watching. Tonight, he was alone.

A flicker of virgin white burst into life on the face of the clouds—a silent tracery of lightning erupting. Clinging to the underside of the sky, it branched and fractured and cascaded across its expanse, reaching with spidery fingers to the horizon. It lasted only a moment, a moment long enough to watch it unfold, but too short to hold the vision in his memory.

Moments later it happened again, the spark struck in a different part of the sky, a new chain of potentials collapsing, the electric fire racing outward along courses invisible until it filled them.

His breath caught in his throat. The lightning had all the fragile beauty of lace—but organic, like the spreading crown of a hundred-year-old oak—but dynamic, like a tumbling waterfall—but evanescent, like a thought. Not a drop of rain fell. No thunder sounded.

Jonathan's feet were rooted, though not by fear. He watched in awe and breathless wonder—

A lucid dream. He remembered the dream, and knew that he was dreaming. He remembered the storm, and knew that it was a memory of an eerie late-summer day, four years ago, when the wind had blown a silent, rainless lightning show across Waterford and away into the night.

Just as the wind was now blowing the storm away—

They had chased the storm across the countryside, he and his friends, chased it down the two-lane highways of the open countryside in Kenny's rusty Ford pickup truck, trying to capture what they were seeing through the lens of Ben and Tracy's camcorder. Though they chased it all the way to the state line before they gave up, they never caught it, never captured it.

This time, he would catch it.

Closing his eyes, Jonathan told himself, You have always known how to fly. As he drew a deep breath, his feet lifted off the ground, and the breeze caught him and spun him slowly like a leaf in a vortex. Opening his eyes, he stretched out his hands and flew toward where the horizon was dancing under electric fire.

He flew over the fields and woods and two-lane highways, chasing the storm. It was the most beautiful thing he had ever seen. If he could touch it, he would know it. If he could catch it, he would own it.

But it ran from him, like a wild thing that did not wish to be known or caught.

It was not enough that he had remembered how to fly. He needed lighter wings, and a vessel to hold the fire.

Here the dream had ended the last time—as always, in frustration.

But this time, Jonathan brought his empty hands together and found between them a crystal bubble so flawless it reflected every facet of the clouds, so light it skated on the wind. Clinging to it, his body was as buoyant as a thought.

Renewed, he resumed his pursuit, chasing the fire in the sky until the ground vanished beneath him, leaving only the dark water of the lake to be lit by the flickers of pure white light. He chased the fire until it was again the roof of the sky, surrounding him, above, behind, ahead, to either side. But the chase had exhausted him, and he could go no farther.

"Now," he said, a plea.

The bubble between his hands mirrored the clouds on its surface, then slowly absorbed the reflection, drawing it inside, capturing the storm in miniature within. He stared as the clouds turned and folded and twisted, drawing in on themselves, still flickering as they collapsed into an echo of a fissured, furrowed human brain, turning slowly in the captured eddies of wind.

"Are you of fire, or earth?" he asked the tiny storm.

When there was no answer, he reached to touch it. But the crystal bubble shattered like glass, the pieces falling into the water below. The storm within unfolded, spread itself on the wind, and faded into the night. He looked up, but above him were only stars. The wind had blown the storm away.

Jonathan woke from the last dream of the night to find himself sitting up in his bed, breathing fast. His senses jangled as though an alarm had shaken him awake, though the glowing numerals of the clock told him it was an hour too early for that.

He felt the fatigue in his limbs, tasted the disappointment.

After a moment's hesitation, he threw back the top sheet and swung his legs over the side of the bed. There was no point in trying to nap until the alarm screamed at him, not with all the thesis notes and reading-to-do spread across the kitchen table.

But as he showered, he knew that he would dream that dream again, and someday catch the storm. And then, finally, he would know what it was, and what he would have to do to hold it.

2

The Intersection of Purposes

The young professor perched on the edge of the table at the front of the lecture hall wore a bright yellow button that asked CAN I READ YOUR MIND?

"One last thing before I set you free to resume your search for used copies of the overpriced study disc for this course," Jonathan said, setting the syllabus aside. "I'm looking—I'm always looking—for volunteer subjects for my own research into the neurology of personality.

"Now, volunteering will not help your grade in this class. It will not improve your sex life, reduce your rent, or alter the point spread for the MSU game. It will not put you on my Boxing Day gift list or tempt me to underwrite your plans for a spring break binge.

"What it will do is give you a chance to possibly help answer a question that neuroscience still can't wrestle to the ground, namely 'What makes you you?' Anyone who's ever had trouble making themselves understood can appreciate the fact that no two people think alike. I'm interested in uncovering why that's so.

"I'm asking for two hours that you'd otherwise spend watching television or playing VR. You'll have nearly as much fun and go home with ten dollars for pizza, besides. I promise you that it's completely painless and noninvasive—all you need to do is sit in a chair with a big SQUID on your head and think clean thoughts."

Four years of practice had polished the pitch to carny smoothness, and they were with him, smiling and laughing at all the right spots. "If you're interested in lending your brain to what passes for science here, please take a scheduling form on your way out. You can turn it in next class, or sign up on the Web. My lab is Room 1110 in the basement of Neuroscience, behind the freight elevator. If I'm not there, my lovely assistant Eric will help you. Bring him food and he'll tell you most anything—except the date of the first pop quiz."

A handful of students in the two-hundred-seat lecture hall groaned, and Jonathan grinned up at them. "Now we see who was planning on letting the reading go until the last week of the semester. Don't worry, I have all your names, this will become part of your permanent record. As for the rest of you—shore leave for everyone. Be back on board by ten Thursday."

While the exodus up the aisles began, Jonathan was tied to the podium by the knot of students that formed around him. When he had answered all their questions, a thumb riff through the stack of remaining forms told him that Human Neuroscience 1 had been even more receptive than he'd thought. Of course, the appeal for volunteers always went over best with the lecture courses and the undergrads, both of which seemed to generate a certain eagerness to be noticed.

Jonathan regretted taking advantage of student insecurities—there was no doubt that many heard him say, "It won't help your grade" and thought to themselves, It couldn't hurt, though—but he had little choice. The amount of hardware needed to capture the dynamic human mind in vectors, bytes, and pixels made Jonathan a prisoner of the basement. He had to coax his subjects to come see him.

And since there had never been enough money to pay subjects more than a token (though ten dollars seemed like more than a token when it was coming out of Jonathan's own pocket, as it frequently did), he was obliged to rely on good-natured begging and pleading.

Between what he thought of as "pledge week" and mid-semester ads in the *Michigan Daily,* a thousand or so students a year took Jonathan up on his offer. Beyond that, Jonathan had cheerfully wheedled nearly everyone in the Neuroscience Building into coming downstairs, and was working his way through the Medical Center directory as well. Many staff members had become friendly "procurers," regularly sending him their in-town friends and out-of-town visitors.

Despite the easy atmosphere in the office, the pace had burned up a doctoral research assistant, three graduate assistants, and four teaching aides. Since setting up the vector lab, Jonathan had averaged eight mind maps a day, forty-five weeks a year—more than seven thousand all told. His current doctoral student, Eric Lutton, updated the total every week on an old fund-raising "thermometer" chart hanging on the back of the office door. The goal at the top was ten thousand vector maps—three years away.

Outside the med school lecture hall, Jonathan found that the morning gray had turned into a misty drizzle. Dodging traffic in the bikeways, he hurried his steps on his way back to the lab's street-level basement entrance.

The smell of preservative and alcohol that hit him as he entered seemed stronger than usual. Dr. Kosslyn must be cutting this morning, Jonathan thought. As he turned the corner by the freight elevator, he heard a woman's familiar laugh from inside his lab suite. He found Elizabeth Froelich in the office with Eric, sipping a mug of coffee.

The office was large enough for a lab table, a few file towers, two workstation desks, and a moderate amount of clutter. "Captain, my Captain," Jonathan said, depositing his wet portfolio on top of a file tower.

His light tone had a hint of an unspoken question in it—a casual visit from Froelich was hardly a curiosity, but late afternoon was more typical of her habits than midmorning.

"Hello, Jonathan," she said, gesturing with her cup. "How goes pledge week?"

"Okay. I think we can count on enough traffic down here to cement the suspicions of Dr. Kosslyn that we're running drugs out of the lab," he said, reaching across Eric's desk and dragging the doughnut box toward him.

Froelich smiled. Out of professional etiquette, she would not join him in his jibes at the current occupant of the Benjamin and Adele Holtom Laboratory, but she always seemed to appreciate them silently. "Eric was telling me about the new student services clerk losing it on her orientation tour this morning."

"Why? What happened?"

"No one warned her about the freezer in the basement," Eric said. "Apparently the prospect of 250 brains waiting on ice under her feet all day—"

"—Thinking little frozen thoughts at her—" added Froelich.

"—inspired her to reconsider her career plans."

Jonathan laughed and bit into a cinnamon roll. "Sounds like a Fox midnight-movie-of-the-week. Tonight, *Sex Slave of the Zombie Brains*—" He summoned his best monster-movie voice. " 'She thought the frozen brains were harmless, but there's nothing colder than an evil thought'—"

"People are weird," Eric said.

"Amen," said Froelich. "Did you hear? Last semester a student in the psych department accused her advisor of psychic sexual harassment and molestation."

"Are we talking about a formal complaint? A Form 230E?" asked Jonathan.

"We sure are."

Jonathan shook his head. "Sounds like someone who's bidding for a free tour of all the trash-TV shows."

"At least she picked the right major," said Eric.

Froelich laughed lightly, then set her coffee cup aside. "I actually came down here to share some good news—departmental e-mail just doesn't make it for some things. I got a call first thing this morning—the International Foundation for Brain Research accepted our bid to host next year's Machinery of the Mind symposium—"

Before she could finish, Jonathan slapped the top of his desk. "All right! That's terrific. Congratulations, Elizabeth. That's a real coup—a real credit to you and the U, and a big plus for the department." He looked to Eric. "MOM's the top event on the neuroscience calendar."

"I don't know how much of a coup it is," she said, standing. "The truth is that I had to call in about every favor I had coming to get past the board's lack of enthusiasm. And they insisted it be a satellite symposium, with three remote teleconference sites."

"So no one who doesn't want to come here has to," Jonathan said with a frown. "Too bad."

"But this gives us an opportunity to sell ourselves to the community, and that's what I wanted. Which brings me to the other reason I came down here. I want you presenting, Jonathan. When the call for papers comes, I want one of the applications to be from you."

Jonathan's expression darkened. "Elizabeth—you know we're not ready. I need at least three thousand more maps. And I need to do more special populations—families, twins. The oldest longitudinal studies are only four years old."

Froelich frowned. "Eric, could you give us a moment, please?"

"Sure," he said, gathering his limbs and easing past her on his way out. When the door closed behind him, Froelich took her seat again.

"Jonathan, I've helped you all I can, and more than I should have," she said. "But there's a limit to how long I can make allowances for you. There's a limit to my ability to defend special treatment for you. How many new med school profs do you think get away with not publishing so much as a letter to the editor?"

"Not many."

"Not any," Froelich said. "And this being your tenure-or-out year, the U grant board and the director of the medical center have both been asking about you. You need to do something to help yourself. And it would be very helpful if you were to present at Machinery of the Mind. It would go a long way toward securing your lease on this lab."

Jonathan sighed into his hands. "I'm not overly comfortable with the idea of putting this before a jury now. There's so much still to be done—"

"Jonathan, you're starting to worry me. Is this just creative insecurity, or do you have something to hide? Did something happen? Don't you believe in the work?"

Flustered, Jonathan said, "No, it's—I believe in the work. I—look, you know they're not going to like this. I want it to be bulletproof."

"It can't be. And I think you're wrong, Jonathan.

Frankly, I think a lot of people in the community want to believe what you're trying to prove. They're hungry to hear someone make a case for the whole being greater than the sum of its parts. Besides, you don't want to wait so long in the quest for perfection that you end up playing Darwin to someone's Alfred Russell Wallace."

"No. No, I don't want that." Jonathan thought a moment, pivoting side to side in his chair. "I suppose we are in the piling-up-the-proof stage. The redesign we did on the SQUID, the vector map paradigm, the storage and classification system, the analysis tools—I could talk about all of that. I could walk through a single subject profile, or some basic correspondences."

He flashed a wry smile and shrugged. "The work is more ready than I am, I suppose. All right. Do you have any idea how much time I'd have?"

"First call for papers will probably be January 1. Four months," she said, standing.

Jonathan rose with her, and buried his hands in his pockets. "Okay," he said with a brave smile. "We'll see what MOM thinks about what we've been up to."

For the two minutes or so that it took Jonathan Briggs to read the letter from the IFBR, the only sound in Dr. Froelich's office was the sound of sleet pelting the windows.

Finally, he looked up, his mouth twisted by a frown. "Well, that's that, isn't it."

Froelich shook her head in commiseration. "I'm sorry, Jonathan. Angry, too. And more than a little shocked. It's a good paper."

"And up against the best. Only twenty-four slots in the schedule. Lots of heavy hitters," he said, dropping the letter back on her desk.

"You're right about that. I was told there were more than two hundred proposals submitted."

Jonathan settled back in his chair and folded his hands in midair. "Probably needed a catchier title. 'Functional Patterning and Individuation in Anderson Vector Matrices.' What was I thinking? I should have gone with 'The Invasion of the X-Ray Telepath Squids, Or, I Know When You're Thinking About Sex,' " he said, and forced a grin.

"I don't know how you can laugh. And I feel terribly guilty for putting you in this position," Froelich said. "You didn't want to do this now. I admit, I was selfish—I wanted your name, U of M's name, in the Proceedings volume. I want the community to know we do good work here, that we know how to do more than send out invitations and cater a banquet."

"Well—Dr. Kosslyn will be on the program."

"Dr. Kosslyn's work is boring. Dr. Kosslyn is boring." She frowned. "You didn't hear that."

"*Gesundheit*," Jonathan said agreeably.

Froelich nodded her appreciation. "But it isn't just institutional ego. Jonathan, I'm damned impatient for you to start talking about what you've been doing. No one's working on synthesis. No one's working on the brain as a system. Your work could change the whole focus of the field in a year."

"Maybe. When it's ready," Jonathan said.

"Someone will publish that paper. *Behavioral Neuroscience. EuroJournal of Neuroscience.* Don't give up."

"I'm not going to send it out," he said, shaking his head. "It was a rush job, Liz. I'm glad they rejected it. I can't do what I need to do in one paper. I have to be ready to follow it up."

"Do I hear a campaign in the planning?"

"Not a campaign. Not even a plan. Just a wish,

about how I'd like it to be. Three papers—all three big journals. An article in *Scientific American*. A book to pull it all together for the general reader. Dreamland, though."

And then she said it: "You know, you should do to the symposium what you've done to us."

"What do you mean?"

"Co-opt them. Get as many of them as you can down to your lab, sit them in that chair, and make them part of it. Just like you made yourself the department's favorite son."

"I never—"

"Oh, I know, you didn't plan it that way—that's the greater part of why you pulled it off." She smiled. "When I hired you, I thought all the black-box psych people and the wet-brain cutters would end up your enemies. I expected I'd have to protect you from them. But you managed to turn that around. The truth is that they protect you—if I were to spank you as hard as I should, I'd be facing a mutiny in the department."

Bemused, Jonathan said, "Gee, that's useful to know."

"If you were the kind of person who'd try to use it, we wouldn't—couldn't—be friends." She plucked a Dove miniature from a small bowl on her desk, and slowly and precisely unwrapped it. "I'm serious about this, Jonathan. You'll be way ahead if you can start getting people on the outside even a little bit invested in what you're doing."

Jonathan shook his head as she made the candy disappear. "It ought to be enough to be right."

"Yes," she agreed. "It ought to. But it isn't. Personal politics counts in this field. It affects who gets grants, who gets cited, who gets into the top journals, who gets a pass on peer review, who gets read, who gets listened to, who gets the awards, who gets the buzz."

"I don't want to play that game," Jonathan said.

"It's not a game. It's tilling the soil. I'm not insisting that you sell yourself," Froelich said. "But, if you want, I can get you the conference registration list. You can be in touch with people and line them up for appointments before they even get here."

"I don't think so, Liz."

"Think about it some more, please?"

He did. It took him two days to work through his misgivings. And ultimately, pride was the solvent for his resistance. Hours after Eric had gone home, after the janitor had made her pass down the corridor and the building's lights and heat had dropped to their evening setback, he sat staring at the 100cm monitor, at the Technicolor lightning dancing within an infinity the size of a human skull.

His skull. His mind at work, thinking about thinking. Was this it? Was this the flame that burned within the vessel? Is this me? Is this what I am? he thought, and watched the vector matrix shimmer and shift colors. Is this real?

He would never know unless he earned a hearing on the main stage. He had sculpted a vision of the reality of being, but it was still green. It had to be offered to the fire.

I have to risk being wrong.

The matrix twitched and shuddered.

He called Froelich at home. "I'm ready to whore myself, madam," he said cheerfully. "Send me your client list."

Spring came to Ann Arbor on a Monday as cold, wet, and gray as the Michigan winter it ended.

Chewing his lower lip and looking harried, Jonathan ran his staff ID through the new scanner at the back entrance to the Neuroscience Building and drummed his fingers impatiently on the glass as he waited to be cleared through. When the door buzzed, he shouldered his way inside with a distracted wave toward the camera.

The long corridor leading to Jonathan's office was deserted, and he half ran its beige-floored length, arriving at his door breathless, feeling the tiny first beads of perspiration starting to form on his forehead. A fine way to start the week, he thought as he let himself in.

As Jonathan entered, Eric Lutton looked up with surprise from his terminal and a cinnamon doughnut. "Doc—what are you doing here?" he asked, rising. "I thought you were going straight to the symposium."

"I forgot the backgrounders we printed up Friday," Jonathan said, sweeping past Eric and into the adjoining lab. "They are here, aren't they?"

"I didn't see them," Eric said, trailing Jonathan into the next room. The vector lab made the office look tidy, congested as it was with tables covered with electronics and the five gray modules of the S-SQ. "But you should have called me—I could have met you with them over at Towsley."

"I would've called you, but my portable's dead. I think the battery's fried—the last charge only lasted two hours. Do we have any more around here?" Jonathan asked, standing in the middle of the clutter and scanning the room. "Ah—there they are," he said suddenly, and pounced on a short stack of printouts nestled atop a rack of amplifiers.

"Any more what?"

"PenCell batteries."

"I'll look."

Jonathan glanced at his watch. "Damn, I'm going to be late. Was there trouble on campus this weekend?

The guard at the Glen Street entrance was more zealous than usual."

"None that I heard about," Eric said. "Isn't this the hospitality hour?" he called back as he disappeared into the office. "I thought the sessions didn't begin until nine."

"Right. But the hospitality hours are actually half the reason to be there," Jonathan said, frowning and peering closer at the master controller's display. "The most effective sucking-up is done in person."

Eric chuckled. "Kind of like the difference between watching a blow job on TV and getting one yourself?" he called.

A grin briefly broke through Jonathan's frown as he studied the numbers on a smaller screen. "Kind of. All the difference in the world, in other words. But it's giving one, not getting one. Take notes, young man. Technique is everything, and your day is coming. Are you all set for our first appointment?"

"As soon as that calibration series finishes running," Eric said, reappearing at the office door and waving a battery pack. "Here you go, Dr. Briggs—I stole it from Kelly's Toshi. It should get you through the morning. When Kelly comes in, I'll get her to track a real PenCell battery down for you and bring it over on one of her shuttle runs."

"Thanks, Eric," Jonathan said, collecting the battery as he brushed by on his way out. He paused by his desk, looking down. "What d'you think, should I wear the button, or not?"

"Depends on whether you're doing Respectable or Approachable."

"Right," he said, and picked up the button.

"Have fun, Dr. Briggs."

"I'll try. The IFBR grant committee will be wearing red carnations—remember, turn the dials up to eleven for them, and whisper 'Repeat after me: Briggs deserves more money—Briggs deserves more money—' "

Laughing, Eric followed him to the office door. "Dr. Briggs?" he called. "Any word? Are we going to get Clement Harris to come down here?"

"I still don't know," Jonathan said. "Wish me luck."

Like the weather, the construction bosses had made no allowances for the fact that there were guests on campus. Walking the four blocks across campus to Towsley Center, Jonathan ran a noisy gantlet between the riggers building the gate station for the skyway to North Campus and the road crews beginning the work of turning Huron-Washtenaw into a cross-campus tunnel.

Entering Towsley the back way, he found the blue-draped registration tables set up in the upper corridor, beneath a black-and-white collage of the medical school's class of 1922. Inevitably, there was a line.

But the line was not long. Form had held, despite Froelich's best efforts to lure researchers to Ann Arbor. The collective attendance at the teleconference sites in Cold Spring Harbor, Palo Alto, Amsterdam, and Tokyo would be higher than the head count at the host sessions.

Even so, by the time Jonathan had collected his badge and participant's packet and found his way to the breakfast reception outside the Dow Auditorium, he had had enough time to work himself into a fine state of anxiety thinking about approaching Harris.

Dr. Clement Harris—two-term president of the Society for Neuroscience. Cowinner of the Nobel Prize for Physiology at age thirty-seven for his work in biopsychology. Head of the Emory University research center created for him. Founding partner of Precision

Medicine, the leading "kitchen company" in neuro-psychiatric drugs. Keynoter for the symposium. If neuroscience had a celebrity superstar, Harris was it.

Jonathan had written, faxed, e-mailed, and called Harris at least once at each of his several addresses, but had never connected with him or received a reply. With anyone else, Jonathan would have taken that as a no. But Harris was worth chasing a little harder—and he had a reputation for, as Dr. Kosslyn had put it, not stopping to pick up passengers.

The lobby was bright and moderately crowded with bodies. Cheerful chatter and the rich tang of coffee hovered in the air. Jonathan picked his way mostly unmolested through the milling strangers, looking for Dr. Froelich.

He found her in the back corridor, engaged in a hushed but obviously earnest conversation with a Towsley technician. When she dismissed him and turned toward where Jonathan was waiting, she was wearing a cross expression.

"Problem, Liz?"

"The Tokyo feed is breaking up." She made an effort to wash the annoyance from her face. "Not much I can do about it, though, except let the gnomes do their incantations."

"Perhaps the ritual sacrifice of a remote control, or a Mac—"

Her face cracked. "You'd like to see that, wouldn't you? A real turn-on."

"You bet. So, any late arrivals? Did we break three hundred?"

"About a dozen late cancellations, I'm afraid. A couple of them on your appointment list, too. Check your mail," she said, gesturing at Jonathan's shoulder pack. "I cc'd the lab, so Eric would know."

"Thanks. Have you seen Dr. Harris?"

Froelich shook her head. "I know he got in all right last night, but he passed up the president's breakfast this morning. I have no idea where he is. But I expected the heavy hitters to be the last to arrive, because they really are here just for the coffee." She glanced at her watch. "Jonathan, I need to go play hostess. Good luck today," she said, and was gone.

Jonathan settled in one of the long row of blocky red lounge chairs facing the courtyard windows just long enough to retrieve his mail, update the open appointment list, and call up Harris's picture to refresh his memory.

As he was finishing, he was greeted by a white-haired professor from Iowa, one Dr. Salgmann, ambling alone along the back corridor from the direction of the lecture rooms. They chatted briefly, and Jonathan passed the time remaining before the keynote session mingling and working the room, watching for but never spotting Harris. When the migration from the reception to the auditorium began, Jonathan resignedly joined it.

To avoid getting caught in the congestion at the end of the session, he took an end seat halfway down the pitched aisle, opposite one of the red fire doors. That obliged latecomers to sidle past him to reach the many open seats in his row, but the auditorium would not be crowded, so few challenged his claim to it. About half of the Dow's green velour seats were filled when Clement Harris entered through the fire door at the stage level and settled in the front row.

A large man with a larger personal space, Harris took up three seats. His portfolio and topcoat spilled into the space to his left, and he himself crowded the space to his right. He did not look around the auditorium, nor acknowledge Froelich with much enthusiasm when she crossed the stage to greet him.

Sighing, Jonathan unlimbered his notepad and logged on to the university net to check in with Eric. While he was occupied, a late arrival stopped by his row and said, "Excuse me." Without looking up, he tucked in his legs to let the speaker by.

Only after the fact did he realize that the voice had been female, and the presence passing close to him a very pleasant and congenial one. He looked down the row and saw a woman he had not noticed at the reception settling four seats away.

If she had been there, he thought he surely would have noticed. She wore a thin-ribbed black turtleneck sweater and blue jeans rolled up at the ankles, which made her stand out among the tweed suits and white shirts, the navy-blue dresses and linen pantsuits. And though she looked young enough to be a student, she also defied the sorority-hooker look that had taken over campus. He couldn't imagine her flashing black lace and spandex (though it was pleasant to try) or wearing a big bow in her hair.

But it wasn't just the clothing that set her apart. She was nearly the only woman in the room with hair long enough to reach her shoulders. Hers, light brown and wavy, spilled like a waterfall to the middle of her back. The scent of it was still in his nostrils, almost familiar.

She seemed somehow elemental and unaffected, as though she'd escaped all the shaping and molding from those who would tell her who to be. And just as he realized he was staring, she glanced his way in time to catch his deer-in-the-headlights expression, and smiled in a friendly way. She had dark eyes and a rich smile.

Jonathan tried to smile back, felt his face freeze, and quickly looked away. When he did, he discovered

Froelich was already at the podium, addressing the gathering. He gave her meaningless words his devoted attention until he finally stopped feeling painfully stupid and self-conscious.

He scrawled to Eric, I just broke University Sexual Harassment Rule No. 16.

Good for you! came the reply. Any chance of breaking any more rules?

Jonathan risked a quick sideways glance toward the woman. No. But a fellow can dream—

Dr. Clement Harris gave exactly the kind of presentation Jonathan had been led to expect. It contained not a hint of what, if anything, Harris himself might be working on. Instead, he offered the kind of highly quotable senior-statesman "vision" speech that was sure to earn him a few lines in the front matter of *Science*.

A clearly envious Professor Salgmann had offered the uncharitable explanation that Harris cared more for protecting his reputation than advancing the field. "I hear he hasn't gotten his hands dirty in a lab for ten years," Salgmann had told Jonathan confidentially. And it was true that Harris had nothing to gain and everything to lose by bringing a new dog to the pit.

But it could also be that, now in his fifties, Harris was more businessman than researcher. He talks like someone who has a patent attorney on retainer, Jonathan thought as he listened. And maybe a publicist, too.

"—As Copernican astronomy was to the sixteenth century and Darwinian evolution to the nineteenth century, neuroscience has become the defining intellectual revolution of the twenty-first century," Harris was saying. "We are helping dismantle the last vestiges of the Empire of Human Egocentrism."

"There are more than a thousand neural disorders affecting a hundred million Americans, a billion people worldwide. We owe all of the progress we've made in fighting them to our willingness, beginning at the end of the last century, to put ego and mysticism aside and view the brain as a machine, a system, a chemical computer.

"Afflictions once beyond our control are yielding to the new power of that vision. We have finer tools now—precision tools." He smiled, letting them know that the allusion to his company was intentional. "We attack human misery not with myths, mysticism, or metaphors, but with molecular science.

"Neurochemical therapy can now preserve the memory of an Alzheimer's victim, replace a suicidal teen's depression with joy, or reinvigorate the sex drive of a desire-deficient spouse. Neuropharmacology can unlock the doors to learning and liberate the prisoners of addictions, compulsions, and phobias.

"Within another decade, psychiatry will be wholly transformed by a new generation of practitioners into a true medical science—a status it's long claimed but not deserved. Another decade beyond that, and I expect to see psychology finally recognized for the superstitious folk art it is, and to see it vanish from the intellectual stage just as phrenology and palmistry did before it.

"Beyond that, as our new vision of human nature filters out to the general population, a conspiracy of destructive myths linked to the old vision will finally begin to lose their hold on us. I'll mention just three.

"The myth of individual consciousness. The fact is that each of us is a committee. Impulse negotiates with intellect, heritage with learning, hindbrain with cerebrum. What we see intersects with what we've already seen and what we foresee. We can never understand ourselves until we realize that we literally embody contradiction.

"The myth of the soul. The fact is that what animates us is not something trapped in the flesh, like a moth in a bottle. It is something of the flesh. We can never properly value life until we realize that life isn't just the overture, it's the whole opera.

"The myth of dualism. The fact is that mind is brain, and brain is body. All distinctions between them are artificial and misleading. We can never accept our place in the universe until we realize that every human quality—both base and noble—is part of our animal heritage.

"This is the real promise of neuroscience, the gift we can give the world.

"A hundred thousand years ago, our ancestors bored holes into the skulls of madmen to allow the demons to escape. The human species still has its demons. But we now have the power to exorcise them humanely. We can lighten the lives of a billion people, and enrich the lives of the rest. We can commute the cruel sentence passed on those whose neurochemical dysfunctions make them experience the world as irrational, unpredictable, terrifying, or simply joyless.

"I hope that you are proud of your part in that, as I am proud of mine. May this conference take us all farther toward our goals." He stepped back from the podium, and the applause began.

There were twenty minutes left in the hour, and Jonathan was caught unprepared by the abrupt end of the session. Harris bowed his head once, then returned to his seat without lingering to milk the applause. When Froelich walked to the podium, Jonathan was still sitting back in his chair, expecting a question-and-answer session. But she merely thanked Harris warmly, announced a room change for an afternoon session, and dismissed them. Harris was the first one on his feet.

Jumping up and frantically gathering his notepad and bag, Jonathan watched Harris sweep out of the auditorium by the same fire door he had used to enter. It could not have taken Jonathan more than thirty seconds to get his things in hand and push through the fire door to the long stair-corridor beyond. But by the time he did, Harris was nowhere in sight.

Jonathan stood there, stupefied, while the corridor slowly filled with people and sound.

"This was not meant to be," he muttered with a sigh.

Out of pure stubbornness, he picked his way down through the migration toward the surviving pastries and searched the first floor. Finding no one but a Towsley staffer at a copy machine, he ran back up the stairs and scouted the reception lobby.

The hell with it, he thought. The morning's coffee was boiling through him, and Jonathan retreated toward the rest room on the stair-corridor. He was within a couple strides of the door when it swung open and Harris emerged. The two men nearly collided.

"Dr. Harris," Jonathan said, stepping back. "Excuse me."

Harris squinted at the younger man's badge. "Briggs. Are you the one who's been pestering me?" His voice seemed as loud as it had in the auditorium, the brick walls as effective as a microphone.

"My apologies, Dr. Harris. I didn't mean to 'pester' you—I just didn't quite know where or how to reach you—"

"What was it you wanted, again?"

Jonathan swallowed. "I was hoping I could interest you in coming over to my lab while you were here and taking a look at what I'm doing," he said, digging in his bag for one of the project summaries. "In fact, if you have an hour to spare, you could be part of the study. We have several people coming over, but I kept an appointment open today and another tomorrow with you in mind. Two o'clock."

Harris gave the summary a cursory glance and handed it back. "Why did you think I would be interested? This is not cutting edge. You're playing with old technology, and old ideas."

His voice was carrying all up and down the tunnel-like corridor and had collected an audience of a dozen or more people who were lingering and trying to look like they weren't listening. "I'm sure you're collecting some pretty pictures," Harris went on, "but any ten-dollar-an-hour radiology technician in Two Sticks, Idaho, can make pretty pictures of brains these days—and those pictures even have some utility."

Struck dumb, Jonathan could neither escape nor defend himself. Harris reached out and grabbed the cheery yellow CAN I READ YOUR MIND? button pinned to the young professor's jacket long enough to read it. Then he tapped the button sharply with a forefinger, twice. "The answer is no. Not mine, not anyone's. Did you hear my address, just now?"

"Yes," Jonathan managed.

"Then I can only assume you did not understand it," Harris said. "This prattle of yours about 'directly observing consciousness as a property of living systems'—ludicrous."

Sucker-punched, Jonathan gaped, staggered. The quote was not from the sheet he had handed Harris, but from his submission to the symposium's review committee.

Harris was not finished. He leaned closer, crowding Jonathan and looming over him at the same time. "You might as well be trying to photograph fairies or phlogiston. Listen carefully, and you might rescue your career: Mind does not exist. Only the brain exists. You are wasting your time, Dr. Briggs—and mine. Now, you will excuse me."

As Harris brushed past and headed up the stairs, Jonathan became painfully aware of the embarrassed silence in the corridor. His cheeks burning and his mouth a tight line, he started toward the rest room to escape the eyes he felt on his back.

"Dr. Briggs."

He turned toward the voice, blank-faced. It was her—the woman from the morning session. "I'll take that appointment," she said hopefully.

It was a delicate moment. Had there been so much as a hint of pity or insincerity in her tone or expression, the humiliation would have shredded him. But there was no hint of that. And in her hand was a copy of his project summary—though where she had gotten it, he could not guess.

"If that's all right," she added. "Alynn Reed."

Her voice was strong but soft, and made him feel like they were alone. But his emotions were a snarl, and his reactions molasses. "Jonathan. Jon Briggs." He swallowed. "If you really want to take part, I—sure. Of course. Thank you."

"Terrific. Two o'clock?"

Royal manners, he suddenly thought. It was as though she were pretending to have overheard a much more civil conversation—a tack that worked much better than pretending she'd heard nothing at all. "Right. Two o'clock. We'll need at least an hour—"

"That's fine. There's nothing on the afternoon schedule that interests me," she said. "Is there someplace I should meet you?"

"Eh—the Taubman entrance? Ten till?"

"I know where that is. I'll see you then. Oh—and, Jonathan?"

"Yes?"

"I think Harris is an ass." And she smiled that friendly smile again before she walked away.

Hiding in a rest room stall, his body leaning heavily against the inside of the door, Jonathan tried to collect himself. He did not begin to understand everything that had just happened.

How had Harris seen his paper? Someone on the peer review panel must have sent it to him, but why? And the calculated viciousness of Harris's rebuff—it was almost as if he'd been lying in wait. Hunting squirrels with a buffalo gun. It just made no sense.

And Alynn—he couldn't read her at all, but she seemed to read him perfectly. Somehow she was attuned to what he needed, even to excusing herself before he went to pieces in front of her. But he knew nothing about her—he could not remember if he'd even glanced at her badge to see where she was from. He could hardly believe she had been looking for him, and had just happened to witness his public evisceration.

As he washed his face at the sink, steeling himself to return to the symposium, all he was really certain of was that in the space of ten minutes, his tranquil life had been turned upside down twice—and that thinking about Alynn Reed was a pleasant antidote to thinking about Clement Harris.

Eric Lutton seemed both surprised and glad to see Jonathan. "Doc, do you have any idea what's going on? Kelly said that the one o'clock never showed, and there've been three other cancellations."

"Yeah, I have sort of an idea," Jonathan said, picking his way through the office toward the lab. "No point in worrying about it, though. Have you had lunch?"

"Well—nothing more substantial than I can get from raiding the vending machines."

Stopping in the doorway to the lab, Jonathan folded his arms over his chest and said, "Why don't you take a break, then, and go get yourself something civilized from the Fleetwood, or Krazy Jim's?"

"You have an odd idea of civilized food, Doc."

Jonathan shrugged and smiled back over his shoulder. "What do you expect? My best friend has brains in her freezer."

"You have a point," Eric said. "All right, I'll go get some lunch, so long as I can pick my own caterer."

Distractedly waving a hand in assent, Jonathan said, "Find Kelly and take her with you, why don't you?"

Eric frowned. "Doc, are you trying to get rid of us?"

"Yes."

"Is Harris coming?"

Jonathan's chuckle was short, sharp, and bitter. "No. He's not coming. He's the reason some of the others aren't coming, either."

"Oops," Eric said with a grimace. "Okay. Translator's working now. I'll clear out and take Kelly with me. When do you want us back?"

Jonathan glanced up at the clock. "When's the next appointment?"

"Four."

"Four, then. Or thereabouts."

"Check. Doc, are you all right?"

"I'll be all right," Jonathan said, turning back toward Eric. "I guess. You know, Eric, I never had the least interest in being a salesman or a politician. And I never thought I'd have to be both to do a little science. I should have learned from my father."

"How do you mean?"

"Back when, Dad wanted to be a musician. That is,

until he and his band started to have a little success, and he got a square look at the business side—leg-snare contracts, touring, agents, promoters, image consultants, payoffs, bare-skin formulas for the videos—" Jonathan shook his head. "He decided he'd rather just make music. Still plays every Thursday night in the garage with his friends, and every other Saturday at a retro bar, for free beer and the love of it."

"Sounds like a pretty cool guy, your dad."

"Yeah—I guess he is. Anyway, what it comes down to is I've had it with all the 'business' crap. Too much talking, not enough doing. Time for me to get back in the lab, get refocused on the work. I've got someone coming over at two—I want to run her through the series myself—"

Eric perked up. "Miss Rule Sixteen?"

"Yeah," Jonathan said with a wry and embarrassed grin. "As it happens. But this is strictly professional." He saw Eric's dubious look and added, "No, really. She asked to be mapped."

"Right. Strictly professional," Eric said straight-faced. "I don't doubt it for a moment."

"All right, all right—nine-tenths professional."

"Half."

"Two-thirds, and that's my final offer."

"Sold," Eric said. "So who is she?"

"Alynn Reed. She's from some company called Arcadia, in Pennsylvania. Not part of the community, apparently. Not sure why she's here, to be honest. I have a search running on the net, trying to find out more."

"You could ask her."

"I just might get a chance, if you ever snag Kelly and clear out of here."

"Going, going, gone," Eric said with a mock salute as he retreated out the door. "You want Kelly to pick up your two o'clock?"

"No. I'll take care of it."

"Okay. Think about Rule Nine, Doc. That's my personal favorite—"

Jonathan smiled, but the smile vanished as soon as Eric did. Thank you, but no thank you, he thought ruefully. Sorry to disappoint, but I've never made a play for a student or a subject, and I'm not going to start now. 'Sides, I've already had my quota of rejection for today—

The testing room was walled off from the rest of the lab by canvas curtains and painted particle board, with its own door off the suite's short hallway.

"In here," Jonathan said, turning and standing aside at the open door. Alynn smiled as she passed him, and he swallowed hard as he followed her into the room. On the way over from the conference center, he had discovered that it was hard to be close to her without jangling. He was at a loss to explain it or even to properly describe it, but he was finding himself unnaturally aware of her. Her presence pressed in on all his senses, including some he had been previously unaware of possessing.

Two steps into the testing room, she caught sight of the SQUID's scanning unit and, stopping short, burst into laughter. "That's terrific," she said, her eyes bright and bemused. "Exactly as promised. That must help put people at ease."

The silver-and-black scanner approximated the shape of a huge helmet with a bulge at the crown. But it was painted to look like a goofy lavender sea creature sitting on a tangle of its own arms. The scanner was perched in the retracted position at the end of a telescoping positioning arm, above a weary but cozy garage-sale armchair.

"The kids, especially," Jonathan said. "And older adults, mundanes. That's the third paint job it's had, actually. The first one was the best one—she made it look like a giant robot's head with open access panels, and all this Rube Goldberg gearing and gimmickry inside? It was really very clever, but it weirded some of the subjects out."

"She?"

"Rebecca—Rebecca Walsh, my first grad assistant. She's at Texas now, working with Brandleigh."

Alynn had crossed the room to examine the scanner, peeking past the curtain through which the cabling disappeared and then peering up into the cavity at the grid poles. "So why don't you tell me what this is all about," she said, clambering onto the armchair to get a closer look inside the scanner. "Without the journal-jargon, if you can."

"As many times as people have asked that, you'd think I'd have a ready answer—"

"Just pretend you're trying to explain it to your mother."

"Well, since my mother is a quality-assurance chemist for Merck Canada—"

"All right, then pretend you're trying to explain it to my mother," Alynn said cheerfully. "She was an English major before becoming a four-stripe mom."

"An English major? Oh, make it easy for me, why don't you." He paused to consider. "I'm trying to take a picture of a thought—and find out if there's a way to tell whether it's your thought or mine. I want to find out if personality leaves fingerprints on the brain."

Sitting on her heels, she turned and cocked her head at him. "Do you believe in the mind, Dr. Briggs? Or is that button you wear another paint job, to make people comfortable?"

Jonathan frowned. "Any neuroscientist who doesn't

want to be laughed at is supposed to say, 'No, I don't,' " he said, wondering at his own honesty. "We're all supposed to be reductionists. As you saw this morning."

" 'There is no mind, only brain,' " she intoned.

"So—you were listening," he said with a sorry smile. "When I started this work ten years ago, my answer was 'maybe.' Now—now I think I have to say yes. Something's going on in here"—he touched his temple—"that the reductionists haven't accounted for. I'm trying to figure out what it is."

She nodded approvingly. Lifting herself for a moment on the arms of the chair, she unlimbered her legs and settled into a more normal seated position. "So now that we've agreed that I have a mind, how exactly do you plan to read it?"

"The basics are pretty straightforward," he said, coming forward and unlocking the positioning arm. "I present you with a series of images, sounds, words, questions—"

"No touching?"

He determinedly blocked any thought that she was flirting with him. "I'm just beginning to fool around a little with touch, smell, and taste. The experimental controls are ten times harder, though."

"Because no one knows if they have twenty-twenty taste, or red-green scent blindness?"

"And because presenting a consistent test suite is a lot harder when you can't give the job to a multimedia computer." He smoothly drew the scanner down until it was only a few inches above her head. "Anyway, what I'm going to do is present you with the test suite, and monitor your brain's activity as you process and react to what I show you. The hard part comes after you've gone home—analyzing the session."

"And the product of this is a map?"

"That's what I call it. Technically, it's an Anderson

vector matrix—a mathematical portrait of the functional links in the conscious regions of your brain."

"Is every map unique?"

"That's one of the questions I wanted to answer. So far, yes."

She looked happy at that. "I don't think you should tell me much more until we're done. How long will this take?"

"How much time can you give me?"

"How much of my time do you want?" There it was again—or was it? Her eyes were guileless, but far from innocent.

"There are four test suites, but I only have to have the first two—"

"How long will all four take?"

"With filling out the biography, you're looking at two hours, plus-or-minus fifteen minutes."

Alynn frowned. "With or without potty breaks? I drank too much coffee this morning."

"With," he said, smiling. "We always stop at the end of every suite, let the subject get up and move around."

"Fine," she said brightly. "Shall we get started?"

"Okay. Get comfy—"

"Do I have to keep my head still, like in a CT scan?"

"No," Jonathan said. He showed her a white paper disc with a black cross, about the size of a quarter. "We record the whole session digitally," he said as he placed the sticky disc in the middle of her forehead, "and we use this as a registration mark to correct the readings for any head motion."

"Straightforward 3-D transformations," she said approvingly. "I know all about those. What's next?"

"The spiff science-fiction part," he said, pulling the scanner down until the "helmet" settled over her head and rested lightly on her shoulders. "You okay? Any claustrophobia?"

"No."

He stepped aside and lowered the scanner's display visor over her face, thumbing a switch as he did. "Still okay?"

"I feel like a deep-sea diver," she said, her voice slightly muffled. "I want a picture of this."

"Can do," he said. "We keep a camera in the office. Okay. I have to go next door to start the first suite and monitor everything. If there's a problem, say something—you're miked, I'll hear you. Otherwise, I'll see you in about twenty minutes."

Once he had settled at the control station, it only took Jonathan a few moments to verify the scanner's video feed and the audio level. Then he queued up test suite 1 and sat back in his chair to watch.

The wide-screen HDTV monitor was divided into thirds. On the left was Alynn's face as it appeared to the visor's tiny lens, the arms of the registration mark on her forehead highlighted with fine red crosshairs. It was Jonathan who'd dubbed that part of the display the sniper window, but the joke didn't seem funny today, and he quickly deleted the hairlines.

On the right ride, a slave window showed the progress of the test suite, echoing what Alynn was seeing. At the moment, the suite was walking her through the alphabet, beginning the process of locating and identifying her basic synaptic vocabulary.

And in the center of the big display, the real-time data window was painting the dance of the potentials inside Alynn's cranium, in a Technicolor palette. Jonathan folded his hands in his lap and focused his attention there. Each new image placed before Alynn's curious eyes became a hot blue spike in her visual cortex, and then a furious spectral cascade through the cerebrum. The lightning of her thoughts was bottled within a ghostly gray wire drawing of the structures of her brain.

All three windows were locked in synchrony: how she looked, what she was seeing or hearing, and the matrix of her thoughts, microsecond to microsecond. How old are those memories being tripped? Kindergarten? A, B, C, D, E, F, G... The senses live in the present, but the mind lives in the past.

Test suite 1 had moved on to number concepts, but Jonathan's own thoughts were elsewhere. He reached for the keyboard and deleted the wire drawing from the center window. That left the animated tracings of Alynn's thought-vectors playing against a black background, as though suspended in space.

The sparkling web of lines was deceptively and artificially thin, as if Alynn were only thinking one plodding thought at a time, one after another: Q, 11, two times two, tree, mother, cat. But the human brain is a far busier place than that—a series of data filters was suppressing the swirl of activity unconnected to the experimental inputs.

One by one, Jonathan disabled the filters, until the tracings expanded to a rich, almost frenetic swirl of activity, like a great ball of lightning yarn with an electric cat inside. He fiddled with the trace decay until the display lost some of its clutter but none of its complexity, and then settled back in his chair once more.

Before him was the whole of Alynn's thoughts and emotions, bright and dark, conscious and concealed—a global vector map. Jonathan did not have the tools or the knowledge to decipher so much as a thousandth part of it. There was no scientific value, no practical reason, for such a view of the data stream from the scanner.

But there were other reasons. The global map was the only view that offered Jonathan his subject in wholeness, as a person and not a process. Here was consciousness, learning, personality, emotion, and the billion-year-old neural machinery of instinct, all merging into one interconnected Self. It was, Jonathan thought, like watching a meeting of the Committee of the Whole. I am large. I contain multitudes. Involution balanced against essence. This defined Being. This was what it meant to be human, and alive.

It was with profound wonder, then, that Jonathan contemplated the view through his window.

Yet even that was not why he had brought Alynn's map to the screen.

Jonathan could not speak of it to anyone, but in the course of viewing so many minds in such unguarded intimacy, he had discovered—or, he thought, more likely invented—an aesthetic of the inner self. When he looked into someone's working mind, he found himself responding to what he saw. He knew his response was emotional, subjective, and wholly unscientific—but still, it was impossible to avoid. Like Rorschach blots and astrological charts, the mind maps invited divination.

Some people were—there was no other way to say it—ugly on the inside. Others were frightened, or angry, or lonely. Some minds were chaos. Some were as tranquil as long swells on the ocean. This one was sharp and alert, that one pale and sluggish. Some said to Jonathan, "We could be friends." Others, he despised on sight.

Rocking ever so slightly in his chair, Jonathan gazed at the display and contemplated that which was Alynn. The palette had given her map a generous shading in warm blue hues, shot through with murmuring webs of new-grass green and fire-spark threads of hot amber, all tied together in a delicate violet nebula that pulsed with the base rhythms of her being.

Now this is pretty sad, eh?, he chided himself mockingly. Standing in the bushes outside her window, wearing your X-ray shades. Briggs, you have to get out more—

Shaking his head and smiling with wry self-consciousness, Jonathan reached out and restored the standard test display.

As if you even needed to peek. As if there was any chance you weren't going to find her beautiful.

But she is, you know. You can see it, can't you?

Stop that right now. Man, you'd better hope Eric comes back early.

Early? Ha! I'm hoping he gets hit on the head by a giant hoagie and forgets to come back at all.

Danger, danger, Will Robinson! Captain, she kinna take much more o'this! Mayday, mayday! Ten seconds to self-destruct—

Which would make it only about ten years past due, eh?

Jonathan steepled his hands over his mouth and swiveled slowly in the chair. The first test suite was almost over—almost time to go free Alynn from the confines of the scanner. Just another test subject, maybe a little more kindhearted than most. A stranger, who'd be out of his life by nightfall. File number 7414. Best to keep it in perspective, especially on a day like this.

Aw, fuck perspective. Life's too short. Let's have another look—

"Thank you, Alynn. Now, please tell me about a place that you'd like to visit again," Jonathan said, and checked off that question on the suite 4 script.

"Mammoth Cave," Alynn said, and smiled happily at the memory. "When we moved from Kansas City to Cincinnati—I was seven—my mom flew ahead to get the house ready, and I got to ride with my dad. We had a minivan packed to the liner with plants and breakables Mom didn't trust to the movers—her mom's china, more Hummels than I want to count, some stained glass, that sort of thing. Mom collected tchotchkes.

"Anyway, we were already on the road when we heard from Mom that there was some sort of problem about the house not being ready. So Dad decided he and I would just dawdle and sight-see. We had a stack of AAA guidebooks, and he told me to pick out anything along the way that sounded half-interesting, and we'd give it a try.

"We went to Cahokia Mounds—which was a big disappointment, just stupid little hills that didn't look like anything—and to some little classic car museum in the middle of Nowhere, Illinois, because I knew Dad liked that sort of thing. We went to Lincoln's boyhood home, after which I swore off historical sites forever. And we went an hour out of our way to Mammoth, because I'd never been in a real cave and wanted to see what it was like.

"It was October, and really cold—half of Mom's plants froze sitting in the van all day. I remember being surprised that it was in the middle of a forest, except there were hardly any leaves left on the trees, and we had to drive up a mountain to get there—I wasn't expecting that. And I remember being surprised that it was warmer inside the cave than it was outside—not warm, mind you, but warmer.

"But mostly I remember how huge the first room was, and how quiet, and how very old and magical it all seemed. We took the standard tour that everyone goes on, and the guide—his name was Ranger Guy, which, being seven, I thought was very funny. Since it was October, the park wasn't crowded, so Ranger Guy let us take our time, and told us great stories about the cave and the people who'd used it.

"Dad and I both thought it was such a kick that when we'd climbed up the tower from the Ruins of Karnak, we resented the guide making us leave. So we went and got a hot lunch in the motel, and then bought tickets for an even longer tour that took us to see the flowstone. Frozen Niagara. Dad and I were both wiped when we got back to the van, and we crashed at the first motel we saw. Ate pizza in bed watching an old movie on sat-vee. That was our last night, our last detour. The next day, we joined Mom in Cincinnati."

She paused and looked away, and for a moment Jonathan thought she was done. But then she added, "Mom and Dad had some problems, and Dad left about two years after that. He moved to Cleveland and was killed in a car crash when I was eleven. So that trip is just about the nicest memory I have of being with him. I always wanted to go back and see what Mammoth looks like in the summer, and walk through the woods—he and I talked about how pretty it must be. But I haven't done it. I don't know why." She smiled brightly. "Maybe I'm afraid of what I'll do the first time I see a seven-year-old kid with her parents."

She showed him her scar matter-of-factly, almost proudly, as though she wanted him to see that the wound no longer hurt. But he was not convinced, and he hurt for her in any case. "I bought the *National Geographic* VR discs of Mammoth," she was saying, "and I've taken all the tours that way, even gone free exploring, but it's just not the same as getting wet feet and cave mud on your clothes, and knowing that you're five hundred feet under the mountain. So— someday I'll go back."

Jonathan waited until he was sure she was finished,

then said, "This is the last question. Tell me about a day that you never want to forget."

Alynn laughed lightly. "This must be the part where you get to hear a lot of men tell you about losing their virginity, and a lot of women tell you about their weddings."

He smiled, but said nothing as she considered her answer.

"I'm pretty sure this isn't the kind of answer you were looking for, but I try not to spend too much time looking back," she said slowly. "The day I never want to forget is tomorrow—tomorrow and tomorrow and the tomorrow after that. I never want to forget that it's coming, because that's where all the promise lives. You can't change the past, and sometimes you can hardly bear the present, but if you remember that tomorrow's coming, you can get through anything, and even allow yourself a dream or two."

She wrinkled her nose. "That sounded like the last act of a sappy musical, didn't it? I hate it when I open my mouth and Pollyanna comes out. Sorry to inflict that on you. I'm done."

"Then so are we," Jonathan said, putting up his datapad. "Thanks, Alynn. No apologies required. That was all terrific."

"Can I take a peek behind the curtain now, Oh Great and Powerful Wizard of Squids?"

"Sure," he said. "Come on over."

Alynn was no wonderstruck child. When she entered the lab, she looked over the clutter of hardware with the knowing eye of a mechanic on a used-car lot, a swap-meet veteran sizing up the aisles. Her gaze fell on the bank of workstations that were the heart of the lab's data-processing LAN, and she stopped to shake her head.

"Oh, my," she said. "Those are SGI Octanes, aren't they? I haven't seen an R10000 used for anything more demanding than talking to the Library of Congress for at least five years."

Jonathan's smile was faintly embarrassed. "If you think that's bad, go look at the Dumpster-edge technology sitting on our desks."

"I don't think I could take it." Her face twisted into a sympathetic expression. "You really are doing this on a shoestring, aren't you?"

"Beggars and choosers—I'm the original second-hand Rose," Jonathan said. "Believe me, if I could get my hands on any faster gear, I would. The analysis program runs twenty-four hours a day on three nodes, and most days we're still falling behind."

"Forgive me. I'm being horribly rude—"

"No, you aren't. It's no secret to us that we're doing this on a shoestring."

Alynn had reached the center of the room by then, joining him at the control station. "I'm experiencing culture shock," she said with a shake of her head. "When I need something for my work, I just go order it."

"Academia is a different animal from the business world. Not as much different as it used to be, but, still—"

"Oh, it's me, I know, not you," she said. "But I'm afraid that when I think of a research lab, I still think of something pristine and state-of-the-art, all gleaming tile, crepe soles, and glowing lights. Like something out of *The Andromeda Strain*, or those DuPont ads."

"None of that here," Jonathan said. "This is garage science."

Something new had caught her eye—she was peering curiously at a cartoonish sketch taped above the control station. "Complete with pornographic pin-ups," she said. "What in the world? 'Dr. Briggs's Trisexual Pet Squid'?"

The playful drawing, hand-rendered in marker on plotter paper, showed an imaginatively equipped squid in simultaneous sexual congress with a variety of partners and objects, including a marching-band tuba and a tricycle. Jonathan flushed. "I'm sorry. That's been here so long I don't see it anymore—"

"Oh, I'm not offended," she said, and underlined it with a smile. "It's kind of kicky, actually. But I want to know the story."

"One day in class I said 'trisexual' instead of 'triaxial,' " Jonathan admitted sheepishly. "The next morning, we found someone had graced the testing room door with that."

"Clearly, you're not working your students hard enough," Alynn said, her smile widening. "Well, do I get a peek inside my gearbox?" she asked, and touched her temple.

"Sure," Jonathan said, surrendering his chair. "Sit here. I'll replay part of suite 3 for you."

When her face came up on the left side of the display, Alynn wrinkled her nose. "Ugh," she said. "You had to look at that for two hours?"

With pleasure, he thought. "I can blank it, if you'd rather."

"Please."

"Done. Okay, here's suite 3, time normal."

She leaned forward on her elbows and studied the rainbow matrix of her own thoughts, captured as she responded to the questions just audible in replay: What is your name? What color is the triangle? Pick a number from one to ten. Think about the smell of coffee. How many are there in a dozen?

"What do you call this?" she asked, pointing at the swirling matrix.

"That? We call that *Homo screensaver*."

Alynn laughed brightly. "I like that. Two points."

"I've been waiting a year to use that on someone," he said, breaking into a relaxed smile. "Actually, what you're looking at is a restricted vector matrix—theoretically, only the neural activity directly related to the test suite."

"There's more, then? That's not everything I was thinking?"

"No. Here, I'll show you the whole picture." He reached across in front of her, blocking her view for a moment. When he straightened up, the center display was showing the same violet-haloed map that earlier he had been guiltily watching alone.

She stood so she could peer closer at the display, and reached out a finger to touch the glass. "That's me?"

"That's you," Jonathan said with a pleased little smile. "Science fiction. Just like in all those *Star Trek* episodes. 'Captain, it's—it's a creature of pure energy!' "

"No—magic," she said, her wide-eyed gaze fixed on the screen. "The genie in the bottle." She swept her finger in a circle over the display. "Do you know what this all means? Can you read all these thoughts?"

"Hardly. I don't think anyone ever will," said Jonathan, sitting on the edge of the console. "We mapped about four thousand high-level vectors in the last two hours. But compared to how many connections there are in a human mind—trying to read a complete matrix with four thousand vectors is like trying to get along in Montreal on three badly pronounced words of French. It's just a pretty picture. Your thoughts are still your own."

"I don't know if I'm glad or disappointed to hear that. But it is pretty, isn't it? Like one of those plasma lamps." She turned toward him. "I was afraid it would be like dissecting that poor pig in high school biology."

He nodded. "All the wonder in a living thing disappers when it dies," he said. "I've never seen anything in a specimen jar that I found half as interesting as a cat playing with his toy du jour."

"Butterflies," she said. "Butterflies are still pretty when they're dead. But that's it. I never understood people who decorate with dried flowers. It's like saying 'I can't win, I can't break even, so I give up.' "

Jonathan shifted into a mock ring announcer's voice. " 'And in this corner, weighing in at a million pounds even, fresh from his triumphant tour of children's bedrooms everywhere, it's your favorite bad guy and mine, Cosmic En-tro-py!' "

She laughed delightedly. "Jonathan, can I ask you a question about what you've been doing?"

"Sure."

"What about turning the whole process around?"

"How so?"

"What about playback? Is there any possibility of letting people see and think and feel all over again what you record—of putting it back in their minds?"

"Oh—not with the SQUID. Probably not by any means. It hasn't even occurred to me to think about it, honestly. It's a one-way street."

"Does it have to be?" she said.

"I think so." He turned his head and tapped the side of his neck with his fingers. "No jacks. Unfortunately, human beings don't come with a data port. —Well, we do, five of them, but they're old-fashioned—analog, not digital. Incompatible."

Alynn wrinkled her nose in a frown. "I guess I thought you'd say that, but I still don't want to believe it. Playback would open up wonderful possibilities."

"Some pretty dismal ones, too. It's already too easy to brainwash people."

"I suppose," she said, sitting back. "Well, I guess you'd better give me that questionnaire to fill out, or I'll be here all night."

The palmtop holding the questionnaire was waiting on Eric's uncharacteristically clear desk. Alynn needed no help with the machine, so Jonathan retreated to the lab, nursing his unhappiness about her imminent departure and blaming himself, wondering why he'd chosen that particular moment to launch into a lecture on social responsibility.

But a few minutes later, his ship of gloom grounded on old-fashioned stubbornness. *Carpe diem*, he thought, and determinedly returned to the office. Alynn looked up as he neared the desk, and he dropped into a crouch beside it, putting himself at her eye level.

"Do you have any plans for dinner?"

Her face brightened. "No."

"Then could we make some? Because I'd like to hear more about those possibilities you were seeing. And I need some more time to figure out why I've been just a little dazed since I saw you in the auditorium this morning."

Her slow smile on hearing that surprised him—it was shyly pleased, and gave him just the tiniest peek past her easy self-assurance. "I'd like that," she said. "I really don't know anybody here, except you—or where to go to avoid crowds and food poisoning both. How much longer do you have to stay in the lab?"

Jonathan smiled back, and pointed at the palmtop. "That's how much longer. I'm the boss, remember? Say boo when you're done, and we'll lock up the garage and see if we can't find civilization."

* * *

Kirby's Upstairs occupied the second floor of a newly restored hundred-year-old brick building located on a side street a block from Main. Bucking both the declining local economy and the wisdom that an Ann Arbor restaurant had to appeal to the Lexus crowd or be on the campus's doorstep to survive, Kirby's was staking its survival on the formula that had made Kirby's Back Room a success cross-state, in Grand Rapids.

That formula included a menu heavy in please-your-mouth retro grill, a bar well stocked with North American alcohol, and the illusion of privacy. The restaurant was a maze of nooks and high-walled booths cleverly arrayed so that it was difficult to see or be seen by other diners, and to hear or be heard by them.

"I've been in A-squared long enough now that I know a lot of people around campus," Jonathan explained to Alynn as they were seated. "Every now and then I want to be able to go out and catch a meal without having to deal with that."

"So this is the romantic hideaway where you bring your girlfriends," she said with a smile. "What do the matchbooks say? LET US CATER YOUR NEXT AFFAIR?"

He laughed. "What girlfriends? You must have mistaken me for someone who has a life. No, I just come here when I want to get out and not be elbow to elbow with eighteen-year-olds planning to get drunk, or already drunk, or trying to get laid, or bragging about getting laid, or being breathlessly political, or complaining about the profs—"

"Or complaining about getting drunk with a breathlessly political prof and not getting laid—"

"Exactly. Don't get me wrong—I like teaching, and I love the energy of a big campus. But sometimes I have to get away from it. Besides, you have to like a place that serves Upper Canada beer and a half-pound Cardiac Burger." He glanced down at the menu. "Will you let me be old-fashioned and get this?"

"The check? Oh, no. I'm on business. My company will pick it up." He could not keep his disappointment off his face. Seeing it, she added, "But you can buy me an ice-cream cone afterward, if you like."

"Ice cream?" Jonathan said disbelievingly. "It's eleven degrees outside."

"No better time."

"How about summer?"

"No, thank you. Don't ask me why, but having yellow jackets grazing on the mint-chocolate-chip trails running down my forearm never appealed to me."

His broad smile chased the disappointment from his eyes. "Fancy that. All right, dessert at Washtenaw Dairy is on me."

When they'd ordered, Alynn sat forward and propped her elbows on the table. "I feel like you know so much more about me than I do about you—"

"All the important stuff, like whether you think left to right or top to bottom."

"—So I'm declaring it my turn to ask the invasive personal questions."

"I'm braced. Fire away."

"Who was the guy on the baseball card?"

"The baseball card?"

"Tacked to your bulletin board, in the office— Johnny Briggs, Philadelphia Phillies? Relative?"

Jonathan chuckled. "Oh, that. Only related in the sense that we're all relatives—oh, I don't know, he could be my thirty-second cousin, nineteen times removed, or some such. One of my students gave me the card. He was amused, and so was I. Souvenir of my first term."

"It's not a very close resemblance. You look more like LeVar Burton."

Jonathan shuddered and flashed an exaggerated grimace. "You just evoked a painful childhood memory involving an itchy gold costume, a girl's hair band, a media convention in Toronto, and an eight-year-old boy."

She laughed. "Are there pictures?"

"No," he said emphatically. "Not since the mysterious problem with the family file server. Which was right after my brother printed them out for my first girlfriend."

"Maybe there are relatives who still have copies," she said teasingly. "So does anyone call you Johnny?"

"Nope. Dad calls me Jon, Mom calls me Jonathan, my brother called me—well, it took me years to shed it, so you'll excuse me if I don't tell you—and everyone else lined up behind one of them. Where does 'Alynn' come from, anyway? I like it a lot—"

"My mother hates it."

"—but it's really unusual. She does? Why?"

A little sigh. "It comes from Alexandra Lynn," she said, settling back against the cushion. "That's what's on my birth certificate. But I didn't like my aunt Alexandra and I didn't want to be a Sandy. So in ninth grade I started writing A-period-Lynn Reed—like F. Lee Bailey, you know?—on all my papers. But it was too pretentious, so I dropped the period." She smiled faintly. "My father's name was Lynn."

"I think I'm getting a picture, now."

"My mother won't call me Alynn, says I've rejected her family in favor of his. My mother is one of those women who can make a naked pronoun sound nastier than a New York hack pilot effing his way through a bad day. Anyway, she's right, but she hasn't figured out yet what her part in it's been."

"Sounds like she's still holding a grudge."

"A bagful. I don't know if she hates him more for leaving or for dying—which she considers a nasty trick on his part to escape the grief she hoped to give him." She stopped and thought. "Do you know what an ant lion is?"

"Eh—isn't that the critter that digs a little pit in the sand and sits at the bottom waiting for lunch?"

"Right—except that it doesn't just sit there waiting. When the ant tries to run up the side of the pit and escape, the ant lion uses its claws to cause little sand avalanches. Poor ant runs as fast as it can and gets nowhere. And if it stops running—crunch. That's my mother. An emotional ant lion. She likes to keep the people around her off-balance. And I don't think she's said 'I'm sorry' or 'I forgive you' in twenty years. Certainly not to me."

"I'm going to go out on a limb and bet you don't go home very often."

"That isn't home," Alynn said. "The last home I had was Kansas City."

Jonathan swallowed, and couldn't find any words with which to reply. She was still displaying her scars stoically, as though she wanted to show him how strong she was, to say "That? That didn't hurt." But he knew that game for the fraud it was, and hurt for her.

Mercifully, the waiter arrived with their salads before Jonathan's tongue-tied silence became obvious. When they were alone again, she smiled brightly and said, "You're very sneaky. How did I end up answering the questions again?"

"I don't know. I have a lot of practice asking them," he said. "And I like hearing about you. I'm sorry some of it's unhappy."

"It isn't, really." She glanced down at her hands in her lap. "Doesn't everyone's childhood feel normal to them, no matter what it's like? I just know that 'family' doesn't mean the same thing to me as it does to some people. And that I don't identify with all those at-least-we-have-each-other loving-family-faces-crisis dramas. Does a blind kid miss color, or is he just puzzled by the idea?"

"Well, I guess that rules out our going to a play tonight," Jonathan said with a rueful smile.

"Why?"

"The U theater department is doing a revival of *The Waltons*—"

She squinted at him. "Did I hear that right? The student theater group is doing a live-action revival of a television show?"

He looked surprised. "Oh, sure, they do one every semester—a different episode every night, two for a half hour show. M-TV, they call it. The audiences really come out. I caught one night of *Cheers* in the fall—they did a nice job."

"I must have been looking the other way while this caught on," Alynn said, shaking her head.

"I was a bit taken aback the first time I heard about it, too. But I've heard the head of the department say that most of the best plays written in the last fifty years have been teleplays—and most of the jobs waiting for his theater majors are in front of a camera, anyway," he said, then frowned. "The only part that still bothers me is that they can fill the auditorium for *The Simpsons*, but they can't for Shakespeare or Shaw."

"Ack," she said. "Enough. You're going to make me lose my appetite. Why don't you tell me about your family." A playful smile spread across her face. "And if you don't have anything awful to say about them, please feel free to make something up."

"Okay. American mother, Canadian father, 2.2 children—my brother is the .2, and half of that is pure courtesy on account of the fact that he's technically human—"

* * *

By the time the plates had been cleared, Jonathan and Alynn had killed off a bottle of '00 Cabernet and the better part of two hours and a pound of marbled prime rib. There had been no lulls in the conversation save those forced by table etiquette, and no taboo subjects.

They talked and laughed together about religion. She called herself a Catholic in recovery. "My parents were devout Unitarians, if there is such a thing," he said, "but only the rationalism stuck. I never got the rest of it."

They talked and laughed together about sexual politics. "I'm not one of these people who think that women are just men with better morals," Alynn said. "I defy anyone to compare the afternoon TV ads with the after-midnight ads and tell me that men and women hear the same siren songs."

Jonathan allowed that, seen from the point of view of neuroscience, men and women were as identical as two computers with different CPUs and different operating systems. "And nearly as compatible," he added, and she laughed.

They sparred lightly over the president's call for a national police force—he was mildly for, she suspiciously against. She surprised him a time or two with a glimpse of a playful wickedness in her smile and her thoughts, though he was too cautious to flirt with her openly.

But he was feeling good about having negotiated the dinner without running aground on any conversational shoals—right up to the point that Alynn drained her glass of the last of the wine, gathered her red cloth napkin from her lap, and sat back against the bench padding, eyeing him with a little frown.

"Jonathan, I have to ask you something."

"What's that?"

"By my count I gave you three chances, and all three times you studiously avoided asking what I'm doing here at the conference—or anything about what I do, period."

Jonathan sat back and dabbed at his mouth with his napkin before answering. "Caught me," he said. "Guilty as charged."

Her surprised-turning-to-hurt expression told him she would have preferred a denial or an apology to a confession. "Why?" she asked with a touch of anger. "Is what I do not important?"

"The truth is that I'm terribly curious," he said with a rueful smile. "I'm just afraid that if I ask what you're doing here or why Arcadia is interested in me, I'll find out you're a front man for the CIA or something even worse—like a televangelist, or a venture capitalist. If this really was just a business dinner for you, I didn't want to know."

She looked at him thoughtfully. "Do you have something against making money, or people who do?"

"No—I just have enough masters to please already, without leasing myself and my lab to some company that does its long-term planning on a three-month calendar, or to someone who's looking for a better way to sell soap or religion. That's not why I'm doing this."

Her smile gave forgiveness for the slight. "Well—I came to the conference for Arcadia. I even came to your lab for Arcadia—mostly. But coming to dinner was for me—mostly."

His answering smile was nervous. "I'm glad."

"And there's less difference from what I do for myself and for Arcadia than you might think, anyway."

Jonathan cocked his head at her. "Now I'm confused."

"For all practical purposes, I am Arcadia," she

said. "Just me, a lawyer, an accountant, a librarian, and a tech."

"What do you do?"

"You really don't know the name, do you?" She shook her head. "Glory is so fleeting—"

"I'm sorry—"

"Don't be, I'm teasing you," Alynn said with a quick smile. "Well, you finally gave your curiosity a tongue. But I think it's only fair for me to keep you waiting a while. Back on campus, you promised you would show me what a thought looks like. Do I get the same chance?"

At once puzzled and intrigued, Jonathan nodded. "Of course."

"Good," she said brightly, and called up the bill on the touchpad. "We'll need to go to my hotel, though. I didn't want to carry everything around with me today on campus."

"That's no problem—wait a minute, you're not in the designer drug business, are you?"

She just laughed as she slid out of her coat. "Come on. You'll see."

Alynn Reed's hotel was the Bell Tower, a small full-service hotel nestled up against the northwest wall of the main campus, only a few blocks from the Neuroscience Building and in easy walking distance of the conference center. Jonathan had been past it a hundred times without ever setting foot inside, and confessed so to Alynn as they approached the entrance.

"The only time I ever rented a room in town—when I was here for my interview—it was at the Star Motel, for thirty bucks."

"I didn't want to have to fuss with either a rental car or taxis while I was here," she said, showing her keycard to the doorman, who passed them through. "Should I have warned you that Clement Harris is staying here, too?"

"No. I haven't thought about him for hours," he said, and realized it was true.

"Good. You know, I had advance warning that he was a self-important jerk," she said as they reached the elevator. "I saw him reduce a waitress to tears at breakfast, in the hotel restaurant, because something or other wasn't to his satisfaction. I almost skipped his keynote because of it."

He smiled. "I'm glad you didn't."

Her room on the fifth floor was modest in size, but plush in an old-fashioned manner, after a guest bedroom in a mansion. "Nice," he said, glancing out past the brocaded window drapes. "And a view of Burton Tower and the League. I'd guess you can hear the carillon from here."

"When does it play?"

He turned away from the window. "On the hour, with a recital every Friday afternoon. But come to think of it, I haven't heard the bells for several days. I wonder if the tower's been locked up since the last suicide."

"The last suicide? Is that a regular occurrence around here?"

"Oh—about once a year, since I've been on campus."

"No connection, I hope."

"None yet, thank chance," Jonathan said with a grim smile. "I'd hate to lose a student that way. The last suicide was someone from the comptroller's office, though."

"Light fingers?"

"His wives found out about each other," he said. "What do you have there?"

Alynn had burrowed into a soft-sided carry case

and retrieved what looked like a game system—a silver-and-black unit the size of a keyboard porta-comp, and two sleek black "bug-face" vEYEsors, which reminded Jonathan more of skiing goggles than insects. The unit went on the nightstand, connected to the phone with an optic cable. With the bug-faces in hand, she climbed onto the bed, stretching her legs out and sitting back against the headboard.

"Draw the curtains and come here," she said, patting the mound of pillows beside her.

He did, pausing to kick off his shoes before clambering onto the flowered comforter beside her. Alynn handed him a bug-head, which he held delicately, as though it were something fragile or unpleasant. "I hope you don't mind the leashes," she said, rescuing the free ends of the trailing cables and jacking in to the base. "The wireless versions just don't have the fidelity I need."

"This is VR—"

"Right."

"I don't own one."

"Really? But you've used them, right? VR parlors? Arcades?"

He shrugged apologetically. "Twice, maybe."

"Huh. Well, I guess you're not going to be able to claim me as a dependent, are you? Here, I'll show you—"

The bug-face adjusted itself to the contours of his head, completely enclosing his ears and covering his eyes and nose. "I can still see you," he said in surprise.

"Latest feature in the top-of-the-line gear—a transparent display matrix. Ready?"

"Um—sure."

Jonathan saw her pull her own visor on, then reach out and touch the unit. Then his visor darkened, and the room faded away. He jangled—it was like waking up in pitch-darkness and not knowing where he was.

A pair of electric-blue chevrons appeared at the extremes of his field of view and glided toward each other. As they crossed in the center, the space between them filled with what looked like mottled blue marble. Floating above the marble wall in black script were the words:

Ideation V
by Alynn Reed

He had thought the wall to be in front of him, like the screen of a television. But suddenly he sensed himself to be suspended in midair—no, falling toward the wall, the rush of air at his ear marking the ever-increasing speed of his descent. He clutched a handful of the bed's comforter with each hand, but that did nothing to shatter the illusion.

Below him, the lettering was fading to gray and dissipating like smoke in a breeze—all but the dot of the "i," toward which he was plunging. It rose up to meet him, swallowed him in blackness like a tunnel, and spit him back into a world turned inside out.

In the end, Ideation V was indescribable.

The television metaphor failed Jonathan almost at once. From the moment the credits ended, he could turn his head in any direction he chose, and his line of vision would sweep through a three-dimensional unreality that completely enclosed him. He did not seem to have a body, but his consciousness occupied a space in that realm, floating in the center of the universe.

It was a universe with few familiar sights or references. Neon bubbles of nothingness formed, swelled lazily, and burst. Sometimes they released a shower of light, sometimes they freed a shape that darted restlessly like a water spider, or tumbled eccentrically like a butterfly in zero G.

Like paint flung on glass, the showers of colored light splattered themselves against invisible shapes and limned them. The shapes pulsed like living things, metamorphosed defiantly, then shed their color and vanished when rain washed the light down the sides of the universe. It collected in a swirling rainbow pool beneath where Jonathan floated. The swirls became a spiral, the spiral a vortex, the vortex a hole that collapsed the universe on itself until it had but two dimensions, time and color.

For those first few minutes, Jonathan fought to make sense of it, to find meaning in it and to understand that message. But it was not a story, or any sort of didactic structure. It was not a journey. It was a visual and aural dance, sometimes languid, sometimes frenetic, and frequently startling.

Before long, the sights and sounds overwhelmed his ability to analyze them. He fought for control, but control was wholly beyond his powers. His remaining choices were flight or surrender, but he had forgotten that there was somewhere to flee to. He surrendered.

And surrender was a liberation. When he stopped trying to fit what he was saw and heard into familiar patterns, he began to experience it directly, unfiltered. Sensation superseded sentience. Wonder displaced wondering. The space occupied by his consciousness expanded until his experience was his consciousness. And from that point on, he could no longer think about what was happening, or talk about it afterward.

When the final image—an undulating electric sea stretching out to infinity—was slowly wiped away to black by crisscrossing chevrons, and the visor brightened slowly to return him to Alynn's hotel room, Jonathan found himself wide-eyed and breathless. He looked in Alynn's direction. "Wow," was all he could say.

She smiled shyly, pleased, and shed her visor, finger-combing her hair.

Clumsily, Jonathan slipped off his own visor. "You wrote that?"

Nodding, she said, "Last month."

"You write like I dream."

Alynn sparkled. "What a wonderful thing to say. That's as close as I've ever gotten to capturing something in my mind and letting someone else see it."

"Well—you said you were going to show me what a thought looks like. I think you did. And I think I'm starting to understand why you are interested in what I'm doing."

She nodded and turned toward him, sitting on her heels on the bed. "Those recordings you have—thousands of them—just think of the lives they represent, what it would mean to be able to read them in detail. If you could play them back in the mind instead of on a screen, it'd be the ultimate diary of a life, wouldn't it?"

"Go to your Sears Mind Center once a year, have your picture taken—"

"You're teasing me."

"No. I don't think it's possible, but I understand—"

"Don't you ever wish you could go back and see yourself being seven again? Or it could be a dream catcher—all those times when you wake up and a dream that you're sure meant something slips away faster than you can remember it." Her enthusiasm lit her eyes. "What if you could read someone else's, and not just your own? What if two people could use it to share consciousness, to tear down the walls that keep us apart? Self is so lonely—what a gift it would be to let people touch that way. Have you thought about any of that?"

"Not until now," Jonathan said.

"Then it's a good thing we crossed paths, isn't it?" she said with a smile. Then she added, with a shrug, "At the very least, a visit to someone else's mind'd be the ultimate in VR."

"I can't imagine it being any better than that," he said, gesturing with the visor. "You do good work."

"I'm glad you liked it. You're the first person I've let see number Five—"

"I'm flattered."

"—But that wasn't work," she said. "When I'm working, I write what the market's buying—mundane VR scenarios. Games."

"Popular ones, I'm guessing," he said. "You were surprised I didn't know you, or Arcadia."

"I have two of the five best-selling games at the moment," she admitted. "And two of the other three are VR porn. But Ideation isn't commercial. That's something I do for me."

"I don't see why it couldn't be commercial."

"Because most VR users think of themselves as players. VR scenarios are built around adventure motifs. That's what gives them high replay value. With Ideation, I'm trying to make sensation the structure, to see if I can capture the ecstatic experience. I haven't, quite—though I still like this one. But there's no market for it."

"What do you mean, you haven't?" he demanded in mock indignation. "Look, don't take this wrong, but one of the words I keep coming back to to describe what it felt like is, well, erotic."

"Sensual."

"No, that, too, but I meant erotic." He frowned as he collected his thoughts to explain himself. "Erotic like getting lost in a kiss, or a dancer completely in tune with the music and the rhythm. Erotic like—this is probably starting to sound like a come-on, isn't it? Never mind. Is there more? What about numbers One through Four?"

"I gave you the best first. It's all downhill from here."

"I don't care," he said cheerfully. "See, Alynn, you have to realize that I'm one of those people who harbors a dark suspicion that virtual reality is sucking my students' minds out through their eyeballs. You'll never get a better chance to convert me than this. Because what you just showed me—that's art."

Her smile mixed embarrassment with pleasure. "If you're really interested—"

"I am," he said. "I like where your thoughts go."

"Then I guess I could find somewhere else to take you."

They visited Ideation II, Firefly, and played tag in Alynn's game world Devil's Keep. When they finally took the visors off for good, it was well past midnight, and the bright lights of the hotel room made Jonathan's eyes ache. He reached out and turned off one nightstand lamp.

"Are you a player, too?" he asked. "You must be, or you couldn't write for them."

"Not as much as I used to be," she said. "It's kind of funny, but most of the designers I know don't play much anymore. When I was younger, though—it was a place I could be in control. It was a place where I could do anything I wanted and still be safe. I needed that for a while."

He tried to look past her at the clock. "What time is it?"

"Almost two."

"I guess I'd better go." He smiled. "Thanks for rescuing my day."

"Are you okay to drive?"

"Sure," Jonathan said, pulling on his right shoe. Then he stopped, left shoe in hand, and added, almost to himself, "But I wish it'd been sleeting ever since I got here and the streets were skating rinks, so I'd have an excuse to turn around at the sidewalk and come back up here and knock on your door."

He twisted sideways so he could look at her. "I'm probably making a mistake saying it, but what I really want to do now is fall asleep holding you in my arms. And you're probably going to throw me out of here all the faster for having the arrogance to think that just because you invited me up to your room you wanted to be asked, even though that's not what I thought at all, or what I'm asking. Alynn, I just don't want to say good-bye."

It was her turn to stare at him like a deer caught in the headlights, her eyes blinking, her brows knit in a slight frown. But she said nothing for long seconds. He smiled as brightly as he could manage and returned to the task of putting on his other shoe.

Then she touched him on his arm, and he looked back toward her. "I think I'd like it if you stayed," she said.

Alynn slept in a long T-shirt that said WAKE ME AND DIE, but also in the warm cradle of his arms. Jonathan kept on his boxer shorts, so there was hardly any bare skin touching beneath the blankets. But the sleepy warmth that flowed between them filled the bed all the same.

"Where do I know you from?" he asked in a whisper.

"I don't know."

"I keep looking at you and having that bell of recognition go off, and I can't explain why. I've been doing that since I saw you in the auditorium. I know I know you. I just can't figure out where from."

"Did you go to the Norman conference?" she asked. "Or Mt. Mercy?"

"I was at Mt. Mercy."

"That must be it, then."

"But the thing is, I can't imagine that if I really had met you, I'd be having trouble remembering when. Is this crazy?"

She found his hand and laced her fingers with his. "Maybe. But it doesn't matter."

The truth of that seemed clear to him, and his thoughts drifted to other matters. "We forgot the ice cream."

"Don't think you're off the hook," she said. "You owe me."

"Tomorrow," he said.

"Tomorrow," she agreed. "I insist."

Outside, an ambulance whined through a nearby street. The blower for the room's heat pump started, masking the sound of their breathing. Though neither was practiced at sharing a bed, they slipped easily into a comfortable lie—spoon-fashion, her head pillowed on his arm. She felt small in his light embrace; she and the moment both seemed fragile. How long can I hold you? Jonathan thought.

"I think I'm in love with you, Alynn."

Her voice was drowsy. "You don't have to say that to stay."

"I know," he said.

Alynn said nothing for a time, and Jonathan wondered if she had fallen asleep. Then she turned and kissed him softly, as though she had thought on it all night and only just decided. "That's a loaner," she said. "Give it back to me in the morning?"

He breathed her in with a contented smile. "I'll take good care of it."

They both slept as though cradled in the clouds.

3

A Discontinuity in the Continuum

Angelo's was nearly filled with late breakfast trade, but Jonathan Briggs had no trouble spotting the woman he was meeting there. He tossed his gloves onto the empty seat of her booth and slid himself along after them. "Hello, boss," he said sheepishly.

Elizabeth Froelich lowered her *Ann Arbor Observer* and shook her head at him. "It wasn't your boss who was calling you all weekend," she said as she folded the paper and tucked it beside her. "It was your friend. Jonathan, are you all right?"

Her voice carried a shadow of anger along with the concern, and a flash of memory put him in mind of how, after any number of his misadventures, his mother would take pains to determine that he was unhurt before launching into a scolding. Despite himself, Jonathan smiled. "I think so."

"You could have let someone know, then. No one's seen or heard from you for three days. And considering the circumstances—" She glanced away, then sighed. "I wasn't completely sure I was going to see you again."

"I'm sorry," Jonathan said, the amusement chased from his face. He shook his head. "I'm sorry if you were worried. But Clement Harris isn't nearly reason enough for me to kill myself."

"Evidently."

A young blond waitress appeared at their table, and they sent her away with their orders. "You blew off the conference," Elizabeth said.

"Yep. Hardly even thought about it, to be honest."

She looked curiously at him. "There's something you're not saying. You seem—buoyant."

He sat back against the cushion and smiled broadly. "Light," he said. "I feel light." He shrugged apologetically.

"And you're not your usual voluble self, either. Where did you go, off to an ashram? What's going on?"

"I met someone."

"Oh!" Taken aback, Elizabeth looked for more to say, but found her way blocked by etiquette. "She— she must have made quite an impression."

"My endorphins like her endorphins."

Elizabeth raised an eyebrow.

"Well—being in love is being on drugs, right? Who knows that better than us?"

"You're such a shameless romantic."

He grinned. "All I know is that I spent three days with a woman I can't stop thinking about. What is it the pushers say—the first fix is free?"

"This is serious, then."

"It is for me," he said.

Their meals arrived, his a country platter, hers an omelet and raisin toast. Jonathan sprinkled salt from the shaker into his hand to measure it, then scattered it over his eggs. "It's funny," he went on. "I think you learn half of everything that matters in the first hour you know someone, and spend a lifetime trying to get the rest. Don't you think?"

"I think I'm the wrong person to ask that," Elizabeth said, her smile fragile. It was Jonathan's turn to be taken aback, but she did not leave him an opening to probe. "I'm happy for you," she said. "And I'm glad you had someone to pick you up after what happened Thursday. Have you thought about what you're going to do?"

"About Alynn?"

"About your work."

His brows knitted. "Keep going. What else?"

"You still believe in what you're doing, then."

"Of course." He spun a forkful of pancakes in a puddle of syrup. "I don't think I ever told you where this began. When I was an undergrad at the U of Toronto, I read Dennett's *Consciousness Explained* for a psych class. Coming from my background, I should have taken to it like water. But it upset the hell out of me."

"It upset a lot of people, in the beginning."

"Well, most of them apparently got used to the idea that they don't really exist," Jonathan said. "I never did. I read *Consciousness Explained* three more times, back to back to back, before I finally decided that he hadn't and it wasn't. He explained it away, if anything."

"You wouldn't be the first to raise an objection along those lines." He noticed then that her eyes were bloodshot, her cheeks pallid, and realized how different her weekend must have been.

"No. But I hope to be the first to make one stick. That's what started me on this path. Liz, I don't want to have to believe that the Dennett school is right. Reductionism is—too cold to be right. Intellect without heart."

Jonathan sipped at his coffee and went on. "When

it was time to leave Toronto for postdoc, I deliberately went looking for someone who wasn't under Dennett's spell. But I never forgot which piper calls the tune. And I never deluded myself into thinking that I was going to be beloved for trying to snatch the piper's pipe away."

"That's good," Elizabeth said. "Because I don't want to see you become the Walter Pitts of your generation. Do you know Pitts?"

"No."

"Not many do anymore. That's because he stopped believing in his own work. He burned all of his unpublished papers in logic and mathematics, and drank himself to death afterward."

"Ouch."

"Ouch, indeed. Jonathan, if you don't already realize it, I have to warn you—last Thursday was just a skirmish. Are you tough enough for what's to come?"

"I guess we'll see, won't we?" he said with a too-easy smile. "What alternative is there?"

"Change your direction. Fold your hand."

Jonathan was shaking his head before she was finished. "No. I can't do that without giving up my whole view of what it means to be a human being. Maybe we really are evolution's androids, as Harris says. How did he put it? 'Biomechanical imitations of the idea of a self-aware organism with free will.' But I'll be damned if I'll concede him the point just to avoid an argument."

A pleased smile. "Then I need to put on my boss hat."

"Go ahead."

"Even though it's detestable and thoroughly unprofessional gossip, your encounter with Harris has complicated things for me. It's weakened my position that you deserve some latitude. There's another round of budget cuts on the horizon, and I don't think I can protect you as things are today."

"What do I need to do?"

"What you've been resisting doing. You have to leave the lab in Eric's hands, hide away in your little cave office, and get that first paper ready for daylight. And that's as close to an order as I'm given the authority to issue."

Jonathan pursed his lips. "I have to confess I've been trying to think of a good way to send a message to my pal C.H. that this particular bug didn't stay swatted."

"I'll give you something else to think about—speaking as your friend, now," she said. "Harris could hardly hold a conversation all weekend without bringing you into it, to ridicule. If he's trying that hard to swat you, he must be worried that there's something to what you're doing. I wouldn't be surprised if he went back to Atlanta and put two or three of his rent-a-docs to work on it. You really can't wait any longer, Jonathan. You have to publish."

"I wanted to make it bulletproof," he said with a sigh.

"It never will be."

"If I had another year, even—"

"You don't," she said bluntly. "But you have enough data to stop whispering in the basement. And somebody who tears your paper to pieces will say something that'll open your eyes to something you missed, and your work will be the stronger for it. You don't want your intellectual children to have that inbred look, after all."

Jonathan laughed. "All right. I'll start work on a paper, and you start trying to figure out who we'll have to bribe to get it published."

"We'll find some way to get it out there, Jonathan.

Just get it written," said Elizabeth. She glanced at her watch. "I have to be going—I have a meeting at nine."

"I'm going to finish this," he said, gesturing at his half-filled plate. "Don't worry about the check, I'll get it."

"Thank you." As she stood and began donning her winter armor, she asked with studied casualness, "Where's Alynn this morning?"

"Pennsylvania," Jonathan said. "She flew home last night, late."

"Ah. Too bad—I would have liked to have met the woman who could do this to you."

"You will," Jonathan said. He looked up, a foolish grin sneaking onto his face. "She's coming back—with her stuff. To live."

Elizabeth stiffened and blinked in surprise. "Well. I guess her endorphins like yours, too. Congratulations."

"Thanks, Liz." He shook his head in wonder. "It's been so strange. I had no idea that I was lonely until I met her. Does that make any sense?"

"Don't ever ask love to make sense, Jonathan." She smiled faintly as she retreated a step toward the entrance. "It's the wrong part of the brain, after all."

The new sign above the entrance to the suite said The Squid is OUT. But that morning, Jonathan's view of it was partly blocked by the head-high double stack of white boxes that narrowed the corridor by half. Easing past them, he called, "Eric, your order from the Chinese restaurant is here."

He was answered with a distant chortle. "Hey, Captain—isn't this the day? I didn't expect to see you here."

"I didn't expect to see me here, either."

Eric emerged from the lab and followed Jonathan into the office. "What happened, some delay?"

"No, Alynn's moving in today, right on schedule."

"Um—I'm not trying to meddle, but shouldn't you be there helping?"

"No need—I'd just be in the way. She paid for shelf-to-shelf, cupboard-to-cupboard moving. Designer Relocations, Inc. I offered to hurt my back for her, though."

"Hey, it's the thought that counts. Designer Relocations, eh? Those guys are fun to watch. My father's company paid for a turn-key mover when he was sent down to head up the Orlando division. A woman came in with a digital camera, photographed everything before it was packed, then went down to Dad's new place and planned where everything would go. And you're right, you'd have been in the way." Eric pointed past Jonathan toward the boxes in the hallway. "Speaking of 'in the way,' were you expecting anything?"

"Huh? No," Jonathan said, looking back. "Is that for us? I thought it was just waiting for the freight elevator."

"It got tired of riding and got off here. And it has your name on it."

"My name?"

"Yep. I had to sign for them. And FedEx almost didn't settle for me."

Jonathan frowned. "I'm confused."

They went together out into the corridor and inspected the boxes. "If these are what I think they are—" Eric said, and shook his head. "You sure you didn't commit fifty thousand dollars of grant money and forget about it?"

"Why, what do you think they are?"

Eric pointed to the corporate logo in the center of the side of the nearest box—a stylized carbon ring enclosing the initials ML. "Molecular Logic makes a deskside supercomputer with a massively parallel bus. A thousand twenty-four processors clocking twenty gigahertz, and it'll run any operating system ever made."

"Been window-shopping again?"

"I saw the one over at the meteorology department a couple of months ago. They're using it to test weather and climate models for NOAA. I'd love to see what it can do with Flight Simulator 3000."

As Eric was speaking, Jonathan found the packing slip glued to one of the largest boxes and tore the plastic envelope open. "Something called a Model 1?"

"That's it."

Jonathan handed the packing slip to Eric as he passed him, heading back toward the office. "I have to make a phone call. Don't touch anything," he said, and closed the door firmly behind him.

Since he wasn't sure where she was at that hour, he used Alynn's 700 number. When she answered, he could hear other voices and a hollow metal clanging—someone running up a loading ramp, perhaps—behind her.

"Hi," he said. "Sounds like the truck's there. Um—did some of your stuff maybe get misdirected over here?"

Alynn laughed happily. "Oh, good—you got your surprise on schedule. So now you've got something to unpack today, too."

"I don't understand—"

"I want you to have what you need to do your work. I was going to see if you could use my old Octal, but I decided half measures wouldn't do. Will the Model 1's do the job? I described your situation to my Arcadia tech and that's what he recommended."

"Lynn—I can't take this kind of gift from you."

"Oh, don't worry," she said. "None of the papers even mention the university. So nobody from the controller's office is going to be able to come say, no, we want those for the School of Family Ecology. And they're all paid for, including a year of on-site service. All you have to do is put them to work."

"Lynn, I—thank you. I'm—completely stunned. This is an incredible, an incredibly generous impulse. But we have to talk about this."

"All right," she said. He wondered if he heard a touch of impatience in her voice. "They need me upstairs right now, though. Is tonight soon enough?"

"You're coming back to Village Green? Or should I come over there?"

"That's the plan—to finish up at your place. And, Jon? We'll talk tonight, but those boxes aren't going back—so there's no reason to wait to open them up. Dive in and have fun."

When the connection was broken, Jonathan sat back in his chair for a long moment, blowing a long sigh through his hand, then scratching his cheek. Then he went out to rejoin Eric.

"Well, this stuff is ours," he said. "On loan from Alynn."

"I figured as much, from the 'Ordered By:' on this," Eric said, returning the packing list to Jonathan. "There's two of 'em, Doc," he went on, excitedly. "And they've got the extensible bus with Niagara optical interconnects—we can run them as one unit if we want. Doc, I'm worried. Once these puppies are wired for sound, I might actually get caught up on processing the archives."

"Why does that worry you?"

Eric shook his head, his expression gravely earnest. "That backlog—why, it's the only thing that's given meaning to my life. It's been the defining focus of my existence. What do you do once you've seen Disney World? What did Armstrong do after his stroll on the Sea of Tranquility? What does Sisyphus do on federal holidays? I see a crisis coming, Doc. I don't know if I can cope with leisure."

Laughing, Jonathan captured the top box of the nearest stack in his arms. "Come on. I want to see you sweat."

"Think one of these boxes has a factory technician in it?"

"It's not on the packing list."

Simply making room for the new systems in the crowded lab was a challenge in itself. Before long, the chronic shortage of clear flat surfaces exploded to a full-fledged crisis.

Midmorning found Jonathan and Eric sitting on the floor in the midst of a chaos of packing and immaculate eggshell-blue components, studying different volumes of the Molecular Logic documentation set by means of laptops perched on laps. When visitors peeked in to see if the rumors circulating upstairs were true, the two men seemed as oblivious to the clutter as a child on Christmas morning is oblivious to the pile of discarded wrapping paper and bows, and easily as happy.

By noon, they had the first system up in diagnostic mode, its configuration daemon pulling down gigabyte-sized blocks of operating system. They also had a call out to Eric's friend in the meteorology department for help. While they devoured a lunch of Caribbean conch roll and paté turnovers courtesy of Takeout Taxi, they marveled at the spectacular screen displays of the Model 1's Graphics Obstacle Course.

"We'll have to get some VR 'sets in here. We may never use a flatscreen again," Jonathan said.

"Your lady does come from another world, doesn't she?" Eric said respectfully. "I mean, normal people have a couple of extra calculators in the kitchen drawer—"

"—including one that uses a battery nobody sells anymore," offered Jonathan, "and another that has a 7 key that sticks every third time you press it—"

"—and maybe an orphan Compaq in the garage, that used to belong to their father when he was in college—"

"—which they can't quite bring themselves to throw out because it still works just fine, even if the kids can't be bothered with anything that won't run Killer Elite."

"That's the one," said Eric. "It's in the box next to the turntable that they kept in case they ever wanted to play any of the records that seem to have disappeared the last time they moved. Pass me the chips?"

Jonathan complied and took up the theme. "Normal people have a cabinetful of kitchen appliances their parents thought looked really useful and turned out not to be."

"Normal people," said Eric, wiping crumbs from his mouth, "have one more car than they really need, sitting in the driveway dripping oil onto a piece of cardboard and waiting for Jennifer to come home from college for the summer."

"Normal people still have the discs for the last three upgrades to their favorite software, just in case."

"Rusty padlocks without keys, and keys to places they used to live."

"Three corkscrews—five if they don't drink wine."

"But normal people," Eric said, "do not have extra pianos, spare forced-air furnaces, or surplus deskside supercomputers. Am I right?"

"Unquestionably. Not even one, much less two."

"So, it's settled, then. You've managed to find a

woman as strange as you are, you lucky dog. Ching, ching, ching—jackpot!"

His mouth full of steak sandwich at the moment, Jonathan smiled and raised his paper cup as in a toast.

"She's going to have her own apartment in Huron Towers, right?"

"Yep. Eighth floor, view of the river. More her office than her apartment, though—I think."

"How's that going to work, exactly?"

"We'll probably be making it up as we go along," said Jonathan. "You know, neither one of us has lived with anyone for a long time. She said she wants a place to work where she can get away and completely control the environment. And she needs a place for her cats."

Eric cocked an eyebrow. "You have something against cats?"

"Village Green doesn't allow pets, and I just started a new two-year lease. But I don't think that had anything to do with her decision," said Jonathan. "The cats keep her honest, she says—having to feed them and such. She said Archimedes and Hypatia are better than any scheduler at making sure she works every day or two, and comes back eventually when she runs away. I guess that sounds strange, too."

"Actually, not to me," Eric said. "I had an uncle who bought a macaw after my aunt died. He said it gave him a reason to come home, and someone to talk to when he got there." He grinned. "Of course, maybe she just doesn't want you to have a relationship with her cats. And who could blame her for being careful, after all?"

Jonathan wadded up the waxed paper that had surrounded his sandwich and hurled it in Eric's direction. "Just remember, you're going to want a letter of recommendation from me someday."

Eric caught the missile and flipped it into a nearby

trash can. "As I was saying, Doc, she's obviously a sterling judge of character, a woman of impeccable taste—"

"And don't you forget it."

"Good God, Eric," a new voice said. "Who's your decorator? It looks like you set off a ten-kiloton mess bomb in here."

"Hey, Archie," Eric said, scrambling to his feet to greet the newcomer. "Thanks for coming over. This is Dr. Briggs. And these—these are our new babies. You may drool enviously at will—"

They worked through the afternoon, backing up the Vector Integration Counter programs on the Octanes, substituting the Model 1's in their place, and bringing the router and storage subsystems back online. Their progress was slowed by the need to rebuild several automated routines, solve timing and interface problems, and test and retest. Archie left them a little after four, but Eric and Jonathan pushed on well into the evening.

"Unless I've missed something," Jonathan said finally, "all that's left to do is bring up VIC and let him at the matrix library. Have I missed something?"

Eric plucked a micro DVD from his vest pocket and held it up with a hopeful look on his face. Jonathan squinted to read the logo, then smiled tiredly and sat back in his chair.

"Right. It occurs to me," Jonathan said, glancing at his watch, "that we need to do some certification runs before we bring VIC up full-time. Put some of last week's work through the grinder again, so we can A-B the results and know that we've got everything set up right. Which means getting into the backup cabinets. What do you say we leave that for morning, and let this rig burn-in overnight?"

"Fine by me."

"And if you want to do a little—eh, independent testing between now and then, I don't see where that'd do any harm."

Eric grinned. "Thanks, Doc."

Jonathan left Eric happily introducing the new computers to Flight Simulator 3000. When he reached his apartment, he found it quiet, and Alynn and the cats all curled up in bed together. His bed. Their bed.

Of the three, only Archimedes, the sable tiger, seemed to notice his arrival. Lying curled in the small of Alynn's back, he raised his head, ears cocked alertly, and studied Jonathan suspiciously. But Hypatia, her purr audible across the room and her orange fur warm in the glow from the reading lamp beside the bed, did not stir from the pillow she was sharing with Alynn. And Alynn herself, fully clothed but for shoes, lay on her side atop the bedspread, hugging a pillow in apparent restful sleep.

Jonathan stood silently and watched them for a long minute or more, memorizing the sight with a small happy smile on his face. Then he tiptoed out, closing the door to a crack, and went to the kitchen to make himself dinner. There were strange appliances on the counters, a surfeit of silverware in the drawers, and a stack of three boxes beside the refrigerator, the top one opened to reveal glassware wrapped in tissue paper.

After a survey of a refrigerator uncommonly crowded with unfamiliar foods, he started construction on a sandwich. Before he had finished, Alynn came up behind him, her arms going around his chest and her cheek against his spine. "Hi," she said. "You must be the papa bear. Sorry, but I ate all the porridge."

"Hi," he said, turning into the embrace and kissing her forehead. "Sorry if I woke you. It's hard to be perfectly quiet in a kitchen."

"I didn't mean to fall asleep. It's only nine o'clock. For some reason today just wore me out."

"Stress. Moving's one of the top ten stressors in everyday life. Right up there with new relationships." He advanced his kiss down the bridge of her nose to her lips. "If I'd known I was going to find you in bed, I'd have been home hours ago."

"For all the good it would have done you," she said with a smile, breaking the embrace. "Go on, finish making your dinner." At that moment, Archimedes appeared and rubbed himself on her ankles. "Is it all right about the cats? I didn't want to leave them alone tonight, they're both still spooked by the move. Once I spend some time with them there tomorrow, they should settle down."

"It's fine," he said. "The management will never know unless they both decide the living room's their sandbox. How did everything go today?"

They sat together at the dinette while he ate and she related the Case of the Disappearing Pentagram. A wall hanging that appeared in the photographs and on the inventory had come up missing from the truck. The move supervisor, the driver, and Alynn were mystified for several hours as calls and faxes bounced back and forth between Ann Arbor and Pittsburgh, until finally the story unfolded.

"Do you know what a woman's star is?" Mouth full, Jonathan shook his head. "Sure you do. The mirror of Venus, the astrological symbol? With a pentagram inscribed in the circle. Mine was hand-carved from rosewood, unfinished, about this tall." Alynn held her hands a foot apart. "I had it by my front door.

"Well, it seems that the packer assigned to the living room—a brand-new employee, on his second job—was a Liberty Cathedral member. And all his training about packing without prying and treating what you handle like your own went pffft. He decided my woman's star was satanic and blasphemous, and disappeared it."

"Oh, no—"

"Oh, yes. Threw it in the Unreclyclables Dumpster for my cottage circle."

"That's outrageous. He confessed to this?"

"I think 'boasted' is the word you want."

"Any chance that they can find it?"

"Oh, they already have. It's on the Pittsburgh district manager's desk. If we'd been on a twice-a-week waste pickup schedule, it would've been gone. But it's been rained on, and I guess it drew up some stains from Lady-knows-what in the Dumpster. Maybe it can be saved, though."

"They'll pay for that, I assume. And so will he."

"He's now looking for work. And DRI's been very apologetic. Since what happened wasn't exactly accidental, they're taking 15 percent off my bill, plus covering repair or replacement, price no object. And my poor little star will be here in the morning, air freight," she said.

"I think I'd be a lot more upset than you seem to be."

"It's a thing, Jonathan," she said, then smiled. "But just think if that Bible-blinded wunderkind had been assigned to my library. Or the chest at the foot of my bed. I'd be missing a lot more than a hundred-dollar sculpture from a craft fair."

Jonathan drained his glass of birch beer and set it aside. "So when do I get to peek into your library?"

"I was thinking you might pick me up tomorrow after you're done at school. You can come up and see the office, and then you can take me car-shopping. I sold the SUV to my old landlord—I need a little town car."

"Sounds doable," he said, rising and carrying his plate to the kitchen.

She followed him as far as the refrigerator. "If you're ready to talk about your day, I think I'm awake enough to have that conversation now."

"Oh—" Jonathan shrugged. "It can keep."

"No, no. Bad precedent. This is our first night together, and I don't want to start out that way," she said. "I don't want you afraid to tell me how you feel. I don't want to have to think that what we've started here is that fragile."

"So—truth time?"

"Please."

"Let's go sit down somewhere," he said.

After displacing some boxes that had settled there first, they settled on the couch. Alynn waited for him to start.

"When I called you this morning, I was—" Jonathan searched his thoughts for a word both truthful and diplomatic.

She waited several seconds, then offered, "Angry?"

"No. Finding it hard to be grateful. Finding it easier to be a little suspicious."

"Was that because you started wondering what I was up to? Did you think I'd sent those workstations to you for me—for my purposes?"

"I wondered, anyway."

"Because it's too big. Too much. Makes you feel like you owe me."

"I guess."

"I thought so." She sighed and sat back against the arm of the couch, facing him. "I thought we'd have to have this conversation, and I hope we don't have to have it twice. Jon, I could do that for you without a second thought or an ulterior motive. There doesn't have to be an angle for me except wanting you to be happy."

"That's $100,000 worth of happy you dropped on my doorstep."

"More like 120, if you're counting—Boone slapped new tariffs on Korean electronic components, effective January 1. But Jonathan, Ant Wars alone earned me half a million dollars last year, clear. And it was the runt of the litter."

Jonathan was blinking in surprise. "Really?"

"Really." She drew her legs up on the couch and crossed them beneath her. "I'm not rich—I've met rich people, and I know the difference. But I've made more money than I had plans to spend. You know, like those poor folks who win the lottery and keep working, because they don't know how to live any other way? That's what I did—I hit the lottery."

"It's not like it was luck, Lynn—" he protested.

"Wasn't it? I didn't pick my talents from a menu, after all. Luck of the draw. Please—don't try to talk me out of thinking this way. If I start to think I deserve it, I won't be fit to live with."

Jonathan yielded. "All right. But if you're not rich, if you're just Fortune's child—"

"There's a limit to how much I can spend without turning into my mother," she said. "I don't want the Big House on the Hill—it just makes me feel small. I don't have enough ego to fill it. I don't want to trade in my jeans for thousand-dollar dresses. I don't want to start collecting Hummels and jewelry, like the curator of some private museum of kitsch."

"Do you do anything for yourself?"

"Of course," she said cheerfully. "I buy every neat new gadget I want without waiting for it to come down to commodity prices. I throw as much as the IRS will allow into a pension plan that I think of as bottled luck. I indulge myself with weekly professional massages, a Skynet subscription, wild-hair weekenders in strange cities, and having Kansas City barbecue flown in once a month.

"And every now and then, I do something for a cause—or a friend—I believe in." She smiled almost shyly. "I love you, Jon. That's all the reason I need. Please let me do this."

Finally, he understood. It was a selfless gift—the expression of a selfless spirit of a kind that was new and almost alien to him. He scooted along the couch toward her and drew her into his arms. "I'm sorry I was such a dunce," he said. "Thank you, sweet."

"My pleasure," she said. "You big jerk."

Jonathan answered the insult with a kiss, to which she did not seem to object. "Can I get you to trade in your jeans for a ten-dollar set of washed-into-submission percale sheets?"

"Maybe—if the sheets have ugly flowers on them."

He gaped at her with dumb suspicion. "Why?"

"Why? Everyone knows ugly flowers are the Western world's one true aphrodisiac."

"They are?"

"Well, they must be," she said with deadpan earnestness. "It can't be an accident so many people have worked so hard to fill our bedrooms with ugly flowers—can it?"

A grin broke through his uncomprehending stare. "I can safely say that I've never considered the question," Jonathan said with a shake of his head. "But I think we should go test your theory on a bed of faded—eh, I think they might be peonies. Purely in the interest of science, of course."

"Why, Jonathan, you silver-tongued romantic, you."

"What can I say? You inspire me."

She smiled piquantly. "Well, I can try."

They made slow, quiet, intense love under the watchful and possibly envious eye of Archimedes, who perched determinedly on one corner of the bed while they were so engaged, then insinuated himself between them when at last they stopped moving in unsettling ways.

As sleep crept up on him, Jonathan was filled with a profound contentment, and the apartment seemed bathed in peace. There was a rightness about Alynn's presence in his life, his spaces, as though she brought to them all that had been missing from them. It was a feeling and a moment he wanted to remember.

"If I'm going to be held responsible for anniversaries, I want advance warning," he said, nudging Alynn. "What do we count tonight as? I'm going to have to write these things down, you know."

She opened her eyes and smiled at him. "Count it as Flowers 1, Forces of Chaos and Entropy nothing."

They lived out of time-sync. She was an owl, he a lark, and they made their lives together in the twilight.

The pattern of their days that spring was this: Without benefit of alarm, no matter how late he had been up, Jonathan would awaken shortly after the sun first struck the panels of the bedroom's vertical blinds. Slipping out of the room, he would eat a simple breakfast with the overnight news. Then, still wearing only the T-shirt he had slept in, he would closet himself in the second bedroom and go online to the lab to wrestle with his paper for a few hours.

As noon approached, he would rejoin Alynn in bed, or she would come find him at his desk. They would eat together, breakfast for her and lunch for him—or, sometimes, make love in the warm light that bathed the bed. Then he would have to hurry to the earlier of the two afternoon classes he was teaching that semester. The balance of his afternoons he kept for office hours and class preparation, leaving the lab in Eric's hands.

Alynn spent her afternoons in her own apartment-office. Jonathan knew little about what she did there—she would only work when she was alone, and would not talk about her projects until they were finished. He imagined her in her rooms high above the river, looking out from her balcony with a cat on her shoulder, and saw her as a twelve-year-old tomboy perched in a tree, imagining a more interesting world to inhabit.

Jonathan could not call her—her voice mailer intercepted any interruptions from outside—but every day, late in the afternoon, she would call him to make plans for their evening. She had discovered how little he knew about what existed off-campus and bought a coupon passbook, less for the discounts than to serve as a "visitor's" guide. It became the focus of a game they called Recreation Roulette—one of them riffling through the book, the other sticking a finger in at random to decide what they would do or where they would eat.

"With what I do, it's too easy for me to end up staying home all the time with people I made up," Alynn told him. "You have to make me go out and do things if you want to keep me sane. It doesn't matter what we do, as long as it's not canned fun."

So they braved bowling, canoeing in Gallup Park, and even paragliding lessons, and turned miniature golf into a fierce but friendly war for bragging rights. Ice-skating was a disaster of laughter, but riding rented bikes through Nichols Arboretum and along the river was sufficiently delightful that both of them bought twenty-one-speed mountain tourers the next day. And though Alynn expressed disinterest in what she called "looking-at" entertainments, they spent a night at the harness-racing track, another at a comedy club, and several nights taking in live folk music at the Ark.

Weekends allowed for more ambitious adventures. Alynn surprised Jonathan with box-seat tickets for a Saturday afternoon game at Tiger Park, and then Toronto surprised him by stealing a 7–4 victory over the home club. Jonathan talked Alynn into trying horseback riding at the state park in Pinckney, and then had trouble talking her into giving back the horse. There was no lure powerful enough to tempt them into Detroit, but they took the SpeedRail all the way to Chicago and then back to Toronto in the same breathless weekend—just because Jonathan had never been to the top of the Sears Tower and Alynn had never been to the top of the CN Tower.

In mid-April, Jonathan's parents, Julian and Ellen Lee, made curious by something they'd heard from or in their son, came to Ann Arbor for a weekend. Without crowding too close, they joined Alynn and Jonathan for three meals, a long afternoon of flea-market shopping, and a Saturday evening of easy conversation in an outdoor hot tub.

"I like the way they are together," Alynn told Jonathan when his parents had gone back to Toronto. "We could be like that." It was as though until then she'd had no vision of what it might mean for two people to grow old together comfortably and happily.

Life reacquired an intensity Jonathan had forgotten it could have. But his life had seemed full to him before, and he wondered how he kept finding room for so much more. Part of the answer was that he was cheating his classes. Only his glibness and the fact that he had taught both courses twice before kept it from showing more than it did. And he and Eric had temporarily shuttered the SQUID chamber, since neither of them had the time to build or keep up with even a modest testing schedule.

But it seemed to Jonathan that most of the difference was inside him. Everything was lit by a different light, somehow all at once steadier, softer, and brighter. He had not known he was lonely until the day he knew he was in love with Alynn. Perhaps, he thought, he had not let himself know.

Their best times were at the end of the day. Curled up together on the couch or in bed, her head on his shoulder or his in her lap, they would listen to music or the day's news queue, talking quietly if at all. If they made love then, it was languid, unfocused, unselfish, a gentle passion rather than a fiery or playful one.

No matter how they passed the time, most nights, he would be asleep by midnight. In what had become a tender ritual, she would kiss him and whisper, "I want that back in the morning." Then she would leave him to do whatever undone thing most nagged at her—perhaps to test-play a competitor's new product in the living room, perhaps to return to Huron Towers for a few hours' more privacy.

But she would come back in the middle of the dark hours and wordlessly cuddle up against him like a child seeking the security of her parents' bed. He kept that perception to himself, for it was important to Alynn not to need anyone's protection, and there was no hint of need or dependence in what they would admit to each other about their bond. Alynn had bloodied her own hands hammering out her armor, and wore it with a craftsman's quiet pride.

Even so, when Jonathan would wake in the morning and find her small and trusting in the cradle of his arms, or clinging to him spoonwise in a sleep-stilled hug, he felt like her shield and defender, and liked the feeling. Against what dragons he sheltered her, he could only guess; but it pleased him that he could offer her refuge, even if only in a wordless Morphian pact. It was the least that he would have done for her, even if it were the most she would allow.

His own dragons sneered and mocked him as they prowled outside the door; but as long as he held her, they would not enter. So he laughed at them and lingered, listening to her slow, deep breaths, knowing her warm against him, looking on her face in sleep when geometry allowed, until the cool morning called him away.

And those were the very best moments of all.

It was almost predictable. On the morning Jonathan's life blew up under him, rude surprises were simply in the air.

A cup of coffee in one hand and a plastic-wrapped pastry in the other, Jonathan wandered sleepily into the living room. "Good morning, Alfred."

Across the room, red lights winked on. "Good morning," said his digital secretary. "Ready."

"Show me new mail," Jonathan said, settling on one end of the couch. The television panel brightened. He scanned the list that appeared and sat back, raising the cup to his lips. "Defer. Show me my news queue."

It was the morning after Blue Jays pitcher Brian Thomassen threw a one-hitter in Yankee Stadium, and then was killed with one shot by a Yankees fan in his hotel lobby. The fan had watched the game on cable TV in a Bronx bar, where, witnesses said, he had been both drinking and betting heavily.

It was the day after Cincinnati police raided Jaeco Media, publishers of the lesbian videozine Fist, arresting the owner and thirty-one employees—all women. The raid was Ohio's first under the MacKinnon "hostile environment" women's civil rights statute. Mrs. Amanda Pickson, a minister's wife and the complainant in the case, primly told CNN that "the very idea of a woman lying with another woman degrades me as a wife and mother."

And it was the morning that the new Republican administration defaulted on nearly $6 billion in treasury notes held by Korean banks, calling it "not a retaliation, but a warning to all of America's trading partners that we will not sit still and be bled by foreign leeches until all that's left is an economic corpse." The best the president's cheerleaders could find to say was that the move would (momentarily, albeit) reduce the national debt, the first time that had happened in two decades.

The Thomassen murder and the Jaeco Media raid were one-shots, headed straight for the talk shows. But the default story would carry the buzz all day long. Before Jonathan finished his crumb cake and coffee, the European Community called an emergency meeting of the ministers of commerce, and the Korean ambassador was demanding an audience with the president.

As Jonathan rinsed his mug in the kitchen, NBCi announced a flash poll showing 71 percent support for the default. While he brushed his teeth, the New York Stock Exchange, apparently heeding some other poll, suspended trading until 2 P.M. as a "precaution."

Jonathan took it all in without any clear idea what it might mean to him. Alfred had no instructions to show him routine political and economic news, and so he had missed most of the foreshadowing. Dump-and-gouge strategies? Korean-Chinese price collusion? Inflation-stoking? Predatory marketing? He suspected Alynn had paid more attention and would have a better grasp of the ramifications, and thought briefly about waking her.

But he did not have much time to think about it. The phone rang as he opened his office door, even before he could settle behind his keyboard. The caller ID window showed that it was Eric calling, on the lab line, and Jonathan picked up.

"What's up, guy?"

"You are, finally," Eric said, with the impatient ill humor that comes with worry. "I've had a Notify pending for almost an hour and a half now. I didn't know you had a do-not-disturb sign up at night."

"I didn't used to."

"Yeah, well, I was on the verge of riding over there and throwing rocks at your window. Doc, you'd better come in. Molly One kicked out an anomaly report overnight that you need to see."

"What kind of anomaly? What was Molly One doing last night?"

"Deep correlation analysis—the new program."

"And—"

Eric hesitated. "A matrix match. Tweedledum and Tweedledee," he said finally.

"How close?"

"To four nines."

"I'm on my way," Jonathan said with a worried frown.

During the short drive to campus, Jonathan kept his fears at bay by brainstorming a list of ways to explain away the threat now looming over the project.

From the start, he had understood that uniqueness was the keystone of any antimechanist model. Premise: We are different because we think differently. Premise: We think differently because there exists something uniquely individual about each neural matrix, something at once dynamic and stable, something that both distinguishes one from another and provides the unity between the child and the man.

Jonathan did not know quite what it was, but he had glimpsed it, in the dancing patterns of the vectors.

Brains and environments are all that is, said Clement Harris. Consciousness is the membrane of the cell, nothing more—the sentry at the door, the face it presents to the world. When I think a thought about thinking, is there any difference between the "I" and the thought? Where can a thought stand to see itself?

Uniqueness was Jonathan's answer. That all brains "think" alike, following the strict mechanistic rules of neurochemistry, was a reality Jonathan could not dispute. But he hoped to show that all persons do not think alike—thanks to the integrity of process he called personality, because he dared not call it consciousness. We are not the sum but the synthesis and the synergy of our parts.

But if the matrices were not all different—if all personalities were not unique—

"Then I'm fucked," he said glumly to the empty car.

There was a beggar at the north entrance to campus, a curly-haired middle-aged man with a droopy moustache and dead eyes, wearing faded jeans and carrying a cardboard sign that read WILL WORK FOR FOOD. The beggar showed the sign in Jonathan's direction as he waited in line to be cleared through the gate, but it was a gesture empty of hope, calloused to the expected rejection.

Toronto had not prepared Jonathan for such things. He had never grown accustomed to the sight of homeless people, or to the guilty discomfort the sight evoked in him. While in Boston, overwhelmed by their numbers, he had learned to avoid eye contact, almost to avoid seeing them entirely. When he had first come to

Ann Arbor, he had been relieved to find that there were mercifully few of them, and compassion crept back in.

But their number had increased with time, and he had fallen back into his old habit of looking away. This time, though, he found himself staring.

Isn't misery personal? Isn't pleasure? Isn't love? he asked the beggar silently. I'd like to see Harris tell you directly that your pain is an illusion—that you don't really exist to feel the despair you wear on your face.

Jonathan shook his head. What arrogance. What a hollow vision. Dear God, if I had to believe that, I think I'd kill myself. Wind-up machines with push-button controls—there has to be more to being than that. The matrix match has to be a mistake. I can't accept anything else—

Despite his insensible state, the beggar finally noticed Jonathan's attention, and decided to take it as encouragement. Jonathan lowered his window and fumbled in his wallet while the beggar approached.

"Here," he said, and held out a fifty-dollar bill.

The man was slow to take it. "Rather have work than a handout," he said with stiff pride.

"I know," Jonathan said. There were three car lengths open ahead of his car, and a horn sounded impatiently from behind. "But you earned it."

"How?"

By being there, hurting more than I am. But he couldn't say that, so he said, "Someday, somewhere, you earned it and didn't get it. You know better than me when."

Jonathan expected an argument, but the man nodded wordlessly, took the bill, and said a quiet "Thanks" before turning away.

The horn sounded again from behind. Jonathan answered with a contemptuous one-finger salute, held high out the window, and stood on the brake a few extra seconds before pulling ahead.

Even you, he thought. Even jerks are more than programmed responses. I'll give anyone the benefit of the doubt on that. Only children say "I couldn't help it"—adults should be ashamed to take that dodge.

Kelly and Eric were both waiting for Jonathan by the lab door, wearing expressions that belonged in an emergency room lounge.

"Long faces won't help any," Jonathan said, managing a respectable imitation of a smile. "Let me see the anomaly report."

"It's on your desk," Kelly said.

They followed him inside and stood back while he skimmed the single sheet of paper. "All right," Jonathan said. "I'll entertain any possibility except one. That includes any manner of screwup or stupidity on my part or yours, any flavor of software or hardware glitch. The only unacceptable answer is that this match isn't an error."

"We have a few ideas." That was Eric, cautious.

"I have a few of my own. I want a look at it myself first, though. Can you bring these two records—0218 and 6853—up side by side on Molly One and Molly Two?"

"All ready to go."

Jonathan stood with his arms crossed and one hand on his chin, studying the shimmering matrices as the first test suite ran in synchrony at half speed.

"I don't see it," said Kelly.

"Shh," said Jonathan. "I do."

He watched through to the end, though he had seen what he needed to in the first minute, in the intangible gestalt of the matrix about which he would not speak.

When the first suite ended and Molly One's screen went blue, Jonathan was wearing an expression grimmer than either of his assistants' had been.

"It's a closer match than twins," said Eric.

"Let's look at the documentation on those two subjects, and the audit trail," Jonathan said.

"Isn't there any more to compare?" Kelly asked.

Jonathan shook his head. "Not for the early numbers, the old scans I did while I was in Toronto. I added the second suite in Boston and the third here." He sat down at the terminal and called up the first record.

Number 0218 was one Dugan Beckett of Toronto, male, age sixty-one at the time he was tested. "I remember him," Jonathan said, leaning back. "Looked like the perfect gentleman grandpa in the chair. But he had a very dry and bawdy sense of humor when he was out of it—kept us all laughing."

Number 6853 was one Brett Winston of Toledo, Ohio, male, age four when tested. "That was one of mine," Eric said. "Can't say as I remember him, though. We mapped a lot of preschoolers last spring."

"Well," said Jonathan, "let me make perfectly clear what the stakes are. A matrix match would falsify either the definition of personality on which all of our mapping has been based, or—worst case—could falsify the entire premise of the research.

"The reason is that it's an absurdity," he went on, "to say that two different brains possess the same personality, or that personalities are mostly unique, except for the exceptions.

"If an infinite number of mental monkeys types on an infinite number of neural typewriters, and two of them produce *War and Peace* with no more difference between the manuscripts than a few synonyms, commas, and the typeface—" He pointed toward Molly

One. "That's all the differences amount to. Closer than twins, as Eric said."

He tried the smile again, but less convincingly. "So, quick—give me some reasons not to be worried about this."

"What about a file error?" asked Kelly. "We could have copied over part of one file with another, gotten them cross-linked. We've been moving things around a lot in the last couple of months, after all."

"No," Eric said. "Can't be. Those two files never even resided on the same server. And I did byte-for-byte compares on the backups—unless we somehow managed to mung them at the same time, the files Molly matched are the original session records."

"Any other ideas, then?" Jonathan asked.

"Sure. We're running a hundred-thousand-line program on a massively parallel networked platform with which we're not all that familiar yet. Maybe we finally hit just the right combination of routines and data to flush out a bug. Every system's got 'em."

"I was wondering about the possibility of another kind of bug."

"How's that?"

"A cruise virus," said Jonathan. "The lab's not isolated, after all. We're on three nets, you and I both have remote command access to the system manager, and we've all been known to walk a disk in here from time to time. If I wanted to stop us in our tracks, hatching a virus to rewrite a couple of our data files would be a particularly nasty way of doing it. It's a booby trap for publication. Whether we include those data or not, we're wide-open to challenge."

"Doc, you have a devious mind," Eric said admiringly. "I don't think I ever want you pissed at me."

Kelly asked, "But who'd want to do that?"

"Anyone who has reason to want to see us look

like idiots," Jonathan said. "Not that I'm making an accusation, mind you."

"Oh. *That* someone. Of course not."

"Well, you're right enough that the lab's wide-open," said Eric, "despite the virus scanners on all the front doors. And you're right that there's been enough time for a cruise virus to find us. But if you're right, there won't be a trace of it left anywhere in the system, except maybe a hidden marker to tell other copies that it's already been here."

"But it would still be out on the nets."

"Probably."

"And if it was a hardware glitch or a software bug, we should be able to re-create it and track it down."

"Maybe," Eric said slowly. "Not easily. There's no such thing as a perfect diagnostic or debugging tool, either. Sometimes computers get a little quirky and in the end there isn't anyone who can tell you why."

"Well—at the very least, we need to recertify our systems and our procedures," Jonathan said. "If I can't have confidence in the work product, we're all wasting our time here. We have to pull the plug, quarantine the Mollies, and rebuild the system from the bottom up before we continue. And everything we've done since they got here has to be considered suspect until we can do a verification pass on a clean system. How long, Eric?"

"How many hands?"

"All three of us. Hired hands, too, if we need them."

Eric frowned. "Three weeks. Maybe more."

"That's about what I figured," Jonathan said with a little sigh. "In the meantime, we're going to have to find Mr. Beckett and young Mr. Winston and get them both in here for retesting. If retesting doesn't solve our problem, it ought at least to define it." He looked to Kelly. "Can you take on that job?"

She nodded. "I'll find them," she said. "Do you want me to make the calls once I do?"

"Yes. Tell them we'll pick up transportation and lodging—all their expenses. If you have to, offer them a fee."

"How much?"

"I don't think we can afford to have them say no. But I don't want it to look like there's a problem. Make it sound routine, longitudinal studies or some such."

"I can do that," she said, standing. "I'll get on it right now."

Jonathan looked to Eric as Kelly left them. "Can we get anything useful done before my one o'clock?"

"Decide exactly what we're going to do, before we start pulling cables and wiping files. I was thinking that the disaster recovery plan might give us a good skeleton."

Jonathan reached for a tablet. "Let's call it up, then, and take a look."

They were still at work an hour later when Kelly rejoined them. She wore a stunned, wide-eyed expression, as though someone had slapped her. "Dr. Briggs—"

Jonathan and Eric looked up. "What is it?"

"I found Brett Winston. His parents will drive up with him next week—"

"Terrific. Great work."

She shook her head. "Not so terrific," she said. "I found Dugan Beckett, too. He's in St. James's Cemetery, in Cabbagetown. He died of colon cancer five months after you tested him."

"Damn," Eric said softly.

Jonathan closed his eyes momentarily, a slight twitching at the corners of his mouth the only outward sign of his struggle to hold himself together. "Thank you, Kelly," he said, looking away. "We're going to be spending a lot of hours here. Let's put in some munchies and everyone's caffeine of choice. Would you put together a list and make the run?"

"Sure," she said.

"Thanks," said Jonathan, standing. "I'll be back in a while. I'm going to go put Dr. Froelich in the picture, then find a good wall to pound my head on." He grinned ruefully. "Adversity builds character, right?"

"That's the rumor," Eric said.

"Better hope so," said Jonathan, as lightly as he could manage. "I think we're looking at a major construction project."

A low-flying helicopter beat a raucous tattoo against the sliding glass doors of the apartment's balcony, interrupting the conversation under way there.

"No searchlight—probably a scrambulance, headed to the U hospital," Jonathan said, craning his head to follow the lights across the night sky until they vanished behind the roof of the building.

"Sometimes they pass over the Towers so close that it sounds like they're landing Marines on the roof," Alynn said, and snuggled closer to him on the glider. "You were telling me about Dugan."

Jonathan drew a long breath and let it out as a sigh. "When Kelly came in and told me he was dead, I was just crushed. A party balloon the morning after. A 'toon who's had a piano dropped on him.

"All the way over to the lab this morning, I was telling myself, 'You can always get them back in and map them again. That'll settle this.' It never even occurred to me that one of them might be gone."

"I remember when my father was killed," she said, "the biggest shock wasn't that he could be taken away. It was that I was sure I would have more time. It's so

easy to take for granted people who are out of sight—
as if they'll always be there, waiting for when we need
them. It's not how close we are to them—it's the unfinished business we have with them."

"Yeah. That's kind of how this feels," he said, and
squeezed her hand. "You know, honestly, I've had it
easy. All I ever had to do was take the road that was
open to me. Oh, I've worked hard enough, but you can
work just as hard in a miserable job as you can in a
good one." He shook his head. "It's all gone—pffft. I
feel like I've used up all my luck."

She smiled brightly at him. "You'll find a way to get
past this."

"There isn't any. It's a dead end. It doesn't make any
difference, though," he said with a shrug. "There's no
virus. There wasn't any hardware glitch, or software
bug, or file error. We don't need to re-spec the map. A
month from now, Eric and I are going to look at each
other and say, 'Huh. Guess it is a match, after all.'"

"But you said—"

"As soon as I saw the matrices side by side I knew
we were in trouble. Eric said they were closer than
twins. He was right. Lynn, I've seen thousands of these
things. I've learned to see things in them that even
Molly can't. Those two maps are like snapshots of the
same person ten years apart."

"I don't suppose you can just discard those two
data points. Or even just one of them."

He laughed. "Sure we could. And we could get
away with it, too. Hell, who'd know? It's all in the
family. But it'd be like sending a sub out on its shake-
down cruise knowing that there's just this one little
bum weld concealed behind a bulkhead—"

Neither said anything for a time. The steady white-
noise rain of the pond's aerator fountain, masking the
pedal tone of tires and motors from US 23, filled the

space. Somewhere, a keening siren rose and fell away like the call of a night bird.

"Jonathan?"

"What?"

"If you're sure that it is a match, what would retesting them have settled?"

"Where we went wrong," he said. "Now I'm probably going to have to find a second match to explain why we got the first one. And who knows how long that will take?" He sighed, hooked his heels on the railing, and closed his eyes.

"Jonathan—"

"Mmm."

"Maybe they really are closer than twins."

"What do you mean?"

"When did Dugan die?"

"Eh—five years ago, more or less."

"How old is Brett?"

"Four—no, no, no, no," he said, sitting up. "Don't even say it."

"Why not? What if they match because they are the same person?"

"Alynn—look, that's just flat impossible, all right? When you close the refrigerator, the light goes out. If there's one thing everyone in neuroscience agrees on, it's that."

She shook her head. "I didn't expect this from you."

"What?"

"Pulling rank."

He frowned and looked away. "Well, I didn't expect to find out that you believed in reincarnation."

"Why? Because you thought I was too well educated to fall for that kind of nonsense?"

Jonathan made a face. "I'm in trouble with you here, aren't I?"

"No," Alynn said. "I just want you to realize that

you're harboring a prejudice about something you apparently know nothing about."

"What is there to know?"

"That life is a circle," she said gently. "It's everywhere else in the sciences—conservation and transformation, cycles of matter and energy, the planets in their courses, parent to child to parent and death begetting life. And the connectedness of everything, from a beginning that might have been an ending right through to this moment. Why should consciousness be the only reality that never touches anything and always dies?"

Her earnest sincerity did not persuade him, but it squelched his inclination to argue. *No reason I have to try to take this away from her,* Jonathan thought, sitting back in his chair. "I guess science class wasn't the religious experience for me that it was for you," he said with a crooked grin.

"Maybe you missed something, then?"

He covered his mouth with a hand and looked off into the night. "Alynn, I'm in trouble enough already just for walking through the neighborhood where consciousness and personality and the soul hang out. Even if I believed your explanation, the slightest hint that those things have any reality apart from the body would ruin me professionally. The best I'd be able to do after that is tabloids and talk shows."

"You're probably right," she said. "Is that a good enough reason not to look at it?"

"Alynn—I just don't have anyplace in my paradigm for that hypothesis. I don't know what to do with it."

"Think about it," Alynn said, "like you would any other. Maybe it's your paradigm that's the problem, not your results."

"I guess I can do that," he said slowly, then smiled ruefully. "A paradigm is nothing more than a prejudice about the way the world works, after all. But, Alynn, I don't want to deceive you. Much as I'd like to stick a knife in Harris's materialism, I don't believe for a minute that reincarnation is anything more than the wishful thinking of intelligence faced with its own extinction."

"I know," she said. "That's why we've never talked about it before tonight."

"But I will think about it," he promised. "And maybe I'll print out Holmes's Law to hang on the wall in the lab, as a reminder."

"Holmes's Law? I don't remember that one."

" 'When you have eliminated the impossible, whatever remains, however improbable, must be the truth—' "

"Oh—Sherlock Holmes," she said, laughing. "Fair enough." She cocked her head at him. "Can we go in? I'm getting cold."

"Sure. All of a sudden, I've gone from wired to exhausted."

"Then let's go to bed," she said with a tender smile, standing and rubbing the chill from her bare arms.

Jonathan let her lead him into the apartment and into the cocoon of quiet warmth they made together under the thin blanket. Nonsense. Wishful nonsense, he thought just before he fell asleep. But appealing nonsense.

He dreamed again of storms.

4

The Fine Thread of Reason

The long plush starboard corridor of the *Radisson Diamond* was deserted except for Alynn—the man she had been pursuing had disappeared, behind one of the dozens of gilt-trimmed wood-panel cabin doors.

Her sunbrella was not much of a weapon, but she clutched its handle tightly nonetheless as she tried the nearest door. The door was locked—which settled nothing. He could be anywhere.

Alynn could hear the cruise ship's turbines, far away and below in the twin hulls of the catamaran, but faintly enough that she did not expect to feel them. Her own footsteps on the soft blue floral carpet made no sound she could discern.

When she heard distant laughter, she looked back over her shoulder. She saw a drunken female passenger, hanging on the arm of a tall black crewman as she staggered down the corridor.

"Evening, ma'am," he said with a nod as they neared Alynn. She stepped back to let them pass, then watched as they stopped at a door a few paces farther on.

"Here's your cabin, Ms. Macey—"

"You have to come in and put me to bed," she said in a wine-slurred voice as she unlocked the door.

"I'm afraid I can't do that."

She peered up at him. " 'Service is our specialty.' I saw it in the brochure. I jus' wan' a little service—personal service."

The crewman disentangled his arms from hers. "I'm very sorry," he said firmly, and retreated a step.

An angry look crossed her face. "Pansy," she said with a sneer, and disappeared into the darkness beyond the door.

With a shake of his head, the crewman turned and saw Alynn standing there.

"Can I help you, Miss—"

"Margarie Timmons. You most certainly can help me! My purse is missing from my cabin," she said loudly. "I saw a man on the fantail—he was carrying it, bold as you please!—and I followed him down here. But he went into one of these rooms, and I'm not sure which one."

"You're saying your purse was stolen?"

"Yes, stolen!" she said, even more loudly. "And I insist that you search these cabins at once, or I'll be going back to Boston and telling everyone I know that this ship isn't safe for decent people."

"There's no need for that, Ms. Timmons—we won't tolerate theft on board, you can be sure of that."

"Good, then get your keys out and start checking these cabins for the thief—"

At that moment there was a shriek from Ms. Macey's cabin. The door flew open, and a man in a gray sweater dashed out and took flight down the corridor, toward the bow. The crewman ran after him, but Alynn did not follow. Moving quickly, she slipped inside the open cabin before the door could slam shut, which brought her face-to-face with a startled Annie Macey.

"Who are you? Get out of here."

"You seem to have sobered up in a hurry," Alynn said, watching the spy carefully. "I want the portfolio. Those discs belong to me."

"I don't know what you're talking about."

The curtains masking the glass doors to the cabin's veranda were blowing ever so slightly, and the sound of the ship cutting through the whitecaps was clear and bright. Standing safely to one side, Alynn cautiously drew the curtain back with the point of her sunbrella. She could just see one corner of the portfolio, resting against the back of a lounge chair facing the night sky and the sea.

"At least you weren't stupid enough to throw it overboard," Alynn said as she retrieved the portfolio. She circled around Macey toward the door.

"That wouldn't help anyone, now, would it?"

"Tell your partner he can—"

At that moment Ms. Macey, the cabin, and the sea beyond all vanished, replaced in an instant by a flat blue static mask. "Oh, poop," Alynn said, and slouched back in her chair. "Tom? Raider? Are you still out there?"

"Still here," said the crewman's voice. "Did I crash the game?"

"Looks like one of you did. What happened? What did you try to do?"

A second voice. "I think it was me. I clobbered Tom with a room service tray, then tried to slide down the banister of the spiral staircase—you know, the big one, in the atrium?"

"That's his idea of how to fade into a crowd," Tom said with a chuckle.

"Well—wisdom aside, what he did is supposed to be possible," Alynn said. "I'll have to work on it. Would either of you be interested in hooking up later this week for some more playtesting? I'm afraid that this module's been spoiled for you, but High Seas has some other mods that could use wringing out."

"Like what?"

"Oh—there's a scenario that plays like paranoia, where you can't trust anyone and the only way to win is to get off the ship before someone kills you." She thought a moment. "There's a ghost-ship scenario. There's a *Poseidon Adventure* scenario, where the ship hits a World War II mine and turns turtle. There's a time-travel scenario, with the ship boarded by pirates. And there's an add-on module with a UFO scenario— the entire ship is plucked out of the ocean by a giant spaceship."

"Cool," said Tom. "Count me in."

Raider asked, "Can I ask you a question? What would have happened if I'd gone into the cabin with Mrs. Macey? Can you get laid in this game?"

Alynn laughed. "How old are you, Raider?"

"Sixteen."

"Um. Well, the answer is, not with the pseudos, you can't. You'd probably have been conked on the head and had your keys taken. Do you know the best way to tell the players from the pseudos in an interactive?"

"No—what?"

"Proposition them. If it says yes, it's a player."

Raider chuckled nervously. "Why's that?"

"The Malton Code," Tom said.

"Right," said Alynn. "Designers are obliged to

constrain the sexual behavior of the characters. But nothing constrains the behavior of an aliased player."

Raider chuckled. "You can say that again."

"Which doesn't mean that there aren't unconstrained black-channel imports that can be had. So to speak. You just won't find them at the mass-market outlets."

"They're disappearing from the nets, too, now," said Tom. "The thought police have been busy."

"I'm sorry to hear that," Alynn said with a shake of her head. "The Code treats designers and players like children. I'd rather let people make their own choices. Besides, I have some ideas the Code keeps me from working on."

"I have to go," Raider announced. "Will you message me when you want players?"

"I'll pick a time and let you know," she said. "Thanks for your help."

"It was fun," he said. An icon vanished from Alynn's viewer to mark his departure.

Tom asked, "Do you need to get right to work? Because I'd like to do what you do. Do you mind if I ask you a couple of questions? I've never had a chance to talk to a professional designer."

Alynn glanced at the clock. It was nearing midnight, but the chances were that Jonathan was still at the lab—he and his students were debugging a revision of the analysis program, and the earliest he'd been home that week was after 1 A.M. "Sure," she said, leaning back in her chair. "Shoot."

"Um—it seems like you're the only designer who uses realistic settings regularly—"

"Well, there's Matthew Michaelson's simulator stuff, and the Alternities Group, which does all the alternate-history games," she said. "But what I'm trying to do is create games where it's possible to forget you've got the goggles on. I don't know about you, but

I can't do that when I'm wandering through something that looks like Escher crossed with Dali."

"But that can be fun."

"Sure. But it's more like being taken for a tour than it is playing a game. And the surprises come too easily, because there aren't any rules."

"Well—that's true," said Tom. "Where did you get the idea for High Seas?"

Alynn slid her goggles up and reached for her drink. "If you do want to design games, remember that you have to draw a line around the world or the graphics overhead will kill you—"

"Even with the systems out now?"

"Even with. We all use dynamic generation now, but you still need primitives for building blocks, and high-quality objects eat storage or processor cycles. Did you know that there's a three-tenths of a second lag on most closed-goggle PRG systems? We don't notice because there're no external references."

"I didn't know that."

"It's true. So game designers look for natural bottles. A cruise ship is great because there's a lot of repetition. You only need five different cabin layouts, a few big sets like the atrium, and vistas for morning, midday, and night—plus a few weather algorithms, a storm, rough seas, like that."

"So that's why there're so many quest-in-an-underground-maze and stranded-on-a-space-station clones."

"You've got it. Using a smaller ship like the *Diamond* keeps my character set down, too. It only carries 354 passengers, and I can get 350 good walk-ons with just ten character variables—eight in a pinch."

"Your characters are great. And it's a very rich scenario, too. I like it."

"Thanks. You can pick any of a hundred different

aliases in any of the modules, interact with both the pseudos and live players, up to a dozen—"

"Why only a dozen? A lot of games support a hundred players now."

"I know." She shrugged. "I don't like mob-scene games. They degenerate too easily. Every time I visit the nets, all I find is wolfing and general anarchy. They aren't games, really—just settings, with no rules and no consequences."

"I liked the touch of seeing yourself in the brass at the elevator."

Her face brightened. "Oh, good, you noticed—I was afraid it was too subtle. I try to put reflectives in all my games. I always put my own picture somewhere, too. Kind of my signature."

"Neat. I'll have to look for it, now. Any other tips?"

Alynn thought a moment. "Just one. There's always an alternative to violence in my games. And the person who takes it usually comes out ahead. That's my little reply to the stuff that plays like a shooting gallery, and you win by splattering the most blood."

"I know a lot of women who love your games," Tom said. "Maybe that's why."

"Well—I'm a woman, and I like my games," she said, smiling. "Look, I need to take a peek at the transaction log for that crash—"

"Sure," Tom said quickly. "I understand. Thanks for talking to me."

"Glad to," she said. "You should hear from me about the testing in a few days."

Logging off, Alynn stood up and stretched her arms ceilingward, fingers intertwined high above her head. "Cassandra, attend."

"Yes, mistress."

"Cassandra, is Jonathan home yet?"

There was a moment's pause. "Jonathan is not home," her digital secretary reported.

"That's too bad," she said, with a restless sigh. "There's nothing like a couple of hours in goggleworld to make you appreciate being touched by a real person."

Alynn went to the glass doors that opened onto the balcony and looked out on the city. The night sky was a shadow of clouds, lit from below by streetlamps and from within by silent flashes of heat lightning. She cracked the door open and tasted the air. It was hot, a simmering breeze carrying a burned tang. Her eyes found the leaping yellow demons of a fire off to the west, somewhere downtown. The light played crazily off the faces of buildings.

"Cassandra, attend," Alynn said, closing the balcony door.

"Yes, mistress."

"Cassandra, what's burning in Ann Arbor?"

Several seconds passed. "I have a news report. Waiting."

"Hold," Alynn said, and turned away from the window. She sat down in the padded wooden rocker that had been her grandmother Reed's, and almost immediately Hypatia appeared and sprang lightly onto her lap. Alynn stroked the long-haired cat between the eyes with her thumb, and was rewarded with an answering purr. "Going to hold me down, golden lady? Cassandra, show me."

The monitor flickered on.

"This is Barbara Sawicki, reporting from Ann Arbor for Michigan NewsNet. The saga of the controversial gentlemen's club Boots, target of protests and lawsuits in recent months, came to a fiery end earlier tonight when two masked men firebombed the lobby—"

"Craziness," Alynn whispered.

"—About two dozen customers and employees escaped out a rear entrance.

"As you can see, the fire is still burning at this hour, and the club appears to be a total loss. Two adjoining businesses have also been damaged. Police say they have no suspects in the incident. According to a witness, one of the men shouted 'Death to whores and harlots' before hurling his bottle bomb against a display of videos featuring the club's dancers—"

Alynn shook her head. "Could that be more Freudian, Patti?"

"—The Reverend Donald Jakes, whose Christian action group organized two of the protests against the club, released a statement which said, 'Michigan Citizens for Decency does not condone violence, and categorically denies any responsibility for this unlawful act. At the same time, we cannot help but celebrate the elimination of a cesspool of evil and sexual degradation from our community'—"

"Stop," Alynn said sharply. It made her so angry— the chaos and foolishness and fear everywhere. Hide your bodies, hide your thoughts, hide your children, hide your wealth—from envy and meddling and a cold and arrogant intolerance. The richness that could be was being beaten down into a gray gruel of joyless sameness.

"Patti, you have to let me up," she said. "I've had all I can take tonight. I'm going home." She gathered the cat in a cradle of her hands and set her on the floor. "Cassandra, attend."

"Yes, mistress."

"Call it a night."

Those words set Cassandra to work closing down the netlinks, saving Alynn's workspace and files, and backing up everything to a remote archive. The lights dimmed to half, the element under the teakettle began to cool, and several appliances dropped into sleep or setback mode.

Alynn crossed to her altar and blew out the white candle, cupping her hand behind it so the wax would not splatter. Then she changed her mind and relit the candle. Sinking to her knees on the carpet, she let out her tension in a puff of breath, closed her eyes, and began humming a throaty chant.

The rosewood woman's star hung on the wall above the small table. On the table, beside the fat pillar candle, a long-haired bronze nude sat perched on the curve of a crescent moon.

Alynn did not ask anything of the goddess-figure— no wish or promise. But she held its image in her thoughts as she searched for a peaceful place, a balance, and the sound of her own voice drew her into the light.

Hate was a poison, anger a drug, and when she let them touch her and enter her thoughts they made her feel dirty and small. She had lived too close to both hate and anger—virulent, impotent, unrelenting—for far too long, and seen how they shriveled living things. She had gone a long way to escape them, and would not let herself invite them back into her life. There were better ways to live and brighter thoughts to embrace.

Alynn knelt, chanting almost in a murmur and rocking on her heels, until the tightness had left her shoulders. Opening her eyes, she wet her fingers and deftly quenched the candle flame between them. Then she rose to her feet, swept up her belt-pouch from an end table, and headed for the door.

"Cassandra, mind the store," she said as she let herself out. "I'm going home." The door locked behind her.

A slow elevator ride down, a nod to the security guard lounging in the lobby, a shoulder against two sets of double doors, and she was outside on the plaza. The hot breeze had blown a few star-littered tears in the canopy of clouds, but the air still smelled of smoke.

Alynn had been in early enough to beat the commuters home, and had found a parking place close to the east tower, in the southwest corner near a wall of trees and the walkway to the pool and the river. As she stepped off the sidewalk and approached her car, she fished in her pouch for the wireless key fob and thumbed the switch.

There was an answering chirp from the Saturn, and then a popping sound. Alynn cried out as bloody fire ripped through her right shoulder. As her knees buckled, her hand flew to the spreading wetness, slippery as raw meat. Stunned, she slumped against the nearest support, the hatch of a bright red van.

"Do it, come on!"

Twisting toward the high-pitched voice, Alynn saw two girls, sixteen years old, maybe younger. They were standing twenty feet away, near the concrete walls flanking a service stairway to the tower's basement. One of the girls clutched a black pistol in a tight, two-handed grip. Her eyes glowed with excitement.

In a long, frozen instant, Alynn's mind jumped from thought to thought. She had walked right past the stairway—how could she not have seen them?—If she could just scream, surely the guard would hear her—Pain broke through the numbness with such force that she was nearly sick.

"C'mon, c'mon," one girl urged the other. "Get on."

Alynn looked at the girls in disbelief. She let the key fob slide from her hand and land with a tinkle at her feet. It was all she could do. She had never known agony, violation, like this before. The burning in her shoulder and chest had turned to a slashing knife that scored her with every minute movement. She looked to the girls with childlike hope, for mercy.

There was no mercy in them.

Pop. Pop. Pop. With a strangled cry, Alynn tried to run, but her legs would not hold her. She fell hard against the trunk of the car parked beside hers, and then slid down it to the ground.

Pop. Pop. Pop. Pop. Glassy-eyed, her cheek hard against the oily pavement, Alynn felt her body twitch as though it belonged to someone else. Enough, she pleaded, enough. They danced right over her, shadows, and car doors slammed. She heard their callow laughter as they roared away into a night growing ever darker.

The fire downtown had been extinguished by the time Jonathan emerged from the lab. Though it had been only blocks away, a freshening breeze from the south carried the smoulder away from his nostrils, leaving him no clue as to what had happened while he had been cocooned.

As Jonathan drove east on Fuller in his Imp, he passed two police cars parked *soixante-neuf* in a driveway, and a third beside the road a half block past Huron Towers. The two officers standing by its bumper looked hard at Jonathan as he passed, in a way that made him markedly uncomfortable. He checked his speed, and wondered nervously, glancing in his mirrors, if he had missed a stop sign or run a light. Guilt adrenaline grabbed him and did not let go until he was sure the police were not going to follow.

When he reached Village Green, he was surprised to find himself alone there, but also relieved. Exhausted by a long and frustrating day of system glitches and bug-hunting, Jonathan welcomed, with guilty pleasure, the quiet of solitude. He felt brain-burned, weary of talk and of people, and doubted he could muster even enough energy for a friendly smile. Instructing Alfred to intercept all calls and to wake him at noon, he fell into bed without wondering where Alynn was.

But when Jonathan woke to find bright sun beating on the bedroom blinds and the bed beside him still empty, that was enough to furrow his brow with curiosity. He padded out to the living room in bare feet, his hair mussed and his face still lined by the wrinkles of his pillow. When he discovered Alynn was nowhere in the apartment, puzzlement displaced the curiosity.

Still, he was not concerned. He called Alynn's 700 number, fully expecting her to answer. When Cassandra answered instead, Jonathan called the office-apartment directly, still expecting to hear Alynn's voice. Cassandra answered again, and the first hint of concern darkened his gaze. But his first thought was What did I do? Had he missed a rendezvous, broken a promise, given some insult, exhausted her patience? What was keeping her away?

"Alfred," he said. "Messages."

"One message waiting, sir," his secretary reported. "Elizabeth Froelich, voice."

"Isn't there anything from Alynn?"

"No, sir."

Now thoroughly confused, Jonathan scratched the stubble along his jawline. "Play Liz's message."

At first, she seemed to be talking under her breath. "Oh, damn—it's the machine." And when she spoke up, her voice was thick and tremulous, uncharacteristically full of emotion. "Of course it's the machine—like you have nothing to do now but answer the phone. I'm an idiot, forgive me. Jonathan—I just want to say that I'm so sorry. If there's anything I can do to help you, to make things easier these next weeks, don't hesitate to ask. You don't have to carry it all on your shoulders, or tough it through alone.

"And please, don't give a thought to anything over here. As of this morning, you're on emergency family leave—all the clocks have stopped ticking. Do what you need to now. Everything else can wait." She hesitated, then added, "I'm just so sorry. I don't know what else to say. Call me when you can. I want to help."

The silence was filled with a terrible dread. Jonathan's mouth had gone dry as he listened, even as he struggled to understand. How would Liz know if Alynn had left? She's talking like— She was talking as though— His mind rebelled at completing the thought.

"Alfred, news queue," he said.

Jonathan had given Alynn's name and the name of her company to Alfred's knowbots months ago, partly out of curiosity and partly as silent penance for not knowing who she was when they met. Now he scanned the list of nuggets panned from the stream of news, hoping against hope not to find her mentioned there.

"Next page," he said, hugging himself. "Next page," he said a few moments later. The queue was nearly a hundred items long, for it had been several days since Jonathan had last cleaned it. His blood hammered in his ears as he scanned down the list. "Next page."

And then, "Oh—" It was a small sound of surprise, almost a grunt, that belied the power of the blow. His skin tingled all over. There was a roaring in his ears, and his legs would not hold him. He sank to his knees on the carpet.

"Show me sixty-four," he whispered.

The header said On the Scene, the time stamp 05:00.

"Bobby Thurman, On the Scene in Ann Arbor. They'll be crying in Ant Town, in the Devil's Keep, and all through the digital kingdoms tonight—the Queen of Imagination is dead. A few hours ago, superstar VR imagineer Alynn Reed was found on the sidewalk outside her Fuller Road apartment, lying in a pool of her own blood, murdered by unknown assailants.

"Ann Arbor police refused to talk to your On the Scene reporter, but our Hot Scene tipster reported hearing semiautomatic gunfire. Reed's shocked neighbors say it looks like another of the parking-lot carjackings that have terrorized this city for months—"

Jonathan could only stare numbly. Disbelief had stolen all feeling from him. He had driven right past without knowing. He thought of the police, lingering, waiting perhaps for the forensics experts, thought of her blood still wet on the ground as he fell into bed. But for a matter of a few minutes he might have driven into the middle of it. But for a matter of a half hour, an hour—

"—her late-model Saturn Zephyr was later found abandoned near Parker Mill County Park, just a few miles from the gruesome scene—"

There was a floodlit shot of the car being towed tail first out of a grassy ditch. Alynn's vanity plate KC KID was clearly visible. He wanted Alfred to stop the playback, but his mouth had gone dry, and he could not make a sound.

"—The assault took place within sight of two hospitals, but, even so, by the time EMTs reached her, it was too late—"

The On the Scene camera had caught it all, and the editors held nothing back.

The dance of the red-and-blue emergency lights on the trees, the parked cars, and the lonely dark street.

The police photographer, leaning over Alynn's motionless body and lighting it with the cold light of her flash.

The faces of neighbors, looking down from their balconies with a mixture of horror and relief that whatever had happened had happened to someone else.

The covered stretcher, disappearing into the back of an ambulance.

The black puddle of blood in the gutter.

It was the last that catapulted Jonathan forward onto his hands and knees, his stomach suddenly convulsed by dry heaves which for all their exquisite violence produced nothing but shame, a bitter taste in his mouth, and an empty ache. As the wrenching spasms eased, the tears began, great racking sobs that became raw, wordless, abandoned wails of anguish and loss as bitter as bile.

Jonathan cried with rage and blind hate, cried for lost dreams and selfish hopes, cried out from the deepest parts of his being in protest, cried for Alynn, in her agony and terror.

The news clip played on, and Bobby Thurman went on talking, unaware of the wound he had opened. "—This is the latest in a series of black eyes for the once-proud city of Ann Arbor, which ranked among the country's most desirable addresses as recently as 2008. But tonight, it's a war zone, with moral zealots filling the air with smoke and amoral predators spilling blood in the streets.

"The irony is compelling—Alynn Reed's VR games gave millions of would-be spies, gunslingers, and warriors thrilling adventures in fantastic settings. But when virtual violence spills over into reality, living becomes the most dangerous game. Some might say that Alynn Reed reaped what she and her peers have sown. True or not, millions of her fans are learning tonight that when the guns and bullets are real, death is for keeps."

"End of item sixty-four," said Alfred. "Keep or delete?"

Curled in a trembling ball in the middle of the floor, Jonathan did not hear the machine, and could not have answered if he had.

It was not standing or even stopping the tears that was hard. It was facing the question, What now? Jonathan escaped it for a time in a long scalding needle-spray shower, leaning against the tile with eyes closed and letting the water beat on his body. The heat seemed to boil away some of the poisons, and the pounding numb some of his pain.

When he finally emerged from the shower, Jonathan knew the answer to the question. He knew he needed to find Alynn—and then try to find some way to say good-bye.

It didn't take long for Jonathan to learn that in the eyes of the law, being in love and making love with someone confer no status at all.

"Detective Division."

"This is Dr. Jonathan Briggs." Acid rose in his throat, and he swallowed it down. "I need to get some information about Alynn Reed."

"You have information about the Reed case? Just a minute."

Shortly, a new voice came on the line. "This is Detective Anderson."

Jonathan repeated his introduction.

"What kind of information are you looking for, Dr. Briggs?"

"Anything I can—I want to know what happened." He drew a deep breath. "And I need to know where her body is, so I can start working on—on arrangements."

"Excuse me, but I didn't catch your relationship to the victim?"

"We lived together."

"Where exactly did you do that?"

"Here—Village Green."

"You were registered as domestic partners, then."

"No—we hadn't gotten to that. Isn't there a six-month waiting period, anyway?"

"But her name is on your lease, then."

"No—"

"Is your name on hers, then?"

"No, that was her office—she just went there to work."

The detective's voice dripped skepticism. "Let me see if I understand this, Dr. Briggs. You had separate apartments, separate finances, you weren't registered—did you buy anything together? That new car of hers, is your name on that? Is there anything resembling an official document on which I'd find both of your names?"

"No. None of that means anything," Jonathan said with frustration. "We've only been together a few months, and that wasn't what our relationship was about. Wait, she bought me some computers—"

"I'm afraid a gift isn't enough to establish a relationship existed, Dr. Briggs," Anderson said. "And keeping a toothbrush at your girlfriend's doesn't make you family, even under the city's generous definition. I'm afraid I can't discuss the details of the case with you. You're free to request a copy of the case report when it's filed, of course. You can make your request at central administration, six weeks after the case is closed."

Jonathan was certain that Anderson was about to

hang up. "Why are you treating me like this?" he demanded. "I just lost the woman I loved—love—and you're acting like I'm some kind of—I can't even imagine what you're thinking."

"Can I be blunt?"

"Please, by all means."

"Dr. Briggs, I've been working on this case since about three this morning, and your name hasn't come up once," said the detective. "I don't know you from Adam's off ox, and everything I have so far says that this girl was a loner. Now, when someone calls out of the blue on a high-profile murder, and he wants to get info, not to sell me a tip or try to confess, I smell a phony FVCA claim coming—"

"What the hell is FVCA?"

"Families of Victims Compensation Act." The question seemed to give Anderson second thoughts, for his tone softened. "Now, if you really were close to Ms. Reed, you have my condolences and my apology. But I'm not a social worker, and I don't do PR for the department. My job is to solve felony crimes and put the criminals in front of a judge. So if you know anything that might help me do that job, I'd like to hear it."

Jonathan hesitated. "I don't know anything. We were both working late, and she just never came home," he said, a wobble in his voice. "I found out why from the news."

Anderson made a sympathetic noise. "That's hard," he said. "All right, I've got your number and address off caller ID. If anything develops that I can share, I'll get ahold of you—"

"Why would anyone do such a thing?" Jonathan blurted out. "They didn't even keep the car! You kill someone for their car, and then toss it away again, ten blocks down the road? Does that make any sense?"

Sighing, Anderson said, "Dr. Briggs, don't try to

make it make sense. A lot of what happens out there is as near to pointless as can be. The people that do these things, they're not like you and me. They just don't care."

"But a two-mile joyride—"

"Some of them'll kill you for looking at them wrong. They'll do it for a dollar, or a bet, or to show off to a cunt—" Anderson stopped short. "Excuse me. This is why I don't do PR. My guess is that this was probably a gang initiation—someone showing that they have what it takes to wear the colors. That's why they didn't keep the car. I'm sorry. I know that's probably hard to hear."

Jonathan fought back his emotions as he listened. "Where is she now? That's what I really need to know."

"That I can't tell you. That we don't tell anyone but family."

"I'm all the family she had," Jonathan said hotly.

"Well, now, that's not exactly so," Anderson said. "How well did you say you knew this girl? Her mother is on her way up from Ohio to collect the body."

Neither the pathology department nor the cold room appeared on the maps given to visitors, as though University Hospital preferred not to remind them that sometimes patients die. But Jonathan knew the unmarked corridors of the catacombs, Basement Level 2. He hesitated outside an open door, steeling himself, and then entered.

"Hello, Peter."

The chief pathologist looked up from his desk with an uneasy expression. "Jonathan. I was hoping not to see you."

"Is she here?"

Dr. Peter Ash leaned back in his chair and folded his hands in his lap. "Yes."

"I wondered. I thought—this is the closest, if they tried at all to save her. I didn't think they would take her to the VA." Rubbing his arms, he tried to smile. "I guess everyone knows by now, huh?"

"You know the grapevine. Tragedy and scandal, they get priority handling. I'm very sorry, Jonathan. I can't imagine how this feels for you."

"Peter, I want to see her."

"No, you don't."

"You don't understand, Peter. I never got to say good-bye—"

The doctor acknowledged his words with a nod. "Jonathan, think. We have a presumed-consent law here. Alynn didn't have a refusal on file."

"So?"

"Do I have to spell it out? The EMTs brought her into the ER on life support. As soon as she was pronounced dead, we autopsied, then the surgical team harvested—whatever wasn't damaged, at least. They try to respect the body, but—" He shook his head. "Besides, the remains are already prepped for transport."

A knot formed in the pit of Jonathan's stomach. "What did you take?"

"Christ, Jonathan, why beat yourself up—"

"Please."

Frowning, Ash rocked forward in his chair and clicked a mouse button. "Both corneas, both cochlea, the middle ear bones," he recited, looking at the monitor. "One kidney, about three meters of small intestine. Skin grafts. The aortic arch, one ovary, lymph nodes, the pituitary. Four teeth—" He wrinkled his nose in discomfort.

"What? And what?"

"You know Dr. Kosslyn has a standing request for brain tissue, for research—"

Jonathan bit down hard on his lower lip and looked away.

"Oh, hell, Jonathan, they didn't know who they had on the table. Somebody would have called you. I knew a surgeon once who was halfway through a harvest before he realized it was his own daughter. Please believe me, you don't want to see her."

"I can't let you make that decision for me."

"I'm afraid you have to. You're not kin, 'next of' or any other kind," Ash said. "I don't have any grounds to give you access."

"You're going by the book on me?" Jonathan whispered, incredulous.

"Believe me, Jonathan, I'm doing you a favor. Go home and get out your pictures. Remember her that way."

"Just five minutes," Jonathan pleaded. "No one has to know."

"I'd know," said Ash. "On top of which, we're expecting the chaplain with her kin anytime now."

"Where are they going to take her?"

"I don't know, Jonathan—they're not obliged to tell us. Why do you want to do this to yourself? What do you think you're going to get out of it?"

His eyes went bright with water. "I don't know. I just don't know what else to do."

Ash pursed his lips and studied the younger man. "Have you ever lost someone close to you before?" he asked finally.

Jonathan shook his head wordlessly.

"You're in denial, Jonathan." He jerked his thumb in the direction of the cold room. "She's not in there. There's no one in there. She's gone."

* * *

Jonathan fled to the only place he could think to go.

The air in Alynn's apartment stank. It was the first thing Jonathan noticed on letting himself in, and a surprise. He followed the smell to the lavatory and found that one of the cats had lost a battle with diarrhea and not quite made it to the litter box.

The most likely culprit was Hypatia, whom Alynn had called her worry-cat. As if to confirm his suspicions, Archimedes came right to Jonathan and watched curiously as he cleaned the mess off the tile floor, while Hypatia was nowhere to be seen.

Jonathan slid the glass door to the balcony as far open as it would go and turned on the exhaust fans. Then, prodded by Archimedes rubbing against his ankles, he rummaged the kitchen cabinets until he found the cats' food.

The sound of the clinking glass bowls coaxed Hypatia out of hiding, but while Archimedes attacked the offering eagerly, she hung back timidly until Jonathan sat down in the rocker. Then she climbed into his lap and curled up into a tight ball there.

"If I didn't know better, Patti, I'd think you were embarrassed," he said, scratching the cat lightly on the bridge of her nose. "It's all right. It's not your fault. You can tell something's wrong, can't you."

It was the first time he had ever been alone in Alynn's apartment. At once, he felt her everywhere around him, and felt her absence keenly. She had filled this place with herself, but the place she herself filled was empty.

He cried quietly for a time, sitting in the chair with Hypatia huddled on his lap and Archimedes on the back of the chair, lightly touching his shoulder. When Archimedes went off to explore the smells at the balcony screen, Jonathan gathered Hypatia in his arms and walked soft-footed through the rooms, as though there were something fragile about them, as though he were an intruder.

Alynn had set up one bedroom as a library, with a quartet of eight-foot-tall bookcases and a recliner with a brass reading lamp beside it. A fine dusting of yellow cat hair on the flowered seat cushion declared it to be one of Hypatia's sleeping spots.

"This must be your little garden, eh?" Jonathan said to the cat, and deposited her gently among the flowers.

He sat on the floor in front of one of the bookcases and began to scan the shelves. About half the titles appeared to be discs—games, visual libraries and gallery catalogs, reference works. He spotted a whole row of *National Geographic* DVD-VRs, with their distinctive yellow endpapers, and briefly fingered the one titled "Inside Mammoth Cave."

The other half of Alynn's collection, taking up most of the shelf space, was comprised of books—as eclectic an array as Jonathan had seen outside of a flea market, and less noticeably organized.

Critical studies of twentieth-century French films, two biographies of John F. Kennedy, and a signed edition of de Camp's *The Ancient Engineers* were cheek by jowl with undistinguished mystery novels and what appeared to be the complete oeuvre of the Victorian novelist Anonymous. A "Calvin and Hobbes" anthology was sandwiched between Shaw's *Pygmalion* and *The Collected Stories of Guy du Maupassant*.

By the window, Jonathan found two stacks of books on millennial prophecies, secret societies, and supernatural phenomena. The top one in the taller stack, Stokes's *A Quarter to Never*, had several torn-paper bookmarks, earmarks of research for a project that now would never be completed.

Looking around the room, he started to wonder

which books she had paged through, sitting cross-legged in the recliner with a cat in her lap, and which ones were unkept promises to herself. The thought cut him, and drove him from the room.

A second bedroom was a sanctuary. The door was always kept closed, and he had never been invited beyond it, though he had never been ordered to keep out. He hesitated, then entered, feeling like a trespasser as he did. Archimedes followed him in—though whether as chaperone or to satisfy his own curiosity, Jonathan could not tell.

It took him a moment to realize that, except for an overhead lamp with no bulb in it, there was no technology in the room. There was also little furniture—a sturdy, ornate oak coffee table in the center of a circular Oriental rug, four smaller oak stands along the rug's periphery, a corner full of cushions, a folding foam mattress beneath the window.

Here was another small library, the bookcases flanking a dark oak sideboard—books on the Aborigine altjiranga, on transcendentalism, on astral voyaging, on reincarnation. *The Wiccan Path for Solitaries, Into the Beyond, Love and Will, Meditation for Moderns, The Sacred Dance.* The titles blurred past his eyes.

The surfaces of the furniture collectively hosted a curious array of ordinary objects—candles fat and slender, sculptures, a ceramic bowl half-full of sand, a crystal stopper-bottle of salt, matches in a wooden box, and more. He tried the drawers to the sideboard and the low table, but found them locked.

An altar. The table's an altar. The realization came slowly, because he had never known anyone—not his parents' friends nor his own—who had any sort of space set aside in their homes for nakedly religious purposes.

Jonathan was wrestling with that alien thought when he heard the apartment door unlock with a buzz and a loud click. Archimedes heard the sound, too, and trotted hopefully in that direction. A moment later, Jonathan heard voices in the living room.

"—you understand that we can't let anyone in un-supervised, and we have to inventory anything that's removed." That was a man, trying to sound sympathetic but only managing apologetic.

"Oh, heavens. Well, to start with, that disgusting cat will have to be destroyed," a woman said. "Can you call animal control and have it taken away?"

"The most we can do is have a pet boarded, if there's no one to take care of it. The laws are set up to protect the tenant's estate, and pets sometimes inherit, you know—"

Jonathan drew a deep breath, and stepped out into the hallway. "The cats won't be neglected, Mrs. Reed."

It was the consummate awkward moment, and it ended with confusion, as all three of them spoke at once.

"Does this man work for you?" Stacey Reed asked her escort, eyes cold and wary.

"Excuse me, what are you doing here?" asked the assistant manager, puffing himself up and stepping forward as her knight.

"Mrs. Reed, you and I have to talk," said Jonathan, who won the floor and went on. "I know who you are. I don't think you know who I am. The important part is that I loved Alynn, just like you, and my world's been turned upside down by this, just like yours. We don't know each other, but I think—maybe—we need each other."

Stacey Reed's eyes remained cold.

"No, he doesn't work for us," the manager said. "Look, fella—you'd—"

"Then how did he get into my daughter's apartment?" she demanded.

"I live here," Jonathan said. "I let myself in."

The manager retreated a step, and Stacey Reed shot a hard questioning look his way. "I thought you said the apartment was sealed. I thought you said my daughter lived alone."

"Well, we'd have changed the key codes by now, but your daughter had her own locks, and our security technician's out sick today." The assistant manager looked to be unhappy at finding himself in the middle. "I suppose she might have given someone a key—but she is the only one on the lease."

"Then I want him out of here, now."

"Well, now, it's not that simple—"

As Jonathan listened to them talk past him, as though he were not there, or furniture, his face went hard.

"Mrs. Reed, my name is Dr. Jonathan Briggs," he said in a measured but clenched-jaw voice. "I was your daughter's friend and lover, and the reason she was in Ann Arbor to begin with. I know this must be a hard time for you and I have great sympathy for your pain, but you have to respect my loss, too."

Even as he was speaking, he realized he was looking into the face of bigotry. She waited until he was done, and then said coldly, "I do not acknowledge your relationship with Alexandra."

Jonathan shook his head. "You didn't even know she was living here until the police called you, did you? She didn't even want you to know where she was."

"No doubt she was ashamed," said Stacey Reed, unfazed. "She always had trouble facing up to her mistakes."

"This is crazy," he said. "Alynn loved me. There's no reason we have to be on opposite sides. We should be able to talk about what she would have wanted. We should be able to mourn her together."

"Alexandra is on her way home for a Christian burial," said Stacey Reed.

Jonathan swallowed down anger. "Then I'd like to know where and when."

"No," said Stacey Reed. "You are not welcome to involve yourself in any way. Now, if you'll excuse me, I need to get her clothes."

"She didn't keep clothing here," he said. "Those things are at our place—where she slept."

For just a moment, Jonathan thought that he'd gotten to her. Then her mouth twitched, and she said, "Clothing can be bought." She turned her back on Jonathan. "Mr. Mitchell, I'm finished here. May we go?"

The anger Jonathan had swallowed blew back up his throat. "How can you do this? You don't even know her! What colors did she wear? How long was her hair? Where was she pierced? What did she like on her pizza? She wasn't even a Christian, for God's sake—" He pointed down the hallway toward the sanctuary. "Go look for yourself! If you're doing this for her, at least honor what she believed. These cats were her children, and your first order's to kill them? No wonder she despised you."

Stacey Reed glared back over her shoulder at Jonathan, the ice having melted in fury.

"I don't care what she professed under your influence," she said. "Alexandra was weak about men, naive, and too eager to please. But my daughter was baptized in the Episcopalian Church, and I will remember her as she was, and pray for God's forgiveness as to who she became."

Turning back to the assistant manager, she

snapped, "I want him out of here. I want those stinking cats out of here. I'm her mother, and I have rights. If anything of my daughter's is stolen or destroyed by this man and his friends, I'm going to hold the management of this building responsible. I'm telling you, get him out, today."

On that note of high dudgeon, she stormed out of the apartment, without looking back to see if the assistant manager was following. The two men looked at each other for sympathy, and, finding none, to displace blame. "It would really make things so much better for everyone if you'd just leave—" the assistant manager started to say.

"Get out of my apartment," Jonathan said, in a voice shadowed with threat.

After a moment's further consideration, the assistant manager opted for a strategic withdrawal. "You'd better think hard about saving yourself some trouble," was all he said in parting.

When he was alone again, Jonathan began to shake and collapsed into a chair. "Cassandra, attend," he said.

"Ready, sir."

"Lock the door," he said. "Change the key."

"Door locked," Alynn's secretary said. "I will need the mistress's permission to change the key."

That was the breaking point. Without thought, he snatched up the nearest loose object from the end table—a ceramic bear holding a basket of candies—and hurled it in the direction of the workstation.

His aim was high. The candies scattered like mines on the carpet, and the bear crashed against the wall and shattered spectacularly. Both cats fled the room. Jonathan buried his face in his hands and began to weep anew.

* * *

Jonathan stood on the balcony of Alynn's apartment, looking by turns out into the night and down over the railing toward the concrete walkway to the plaza, eight stories below. He was hugging himself, arms crossed over his chest, with Alynn's portable phone cradled in one hand tucked against his cheek. "Liz—"

"Jonathan?"

"Can you help me?"

"Of course—just tell me what you need."

"I need you to pick some things up for me from my place. I'm afraid that if I leave here, they'll lock me out."

"Where are you?"

"Alynn's place. Eight-oh-one, in the east tower." He found himself leaning against the railing, looking down at the walkway.

"Jonathan, are you all right?"

"Everyone's trying to take her away from me, Liz. I'm not going to let them. They can't make me let go of her." He felt himself swaying and closed his eyes. "In my whole life, I never met anyone like Alynn. All the places I've lived, there was never anyone who—she filled all my emptiness, Liz. Did you realize that? She made me feel whole."

"Jonathan—"

His legs were folding under him, until he was sitting on the balcony with his back against the railing. "I wanted to be with Alynn forever. Not 132 days. That's not enough, Liz. That's just enough to make me crazy."

His voice suddenly turned hard. "And don't tell me that life's not fucking fair. I know that. I know that. But why not someone who hated being here? Why not someone who was just marking time, plugging in and drugging out? Why should some—" Jonathan could not find words with enough venom. They were all too shallow to carry the depth of his contempt, and his hate. "It just shouldn't be possible for someone so small to destroy something so beautiful."

There was a long silence from the other end. "I'll need your key."

"Last six digits of your phone number, then your middle initial. I already had Alfred change it, so you wouldn't have to remember."

"Tell me what you need."

It was an effort to think such simple thoughts. "The pillow on the right side of the bed. Eh—my toothbrush. I don't have a toothbrush here. Clothes. It's the blue one. My toothbrush."

"What kind of clothes do you need?"

"Her clothes. Yesterday she wore—" He winced. "I can't remember what she was wearing. In the movies, he can always remember what she was wearing, what was playing on the radio, what she said, her exact words." His voice broke. "I don't have any of that, Liz."

"Whatever's important will come back," she said. "I'll be there as soon as I can."

"Please," he said, and let the phone fall from his hand.

The glowing red numeral above the doors changed from 4 to 5. "Come on, come on, even I could climb stairs faster than this," Elizabeth Froelich muttered to herself, shifting the large soft-sided bag she carried from one hand to the other. Still chafing from being stopped in the parking lot by a zealously officious rent-a-cop, Elizabeth Froelich had little forbearance for the painfully slow Huron Towers elevator.

But when the doors at last opened to the plain and narrow eighth-floor corridor, she felt a sudden twinge of apprehension. It was strong enough to slow her footsteps as she approached the door at the south end. Jonathan had buzzed her in, so he was alive—but beyond that, she had no idea in what state she would find him. He had sounded so fragile on the phone, so unlike himself—almost as though he was riding a carnival ride that was about to whirl itself to pieces. She was frightened for him, and just a little bit frightened of him, as well.

The door to 801 opened before she reached it. Startled, she took a step backward. Jonathan emerged far enough to snatch the bag from her hand, then turned his back on her and disappeared into the apartment, leaving her to follow him. She found him in the living room, sitting in the middle of the floor with the bag's contents on his lap and picking through the pile.

"I didn't know what to bring, so I just filled a bag with anything that looked clean," she said tentatively. "I brought some of your clothes, too."

He held up a black knit top with shoulder cutouts and silver trim. "This is what she should be wearing. This was her favorite blouse. And jeans." He shook his head. "I just know she's going to bury Alynn in some sort of prom-fabric dress with a flower print and lace collar, like she was some sort of fucking Barbie doll—"

"She?"

"Mrs. Stacey Reed." Jonathan scowled. "Alynn's mother."

"She's here? Was here?"

"She took Alynn away. To Cincinnati, so a bunch of people Lynn didn't know can come and make sympathetic noises to Mrs. Fucking Stacey Reed."

"Why do I get the idea that you two didn't hit it off?" She hoped for at least a wry smile from him, but his usual easy humor was beyond reach.

"I don't care. I still want to go to the funeral," he said.

"Well—of course. When is it?"

"Tomorrow at three. I found the announcement on a mortuary site in Cincinnati."

"If you need someone to go with you—"

"I'd need someone to stay here, so they can't lock me out."

She was not so quick to offer this time. "All right. But if you're going to go, you should fly, or have someone to go with you. You're in no shape to be driving three hundred miles."

"It doesn't matter," he said, standing and letting the black top fall from his hand to the jumbled pile of clothing. "I'm not welcome. I'm not invited." He walked to the balcony door and let himself out. She hurried after.

"I should go anyway," he said when she joined him at the railing. "What's she going to do, have the bouncer throw me out? Have me arrested? Aren't there people who go to funerals all the time, like court watchers?"

"I think you're thinking of *Harold and Maude*."

"I guess I am," Jonathan said, and a welcome hint of a wry, crooked smile appeared. "Still, they don't check your ID at church doors now, do they? You don't need a pass to get into a cemetery."

"But if you and Mrs. Fucking Stacey Reed—did I get that right?" She was poking at him now, like a parent tickling a sulking child.

He smiled tiredly, and shook his head.

"—If you and the effing Mrs. effing Stacey god-damned Reed—"

This time he laughed despite himself, his chest rising and falling with a sound that was closer to a grunt than a chuckle.

"—If you two aren't able to be civil to each other, then what good will your being there do either of you?

You can have your own ceremony for Alynn," she said. "You don't need a box in the center aisle for that. You could do something here, with your friends. I'd like to be part of it."

"Maybe that *is* what I should do." He turned and sat down on the balcony, his back against the railing. "I can't help thinking that we should have been able to hug each other, like two people who loved someone and lost her. But she made me feel like a nigger, Liz. Maybe other people are used to that, but it hasn't happened to me very often."

She reached across and squeezed his hand. It was a mistake.

"No," he said, pulling away. "I don't want to be touched."

But she was certain he did—wanted and needed it. He was clinging to his pain like a drowning man strangling his rescuer. What was the secret to reaching him? He was struggling for control when what would start the healing was surrender. Alynn was dead and he was alive and alone. And he had to know that nothing he did would change that. Jonathan could come to terms with what was, or he could bludgeon himself with his own misery.

The same choice Elizabeth had.

I know about wanting someone who isn't there, she thought as she watched his head loll back against the metal mesh and his eyes close. We're alike in that, now.

And as she thought those thoughts, she wondered in passing why she did not say them aloud.

"You look exhausted," she said. "I know you don't want to sleep, but you need to be gentle with yourself."

Eyes closed, he nodded. "I can't think anymore," he said slowly. "I can't feel anything. I'm just—I guess I'd better go lie down for a while."

"I think that's a good idea."

He opened his eyes. "It's just that I don't want to dream about her."

"You won't," she assured him. "You're going to go a long way down and stay there."

"Will you stay, please?"

"Of course."

She followed Jonathan into the bedroom, which was lit only by the glow from a perpetual candle. Without pausing to turn on a light or turn down the covers, he climbed onto the neatly made bed in his clothes and crawled toward the ornate wood headboard. Pulling a pillow toward him, he collapsed on his left side with his arms wrapped around it.

With no sign or invitation from him, Elizabeth sat lightly on the edge of the bed, near him, but not touching. She listened to his deep, ragged breathing and tried to decide if he was crying.

"Please—let me hold you," she whispered at last.

To her surprise, he reached for her. Finding her hand, he drew her toward him. She was a foot shorter than he, and half his weight, but cradled him as best she could, letting him be small in her arms, sending comfort into him at every point where they touched. She closed her eyes and listened as the rhythms of their breathing approached each other and merged.

And somewhere in that moment, what was for him and what was for her fused, and his needs and hers blurred together in her mind. The first kiss was on his forehead, and tender. It was the kind of kiss that heals wounds and numbs hurts, but it also had its own loneliness and longing. The second, a cautious interval later, was full on his mouth, and at once tentative and hungry.

For just a moment Jonathan kissed back. Then he came up from his drowsy haze as though she had driven a pin into his flesh. He shoved her away and scrabbled backward on the bed. "Jesus, Liz—"

"I'm sorry—"

"Get out," he said darkly.

"Jonathan, I—"

"Don't talk to me. Just get out."

Retreating toward the door, arms crossed in front of her, she pleaded, "Please let me explain—"

"No! I don't want to talk about it. I want you out of here! I want to forget what you just tried to do."

Her cheeks burned with shame, but her eyes flashed anger. "Damn you. Don't make it a mistake for someone to care about you."

"Liz, I'm trying very hard not to hurt you. But if you don't get out of here soon—"

She fled. Waiting for the elevator, Elizabeth hugged herself and bit her lower lip until it bled. When she finally reached the privacy of her car, she punished her face with her fists, muttering "Stupid, stupid, stupid!" under her breath, until tears came.

Then she slumped over the wheel, sobbing. The moment was gone, and there was no undoing it.

Jonathan awoke with his heart hammering in his chest, his senses jangling. For agonizing moments, he did not know where he was, and scrambled for his bearings—darkness inside and out. He was sitting in a big chair, in a strange room—

Then he remembered the look on Elizabeth's face, and his own shame and anger—remembered straightening the bedcovers, as though brushing out the wrinkles would sweep away the guilt, and retreating to the library. Hypatia had yielded the recliner to him, then bounded back onto his lap. He thought he had fallen asleep petting her.

But how long ago, and what had startled him so? He was alone in the chair now. He strained to hear the echo of any sound, to grasp any fragment of a dream that might have jolted him awake. There was nothing.

It was almost as if someone had touched him—but there was no one there.

The chair's mechanism creaked loudly as he brought the back forward and stood up. If there is someone out there— He didn't complete the thought.

He stepped out into the hallway. The only lights on were to the right, in the office. "Cassandra, attend."

"Yes, Jonathan."

"Turn the lights on. All of them."

Night turned to day, and a quick if cautious search of the apartment showed that he was still alone. He settled uncertainly into the chair at Alynn's workspace. "Cassandra, do you keep a sensor log?"

"Yes, Jonathan."

"Cassandra, give me what you have for the last half hour."

There was nothing—no helicopters passing the balcony, no buzzers from the lobby, no cats chasing each other over the furniture. He learned that it was almost five in the morning, that he had been asleep for just over three hours, and that he had cried out as he awoke.

His eyes were burning from lack of sleep, and his mouth tasted foul. He found the toothbrush Elizabeth had brought and used it, then washed his face with cool water. It did not ease the burning, but made him feel a measure more human.

Standing on the balcony, he looked out at the still-sleeping city, and drew deep breaths of cool morning air into his lungs. He gripped the railing with both hands and looked down on the parking lot, on the spot where she had died.

"What do you do the first day after?" he said softly, and went inside.

Sleep was out of the question. He was thoroughly awake, and restless.

"Cassandra, do you keep other logs?"

"I maintain a security log, a command log, and a connect log, Jonathan."

"Cassandra, are any of the logs passworded?"

"Not to you, Jonathan. You are on the family list."

Momentarily undone by the answer, he made his way to Alynn's chair and shakily sat down. She had wanted no secrets from him, even in her private space. Even now. Yet he felt an uncomfortable rush of guilt, as though he had been caught snooping. It was minutes before he could accept that he had permission.

"Cassandra—how do you keep your logs?"

"As recordings, Jonathan."

He covered his mouth with his hand. "Cassandra, do you have recordings of Alynn?"

"Yes, Jonathan."

"How far back do they go?"

"The security log is a seventy-two-hour loop. The command log and connect log are archival, and begin February 26, Jonathan."

That was the day she moved in. He leaned back in the big chair and said quietly, "Cassandra, play them for me. I want to hear her voice."

"Would you like the oldest or newest first, Jonathan?"

"Oldest." He folded his hands over his stomach and sucked his lips between his teeth, steeling himself. "Now, please."

A time stamp appeared on one of Cassandra's small monitors. "—No, all of that goes in the second bedroom. Cassandra, are you up yet? Oh, good. Welcome to Michigan. We have some settling-in to do. Let's put some knowbots to work. We need our netlinks back, I want all the current project libraries pulled down from the Arcadia server, and I'd like to know if there's anyplace in town I can get incense, charcoal, and a good Rolfing—"

The time stamp kept changing, jumping forward now half an hour, now half a day, skipping a night, a weekend. Most of what was logged was wholly inconsequential. But at times, she would chat at Cassandra in a way that turned the log into a makeshift diary.

No matter what the content, Jonathan listened without interruption, sometimes just to the sound of her voice rather than to her words. As he did, he found himself smiling—a smile that darkened to bittersweet regret and brightened to broad delight, but settled most often in warm affection.

He laughed aloud only once.

"—Stop, Cassandra. I've heard enough. Letter to the White House, personal letterhead. But you'd better not let me mail the first draft. Begin: Dear Madam President. Pardon me for asking, but are you out of your fucking mind?—"

A few small surprises were waiting for him, and a few missing pieces fell in place. "—Cassandra, would you find a number for Kelly Mizimi, Jonathan's grad assistant, and see if you can get her to pick up—"

"—Hi, Tommy, this is Lynn. I need to buy a couple of workstations. No, I already know what I want. I just want you to take care of the paperwork. Molecular Logic Model One. Cassandra will send you the details on the configuration. I'm told there's a waiting list for these machines, so I'm not expecting a bargain. In fact, I want you to buy your way to the front of the line, if you can—"

Time compressed, then blurred. The longer he listened, the more he missed her, and the more acutely he knew that she was gone. He had thought he might find Alynn here, but all he had found were shadows and echoes. And he knew that both would haunt him if he let them.

But still he listened, twisting the chair slowly from side to side, his hands folded at his mouth, until the sky brightened and sunlight pooled on the carpet for the cats. This was his vigil, his remembrance, his goodbye. He closed his eyes and searched for a quiet place to begin healing. And when he could not find one, he began to think about stopping the reading of Alynn's diary before the final entry, the last words of her last night.

Then a new emotional note in Alynn's voice called Jonathan back—two parts ebullient joy, a hint of earnest worry, a touch of impatience. But he was too slow to refocus his attention, and couldn't catch the thread of what she was saying.

"Cassandra, go back thirty seconds and resume."

"—He doesn't know what he has, Cassandra," Alynn was saying. "He doesn't know! But maybe we can help him discover it. This is so exciting. There're so many people who've forgotten how to believe, how to let themselves feel what they can't touch and know what they can't prove. He could open the door for all of them, Cassandra—the door to the infinite. The door science slammed shut."

He sat forward in the chair, resting folded arms on the edge of the console and his chin on his forearm, listening intently.

"Oh, sweet Mother, it's so hard not to talk to him about it. This is the next step up. This can restore what's been missing—knowing that everything we do matters. But he has to find it for himself, on his path. He could change so many lives, if only he can find it. If he comes to me—if he comes to me, I want to be able to help him. But he has to come to it himself. If I try to show it to him, he'll run away.

"—Oh, Jonathan, it's right there in your hands. It can only mean one thing. I wish I could whisper the right words in your ear. Oh, sweet, I hope you can take the leap. You see with your eyes, but you understand with your heart—"

"Cassandra, stop." He sat bolt upright and stared at the time stamp. It was from the day after Molly One had kicked out the matrix match and kicked the props out from under the project.

In just a few hours—perhaps because she would think him ready and receptive, perhaps because her eagerness would get the better of her judgment—Alynn would quietly and matter-of-factly ask him to think about the unthinkable.

And he would refuse, just as she feared.

And she would never bring it up again.

"Cassandra, I want you to connect to Molly One at the lab. Grab as much bandwidth as you can. I'll talk you through the security."

It took Jonathan less than a minute to introduce Cassandra to Molly One. On the way in, he deferred a long queue of mail, but took a moment to check what else was happening in the lab. No other users were logged in, and the door was locked.

"Cassandra, I need to talk to Molly directly."

"Yes, Jonathan. The keyboard is now pass-through."

DISPLAY
Ready
CALL RECORD 0218, TIME ZERO, he typed.

Cassandra's giant display monitor brightened, and the now-familiar matrix appeared to fill it.

CALL RECORD 6853, TIME ZERO, AND TILE

Now there were two frozen vector maps side by side on the screen. The one on the right had more bright traces, deceiving the eye into thinking that it was more simple.

VIEW AXIS −Y, AND ANIMATE

Both matrices smoothly rotated to a top-down view and came alive with the dance of the mind. Jonathan pushed the keyboard back and propped his chin on folded hands, his elbows on the edge of the desk. Both maps were familiar enough now that they entered his dreams, like a song that wouldn't stop playing in his head. Even so, he studied the screen for a long time: 0218 and 6853.

Dugan Beckett and Brett Winston.

The old man and the infant.

He found himself shaking. Wishful nonsense. Brain weasels. Lynn, if I invite this thought into my head, it'll drag me down a hole I'll never come back from. Can't you see that? Don't you know how much I'd like it to be true right now?

STOP, he typed, his fingers barely able to find the keys, then pushed his chair away from the desk and fled to the kitchen. He gulped cold water from a hand cupped under the faucet, then splashed his face with vigor, rubbing his eyes as though trying to wake himself up. Water dripped from his elbows to the floor and from his chin to darken his shirt.

Finally, he drew the back of one hand across his mouth and again turned toward the desk. The vector maps of Dugan Beckett and Brett Winston were still visible across the room.

"Cassandra, say good-bye to Molly."

The display went black.

"I guess this would all give Harris a good laugh, eh?" he said, and looked up. "How about you, Lynn? Are you sitting somewhere watching, shaking your head and smiling that indulgent smile at me? I stopped believing in Santa Claus when I was five and heaven when I was eight. Did I ever tell you that? I've never needed there to be anything beyond what I could see—until now." His eyes filling, he frowned and hung his head. "Christ, I don't even know who I think I'm talking to."

Never in his life had he felt so terribly and completely alone as he did in that moment. Neither Cassandra nor the cats had any comfort to offer. No one he could reach could help—not Liz, not his parents, not the scattered friends who hadn't yet even learned of the joy that had been shattered by gunfire in the night. Nothing he could still call his own could fill the emptiness left by what had been torn from him.

No one but Alynn. Nothing but being with her again, a thought so suffused with longing as to be nearly unbearable.

There's still no other answer. How much would it hurt just to look at this one?

"Cassandra."

"Yes, Jonathan."

"In the logs—does Alynn ever talk about reincarnation? Besides the last segment you played."

"Yes, Jonathan. That word appears twice."

"Play those segments," he said, walking back toward the desk.

Alynn's voice, eager and earnest, rose up to meet him. "Let's see what we can pull together for him off the nets, Cassandra. A reading list, or at least a place to begin. Program a knowbot to look for—oh, reincarnation, eternalism, *The Tibetan Book of the Dead*,

Dr. Ian Stevenson, Romy Crees, Sangyyal Dorjee, the Thouless key. Use my reference list from *Immortality*—it's at Arcadia if we don't have it here.

"But screen out anything involving channeling—it'll peg his hooey-meter. I'm really after case studies, and primary sources. Build a table of bibliographic citations and locate as many of the top hundred as you can. Maybe that will help separate the wheat from the chaff. Job name, let's see—A Bouquet of Reincarnations." She giggled. "No, too silly. Job name: Just Trying to Help."

The second entry was short, and Alynn's voice was tired and unhappy. "Cassandra, is that reincarnation job still running? Well, kill it, and purge the work files. Help was not wanted."

It only took him a moment to figure out what conversation lay between the two time stamps. And in that moment, Jonathan realized that he no longer had a choice. Everything was pushing him in the same direction—what he wanted, what he needed, what he owed Alynn.

"Cassandra, can you restart that job, Just Trying to Help?"

"Yes, Jonathan."

"Please do," he said, and went down the hall to Alynn's sanctum.

Crouching before the bookcase, he could only find seven books devoted to reincarnation. He told himself that that meant there was a good chance that they were especially meaningful to Alynn. Taking them down one by one, he paged and skimmed through them, glancing at copyrights and indexes, looking for something that would tell him he was on the right path. Finally, he settled on the least-fragile-looking of the books, a large volume titled *What Survives?*

Then, as the sunlight poured in through the slatted blinds and Hypatia lounged on the windowsill, Jonathan curled up in the corner of the altar room, on the huge pillows from which he thought he could still catch Alynn's perfume, and began to read.

5

The Inchoate Incarnate

I t took only two days for the siege to begin.

The first to try to dislodge Jonathan from his refuge was the manager of the Huron Towers. After his many calls went unanswered, he gave way in turn to a vice president of the management company, who passed the baton to an arbitrator from the Ann Arbor Housing Commission, who threw up his hands and ceded the field to Barr, Anhut, & Reno P.C., Attorneys-At-Law.

But by then, the real estate lawyers had to wait in line. Ahead of them were Hyatt & Garris, representing Mrs. Stacey Reed in an action against Jonathan Briggs to recover Alynn's property, and Fawcett, Donovan, Bishop, & Associates, representing Mrs. Stacey Reed in a wrongful death suit against Huron Towers, with the city of Ann Arbor, General Motors, and himself among the eleven codefendants.

Jonathan ignored them all. It was not possible to harass him by phone, because he had Cassandra to insulate him. With privacy set to high, he did not even have to hear the incoming messages, much less answer or return the calls.

The attorneys kept trying to reach him, all the same, reinforcing their efforts with registered e-mail, certified street mail, FedEx document packs, and finally process servers. It made no difference. E-mail accumulated in Cassandra's in-box, street mail in the key box in the lobby, and parcels in the manager's office. The eviction notice was taped to the outside of the locked front door.

But it was not all the yelping of attack dogs. Condolence calls from colleagues at the university and friends outside it trickled in as word of Alynn's murder spread. And Jonathan did talk to his mother once, his father twice, but only to keep them from flying down from Toronto. Eric and Kelly sent regrets and flowers, then respectfully waited a week to call and ask what Jonathan wanted done about the lab. The question seemed wholly irrelevant, so he did not bother to reply.

Only Liz did not call. And though he thought they should talk, he did not know what he wanted to do about the breach between them, so he did nothing.

Throughout this time, Jonathan never left the apartment. The front door had been opened only to food deliveries, flowers, and one surprise—Dr. Rupert Kosslyn, who showed up Sunday night with a large pan pizza and a larger bottle of Scotch.

"Life sucks," he said when admitted. "Where are the glasses?"

Jonathan would not have counted Kosslyn among his friends. They had never socialized, and barely spoke when their paths crossed. And, behind his back, Kosslyn had been an easy target for Jonathan's barbs.

But Dr. Kosslyn's dour blandness was oddly comforting now, because Jonathan had forgotten how to laugh. There was little conversation between the men, and none of it was about Alynn, or anything else that mattered. They gorged themselves and got drunk together like old friends spared from talking by already knowing each other's stories.

At midnight, Kosslyn rose on wobbly legs to keep a rendezvous with the taxi he had arranged for in advance. "Life still sucks," he said, collecting the near empty bottle in an embrace. "But this is very good Scotch."

Jonathan tried standing with him, but the room tilted, and he quickly sat down again. "Rupert— why'd you do this?" he blurted out.

Kosslyn paused by the door. "Son, you're gonna feel lousy in the morning," he said. "But later on, you'll feel better. I just wanted you to remember that that's possible."

By the end of the week, he was sleeping in Alynn's bed and living at Cassandra's desk. He had read every reincarnation book on Alynn's shelves, but found them wanting—full of metaphysical systems that didn't map in the least detail against the physical universe he knew, of earnest speculations riddled with faulty logic, of unverifiable testimonials and credulous reporting.

To be sure, he also found elegant visions and eloquent, evocative prose. But Jonathan had hoped for more. He needed a reason to believe. Instead, he was finding only fuel for his skepticism.

Still, he persisted, pushing his skepticism away for Alynn's sake. He patiently sorted through the domains of reincarnation and transmigration, of immortality and immortalism, of anatman and annihilationism, until he came to understand that there was no metaphysical Unified Theory of Reincarnation, but dozens of mutually contradictory notions.

There are millions of educated Westerners who believe in this, he told himself. Lynn believed. I have to understand why. I have to understand how they think it works. If there's anything to reincarnation at all, there has to be more at the heart of it than need-to-believe. Somewhere the metaphysics has to touch the physical world.

But it was hard to see where that might be. The popular press, a direct descendant of the carnival freak show, eagerly offered up reincarnation as part of their parade of cults and the occult. And the popular culture was periodically held spellbound—to the tune of millions of copies—by Seth and Michael, Omm Sety and the Thouless key, and the past lives of minor entertainers and first ladies.

Between the gawking and the gullibility, Jonathan had found plenty of reason to keep his distance.

Still, he thought, in ten thousand years and a thousand cultures, somewhere, someone must have gotten hold of a piece of the truth—and an open mind should be able to recognize the truth. Even if their tools are no better than guesswork and serendipity, and the water's muddied by fraud and imagination and wishful thinking, someone will have a piece of the truth—a piece that will connect to the piece I have. And if it's there, I'm going to find it.

Holding fast to that determination, Jonathan turned to the list Cassandra's knowbot had produced. But he soon discovered that most of the books on that list were among the millions of texts that had yet to be published electronically, or even to be released in a scanned facsimile. They simply weren't anywhere to be had, online.

He thought of how his father came to haunt yard sales and flea markets in search of moldering vinyl LPs, which he dubbed to digital minidisc via a Rube

Goldberg record changer so delicate everyone was required to go about the house on tiptoe.

"Vinyl to CD, mono to stereo, 78s to LPs—every time they change the rules, wonderful performances, and performers, sink from sight, never to reappear," Julian Briggs had complained, and pointed to his complete set of Schwann catalogs. "Those are my treasure maps to the Lost World. How many people today have ever heard the real Billie Holiday, or Toscanini conducting the NBC Symphony?"

I understand, Dad, he thought, looking forlornly at Cassandra's list. New technologies did not just replace the old. They also winnowed and widowed.

Prompted by that memory, Jonathan recalled another long-past conversation with his father. Julian's habit was to play his LP recordings at performance volume, for hours on end. And the immaculately reproduced sound of analog tape, mechanical record-cutters, and a diamond stylus scratching across worn plastic was, to the ears of a teenage boy spoiled by digital perfection, a form of torture.

"How can you stand that?" he had demanded one day, confronting his father. "Between the hiss and the Rice Krispies effect, you might as well be listening to AM radio in a thunderstorm."

Faintly surprised, his father had shrugged. "I listen to the music, not the noise."

At the time, he had thought it a glib, annoying answer. But now Jonathan seized on it as a way of thinking about his mission.

Listen for the music. Ignore the noise—

The obvious place to turn next was the university library system. It still owned more than a million books in paper, as well as extensive periodical holdings. Though most of the printed matter was now held in the closed stacks of various special collections, that was no obstacle to a member of the faculty.

But as he browsed the online catalog, Jonathan discovered anew that the two worlds he needed to draw together had almost nothing to say to one another.

A keyword search under reincarnation turned up 155 entries. Under immortality, there were nearly 400. Under soul, half again as many. Promising.

But when he added science to the search criteria, those long lists were quickly winnowed to a handful of books, most written long before there was anything resembling a science of the mind. Using "personality" instead turned up a Jungian analysis of the belief in reincarnation, and not much more.

Jonathan could have all the works written in the foreign languages of Hindi and theosophy he wanted. But when he asked for something from a more familiar culture, he was left waiting while Mirlyn thrashed through long searches that produced short, disheartening reports:

------MIRLYN --

Search Request: K=REINCARNATION AND NEUROSCIENCE

UM Online Catalog

Search Results: 0 Entries Found   No Keyword Entries Found

No Keyword Matches Found

And, he found, this was not merely a matter of the U's undeniable intellectual prejudices being reflected in the library's acquisitions policy. It was the same up the road in East Lansing:

------MAGIC --

Search Request: K=REINCARNATION AND BIOLOGY

MSU Libraries Catalog

Search Results: 0 Entries Found   No Keyword Entries Found
--- D3AB
                    No Keyword Matches Found

It was the same everywhere. It was as though, sometime late in the nineteenth century, the Great Rift of materialist reductionism had created a kind of intellectual continental drift, separating and isolating the cultures of I-Believe-What-I-Know and I-Know-What-I-Believe. There was no intersection between them at all.

The reincarnation books were consigned to the religion, anthropology, and philosophy sections of the undergrad library. The only journal that seemed to consider the subject fit for serious discussion was *Religious Studies*. Even the remaining psychologists, effectively defrocked from the priesthood by Harris's neuroanimatics, were interested in reincarnation only as a belief system and a therapeutic tool.

It seemed to Jonathan as if no one were allowed to hold citizenship in both countries—to be both a skeptic and a believer, to combine the fruits of deduction and intuition. There was a terrible schism, vigorously enforced from both sides. One refused to subject its beliefs to testing, while the other refused to believe in anything it could not test.

And with head and heart not on speaking terms, no one was asking the question Jonathan was desperate to answer: whether there was room in Darwin's naked ape for a touch of the divine, and in a finite, chaotic, temporal universe for an infinite, eternal consciousness. Could what he knew and what Alynn had believed coexist in the same reality?

If it wasn't possible, she was gone forever.

And because that was still an unthinkable thought, he pushed back the wall of frustration and discouragement, and pressed on.

* * *

Hours later, Jonathan finally realized that he had lost his way in the unfamiliar jungle. He was reeling from conceptual overload. Everything was coming through as noise. There was too much new to absorb, much less to process and integrate—from astral physics to oversouls, egregores to zodiacal bodies. He needed a native guide and interpreter.

He was certain there had to be someone nearby. Cassandra's inventory of local resources included a women's spirituality group on campus, two crystal-and-wand bookstores in town (and five more within thirty miles), an active CUPPS group at the local Unitarian church, and a pagan grove in Royal Oak. And if he needed more, Cassandra had located three back issues of an electronic newsletter, *phenome-NEWS*, which was edited in Brighton and filled with ads for esoteric workshops and alternative practitioners throughout the area.

If he could only get out and start talking to people, Jonathan was sure that he could find the help he needed.

But he was a prisoner in the apartment. And he harbored a suspicion that the person he was looking for would not likely be found in the business directory under "Past-Life Counselors," ready to take his money in exchange for telling him what he wanted to hear.

In search of help, he went back to the nets. Somewhere among the tens of thousands of postings archived from the newsgroups, and the threads still current on the commercial data channels, he hoped to find someone who could do for him what Alynn would have, if he had let her.

Even with Cassandra's help, it was a tedious process. There was no substitute for wading through the long, rambling conversations in search of someone whose intellect and sensibilities he could respect. And then he felt obliged to scan every other post by them he could find, to confirm or contradict that first impression.

After three hours, only two prospects were still viable—an Air Force master sergeant who posted under the handle "Sherry," and a Seattle hypnotherapist named Tom Lightfeather. Anyone who claimed a past life as an historical figure was struck off the list without appeal. Several others with promise had lost points by proclaiming a belief in Atlantis, Strieber communionism, halo therapy, or the *Weekly World News*.

Sherry had been convinced by her own past-life memories, which came to her in lucid dreams. Tom had been persuaded by twenty years of watching his clients during regressions. But both explained themselves calmly and measured their claims, with no sign—yet—of the credulous certainty of the True Believer.

When the knock at the door came, a weary Jonathan was struggling to concentrate on a long essay by Lightfeather, his response to an attack from a rabid American Family Church member.

"Go away," Jonathan muttered distractedly.

But after a polite interval, the knock came again—sharp, measured. It was then that Jonathan remembered that he was expecting Kelly or Eric to show up with the first batch of books from the library.

"Cassandra, show me the hallway."

The secondary monitor brightened, and the peephole camera showed a man twenty years Jonathan's senior, balding but trim and well dressed. Jonathan did not recognize the man, but he recognized the look—three-piece suit, expressionless face, hundred-dollar-an-hour billings.

So—it begins.

The man leaned forward and rapped smartly on the door with his knuckles. He peered at the peephole lens. "Mr. Briggs, my name is Arthur Steuben—of Hillerman-Steuben-Welch, in Chicago. I apologize for intruding on you, but you apparently haven't been receiving my letters and messages. It's very important that I speak with you."

A new player, Jonathan noted with idle curiosity, sitting back in his chair. "Cassandra, tell him I'm not home," he said, and listened as Cassandra relayed the message through the security intercom.

The man shook his head. "Mr. Briggs, forgive me, but I know otherwise. I've spoken with your parents, and I understand your situation. I believe I may be able to simplify matters somewhat for you. But I need to speak with you, and sooner is better than later, for everyone."

Jonathan reached out and touched the intercom key. "You lawyers must think the rest of us are idiots. I don't know whose lizard you are, but you can go back and tell them I'm not budging—not for phony fire alarms, not for the neighbors-from-hell, and especially not for a lawyer-of-the-week who says he just wants to help. Fuck off."

The man's eyebrows shot up in surprise as he took in Jonathan's broadside. Then, at the end, a glimmer of understanding washed across his face, and he smiled tolerantly. "Mr. Briggs, I'm afraid you have me confused with some other lizard. The only lawyers at Hillerman-Steuben-Welch are tax lawyers. We're an investment counseling firm—a bunch of hard-partying CPAs."

Frowning, Jonathan touched the key again. "Then what do you want with me?"

Steuben's smile faded, his expression turning serious. "Mr. Briggs, I'm the principal trustee for the estate of Alynn Reed. And I really think you should talk to me."

A shiver ran through Jonathan's body, with no obvious cause or meaning. "Cassandra, do we know Arthur Steuben?"

"Arthur Steuben is vice president of Hillerman-Steuben-Welch, trustees for the Arcadia Trust, an instrument created and funded by the mistress. There are three letters, six phone calls, and a lobby page from Arthur Steuben in the Pending queue."

Sheepishly, Jonathan reached for the key. "Mr. Steuben, I'm sorry about the lizard crack. Cassandra, please let him in."

They settled at the only table in the apartment, the small dinette in the kitchen.

"Mr. Briggs, do you have any identification?"

Brow furrowed, Jonathan handed his visitor his National Health card. When Steuben looked at him expectantly, Jonathan also produced his Michigan Resident Services ID. The accountant studied both briefly, then pushed them back across the table.

"Thank you," he said. "Mr. Briggs, how much did you know about Ms. Reed's finances?"

"Almost nothing," Jonathan said. "I know she's—she was very successful. But we didn't mingle money. I paid for everything at my place, where we lived—I was glad to, I never asked her for anything. She took care of this place. And when we went out together, we took turns. Whoever suggested something usually paid." He shook his head. "I can't remember a money conversation that went much beyond 'I'll get this one.'"

Steuben nodded. "So you didn't know anything about the Arcadia Trust."

"Not a word."

"I had better fill you in a bit, then." As he spoke, Steuben retrieved a pocket PC from inside his suit coat and opened it on the table. "The Arcadia Trust is principally funded by the income stream from Ms. Reed's properties, all of which are held in the name of the trust. She, in turn, drew her living expenses directly from the trust."

"For tax reasons, I assume."

"In part. The current value of the trust assets is"— Steuben glanced down at the computer—"slightly more than $13 million. The annual investment income on the assets is, in a difficult market such as we see today, a little less than $1 million. Income from sales and licensing varies from year to year. Last year, with no new release, it dipped below four hundred thousand."

Jonathan rested his folded hands on the table and cocked his head to one side as he looked at his visitor. "Mr. Steuben, why are you telling me this?"

"Because you are the principal contingent beneficiary, Mr. Briggs."

Jonathan jumped up out of his seat, knocking his chair backward as he retreated. "No, no, no—I don't want this—"

"And my instructions from Ms. Reed are to provide you with what you need," Steuben continued. "That's why I'm here—to discuss the necessary arrangements. I'm sorry if this comes as a shock, but there was no way around it. If you'd been reading your mail—"

"Why me? Jesus God Almighty—"

"Ms. Reed didn't discuss her reasons with me," Steuben said, closing his computer and tucking it away. "It's probably safe to assume that there wasn't anyone she wanted more to have it."

"Do I have to take it?"

"No, of course not. But you can't change the terms of the trust, either—you're only the principal beneficiary, not the owner. If you choose not to draw on the trust, all the earnings will be reinvested, save for the amounts reserved for certain onetime gifts specified in the trust documents."

"Her mother?"

"I'm not at liberty to discuss those gifts, Mr. Briggs, I'm sorry."

"It doesn't matter—her mother will never stand for this." Jonathan shook his head. "I need a drink. Can I get you one?"

"Thank you, yes." While Jonathan opened cabinets and clinked glassware with trembling hands, Steuben added, "I can tell you that Mrs. Reed's lawyers have already been in touch with us. I'm afraid there's very little they can do on her behalf. We're very good at what we do, Mr. Briggs, and a trust is much more secure than a will."

Jonathan brought the glasses to the table, then retrieved his chair. "Speaking of lawyers," Steuben continued, "I understand you've been having some trouble with Huron Towers. You should see the end of that, now."

"Why?"

"I stopped at the management office before coming up to see you, to straighten matters out. It was entirely a problem of miscommunication. They were under the mistaken impression that a personal corporation was involved, not an ongoing trust instrument. We hold the lease, you see."

"So—the trust is technically the tenant?"

He nodded. "I informed them that we'd be keeping the apartment for another three months, at minimum, and I've paid them in advance, to smooth the waters a bit. That will give you enough time to decide what you want to do."

"I'm free to come and go now?" Jonathan stared at him, afraid to believe.

"Entirely free."

A flash of paranoia seized Jonathan. "If this is a trick to get me to leave—"

"—It would be a good one. But it's no trick. I don't play games with fragile people." He sipped at his glass. "This is respectable. Single malt, right?"

"I didn't even look, to tell the truth."

Steuben smiled. "I understand. —Mr. Briggs, I know that you've suffered a terrible blow. I liked Alynn Reed. I suspect you loved her a great deal, and I can see how a man could. It's always hard to deal with the thought that you're profiting from someone else's misfortune—and all the harder under these kinds of circumstances."

"I'd trade every last nickel of it to have her back," Jonathan said, tears suddenly streaking his cheeks. "A million, fifty million, or fifty times fifty. Without a moment's hesitation."

"I know you would, Mr. Briggs," Steuben said gently. "Any decent person would. But that option isn't on the table."

"This just doesn't feel right."

Steuben folded his hands and looked down at them. "I'll tell you the same thing I've had to tell a number of people over the years—you didn't ask for this, and you need not feel guilty about accepting it. This was her choice. This is her last gift to you. And chances are, the last thing she wanted was for you to tie yourself up with guilt over it. She thought you were worthy." He looked up. "So let yourself be."

"What does that mean?"

"It means you can best honor her by accepting her gift and using it well—to realize your ambitions, to help make yourself comfortable and happy, whatever. She probably had some idea what you'd do with it, after all. Clients don't usually come to my office to get help giving large sums of money to people they think irresponsible or undeserving.

"Hard as it may be to accept, Mr. Briggs, she's given you an opportunity. Let yourself be grateful. My father used to say that when one door closes, God opens another one. I don't know if you're a religious man, but I do think it's true. Perhaps in a month or two you'll be able to see it that way."

Jonathan was silent for a long time. He rested his forehead against his fist and stared at the tabletop. "Yes," he said finally, his voice surprisingly collected. "Yes, I can use this to open a door." He looked up. "I suppose there are papers to sign, or something?"

"I'll send you a copy of the terms of the instrument as they apply to you," Steuben said. "But there aren't many. My initial instructions are to provide you with one hundred thousand dollars per year for personal expenses, and an unrestricted renewable grant in the sum of $1 million per year to support your research. Apart from that, this is one of the most open trusts I've written. Your access to the money is essentially unrestricted. You're free to use it for whatever purposes you deem fit. I also have the discretion as trustee to disburse larger amounts if those are not sufficient, though professional ethics require that I strongly discourage you from touching the principal."

Steuben stood, reaching into another inner pocket of his jacket. "I brought you a debit card," he said, laying a small leatherette wallet on the table. "It draws against a starting balance of fifty thousand dollars. The balance of the year's distribution will be added to the account in four months. If you need that money sooner, contact me. You do understand that most of the trust's assets are tied up at any given time? It's not a pile of money in a drawer?"

"I—yes."

"Good." He glanced at his notepad. "Now, the research grant will be handled as a gift to the university, creating a discretionary research account for you. We negotiated a fee of 20 percent for account administration and indirect costs, and will add that amount to the gift.

"I believe this arrangement will keep you clear of all of the paperwork associated with sponsored projects, as well as all of the tax and accounting complexities involved if you handled the money yourself. Alynn wanted to give you the most freedom with the least administrative nuisance." He closed the notepad and tucked it away in his jacket. "I think she also hoped to bolster your status in the department. It's my impression, based on the tone of our conversations with the university, that a gift of this size will likely have that effect."

Reaching down, Steuben picked up his glass and finished his drink. "Good luck, Mr. Briggs," he said, offering his hand. "I'm very sorry about your loss."

Jonathan sat at the table for fully half an hour after Steuben left, staring into his folded hands and glancing uncomfortably at the gift Steuben had delivered to him. The thin wallet contained the distillation of Alynn's hard work and creativity, rendered to its simplest form—the money that people were willing to pay to play in her imaginary worlds.

Is that all we amount to when we're dead? Assets to be disposed of, debts to be paid? A trail of entries in the big record book, ending with unkept promises and unfinished work, an obituary and an estate sale?

Or was it possible that something of Self did survive? How comforting a fiction that would be—but how wondrous a truth.

Jonathan did not want the money for himself. But he could not help but wonder if there were something he could buy for Alynn with it. At last, he reached out and, with a light touch of his fingertips, drew the wallet across the surface toward him.

The debit card bore a hologram of the Visa Express trademark, and a touchmark waiting for his thumbprint. Holding the card by the corners, Jonathan angled it to catch the light. The winged horse sprang into silvery flight. Where do you go in the darkness? he thought, tipping the card away to make the Pegasus vanish. Maybe the body is nothing more than the light that illuminates the soul, and without which it hides from our eyes.

Jonathan peeled the protective cover back from the touchmark and pressed his right thumb firmly onto the square. Then he stood, tucking the wallet into his back pocket. He walked to the bathroom, where he shaved and trimmed his moustache for the first time since Alynn died.

Then he took the elevator to the lobby, and emerged into the sunlight. He stopped to take a white mum from the landscaping and lay it on the spot where Alynn had died, but he did not linger there. The chains had fallen from his limbs, and he had much to do.

Walking into Moonstone Craft House for the first time reminded Jonathan of the first time he'd gotten up the courage to go into one of the Toronto Centre sex shops. He was as unsure of himself now as he had been then, and equally at a loss to understand the uses of much of what he saw for sale.

Moonstone boasted all the usual and expected trappings of a mundane bookstore—a wall full of multimedia, another of books on disc and paper, a Canon self-service demand printer, greeting cards and calendars, software and sharetext samplers. Only the subjects covered and the roster of publishers represented were unusual.

But at least half the store was given over to brass bowls and "singing" bells, earth-tone stoneware and porcelain statuary, and esoteric jewelry in silver and crystal. There were "dream catchers," healing stones, and an array of double-edged knives and swords, which Jonathan eyed with some alarm. The offerings in candles, oils, herbs, and incense gave the air in the store an almost overwhelmingly organic smell, like a forest after a summer rain.

And everywhere there were instruments and noise-makers, from skin drums and rainsticks to rattles, bells, and "moon chimes"—enough to outfit an exotic percussion ensemble.

It's a hardware store for an alternative technology, he thought as he gazed wonderingly at the shelves and displays.

Jonathan had become accustomed to the smotheringly helpful "sales assistants" that were retail's answer to web commerce shopping. But when no one pounced on him while he lingered near the door, he made his way to the register. Tending it was a twenty-something woman with a pentacle and a labrys dangling from her throat piercings.

"Can I help you with something?" she asked as he approached.

"I hope so," he said, trying a smile. "I need to find someone in the area who's knowledgeable about reincarnation, and I thought this might be a good place to start looking."

"Have you looked at the multimedia rack? We just got a new disc in from Aetherius Press that Sharra is very high on—"

"No, you don't understand," Jonathan said. "I

need to find someone who really understands this—I need to be able to talk to them about my questions."

She studied him for a moment. "Someone close to you recently crossed over."

"Yes," he said, not questioning the source of her perception.

"And you've been in great pain," she said, shaking her head sympathetically. "Your aura is awfully weak, and much too yellow. You're going to have to be careful, or you're going to make yourself terribly sick." She played idly with her throat jewelry while she thought. "Are you hoping to try to contact this person?"

"I don't know," he said. "I guess I'm trying to find some way to make it all right. I really don't quite know what that will take."

The woman turned and called toward the back of the store, "Barbara? Is Lady Aryanna still in town, or has she already left for Wisconsin?"

"She left Tuesday," the answer came back.

"Oh, that's too bad," the young woman said, frowning. "I'm sure she would have been good to talk to. But she's gone off to a Midsummer gather, and she's staying on for a month to teach some workshops at Mt. Horeb. I could give her your name when she comes back—"

"I can't wait a month," Jonathan said anxiously.

"I know," she said. "But I don't know what to tell you. We have a networking bulletin board in the back, with the business cards of some metaphysical therapists. But there really isn't anyone I'd care to recommend—"

She suddenly snapped her fingers and her expression brightened. "Wait. You know what I would do if I were you?" Emerging from behind the counter, she led him by the hand to a literature rack near the front door. She plucked a sheet from its bin and handed it triumphantly to Jonathan.

"What's this?" he asked. "Starpath?"

"It's the biggest open pagan festival left in the East, and it's just two weeks from now. They get three or four thousand people in, from all over. And that means just about every path you've ever heard of. It's a wonderfully eclectic mix—that's what it's all about, sharing. I went three years ago and had an incredible time." She gestured eagerly with a ring-bright finger. "Look at the list of workshops, on the back."

Jonathan turned the flyer over. At first glance, he saw at least four sessions that mentioned past lives or reincarnation, each led by a different presenter.

The young clerk edged closer. "See, your problem is that a lot of the local people have gone undercover, with that new state law," she said quietly. "Anyone who's easy to reach wants your money and probably isn't worth it, and the real teachers are going to make you wait at least a month to make sure that you're sincere. Lady Aryanna is about the only one who wouldn't."

"But she's in Wisconsin for a month."

"Right. You said you weren't really sure what you needed. Maybe going there will give you a chance to find out," she said with a nod, and squeezed his hand. "I believe we always find the teacher we need, when we're ready. I hope you find yours."

Jonathan folded the flyer and looked up. "Thank you," he said, tucking the paper in his jeans pocket. "You've been very kind. And trusting."

"I don't believe in secrets," she said. "These things belong to all of us. The problem's not that too many know, it's that too few do." She held open the door for him. "Come see us when you get back."

*   *   *

Once western New York forest, then a hope-and-sweat family farm, the rolling field was returning to forest once more.

Great arcs of young broadleaf trees bridged the Starpath site from one side to the other, subdividing the field and creating ribbons of sheltering shade. But the sun breaks were neither so tall nor so dense yet as to hide the fact that the field was filled with tents and canopies of every color and description.

There were striped beach shelters, towering tipis, nylon dining flys, and sun shields snapping in the breeze, white pyramid-peaked campaign tents with fluttering corner pennants, even a few air-supported TubeTents, with their cushioned floors and humming coolers. The two permanent structures—the "water house," with a swimming pool, showers, and taps, and a covered stage—were lost among the hundreds of transients.

Jonathan was amazed to see so many people already there. He had timed his own arrival to place him at the festival the afternoon before events began. Better to come early to a party where you know no one, he had thought—it's easier to meet people as the room fills than after.

But the party was already well under way. From some unseen corner of the field, Jonathan heard the deep heartbeat pulse of drumming. From inside a tent somewhere nearby, he heard someone singing over the strum of a steel-stringed guitar. There were cooking smells in the air, and laughter and happy voices spicing the bustle of activity.

Shouldering his bags, Jonathan followed the trail flags to East Meadow, to which he had been assigned. He found a place for his two-man pop-up along the border of the Wild Grove forest camping area. There it would catch morning shade from an old oak, but bake in the afternoon. It seemed an agreeable trade-off, considering how much of the space left had no shelter at all. His tent was soon staked and his kit stowed inside.

Jonathan had not brought much of value, but, out of habit, he hesitated to leave it unwatched and unsecured. Standing protectively before his tent, he watched his neighbors moving about their business, setting up camp and greeting friends.

Before long he began to feel foolish for having packed his urban fears along. He zipped the screen door of his tent against the insects and dismissed the thought of keeping out anything larger. Then, with his site map folded in his pocket, he set off to explore Starpath.

The ten largest meadows were named for the compass points, the elements of Empedocles, and the Sun and Moon. Common tents were set up and workshop spaces set aside throughout the camping areas. Sun Meadow, in the center of the site, was home to a tent mall of artists, artisans, and hucksters offering a wide array of esoteric and handmade wares. Jonathan found there the source of the cooking smells—a file of food booths offering an eclectic menu of alternatives to backpack and cooler fare.

Moon Meadow was reserved for large gatherings, and held the stage and little more. A gentle hill provided natural risers. Fire Meadow, to the northeast, was similarly forsaken, dominated by an extensive labyrinth of hedges on the slope above a huge fire circle.

Beyond Fire Meadow, Jonathan found the source of the drumming he'd been hearing since he arrived. A branch-and-vine structure known simply as the Dome housed a small band of trance drummers, apparently exiled from the greater community. The reason for that exile became clear later that night—the trance drummers carried on around the clock, until the relentless rhythms and exhaustion combined to place them in an ecstatic state.

As he wandered, Jonathan stayed within himself, looking without touching, exchanging a few polite smiles but few words. When he realized he was hungry, he wandered back to Sun Meadow and bought himself a plate of curried rice at a booth called Smokey's Grill. He ate alone, sitting in the shade of a tree and watching children cavorting in the pool. He envied them their easy joy, and tried to remember being filled with the same light.

That evening, he sat near the back of a crowd of three or four hundred that gathered on the dew-damp grass of Moon Meadow for an informal concert. Loneliness was an ache in his throat, but he was not able to reach out. Though no one had done anything to force the feeling on him, he saw himself as an intruder, an impostor at someone else's family reunion. Alynn would have been at home, but he did not know how to claim a place for himself.

Without Alynn, I don't belong here—

Jonathan tried to lose himself in the music, which was surprisingly professional. Nine musicians shared the stage—Celtic harp and several acoustic guitars, flute, and African percussion—taking turns and collaborating on tunes. All but one were accomplished performers, and the sound engineer discreetly submerged the hapless guitarist's contribution in the PA mix.

Though Jonathan knew none of the songs, it became obvious that he was the exception. Through "Gently, Johnny" and "Spring Strathspey," "Lord of the Dance" and "Time and Stars," he found himself sitting in the middle of a soft-voiced people's choir, as those arrayed around him on the hill quietly sang along with the performers.

It was like going to St. Andrew's Catholic Church

with his friend Steven, when they were both ten. The music was grand, but he was embarrassed to be the only one not singing. Worse, because here there was no hymnal. And his discomfort became acute when the harpist announced a song called "Circles," and the sound from the throats of the audience swelled from contented accompaniment to a level more appropriate to an anthem:

> "—*Around and around and around turns the good Earth*
> "*All things must change as the seasons go by.*"
> "*We are the children of the Lord and the Lady—*"

But I'm not, Jonathan thought, the realization bitter. I shouldn't have come. He stood, turned away from the stage, and retreated up the hill and into the enveloping darkness. The music followed him all the way to his tent, but long before he reached it he could no longer distinguish the words, and it became only another sound in the night.

One more day, Jonathan thought. I'll stay one more day.

He lay on his foam bedroll, staring at the ceiling of the pop-up and listening to the wind in the trees and the voices of late arrivals setting up camp by flashlight. The gates were closed at midnight, halting the trickle of newcomers. The concert ended soon after, but a furious chorus of insects soon usurped the silence.

Somewhere a few tents to the north, a camper was snoring. Somewhere closer by, Jonathan heard the muted cries and writhings of two people making love—he thought both voices might be female, but he was not certain.

Those sounds, he filtered out, in time. But he could not quiet the distant drumming or his memories of

Alynn, and they conspired to keep him a prisoner of consciousness until dawn.

If there was any doubt in Jonathan's mind that the Starpath community was a culture unto itself, it vanished the next morning.

Leaving his tent when he started to hear the encampment stirring, Jonathan walked through the cool, wet grass down to Sun Meadow and the water house. There were two dozen indoor showers and another dozen outdoors there, and he hoped a long, hot soak would wash the fatigue from his muscles and the burning from his eyes.

But the program had neglected to mention that the showers were both unisex and communal. Jonathan found himself standing in a short line behind a woman of grand proportions wearing naught but the towel draped over her shoulder, and trying not to stare as five men and three women soaped their water-bright nude bodies under the outdoor showerheads.

He soon discovered that the arrangement and the rules inside were no different. The sign on the door said not MEN nor WOMEN, but PEOPLE, and the gang showers, locker-room style, offered no concessions to body modesty. It seemed that avoiding exposure to the morning's breezy coolness, not exposure to strangers' eyes, explained the line.

Jonathan was not particularly shy about his own body, except that he did not quite trust it not to misinterpret the sights. As if to test him, the shower that opened up placed him between two women. On his left, an older woman with olive skin, black hair to midback, and the lush figure of a Reubens goddess. On his right, a tall college-age woman with short-cropped hair and a sleek runner's body.

It was impossible not to look, especially after the older woman smiled at him. The most he could do was not linger, or allow his gaze to.

Now, wouldn't that tickle any university harassment officer's heart—a man afraid of getting an erection in a roomful of wet, naked women, he thought wryly as he toweled off. I do believe Dottie Stone's managed to bob me after all.

For Jonathan, the water house was the beginning of a crash course in the aesthetic of the human form. For, once the gates were closed against the outside world, those inside seemed to quietly set about shedding its conventions and taboos. Defying the odds and the sun, they wandered the meadows in every possible state of undress, revealing bodies of every shape and size.

There were high-collared capes made of zero-transmission fabrics, worn with nothing but skin underneath. Jonathan saw his first zero-modesty breechclout, and his first pierced and tattooed penis. An uncountable number of women were bare to the waist, even several who had had mastectomies. And more than a few men and women went about completely nude but for a waist pack, shoulder bag, head scarf, or a drape of silver-and-stone jewelry.

It was an education—no, a reeducation, adjusting the expectations created by years of camera-perfect models and sex-charged commercial nudity. Jonathan had never been to a clothing-optional beach or a sun resort, or even in a hot tub with more than three other people. The novelty and the variety both captured him.

Where's *National Geographic* when you really need it? he thought, sitting near his tent and unobtrusively people-watching.

Most who chose to shed their clothing seemed wholly casual about it. But some were proudly ostentatious. The lithe hard-bodies, the elaborate piercings and body art, were meant not only to be seen, but admired. And there were any number of carefully assembled outfits that covered nothing, such as the woman Jonathan thought of as the Irish Cherokee princess.

All high cheekbones and high breasts and flame-red hair in a single braid to the small of her back, she wore nothing but jewelry, a few feathers, and a tiny beaded medicine pouch. And, yet, she seemed able to go about unmolested to a degree that her six-foot-tall walking stick didn't account for. Even fully dressed, she couldn't have walked two blocks on an Ann Arbor street without having to fend off an advance.

But after puzzling for a while over what he was seeing, Jonathan caught on to what was happening. A naked woman is a sensation, unless she's but one of five hundred. A bare breast is a titillation, unless bare breasts are commonplace, available to every casual glance. For the women, Starpath had become a place where it was safe to stop hiding their bodies and celebrate them. Here, they could escape the entice-but-conceal games that sexualized every hint of cleavage and every inch of bare leg.

Wittingly or not, the women of Starpath had successfully conspired to debase the sexual currency to the point that it was no longer worth stealing. Desensitization therapy, on a mass scale.

Jonathan found for himself that, within the first hour, the link connecting nudity to the promise of sex had been broken, or at least benumbed. His appreciation of the women he found attractive was undiminished, but it was subtly changed. The teenage eagerness and wish-to-possess seemed muted, or transmuted.

But that was not the only thread of liberation in the nudism. The other challenged the body snobbishness that insisted that those whose appearance deviated too far from the cultural ideal must cover up. The surgical scars and birthmarks, the stippled stretch marks of childbearing, the round bellies and pear-shaped bottoms, the softness and sag from aging, the fullness of a Venus of Willendorf or a Henry VIII—the defiant unveiling of these declared them variations, not flaws.

It seemed to Jonathan that he had come to a place where ordinary people, not just genetic celebrities, were allowed to love their bodies and know that they were beautiful. And in that aesthetic, he found the first thread of affinity with the people around him. It was something they believed in that he could believe in, too. It was a beginning.

He knew his allegiance had changed when a state police helicopter made two slow, obviously voyeuristic passes over the site, and he laughed at them for their foolishness. You poor sorry sods, he thought, peeking through keyholes and up girls' dresses on the stairs. You're up there leering at the freak show and don't have a clue that you're the freaks.

And because he did not know what it felt like to stand naked on a forest meadow in the sun and the wind, Jonathan shed his own clothes, all but his watch and a red sweatband. It was an agreeable feeling, not least because no one around him took particular notice, and he walked to Sky Meadow for the first workshop feeling lighter and more hopeful than he had at any time since he arrived.

With his mane of shoulder-length black hair, intense gaze, short beard going to gray, and belted pirate's blouse, Adek Greystone was well cast for his role as leader of the past-life regression workshop. He looked like a man out of time.

"Without a doubt, the two most important tools

for past-life regressions are hypnosis and meditation," Adek was saying. "I want to focus on the second of those today.

"Many people in the community believe that only hypnosis can produce a true connection to the higher self. I consider this equivalent to the Christian belief that you need a priest or a saint to intercede for you with God."

There was a ripple of laughter, which Adek acknowledged with an easy smile. "Hypnosis is only a tool," he said, "and we PLR hypnotherapists aren't the chosen gatekeepers of the eternal. Much as I like being able to pay the rent, there's no reason why you should need me to introduce you to your inner self. Mother didn't hand out exclusive franchises, especially not fifty-dollar-an-hour ones. There's always more than one way to get to the truth."

He's good, Jonathan thought, listening. Self-assured, likable—draws everyone right in. I want to believe him.

"The truth is that our past lives bump into our present lives all the time," Adek was saying, "and not just in the subconscious realm of emotions and the unconscious realm of dreams. If that wasn't so, our past lives would be irrelevant, and our present lives—our choices, our lessons—would be much easier to understand.

"What I want to do in the next hour is try to guide you through a meditative process that I've found useful for learning to listen with the whole self," he said, walking slowly among his attentive audience. "I believe that anyone can learn this technique. I can't promise that you'll all learn to do it today. Those of you who've been meditating for other purposes will probably come to it more easily. The rest of you will need to take this home with you and work with it.

"The secret, if there is one, is that the fragments of our godhead that lived our past incarnations are dearer to us than a sibling or a parent. No matter how much pain is there, we can't help but love them, and we never let them get very far from us. They whisper in our souls.

"And they can't help but try to steer us toward the unfinished work they started—which is why there are many voices in our heads and why they so often can't agree. The key to meditative PLR is learning to identify your own voice and to mask it—to listen only for the thoughts that don't belong to it. Those are the voices of your past incarnations, whispering in the shadows. And once you know how to listen, they'll tell you who they are."

"Isn't there a danger in this?" a woman called out.

Adek stopped and turned toward her. "Go on."

"My half sister has had multiple personality disorder for the last five years," said the woman, rising to her knees. "And after spending time with her, I really believe that it's a psychic affliction. These other personalities are past-life fragments taking over her body. If we open the channel wider, without someone there to ground us—"

Adek nodded. "I can understand your apprehension. In fact, I have the same suspicion about the cause of multiphasic syndrome."

"Well, then—"

"But I think it happens not when we open the channels," Adek went on, "but when we close them. I think it happens when, for whatever reason, someone breaks the connection, tries to silence their other voices. I have to believe that'd be like watching your one-year-old wander out into traffic. It's not the kind of thing you let happen and chalk up as a learning experience."

"No," said the woman. "You act—you do what-

ever's necessary to snatch them back out of danger."
She frowned. "Interesting. And it fits with what my
sister was doing with her life just before this came on."

Jonathan's curiosity was aroused. I wonder what
we'd find if we put the ol' squid hat on some MPD patients, and compared the vector matrix of one personality with another—

"Good," Adek said. "But don't let me mislead anyone. There are no safe quests. There's always the risk
that what we learn will subvert what we thought we
knew. There's always the risk of having to face something you've been avoiding. When you go digging in
the dark, you never know what you'll turn up.

"But there's a greater danger out there to keep in
mind. And that's the danger of living unconsciously,
with no understanding of how your choices connect
with what's come before, or what's still to come."

Several heads nodded in agreement, and Adek
clasped his hands together. "I think we should probably get started—they haven't given us any too much
time. Get yourself in a comfortable position, something you can sustain for the next hour. It's best if
you're not touching anyone else, and if you are in
touch with the Earth. Mother can be a wonderful am-
plifier—"

Jonathan tried. He tried earnestly and hopefully,
with his skepticism stuffed as far into a dusty corner of
his consciousness as he could manage. He listened at-
tentively, and he followed Adek's instructions faith-
fully. And he failed utterly.

The only thoughts he could hear were his own. He
never achieved the desired state, which Adek called
passive awareness. Every sound from the camp pulled
him back, reminded him that he was lying on his back
in the grass, eyes closed and naked, with forty other

people. He never silenced his own "voice," which insisted on busily thinking about eleven things at once.

"Create spaces between your thoughts, and listen in the spaces," Adek said. "Slow the pulse of your consciousness, and listen between the heartbeats."

But that was not how Jonathan was accustomed to thinking about thinking, and the imagery did not help. He tried instead to envision his own matrix map and let it separate into its elemental components, hoping to find a ghost left behind.

Listen to the noise, not the music—

It was hopeless. And when a woman nearby suddenly cried out and began to sob, Jonathan sat up with a start and stayed up. He watched Adek come to comfort the woman, listened to her agitated voice as she told of her discovery, watched her face and wavered between doubt and envy.

"I was hiding in a tunnel in the dark," she was saying, the words tumbling out as Adek led her away, "a tunnel in the rock, in a mountain, with some kind of gun in my hands—and then fire came pouring down the tunnel, and it stuck to everything it touched, and we were all burning—I could see my friends' faces—it was horrible, horrible—"

It was obvious that something had happened to her during the meditation, something that had affected her profoundly. The question Jonathan struggled with was, where had that experience come from? Why her, and not him? Past lives implied past deaths. Surely one of his had been traumatic enough—

If I was on the inside of that, I'd know if it was real, he thought. That would be enough—that's all I want. Just a little taste of something so extraordinary I can't explain it away. Oh, a hard left jab to the paradigm, ladies and gentlemen, and he's down on the canvas. Folks, I don't think he's going to be getting up—

But it didn't happen. He had had an ordinary experience, while people ten feet away were having extraordinary ones. Was it something about him? Something about them? He was the one in the chair now—his own work said that when you map the experience against the stimulus, what appears between them is the personality. Was he too hidebound and stodgy, or were they too suggestible? Was he preventing himself from touching it, or was there nothing there to touch save the epiphanies of imagination?

There were no answers—nor could he expect any. *It's just going to have to be the front door.* As the workshop drew to a close, Jonathan watched for an opportunity. When it came, he stood and claimed the floor.

"Excuse me," he said to Adek, then addressed himself to the group. "My name is Jonathan. My girlfriend was murdered a month ago. She was shot in a carjacking, and died before I knew anything had happened."

"Oh, no," someone said. All around him, expressions of concern and sympathy leapt to faces. Jonathan shut them out so that he could get the words out. "She's why I'm here. She believed in reincarnation—and I, I don't know what to believe. We only talked about it once, and I wasn't the most receptive audience."

"Don't blame yourself for that," Adek said quietly.

"But I do," said Jonathan. "I've been trying ever since she was killed to understand the way she looked at things, what it meant to her—what it means for me, looking at going on alone. The truth is that I feel like I'm standing on the edge of a pit and I don't know if letting myself believe as she did will pull me down into the pit, or pull me away from the edge.

"None of you know me, and it's not your problem. I know that. But I'm asking for help, because I don't know where else to turn. If any of you'd be willing to come up sometime and talk with me about what you believe, about what you think happens, about where she might be now—well, I'm in East Meadow, in a tan-and-copper pop-up, along the tree line. I'd be very glad to see you, and to buy you a meal or a bottle for your time." He looked back toward Adek. "I apologize for the interruption."

He sat back down, feeling exquisitely vulnerable. The shield he had carried not just for the last month, but for a lifetime, lay on the ground, cast aside. The smallest cut, and he would bleed to death. The slightest breath of air would carry him away.

But almost immediately, the people nearest to him on either side reached out and took his hands, holding tight, holding him down. From behind, someone else laid a comforting hand on his shoulder. The rush of relief was as rain in the thirsty dust, shock and balm both.

"I'll come," said the woman holding fast to his right hand, giving it a squeeze.

"I can, too," said a man a few feet away.

"No apology needed, Jonathan," said Adek. "And I have some time right now, if you do."

Jonathan nodded. "Thank you. I'd like that."

In all, Jonathan took seven people and several more promises away with him from the workshop. The number gathered under the old oak swelled to eleven with later arrivals. To Jonathan's great delight, the group included not only Adek, but the woman who had had the fire vision, and Jonathan turned immediately to her once they had settled on the grass.

"Excuse me—what's your name?"

"Katherine Elaine Carlson," she said, and smiled.

"But I was born on Easter, so everyone calls me Bunny."

Jonathan answered the smile. "Bunny, you had something happen to you down there that's completely outside of my experience. Can you talk about it?"

"Okay," she said, and retold her vision of burning to death in the tunnel, this time with more composure, but no less earnestness. "I can't feel it the way I did then, because I have my shields back up. But it's still vivid. All I have to do is close my eyes."

"What do you think it means?"

"Oh, I don't have any doubts. I was reliving my own death."

"Why that? Just because it was so vivid?"

"Oh, no," said Bunny, shaking her head. "You see, I've always been skittish about fire. You won't see me at the bonfire Saturday. I can hardly make myself light a match. I was always afraid that there'd be a fire while everyone was sleeping—I have five smoke detectors in my house.

"And it's not just real fire that frightens me. When I was little, anything with a dragon in it, even a Disney cartoon, terrified me. That scene at the end of *Raiders of the Lost Ark*, with the German soldiers being melted by the fire from the Ark? I threw up all over my boyfriend's couch.

"I used to think I was that way about fire because I was burned as a witch, in the Middle Ages. Now I know—I was a Japanese soldier, on Corregidor, and I died in a flamethrower attack. And I'm pretty sure that that was my last incarnation before this one."

"Wait—were those details part of the vision?"

"Not at first. They came out talking to Adek, after. See, I don't know anything about military history, or weapons—"

Frowning, Jonathan glanced over toward Adek.

"You're troubled by the problem of proof," Adek said, catching the meaning of the glance. "And my talking to her taints the evidence."

"Well—yes. It raises the issue of how much she got from you and what came from somewhere else. Look, I don't mean to insult anyone. I don't think anyone is lying. But I've had nightmares, too, only no one ever told me to believe in them."

"Jonathan, one thing you have to understand is that the evidence is always tainted," Adek said. "There's no way of knowing what people have seen and learned, but forgotten. And the past isn't usually documented in enough detail, even when a regression is. Besides, any memory that can be verified could be a fraud, just as any memory that can't could be a fiction.

"I've been involved in this for fifteen years, and I don't think proof is possible. That's why it's so individual. The only real gauge we usually have for what's true and what isn't is our inner compass. Something clicks, or it doesn't. The dreamer knows."

"It was horrible, Jonathan, but it wasn't a nightmare," Bunny said. "I was awake. I wasn't dreaming, or making it up. I can understand your doubts, but I don't have any."

Jonathan looked around the circle. "Is this sort of thing common—has anyone else here made that kind of connection between the past and the present?"

A man to Jonathan's left spoke up. "I once lived with a woman who would start rubbing her wrists on her pant legs whenever anyone talked about a suicide. She didn't know she was doing it until I pointed it out to her. But she couldn't stop, even when she knew. She worked with a scryer and found out that she'd killed herself at least three different times. The last time, she'd slit her wrists in her husband's parked car, while he was upstairs in his girlfriend's apartment."

"If not in his girlfriend," a woman added acidly.

"Ouch, Tavis," a man said. "I'll bet he never enjoyed sex again."

"I think that was probably what she had in mind," said Tavis. "Anyway, Toni got a lot of insight out of the scrying. She had a lot of anger toward men, and at the same time a really insecure need to be loved. She'd pull men to her—and, boy, she could do it, too, she was maiden *ne plus ultra*—and then drive them away again. And, of course, then she'd get depressed, and start all over again. It was not healthy."

"And this past-life discovery helped her get better?" asked Jonathan.

Tavis shrugged and laughed lightly. "She's living as a lesbian now, so I guess she worked something out for herself."

"I know a couple back in Albany," said an older man, resting his back against the trunk of the tree. "They've been together for about three hundred years now. He used to have the oddest reaction to crowds—he could go into New York by himself, go to a ball game, ride the subway, walk Fifth Avenue at lunchtime, like he was born to it. But if she was with him, he'd get frantic, paranoid—almost a panic attack. They did some hypnotherapy with a friend of mine in Rochester—"

"Lady Calida?" asked Adek.

"That's her. You know her?"

Adek nodded. "She's very good. I'm sorry, you were saying?"

"Well, what they discovered is that she'd been a Japanese prince, or whatever they call a prince in Japan, and he'd been her bodyguard. She was stabbed to death by assassins, in the crush of the crowd at a festival. A couple of days later, after the assassins were executed, he committed seppuku, out of shame for his failure to protect her."

"Wow," someone said.

"No wonder he came back to her," Bunny said quietly.

"Does everyone have a story like that?" Jonathan asked.

On Jonathan's right was the slender dark-haired woman who had taken his hand at the workshop. "I don't have a story," she said. "I haven't been able to access any past-life memories yet. I may never be able to."

"But you still believe in reincarnation?"

"Oh, yes—"

"Why?"

"Because it makes more sense to me than the big-God-in-the-sky paternalism my parents believe in. And it makes more sense to me than the life-is-short, party-hard nihilism that my brother opted for," she said.

"How so?"

She considered for a moment. "In a world where every drop of rain and every speck of dust goes around a million times, where every ending's a beginning—well, why should consciousness and intelligence, the two most precious elements there are, be the only ones that are squandered? Laws of conservation, right? Life is a circle," she added. "I don't think there are any straight lines, anywhere—not even time."

Jonathan stared at her, stunned. Her ideas were so eerily close to Alynn's that it was as if this stranger had reached into his memory to show them to him again. His mouth worked, but he was struck dumb.

"Are you okay?" she asked, and reached to touch his hand.

"Did that hit something, Jonathan?" asked Adek.

"That was the way she talked about it," he said finally, looking toward Adek.

The hypnotherapist nodded. "Jonathan, do you want to define the problem for us? How can we help you? Do you expect us to try to talk you into, or out of, something?"

"Define the problem," Jonathan echoed. "Yeah, that's usually a good idea, isn't it?" He covered his mouth with his hand and blew a sigh into his palm as he stared at the grass. "I don't want to let go of her. It's—still unthinkable that she's gone forever."

"Then don't think that," said the woman holding his hand. "The chances are she doesn't want to let go of you, either."

"But I also don't want to get caught in a, a foxhole conversion, getting sucked into believing something that isn't true just because it makes life a little easier to face," Jonathan said. "I'm very afraid of that trap."

He looked around him and tried to read their faces. "I mean, these stories I've just heard—sure, they tug at me. They tug at the part of me that wants to believe my life's important enough not to end up on the universe's discard pile. But that's exactly what stops me from believing. Everything has a reason, and there's always a second chance—it makes it sound like the kind of things grown-ups tell children so they can sleep at night. Reincarnation makes everything so easy."

There was sharp laughter at that, which took Jonathan by surprise.

"No offense," the old man at the tree said to Jonathan's puzzlement, "but whoever told you that reincarnation was a blessing? Instead of one life's heartbreak, and one dumb, embarrassing death, you get to go through that drill twenty or a hundred times." He raised his palms to the sky and looked up. "Thank you, Universe—how very thoughtful. You shouldn't have, really."

There was more laughter, which the old man

seemed to take as encouragement. "If you're especially lucky, like Bunny here, you even get to see the highlights film, all the best moments," he said wryly. "And you're stuck with the mastery learning plan—instead of just carrying your lousy grade home to Mom and Dad at the end of the term, you get stuck there at school, taking the same tests over and over again until you stop repeating your mistakes." He flung an acorn away into the grass and grinned. "Nah, you'd be better off being a Christian. Much simpler. Fourscore-and-out, and then you're somebody else's problem."

"Ah, Kyrdwen, you have such a charming way of finding the gray lining inside every silver cloud," said Adek, bemused. "Kyrdwen's in his curmudgeon phase, Jonathan. Don't mind him. Even he doesn't know when he's being serious."

"Do, too," said Kyrdwen, launching an acorn in Adek's direction.

"The thing is," Adek said, his tone now earnest, "we can't make you believe—even if we wanted to. It's your choice what shape you want to give your reality. And if that's what you want from us, to make that choice for you, I'm going to have to beg off."

"No," Jonathan said, shaking his head. "No, I can make my own choice. Just—just show me the world through your eyes. Tell me how it works. You"—he turned to the woman next to him—"what's your name?"

"Kari."

"Kari," he repeated. "Will you show me what that circle looks like—where consciousness goes and what brings it back? Kyrdwen, is it? Tell me how you think your friends found each other again. Bunny, Tavis, Adek—what's on the other side? Who or what decides if, or when, or where you come back? That's what I have to understand. If everything makes sense when you know the context, give me the context. The devil is in the details."

He paused and looked around the circle at their faces, then drew a deep breath. "You see, it isn't just losing the woman I loved that's pushing at me. I'm a neuroscientist. I've been researching personality—mapping brain activity. Photographing minds, if you want. And there's a chance I may have caught a glimpse of the same mind in two different bodies—going out the door and coming back in.

"If that's what it was—I really don't know, and I don't want to say any more about that right now. But, you see, I have two reasons to want to believe, and reason enough to be doubly careful." He frowned. "Alynn thought the work was important, though. So this isn't just about her, it's also for her."

A surprised and delighted smile had spread across Adek's face as Jonathan was talking. The others were looking at him with a mixture of curiosity and hopeful wonder.

"Why don't we get some lunch and liquids up here," Adek said softly. "And maybe some cushions for bottoms, or even some chairs. I think we're going to be at this a while—and me, I've sat on enough acorn shells already. There's a reason there aren't any tents here—"

When everyone returned from their expeditions and settled in, Jonathan was surprised to find there were thirteen bodies instead of eleven. By dinnertime, there were fifteen—after dinner, the number climbed past twenty, loosely arrayed in two circles.

And the roster kept changing. As new people came, they would settle on the fringe and listen until they caught the flow of the discussion. Some would leave without ever joining in, while others would edge forward into the inside circle and the conversation when an opening appeared. Some who left came back later, bringing still others with them.

The faces changed by the hour, and the flavor changed unpredictably from Socratic inquiry to intense argument to speculative discussion to pagan support group, and back again. At one point in the early evening, Jonathan looked around the gathering and realized that he recognized only a few faces from the workshop.

Where did all you people come from? Why are you here?, he wondered.

It was then that he realized Starpath had adopted him, and the Oak Tree Reincarnation Roundtable had become an unofficial minor event of the festival. Whether compassion or curiosity brought them, they kept coming. The numbers dwindled as darkness fell, until the last half dozen adjourned to one of the hot tubs at the water house, but in the morning they were back again. Jonathan returned from his shower to find blankets being spread, a cooler of ice water on a chair, and the question already joined. The roundtable had taken on a life of its own.

Many of the new faces that appeared on the second day belonged to people who'd come not to argue metaphysical systems, but to tell Jonathan a personal story of their struggle and their discoveries. He was struck by how different the stories were, and how shyly and uncertainly many of them were told.

To be sure, there were a few obvious egotists who eagerly paraded glamorous past lives, apparently hoping to gild a mundane middle-class existence with reflected glory. And there were two or three troubled souls whose grasp of reality Jonathan wouldn't have trusted for directions to the nearest fast-food joint. But those extremes were, surprisingly, the exceptions.

"You know," Jonathan confessed to the roundtable over dinner, "I more than half expected that everyone was going to tell me that they'd been Marie Antoinette and Julius Caesar, and I was all ready to say, 'Okay, where the hell are all the serfs?'"

They laughed, and he looked down at the notes he'd been taking. "But the serfs are here, aren't they?" Jonathan went on. "Look, here's a German cooper, a Mayan farmer, a French trapper—six foot soldiers and only a single knight, a Spanish one at that."

"I admit, I have the same reaction when someone says they used to be a famous personage," a man named Gareth said. "And I've sure heard my share of stories I didn't believe two words of."

There were several nods of agreement at that. "You meet your third or fourth Marie Antoinette," said Tavis, "and you start to realize it can't all be taken at face value. Sometimes the young souls have an irresistible need to feel important."

Kyrdwen claimed the floor with a gruff grunt. "I always thought there should be some sort of reincarnation registry—'I'm sorry, all French kings after 1500 are already taken. Please enter an alternate famous person, or select from this list of minor Prussian nobles—'"

Smiling broadly, Gareth added, "But, still, I wouldn't be surprised if Marie and maybe even Julius really are still kicking around somewhere. John Kennedy, John Lennon, that pope, too. Bad deaths bring you back, I think."

"The towers," Bunny said simply, and the gathering grew respectfully quiet.

"Yes. Very bad deaths. They're all among us, somewhere," said Wakanda, looking toward Jonathan. "They were so *surprised*—so confused. They lingered for days over the pit. A lot of them had to be helped to leave—there was a lot of work done in the etheric to guide them."

"If my practice is any guide, people who died in the towers aren't ready to talk about it," Axel said quietly. "They aren't even ready to know."

"Well—we've talked about plenty of bad deaths here today," Jonathan finally offered into the sober silence. "A petty thief, hanged, and a horse thief, shot. Women who were raped and murdered—though not by any killer with a nickname and a serial killer trading card. Women dying in childbirth in Utah and Montserrat—clearly, two of the hot stops on any time traveler's itinerary. We've had a fourteen-year-old boy sent on the Trail of Tears, and a fifteen-year-old girl sold into slavery from the Children's Crusade—a little history there, but no glory."

Jonathan closed his notepad and set it aside. "All in all, a lot of hard lives and nasty deaths. None of them much to brag about, no matter how exotic the surroundings." He tried for a smile, then shook his head ruefully. "If you folks have been making this all up, I gotta tell you, you could do better. I'm really about ready to hear from a sultan beloved of his people and his wives, who fathered a hundred children and died of old age in his sleep—just to make things a little less bleak."

"See—I told you," said Kyrdwen from his perch against the tree. "A fine blessing, reincarnation."

"Amen," said a man who had told of being murdered in a love triangle. "Only masochists would invite this kind of pain into their lives."

"That's not true," protested a pregnant woman—seven months, Jonathan guessed—stretched out on a blanket behind the latest speaker. "I knew my regression work was going to be hard, but I wanted to know my demons by name. I couldn't make sense of this life until I knew about the last one."

"I couldn't make sense of my kids until I knew who they were," said a round-cheeked woman, her fingers flying over the crochet work in her lap. "A young king and an old wizard, sharing a bedroom—Goddess preserve!"

That drew a ripple of knowing laughter.

"That's really what this is all about for most of you, isn't it?" asked Jonathan. "That's the common thread—that everything makes sense when you know the context. That irrational fears aren't irrational—they're old scars from real wounds—"

"Exactly," said Adek, who had rejoined the group in the last hour. "If someone walks in with a phobia, or an obsession, or destructive interpersonal scripts, you try to explain everything you can in the now. But when you run out of answers there, you start looking farther and farther back. That's standard therapeutic practice, ever since Freud."

"You just don't stop at toilet training and birth trauma."

"There's no reason to," said Adek. "The results can be astonishing. If you'd seen the transformations I've seen, in my clients, you'd know just how potent those revelations are. Rediscovering your past can be tremendously healing—tremendously empowering."

"Hardly any of this is about the future, then," said Jonathan. "In two days, no one's talked about where they're going—only about where they've been."

"I don't worry about tomorrow," a woman said simply. "I know that whatever I need to do, there'll be time. And the people that are important to me will be there in my life, to love and learn from."

"There's something else," said a woman who reminded Jonathan of Elizabeth. "There's knowing that we're going to live in the world we create. None of this leave-the-world-a-better-place-for-your-children crap. We're going to inherit the consequences of what we do."

"I'll tell you what this means to me," said Tavis, who was sitting to Jonathan's left. "It doesn't wash away all of my problems, or guarantee happiness. It doesn't pay the bills or protect me against the wolves. But I'm not afraid of dying—which means that I'm not afraid to live."

"That's it," someone said. "That's it exactly."

Jonathan crossed his arms on his knees and rested his chin on a forearm. To the west above the trees, the broken sky was being painted muddy scarlet and pale yellow in wide, sweeping brushstrokes. Booming sound checks for the night's big concert had begun to rumble across the festival site from the direction of the stage, heralding the imminent end of the roundtable. Already, half a dozen people were starting to gather themselves to leave.

But there was one question Jonathan had not touched directly, and could not leave alone. "Let's say something happens and I die tonight—clear-sky lightning, or that old family aneurysm," he said slowly. "When do I come back? And where? What controls it? Who decides?"

Adek chuckled. "That's like asking a Christian what heaven's like," he said. "Really, nobody knows— even though we've all been through it. There seems to be a wall that separates the incarnate from the astral. But I think you'll make those decisions, while you're on the other side." Several heads nodded in agreement. "I think we choose our culture, our community, our parents, our birth sign and aspect, our sex, our issues—with full knowledge of our entire history. The most potent force in the Universe is will."

Jonathan looked at the hypnotherapist thoughtfully. "I think I'm beginning to understand."

Saturday dawned with steady patter of rain on the tent, and an unsettled feeling that nagged at Jonathan more strongly as the morning wore on. The feeling was hard to put into words, even for himself. It was as if he had been busy through the night, and his work was not quite finished. It was as if there was a shadow on his thoughts, though he could not see what was casting it.

Imprisoned by the rain, he opened his notepad and tried to write a letter to Elizabeth. She had left campus immediately after the end of the term—a week after Jonathan was freed from his hermitage, but before he had worked up the resolve to talk to her. The department secretary thought Elizabeth might have gone to Hawaii, but could only say for certain that Dr. Froelich had written herself authorization for four weeks' leave.

Jonathan soon discovered it was much harder to say in phosphor what he had worked himself up to saying in person. He had planned an apology, first, for his overreaction, then something delicate about it just being something that happened, as much his fault as anyone's, but really no one's fault at all—not anything wrong, even, well-meant, just a wrong moment, and unexpected.

In short, he wanted to say, "I'm sorry—can we both forget it and get back to being friends?" But he found it impossible to write a letter impervious to misinterpretation, or that anticipated every possible adverse reaction. Without being there to see her eyes, he could not be sure what he wrote was not making matters worse. It would have to be said face-to-face.

So he filed his failed sketches for the letter and turned to browsing back through his roundtable notes. After a time, he called Cassandra from his pad and asked for some of his files. He spent the morning becoming more and more unhappy with what he had heard and collected.

When he became aware of it, he found himself wondering if the elves of skepticism had crept in during the night and rearranged his mental furniture.

The spores—the spores are gone, Leila, he thought, self-mockingly.

The rain tapered off by noon, and the sun broke through soon after. Wearing jeans and a long-sleeved tee against the dampness, Jonathan went down to South Meadow for the final workshop he had planned to attend. But he had no great enthusiasm for it, nor any sense of hopeful anticipation—it was mere duty, keeping a promise to himself. He sat by himself in the back, making himself as inconspicuous as he could.

But several people who'd been in on the roundtable spotted him soon after he arrived. One came and sat beside him, whispering, "Do you have some time after this? There's someone I want you to meet—"

Worst of all, the presenter—a boyish woman with blond hair clipped so short it was nearly invisible—emerged from a huddle with a woman he recognized and headed directly for him. "Hello. I understand you're Jonathan—of the East Meadow Jonathans?" she asked with a pixieish twinkle.

He nodded, wary. "Yes."

"Wonderful—I'm glad you're here. You're going to be very interested in this, and I'm very interested in talking to you about your research. From what I've been hearing, I think we can help each other. Let me buy you lunch after, if you haven't eaten yet."

She turned away before he could say anything and

addressed herself to the workshop. "Welcome, every-one. I'm sorry the carpeting's so soggy," she said. "I'm Dana Stover, and the title of this workshop is 'Reincarnation and Telepathy.' And what I hope to do in the next hour is offer you another way of looking at the evidence for past lives.

"Like many of you, I've had powerful PLR experiences. However, unlike most of you, I no longer believe in reincarnation."

Jonathan's wandering attention was suddenly sharply focused on her words.

"What I now believe happens in the PLR experience is telepathic communication with the unintegrated dead," she went on. "If you'll join me in a thought experiment, I'll try to show you why.

"Begin with the understanding that substance is intrinsically Mother, spark intrinsically Father—both eternal in their separateness and cocreators of life and consciousness. The Goddess can only know herself through the God. The God can only know himself through the Goddess. Where they touch, creation beholds itself—the greatest of the mysteries.

"Science tells us that the living body is self-created out of simple raw materials drawn from the Earth. At death, the binding force releases and that which has been borrowed is returned to the Goddess.

"I believe that, in just the same way, the living soul is self-created out of the simple raw materials of the God-spirit. And at death, the binding force of will is released, and self returns to the source and merges with the All, like a raindrop falling into the sea—"

Jonathan listened for ten minutes, first with resistance, then with growing dismay. When he could take no more, he stood and quietly walked away, across the meadow, down toward the pond and the woods beyond. He did not notice that someone had followed until she came up alongside him as he reached the woods.

She had been at the roundtable, too—a quiet, kind-eyed woman he might not have noticed but for the unusual suede breast drape she wore both days. Her soft khaki hat spread out over a leonine mane of graying hair. But he did not know her name, and could not remember her ever having spoken.

"Hello," she said. "Can I talk to you?"

Jonathan stopped and turned toward her. "I'm all talked out. I'm sorry," he said stiffly, and started to turn away again.

She reached out and caught his wrist lightly to stop him. "Please—it won't take long."

"I don't—"

"I'm just afraid you're thinking about leaving."

He grunted, and his face wrinkled in a rueful frown. "You're right enough about that." He looked away toward the woods. "All right—since you followed me all the way down here."

Her name was Eleni. They found relatively dry perches on a jumble of broken concrete at the edge of the pond. "What happened, just now, up there?" she asked when they were settled. "What made you angry?"

"Who said I was angry?"

"Your face did."

He stared at the cloudy water, his eyes following the travels of a water strider across its invisible skin.

"What is it?"

"What is it?" He gestured toward the campsite. "I sat under that tree for two days listening to one person and another grope the elephant, thinking I could figure out what it looks like. And now here comes someone who says there is no fucking elephant. You people aren't even all on the same page." He shook his head. "I'm sorry. I appreciate what everyone's tried to do.

But I was wrong—it was my mistake. I can't use any of this. I'm sorry."

"You sound like a different person today."

"Return to reality, I guess." He plucked a tall green weed from the soft ground and methodically began to shred it, peeling the leaves off one at a time. "I've been letting myself be impressed by people's sincerity, and the strength of their beliefs. I haven't been asking the hard questions I should've, didn't even think to do it, like I checked my critical thinking at the door, because everyone's been so nice to me that it would have been rude. Well—this morning I turned the analytical engine back on."

"What kind of hard questions?"

"I don't want to get into a long argument about it," he said, with a weary shake of his head.

"I promise I'll just listen. I do it well, you know."

He studied her face for a moment. "Well—for starters, the problem of population growth. Where do all the extra souls come from? Someone actually tried to explain that one away by saying many of the bodies walking this planet don't have souls."

"I could be persuaded," she said. "Sorry, that's an editorial comment, not an argument. Go ahead."

"Hmm. Then there's the problem of misery—why in hell would anyone choose to be born in the streets of Calcutta, or Los Angeles? Pretty convenient ethic for a world where there's not enough to go around, shrugging off suffering as a life choice. Why don't we all just choose to be rich and happy?"

She said nothing, but her smile had a touch of sadness.

"And there's the epistemological issue—the problem of self-delusion. I actually let a woman tell me she couldn't be making it up because she could never make up anything that detailed and believable, when what I should have said was, 'Come on, don't you ever dream?' " He shook his head again. "I guess I wanted to believe."

"So—what do you think about reincarnation now?"

Jonathan was slow to answer. "I think it's comfort food. I think it's just another human belief born in self-defense against the terrible knowledge that we're going to die." He looked away, toward the brush-covered field north of the pond. "I think she's gone forever."

She unslung a wineskin from her shoulder and took a drink, then offered it to him. "I think you're wrong," she said.

"Yeah, well, so it goes." The contents of the wineskin were sharp on his tongue, all cinnamon and must, and hot in his throat. "What is this?"

"Mulled wine," she said. "I make it strong, to keep off the chill. Jonathan—was your girlfriend's name Alynn Reed?"

The question snapped his head around. "How did you—I haven't told anyone her last name, or mine. I didn't want anyone knowing anything about us. What did you do? Some sort of net search?"

Her expression was guileless and earnest. "I did some work with my cards last night, about you."

"Cards?"

"The Tarot."

He slipped down off the concrete and started walking away. "I don't want to hear this."

"This wasn't the first time you two met," she called after him. "You've been together before."

"I don't care what you believe."

"This isn't what I believe. It's what I know."

He turned and glared angrily at her. "Stop it. Why are you doing this?"

"Because you're about to make a mistake."

"Did your cards tell you that?"

"You think that if you let yourself believe, you'll be giving up something you can't cope without."

"Which is?—"

"The illusion of control. The security of living in an orderly world with clearly defined boundaries. You've tamed the universe by making it small and ordinary," she said. "But the universe is vast enough for dreams to be real—"

"Please—leave me alone."

"And it's wonderful enough for will to survive. Don't be afraid to let creation make you feel small, Jonathan. It's the first step toward seeing the grandeur."

"That's all just words. Nonsense words—"

"No," she said patiently. "You never were in control, Jonathan. It's always been bigger than you knew. You're fighting against admitting that. Being wrong scares you more than giving her up does—so you're going to give her up."

He stood there silent, looking lost. She climbed down from her perch and came toward him.

"Let me ask you this," Eleni said softly. "Did you and Alynn ever discover that there'd been some earlier time that you'd had a chance to meet, but didn't?"

Yes, he thought. "Why?" he asked.

"Because it happens, when we have a bond with someone, or work to do with them. Listen to me, Jonathan. I don't understand it all, but I'm sure of this: You don't have to let go of Alynn. She'll come back to you. You'll be together again."

"How?"

"Because you both want it."

He took a step toward her. "Just that easy—everybody gets three wishes."

"At the very least," she said. "Jonathan, we make decisions on the other side that shape the currents. And those currents push us toward each other, like two thoughts on a collision course. We're given opportunities to find our partners. And if we miss one vector—"

The word slashed through his resistance. He stared blankly. "What? What did you say?"

"If we miss one vector, the currents keep pushing us at each other, until we finally recognize each other. Then we have the choice, to follow through or turn away. The work we set for ourselves—sometimes it's hard work."

Jonathan blinked and ran his hand over his hair. "Vectors," he said. "Signals. Points of connection."

"Yes."

"And what about when someone dies?"

Compassion filled her eyes. "It happens. Sometimes bond-partners miss each other. And sometimes they're already caught up in something else when they meet. Opportunities aren't guarantees."

"Why should it be this way?" he demanded, gesturing angrily. "Why should there even be opportunities?"

"You don't need me to answer that."

"Yes, I do—"

"No. Everything that is, is inside you. And you're part of everything that is."

"I don't know what that means," Jonathan said, and kicked a stone into the water.

"It means the answers are inside you. What you touch, the cosmos touches. When you want, the cosmos wants. We're thoughts in the mind of creation, Jonathan. How can we not be connected? How can we not help shape what is?"

"You're turning me around," he said. "I don't know what to believe."

"That's a beginning," Eleni said, and smiled. "Jonathan, this is the one thing I really came to say to you: Don't let go of her. Throw away everything else, if you want, but hold on to your hope. Life is only a whisper, a whisper in a long dark night. But the whisper has an echo."

He shook his head. "I wish I could hear it."

"You will," she said. "If you keep listening." She stepped forward quickly and kissed him on the cheek. "Good luck, Jonathan."

The woods wrapped Jonathan in solitude and silence, but he still could not hear Alynn's voice. He wandered on until he was stopped by a chicken-wire fence topped with a single strand of barbed wire, then followed the fence north until he sank a shoe to the cuff in soft mud.

As he stood there, indecisive, he started to hear drumming from the camp again. It was louder and more focused than what the trance drummers were capable of by then. He thought it had the sound of a rehearsal, like some metaphysical marching band practicing on a hot August afternoon.

Unwilling to turn back yet, Jonathan decided to make a circuit of the property, even though he had no map and no sense of how long a distance that was. Using the distant drumming as a compass, he picked his way around the little slue and started on a sweeping, irregular arc toward the north.

He crossed several trails but stayed off them, heard laughter once but saw only a splash of red nylon off among the trees. When the drumming stopped, he lost his compass, but still found his way to the east fence without it.

Shortly after, his attention wandering, he stepped on a half-buried rock and rolled his right ankle over. Pain ripped through the ankle, and it would not hold him. He stumbled to his hands and knees, grimacing and grabbing for the injury.

"Damn, damn, damn, damn," he muttered to himself. "Sweet mother of chocolate, I hope I didn't tear it."

Up until then, he had managed to let the business of picking his way through the trees fully occupy his mind. But the longer he sat and rubbed his ankle, the more thoughts rushed into the space swept clean by the pain.

All I want is a decision I can live with. I don't even care anymore what flavor it comes in. Alynn—I'm crazy with missing you. You spoiled me for being alone. I keep turning to talk to you, turning over to touch you—and when you're not there, I die a little. God, I don't want to be doing that for the next fifty years—I can't do that for fifty years—

A few minutes of such thinking was enough to goad him into testing the ankle. But it showed no eagerness to carry his weight, and he settled on the trunk of a downed tree to work the pain a while longer.

They have beliefs without evidence. And I might have evidence of something I don't believe in, he thought. *There's only one place I can go now. I've got to follow the evidence, wherever it leads—even if it leads me someplace I don't think exists, to something I would have laughed at before this happened.*

That's the only road that might lead to you, Alynn. I have to find the proof, or make it—or become it.

The moment he thought it, he knew it for the answer he had been seeking.

All of the people he had met were struggling for understanding, just as he was. But their tools were not his tools. Naively, wishfully, he had hoped he might learn from them some ancient truth overlooked by a blinkered science. But the strength of their paradigm was not in the answers they could give him but in the questions they thought worth asking.

The question was what mattered—what always mattered most. The answerable question. The testable hypothesis. The right question, not the right answer. Ask the right question, and the world can change. And in that new world, the question answers itself.

He had come to Starpath seeking nothing less than salvation. He would take away with him nothing more than direction—but it was enough. For the first time since Alynn had been killed, he knew what to do next. The road had a destination.

Like a fire consuming its fuel, the pain had numbed his ankle. On the second try, it felt better—better enough for him to go on.

The same could be said of his heart.

By the time Jonathan reached East Meadow, the sun was low in the west and shining full on his tent. With the rain flaps still zippered shut from the morning, the air inside was muggy, stiflingly hot, and unpleasantly reminiscent of the inside of a gym bag. He exposed himself to it just long enough to compose and send a short message to Eric:

Had enough vacation yet? Urgent we resume full testing schedule at earliest possible opportunity. Please return to campus ASAP. Double pay and my earnest gratitude await you.

Then he borrowed a sockful of ice from a neighbor on the tree line, and lay on his back in the grass outside his tent, with the makeshift ice pack draped over his throbbing ankle and a forearm shading his eyes.

His body welcomed the warmth of the sunlight, and he dozed, slipping in and out of consciousness and losing track of time.

A now-familiar female voice called him back.

"Hey," it said, and something nudged his foot. "Made up your mind yet?"

Jonathan looked up to find Eleni standing by his feet, wearing a friendly smile and a full-length sea-blue cloak. The sky behind her was violet dusk. "About leaving?" he asked, and nodded before she could answer. "In the morning. It's too late to start home tonight."

"Will you come to the bonfire with me, then? They're gathering down at the stage for the procession."

Only then did he realize how deserted the meadow was. "I think I'll just stay up here," he said, and jabbed a finger in the general direction of his ankle.

Crouching, she plucked the sodden sock off him and inspected what lay beneath. "What did you do to yourself?"

"Exceeded design specifications." When she looked at him blankly, he added, "Twisted the hell out of it. Say—are you still carrying that wine around, perchance?"

"I've switched to the hard stuff—mead," she said. She unslung the wine bag from under her cloak and handed it to him, then sat down and took his ankle in her hands. "I think I can help a bit with this," she said. "Find anything in the woods besides a hole?"

"It was a rock," he said, and drank. A moment later he was coughing. "So that's what mead tastes like. Well, I found thorns and deerflies," he added, pointing in turn to long scratches on his forearm and a lump on the side of his neck.

"You should have someone check you for ticks, too," she said.

He let that pass. Propping himself up on his elbows, he peered curiously at her hands. "I don't know what you're doing down there, but it feels wonderful. What are you doing down there?"

"Smoothing," Eleni said. "Your meridians are unhappy."

"I don't understand a word you just said," Jonathan said, shaking his head. "But please don't stop." He sat all the way up and tried another squirt from the wine bag. "I can only describe this as feral beer."

She laughed. "When I asked if you'd made up your mind—"

"I knew what you were asking," he said with a wry smile. "Eleni—thank you, for the things you said earlier. For coming after me."

"If any of it helped, I'm glad," she said. "What are you going to do?"

"I want it all," he said. "I want Alynn back. I want my orderly world and my illusion of control. I'm not willing to give up either."

"Good for you," she said. "But you can't build a bridge between those two places—you have to fly."

"I can't fly," he said with a shrug of the shoulders. "So it'll have to be a bridge. —Besides," he added, "if I do somehow manage to build a bridge, it'll be there for anyone who comes after."

She looked at him curiously. "So what will you build your bridge out of?"

"I have, ah—I have an experiment in mind."

Below, the processional was beginning. A steady heartbeat of drums began, and was soon overlaid by a thousand voices in chant. Jonathan could see torches bobbing, leading the way. "—Spirit of fire, come to us—we will kindle a fire—"

"Tell me," she said.

"I'd rather not."

"You don't trust me, or you don't think I'd understand?"

"I trust you," Jonathan said. "But I can't talk about it, to anyone. All the blueprints have to say 'observation tower.' There are people who'd try to stop me. Who could stop me. I can't—won't let that happen. When people look at me, they're going to see just what they expect to see. I'm going home, and I'm going back to work."

Eleni released his foot and sat back. "Try that," she said.

He gathered himself to his feet. "That's incredible," he said. "A thousand percent better."

"Good," she said. "Jonathan—what will you do, if you do find the proof you're looking for? If you find your reason to believe?"

He looked down at her for a long time, and her eyes told him that she already knew. With a quick, slight smile, he held out his hand to her. "What do you say we go down to the bonfire," he said. After a moment, she took his hand and let him help her up, and they never spoke of it again.

They met the procession where it entered the labyrinth and watched it pass into the entrance as a parade, torches and drummers and fire maidens dancing. Then they fell in with the throng following, joining the human chain, hand to hand to hand, winding through the darkness of the pathways. When they emerged on the other side, the chain was shattered by exuberance, as they ran down to join the great circle forming around the towering cone of unlit branches and timber.

They found themselves near the drummers, so close that he could feel the rhythm in every part of his body, so close that the sound swept him up. Talking was impossible, thinking barely less so. Pressed in on all sides by other celebrants, they drank Eleni's mead and chanted and clapped with the drummers, while the fire maidens circled and will, given voice, called up the fire.

Higher and higher they built the cry, until the current circling through the crowd had Jonathan vibrating, until at last the torches were plunged into the great woodpile from the four quarters. A bare minute later it was a great light in the night, the chant rising with the flames until the fire had its own roaring voice and the chanting dissolved into a cheer.

Without any cue Jonathan could hear, the character of the drumming suddenly changed, from pulsing, driving heart to happy celebration. And as the heat pouring off the bonfire beat on the faces of thousands and pushed the crowd back, the fire maidens shed their garments to dance naked in its embrace.

Primal, ecstatic, their bodies painted a rich red-orange by the flames, they danced light in heart and provocative in step, circling and passing into silhouette as each in turn briefly eclipsed the bonfire. And others came out of the crowd to join them, men and women both, until there were so many bodies that they nearly walled off the heat.

The rhythms changed, and changed again, the drummers dancing with their hands, on dumbek and ashiko and jimb, and tar. The fire glinted off the copper and silver drums, off jewelry and bright eyes, and threw sparks high into the night.

Sometime after the last of the mead was gone, Eleni slipped off her cloak and handed it to Jonathan as she went to join the dancers. He edged forward through the crowd to watch her, knowing that to do so was to begin wanting. She saw him watching, and her smile sealed a silent pact.

When Eleni returned, breathless and sleek with fire-sweat, she led Jonathan away into the darkness. There she spread her cape on the dew-damp grass and wordlessly drew him down atop her.

And he embraced the warmth and comfort and desire she offered him, and gave back all he could in kind. The ache of aloneness was too acute for him to do otherwise. He craved the healing touch of tenderness, and the cleansing surrender of ecstasy. She understood, and asked no promises of him, and let him cry in her arms without shame afterward.

When the night chill settled on them, he walked her to her tent, and said good-bye with a long hug and gratitude that only eyes could speak. "Blessed be, Jonathan," she whispered.

By dawn, the space under the oak tree in East Meadow where the tan pop-up had stood was empty, and Jonathan was thirty miles west of Cleveland, going home.

6

A Spark Flies Upward

Steaming coffee cup in hand, Jonathan quickly surveyed the lab, counting heads.

"I think this is everybody. It's been so long, I almost made up name tags for us," he said with an easy grin, and took a sip. "I don't intend to dwell on recent history. There isn't anyone here who doesn't know what happened. The project took a direct hit amidships, and then I did. It's been a rough couple of months. But as of today, we're back in action."

"All right," said Eric around a mouthful of doughnut, giving a thumbs-up salute.

"We've done everything we can to explain away the matrix-match as an anomaly," he went on. "From now on, it's a phenomenon to be investigated. We're not going to try to make it go away—in point of fact, a top priority is to find another.

"I'm going to be the point guy on subject contacts—we're not going to be just taking whoever walks through the door. Our sample's too heavily skewed to young, healthy adults, and we're going to be trying to balance it at both ends. If everything goes the way I intend, we're going to have a pipeline to the pediatric and geriatric services in the area hospitals.

"I've brought Stephanie Oroz—Steph, raise your hand. She's going to be our subject liaison, taking the scheduling and accounting off our hands. I stole her from Washburne Travel, and I know she's going to make that end of things run smoothly. For the moment, she'll be operating out of her home, out past Dexter. We'll probably need a second person before long, too, so if you have any hardworking, well-organized, and underemployed friends, point 'em her way.

"We're aiming for a twelve-hour schedule by the end of the first month and round-the-clock by the end of the summer. Eric, Kelly, when the semester starts, I intend to bring on more grad asses, so no one ends up with more than a forty-five- or fifty-hour week. I know some of you still have lives. Eric, as always I'll be counting on you to run the lab in my absence. Kelly, I'm looking to you to supervise a shift, handle training, and generally cover when Eric's not here.

"David Helms is also joining us," Jonathan said, nodding in the direction of a round-faced young man in jeans and a faded I Survived the Millennium T-shirt. "David's going to work on bringing our biographical database up to snuff—"

"What biographical database?" asked Eric.

"Exactly. You probably won't see much of him, since he'll be working primarily out of my old apartment. But he'll be online to the lab and have full access to the subject library.

"There'll also be some strangers in and out of here from time to time to run some tests on the SQUID," Jonathan went on. "I'm probably dreaming, but I want a mapper I can take on the road, even if it ends up filling the back of a van and plugging in with an extension cord as thick as my wrist. This is fifteen-year-old hardware, which is two weeks past forever in geek years.

"And if I can't have portability, maybe they'll at least find a way to give us some useful new functionality or increased sensitivity. I think it's worth a bit of downtime to find out.

"The first new subjects will be here next Monday. That gives you four days to get ready for them. Eric's already started on a full system checkout and catching up on some deferred maintenance. If there's anything anyone else needs, I want to hear the what, the where, and the how much by the end of today."

Jonathan's coffee had cooled while he talked, but he paused for a long draught he barely tasted. "Steph, I'd like to see you for a few minutes before you head back out to the farm," he said, wiping his lips with a swipe of his hand. "And David, I'd like to come by to talk about where things stand. About one?"

"One's fine," said Helms.

"Good." He clapped his hands together and surveyed the room with a smile. "Overwhelmed yet?"

"Heck, no," said Eric. "This is going to be fun."

"I hope so," Jonathan said. "The last thing I have to talk about is discretion. I don't want this project talked about outside this lab. If you can't be a team player in that respect, please get out now. We're going into high gear because we want to get there first. I don't intend to take any hitchhikers along."

"Doc?"

"Yes, Eric."

"Where exactly are we going? Do we have a working hypothesis?"

"The working hypothesis is that the matrix match isn't a mistake," Jonathan said. "Other than that, we'll know where we're going when we get there." He smiled. "Thanks, everyone. That's it for now. Steph, why don't you walk me to my car?"

The stolen Saturn Zephyr had finally been released by the police two days before Jonathan left for Starpath. But Jonathan did not want it, and had told Steuben so. He could not even bring himself to sit in it, knowing that Alynn's murderer was the last to have been at the wheel.

Steuben had not asked for explanations, even when Jonathan told him what he did want. While Jonathan was away, Steuben made the Zephyr vanish, and replaced it with a new dual-power Honda Imago midivan.

That was the "car" Jonathan had parked east of the Neuroscience Building, in a space reserved for campus jitneys and university vehicles. And though he had only been inside a half hour, the Imago had nevertheless collected a ticket.

"One of the great little mysteries of the universe," Jonathan said, folding the ticket and tucking it into a pocket.

"What's that?" asked Oroz.

"Why parking enforcement is always the most efficient department on campus," he said, and she laughed.

They climbed in and used the front seats as a temporary conference room. Oroz jotted notes as Jonathan rattled off the decisions he'd made overnight.

"The rat pay is now two hundred dollars. But we'll be flexible—I don't want to be held up, but if there's someone over sixty or under five we really need to get, we'll negotiate. The University insists on paying human subjects through the payroll office, by the way—but let's do whatever we can to make that painless.

"Out of town, we'll pay mileage up to 150 miles, air or train fare beyond that—"

Oroz was shaking her head. "You won't get many people driving three hours each way for two hundred dollars. Or flying in, for that matter. I know it sounds like a decent day's pay, but settled people who have busy lives won't think it's worth the trouble."

"I know. And I'm going to work on another answer to that problem," Jonathan told her. "But let's try, anyway. Now, for mothers with infants, the base fee'll be $500 plus transportation, plus one room night, and we'll go ahead and map both of them.

"If we can't keep the lab busy at those rates, tell me, and we'll increase them. I'm willing to pay to get the right subjects, and to get them now. Don't let that get out."

"I won't," she said. "You don't have as much money as you think. Have you thought about setting up a budget?"

"There'll be more money after the first of the year," he said, shrugging off her concern. "For now, I'll make the initial contacts and give you names for follow-up—"

"You're going to need some help with that," said Oroz. "You're looking at a lot of calls. And maybe sometimes it will help for the point man to be a woman. Or white. Or not a media celebrity."

"I'm no celebrity," said Jonathan. "I'll handle it."

"I just want you to know I'd be willing to take on some of that, too."

"There *is* something you can take off my shoulders," he said. "Track down some identical twins raised apart and get them in, for a side inquiry. I know that podlings are celebrities in the psych community, but I'm willing to outbid other researchers if need be. I'm even willing to pay a finder's fee to anyone who brings us a set. Can you get the word out?"

"Of course. But a finder's fee? Identical twins aren't that rare, are they? And doesn't someone keep a list?"

"There are dozens of twins registries, but they make you jump through hoops before they'll deign to give you access," he said impatiently. "I want to do this fast."

"I'll see what we can do working the net."

"If I thought we had a chance, I'd love to get some true multiple personality disorder patients in, too," he added. "Now, those *are* rare. And everybody wants to study them." He smiled wryly. "I hear you can make a pretty good living out of being a research rat. The cages are clean and the food's good, anyway."

"I'll see what I can do on both of those," she said. "Now, about that budget?"

Jonathan waved a hand in the air. "Whatever it takes. Get results, and I'm not likely to squawk."

The Village Green apartment looked like it had been stripped by thieves and invaded by squatters. Gone was anything and everything personal, from Jonathan's and Alynn's clothing to the marinayda-style nested ball of Dante's circles of hell. Half the furniture was gone, and the rest had been pushed against walls and into corners to make room for several long tables.

David Helms's workstation was set up on one of them, under the cathedral ceiling of what had been the living room. It shared the table with a page scanner and a page printer. Nearby, a brand-new plotter waited to be released from its shipping box.

The two men settled facing each other at one end of one of the empty tables, and Helms pushed a sheet of paper across at Jonathan. "I've identified thirteen of your subjects who are deceased—two heart attacks, one AIDS, two auto wrecks, one drug O.D., one armed robbery, two cancer, a drowning, the murder end of a murder-suicide, and two suicides."

"Thirteen?" Jonathan said in surprise. "That's good."

"Not really," Helms said contrarily. "If your sample was more representative, you should have close to a hundred by now—nine out of every thousand people die in any given year, and you've got more than seven thousand subjects, some of whom you've been carrying for almost ten years."

"But thirteen's more than I was counting on," said Jonathan. "And it's enough to get started. You're going to maintain an obit watch on the rest of them, right?"

"A newsfilter with seven thousand search terms? They'll clip you for two grand a month, at least."

"Do it," Jonathan said. "Now, these people who're dead—I need as much information as possible about them, especially about how they died and what kind of unfinished business they had when they died."

"Unfinished business?"

"Reasons they would have had to want to keep living—personal, professional, creative, whatever. I wrote up Alynn's for you as a sample. Check your mail."

"Okay."

"And for each dead subject, I'm going to need a separate—well, I've been calling it a target list, and I suppose you might as well, too. What I want is a list of new births associated in some way with the person who died."

"Associated how?"

"Blood. Geography. Children born in the extended family, in the place they were born, the place they died. Something that comes out of the unfinished business. Again, look at the one I wrote up for Alynn."

"I will. Dr. Briggs, would it be nosy of me to ask what it is I'm doing?"

"Trying to rig the wheel," said Jonathan. "Is there a problem? Is what I'm asking for not doable, or outside your expertise, or outside the law?"

"No, it's doable. It's just—a bit unusual."

"That I knew." Jonathan glanced at his watch and stood. "I have an appointment. I have to go."

He took the list of the dead with him.

By the time Jonathan reached the Ann Arbor municipal airport, the sleek twin-engine Raytheon Starship II was already on the ground, and its sole passenger waiting in the terminal's tiny lounge.

"Dr. Jonathan Briggs," Jonathan said, extending his hand as he approached. "Sorry I'm late."

"Tommy Ramirez. You aren't late, we were early. Big storm over Tennessee—we had tail winds goosing us almost all the way here."

"Well—thank you for coming. Especially on as little information as I gave you."

Ramirez jerked a thumb over his shoulder in the direction of the Starship. "Nifty little butterfly, that. Never been up in one before. Worth the trip by itself, I think. Thanks for arranging it. I'd have flown commercial, though." He smiled. "Even into Detroit."

"You heard about the 757 that somebody shot up, then."

"Oh, yeah. Dead Bob had a funny bit about it. 'In the event of a landing in Detroit, your seat cushion can be used as a flak jacket—' I am curious as hell to know what this is about, though."

"Come on, then," Jonathan said. "We can talk on the way."

They headed east on Ellsworth, past an old research

park and into the domain of the prefab metal building and the commercial warehouse. "You were Alynn's hardware specialist," Jonathan said. "She told me you were involved in getting the Mollies for my lab."

"That's right."

"What's your background?"

"Caltech, Carnegie-Mellon, Cooper Union. Ended up with a double bachelor's in EE and microsystems design. Then I put in five years with Agilent working mostly on measurement control, until I went stale. Did contract consulting for a while, but I didn't like being in business for myself."

"Big government fill-out-the-paperwork nonsense."

"Dead on. I already miss working at Arcadia. It was just about perfect for me." He paused and looked out the side window. "I can't tell you how sorry I am about Lynnie."

"Yeah," said Jonathan, turning left onto a side street. "Well, your work might not be finished yet, if you don't want it to be."

"Oh?" said Ramirez.

Jonathan steered the car into the otherwise deserted parking lot at the front of a one-story commercial building. The name of the building's last occupant had been whitewashed, but was still discernible on the concrete wall: PM Technologies.

"Alynn and I were starting work on something that meant a lot to her—a new interface," he said, killing the engine. "We hadn't gotten to the point of bringing you in yet when she was killed. I want to continue with the work. And I want to know if you're interested in being part of it."

"I'd like to hear more. I'm willing to swear silence on a dead lawyer, if you want."

Jonathan shook his head. "Not necessary. Let's go inside."

* * *

Carrying his bulky laptop in a case under his arm, Jonathan unlocked the steel front door and led the way past the bare desks to a conference room. The appointments were plain and functional, the air stuffy and warm.

"Have a seat," Jonathan said, sliding into a chair and starting to unlimber the computer. "Tommy, I won't drag this out. For the last dozen years or so, I've been learning how to map and record human thought patterns directly." He turned the computer toward Ramirez, allowing him to see the sinuous sparkle of the matrix displayed on the screen. "Like this."

"Huh," said Ramirez. "This anyone I know?"

"Me," said Jonathan. "I made this recording with a thousand-pound scanner that cost umpty-million dollars when it was new. I'd very much like to have a portable mapper, if it could be done. But more importantly, this's been strictly a one-way process—record and analyze. Alynn hoped there might be some way to play back recorded data in a human brain instead of on a monitor. A two-way machine-mind interface."

"Mind reading," Ramirez said. "The gearheads have been waiting for that for fifty years." He turned the computer back toward Jonathan. "You know, it's not like this hasn't been tried. People keep running into brick walls."

"I don't think anyone's tried using this door before," said Jonathan. "And I thought you might relish the challenge of picking the lock." He stood up. "Come on. I want to show you something."

Leaving the office area, Jonathan led his guest to a narrow stairway and up onto a small balcony that looked out over the production floor. From there Ramirez could see that the rear two-thirds of the building was one cavernous, metal-roofed expanse, with several smaller rooms nesting inside.

"Two six-hundred-square-foot Level II clean rooms, two eight-hundred-square-foot prototyping workshops, a Nakamachi direct-to-silicon chip-etching station, and two thousand square feet of enclosed production space. Everything they didn't spend to make the offices pretty, they spent out here on good tools. I'd like to set you up here, working on the Reed Interface."

Ramirez pursed his lips as he studied the facilities. "What kind of arrangement do you have in mind?"

"Bring in other people as you need them. You'd have complete autonomy. I'm only interested in results. I want to do this for Alynn. I want to see what we can make out of my research and her vision."

"If we can make anything at all, we can probably make a very big pile of money," Ramirez said, turning to Jonathan. "But I'll bet your pockets aren't very deep right now. And we will have to spend a few bucks between here and there. So I'll work without salary for now. But I want to be paid with a piece of the back end if this goes to market."

"I had in mind a one-third share."

Arms crossed over his chest, Ramirez shook his head. "Twenty-five percent."

"Um—I don't think you—"

"But I want another twenty-five to use as bait to bring in the other people I want," said Ramirez. "If it turns out it's a dead end and the Reed Interface never goes to market, I'll take what I was getting at Arcadia for the time I put in—if I haven't spent all your money already. Fair enough?"

Jonathan offered his hand. "Welcome to Vector Systems, Tommy."

*   *   *

By the end of that first day of meetings, Jonathan knew he would need a confidant.

The truth was the only map on which he could plot the progress of the different wheels he was setting in motion. He would be keeping secrets from everyone, filling the air with lies and partial truths. He feared that if he was not honest with someone, he would lose sight of what the whole truth was.

There had to be someone who would let him say the things he could say to no one else. That would make the truth at least as real as the lies.

But he only needed someone who would listen, not someone who might interfere. He did not want to have to explain or defend himself. It had to be someone he could trust completely.

So Jonathan had Cassandra find a Turing program, and create for him an invisible friend. He named his confidant Stuart, after a stuffed triceratops he had had as a child, and gave him an animated avatar that nodded and smiled and yawned. Cassandra hid Stuart in a voice-locked and encrypted directory that she walled off from all networking. Should anyone break in— through a door or a data line—Stuart would be the first file deleted. Should the power be cut off, the ghost directory would vanish.

But after all that, he found that the sound of his own voice made him self-conscious. Moreover, he realized he only wanted a listener, not an interrogation. So most of Stuart's higher functions were quickly disabled, reducing him to little more than a face for a digital diary. Jonathan's ensuing conversations with Stuart were all one-sided, and as private as silent, solitary keying could be.

How completely laughable this all seems sometimes, Stuart, he admitted. *In a matter of a few months, I've gone from catecholines and neurometric voltammetry of ion channels and Neher-Sakmann clamps to the wish-fulfillment fantasy of the age.*

Completely laughable, except that there's no joke. If I can find where Alynn's gone, I'm going to follow her.

I tell them only what they need to know, and keep them apart, so they can't figure it out. Eric and Kelly are just happy to see me back at work, back to "normal." And the others are just happy to have the work. So long as I'm the only one who can see it all, things can move ahead.

This is a death watch. For me, and for everyone who's ever passed through the doors of my labs. How strange will it be to get up every morning, hoping to hear that another subject has died? I'm suddenly rooting for the other side, because everything turns on finding another match.

I hope I can be patient. I don't want to find out what impatience might bring me to.

If death sends a spark flying upward from the earth, how long does it take to fall back again? It took Brett Winston a year and a half. Was he in a hurry, or dawdling?

Patience and luck both, Stuart. If it's one of the thirteen, maybe it'll only be a year, a few thousand more heads under the SQUID. If it's someone who hasn't left yet—three years? Five years? Ten?

I don't know if I can wait that long. I don't know if I can pretend that long, keep the secret that long.

Maybe we should just kill them all, and let karma sort them out.

I don't mean that. I don't think I mean that.

I'll have to watch the money. I'll have to make sure my position with the U is secure.

Better still I find an answer soon. The thirteen give me a place to start, at least.

And I've given Ramirez a place to start, too. That

door won't open to any combination of ones and ze-roes. The human brain isn't digital. It's analog. And I'm the only one in the world who knows the wave equations of consciousness.

Damn it, why do I still hedge? I've glimpsed the soul. And I'm chasing one that's dearer to me than anything.

I'm not afraid to be wrong, Stuart. If I'm wrong, at least it will be over. I'm only afraid of being stopped.

I feel very calm and focused, clear in my purpose. I sleep well when I sleep. And yet I know the foolish, pathetic absurdity of loving a dead woman this much. I wonder, is this what madness is like to the madman?

Sometimes I think that Alynn will come to me, will come into my mind and help me to find her. But I can't feel her anymore, the way I could at first. I can't keep the memories sharp. I have no way to know that she still exists—if the universe still sings her song, or there's only silence beyond.

What life gathers, time disperses. The real enemy of will is entropy.

But, still, I do believe. We are, like the world we live in, always in a state of becoming. Even Alynn. Even now. And I will never let her go.

The next and potentially thorniest problem was Elizabeth Froelich.

By the time she finally returned to town and cam-pus, the department gossips were entertaining several competing rumors about Dr. Froelich's summer, from interviewing for jobs elsewhere to a beach-blanket romance. She came back the first week of August, tanned, ten pounds thinner, and as tight-lipped as the departmental secretary had been in her absence. All three facts gave credence to the romance theory, quickly amended to have a broken-heart ending.

Jonathan monitored the rumors carefully, but kept his own counsel. The longer Elizabeth had remained absent and out of touch, the more her absence seemed like a ticking bomb in the middle of his delicate plans. There was a real prospect that he had turned a friend and defender into someone who might have reason to want to see him leave—and who could easily make it happen.

Which would be a disaster of the first order.

So, at first opportunity, Jonathan moved to try to defuse the threat. The hour he heard that Dr. Froelich was back, he called her. When she didn't respond to her phone, he followed it with mail asking about lunch. When at the end of a week that, too, had gone unanswered, he went up to her office to see her. But her door was closed.

"Just tell her I stopped by and I'd like to see her when she has a minute," he told the secretary, and retreated.

That evening, sitting in his idling car at the street end of the long driveway to Elizabeth's house, Jonathan wondered if he was about to make a strategic mistake.

He had never been there before. He didn't know anyone in the department who had. Sixteen miles west of the city, Elizabeth's house was a private hideaway, the wooded lot nestled between farmland and a state recreational area. The driveway was not gated, but it was posted against hunting, trespassing, soliciting, snowmobiling, and country music.

Despite the humor of the last, the net effect was not to make the uninvited feel welcome.

But Jonathan put the Imago into gear and eased the van up the narrow, rutted driveway to the house. He parked behind Elizabeth's four-wheel-drive Yukon and climbed out, wondering if—living alone next door to nowhere—she kept a gun.

Elizabeth must have heard him coming. She opened the front door, though not the screen, before he could knock or try the doorbell.

"I hadn't figured you for this persistent," she said.

"I thought we'd been awkward around each other long enough," he said. "Can I come in?"

"I don't think so," Elizabeth said.

"I really think we need to talk."

"We can talk right here," she said. "I'm told that you've really bounced back, have the lab humming. Congratulations on your grant—the provost was impressed. I'm glad for you." But there was no smile. "Oh, I've restarted your tenure clock. You'll be reviewed during the fall semester."

"Thanks," he said. "It feels good to be back at work." He edged closer to the screen door. "But this doesn't feel good—this stuff hanging between us. Liz, I want to apologize. It was my fault. I can't believe I treated you so badly—I just lost myself, lost my compass. It had nothing to do with you. You saw how I was—exhausted, all torn up and turned around. I just couldn't stand to let anyone comfort me. That's all it was." He shook his head. "I wish I could tell you how sorry I am. I don't have the words."

Elizabeth clung to the door, half-hiding behind it. "You have a good heart, Jonathan. But that's not what happened, and both of us know it. I give you points for trying to do the gentlemanly thing and take the blame. Heaven knows I'd like to let you. But we both know better. And excuses won't help me get over this."

Frowning, Jonathan cocked his head and looked at her with puzzlement. "What are you talking about, Liz?"

"Do you know where I've been, this summer?"

"No. Not in Hawaii, I take it."

"I was in the Kincaid Center at St. Luke's Hospital in Tuscon, Arizona," she said evenly. "That's a residential clinic for adult chemical dependency patients. I'm a drunk, Jonathan."

Taken completely aback, he stared.

"I told myself it wasn't a problem, because no one noticed. Except I was working at hiding it, which should have rung the alarm. I told myself I had it under control, because I only drank at home. Except I used to come home alone every day, close this door, and open a bottle.

"I was drunk when you called that night, and I kept drinking after you called, because I was afraid to see you in that state. I almost rear-ended a truck on I-94, almost rolled the Yukon over on the exit ramp by your apartment, taking it too fast."

"I didn't know," Jonathan said.

"I didn't want you to, so you didn't," she said. "I didn't want anyone to know about any of it. I didn't want to know. The Kincaid program doesn't ask for public confessions, and I don't intend to offer any. I wouldn't be telling you now except that you were hurt by my drinking."

"I promise you, no one will hear this from me—"

"I know that."

If there had been no door between them, Jonathan would have tried to hug her. "Are you sure I can't come in?"

"I'm sure."

"I don't understand—if nobody's angry—"

"Jonathan, I have to remember where I am, and what I'm up against. I drank mostly because I'm lonely, and unhappy about it," she said bluntly. "When Donald divorced me—"

That was a second, smaller shock. "I never knew you were married."

"For six years, twenty years ago. We were students. He got his doctorate first and was gone like a shot," Elizabeth said. Her voice remained even, in control as always. "The point is, I never planned to end up alone. It just happened.

"I've been dry for sixty-six days. But I'm still lonely, Jonathan. And I'm not sure that I can keep my feelings about you neatly confined to friendship. I don't want you to become either the crutch I use to stay dry, or a reason I start drinking again."

"Liz—"

"That's why I won't let you in, and why I'm asking you to not come back. I wish I could let you be my friend, because I miss you. But I need to work on being my own friend. Giving up drinking is part of that. So is closing this door with you on that side of it." She attempted a smile, but it never brightened past wistful. "You did me a great favor by chasing me out of your home, Jonathan. I'm returning the favor by keeping you out of mine. Trust me on that."

"Elizabeth—"

The door closed gently, but the lock's snapping into place a moment later made its point firmly enough.

Jonathan drove back to Ann Arbor feeling sharp pangs of sadness for a friend in pain. But at the same time, he realized that she had removed herself from the equation, at least for a time. Her perceptiveness was no longer a threat. And, he told himself, being at a distance would help cushion Elizabeth against what was to come.

It was not what he had expected from the evening, but it was enough.

*   *   *

August brought hundred-degree days and record rains that spilled the Huron River over its banks for a week. Truckers staged a twelve-hour blockade on Detroit's Ambassador Bridge over a two-dollar increase in the toll, and the FBI arrested eight state employees over $11 million in fraudulent charter-school grants. A tornado ripped through Whitmore Lake, and a weekend of arson and gang violence ravaged the south side of Ypsilanti, with the latter doing twice as much damage and the former getting twice as much press. The last adult bookstore in Washtenaw County was firebombed, and "soldier of decency" Marion Neal stepped forward to claim the credit, defying prosecutors to find a jury that would convict him for "protecting women and children from Satan."

Jonathan barely noticed any of it. Jumping from one task to the next like a frantic carnival juggler, he spent most of the month getting all of the wheels spinning. But once they were, a new equilibrium was established, one that almost began to feel normal.

Though he was technically ineligible, he had requested a scholarly activity leave for the fall semester, hoping they would bend the rules to accommodate his circumstances. His request was politely declined, which was a disappointment, but no real surprise.

It made it all the more important, however, for him to spend long hours at Vector Systems with Tommy Ramirez and his "punkworks" team—a blond Californian named Chip, a dark-eyed Canadian woman named Margie, and a Korean superconduction specialist with a shaved head and the culture-clash name Jacob Lo.

Working together, they defined the design concepts for the two projects on the table: prototyping the portable mapper and a direct memory player, which Chip dubbed "Mind TV." When that task was complete, they spent an intense weekend identifying the technological and theoretical hurdles and trying to settle on a strategy.

"Here's how I add it up," Ramirez said at the end of it. "The portable—six weeks to prototype, sixteen to twenty to program for garage quantities. Mind TV—I'm guessing, but I'd say a year just to find out how to do it. If we can do it."

"That's too long," Jonathan said.

"So we concentrate on the portable?"

"No," Jonathan said. "I need them both." They looked at him in surprise. "The portable would be a convenience," he said, standing and closing his notepad, "but we have the SQUID. I want my MTV. I have to know that we can have direct access to the recordings."

In the days that followed, he supplied Ramirez & Co. with the most current research on induction of Hebb synapses, precipitation of matrix cascades, principles of active neuroammetry, and the like. He taught them the basics of reading a matrix, and provided them with access to the SQUID to record a series of simple one-concept maps of single colors, images, words, and sounds, for testing purposes.

"If you crack open a man's skull, you can touch his brain with a probe and cause him to see, hear, crave, remember—all according to where you touch him," he told them, in what amounted to a pep talk. "If you let a man sleep, his brain will create a dozen imaginary realities a night, out of nothing more than his neurochemistry at idle. What we want is a way to get inside the skull without a bone saw, a way to give that man a waking dream. We know how to listen to the brain at work. All we need now is a way to talk to it. Find it, and we can change the way people live."

Then he got out of their way.

* * *

At the lab, Eric and Kelly had risen to the challenge he had dropped in their laps, relieving him of the need to spend time supervising the testing and analysis. But as September approached and the students returned to campus, they were nowhere near his goal of keeping the lights on and the test chamber seat warm around the clock. And with the odds against them as long as they were, 30 percent of capacity—forty or fifty new subjects a week—did not satisfy Jonathan's sense of urgency.

The fault was not with Eric and Kelly, or even with Stephanie Oroz and David Helms. David had assembled a criterion list for new subjects, based on the profiles of the thirteen "volunteers" (as Jonathan, with morbid humor, now referred to them). But, so far, the list was proving to be a filter that caught either too much or nothing at all.

The one criterion about which there was any certainty was age. The earliest death of a volunteer had been seven years ago, which meant that anyone under the age of seven was a prospective match. But with 4 million births a year over that span, the candidate pool numbered well over 25 million—an impossible number. The odds so favored the house that there was hardly any point in playing.

I might as well be buying lottery tickets and tearing them up on the way back to the car, Jonathan told Stuart.

So Jonathan began looking to geography to shorten the odds. Brett Winston had been born 244 miles away from where Dugan Beckett had died—an interesting factoid, but only wishful thinking could find any logical necessity in it. Wishful thinking or not, six of the volunteers had died in Michigan, and Jonathan could not help hoping that one of them had returned there.

But even if that was so, there had been three-quarters of a million births in the state since the earliest Michigan death, and a circle with a radius of 250 miles enclosed Chicago, Cleveland, Columbus, and at least a million more births. The house still had no reason to worry.

And what if they've already come and gone, Stuart? What if they died a second time on the preemie ward, or in a Woodward Avenue Dumpster, or at the hands of a kid-stalker? There has to be a better way—.

But other, more substantial connections between Winston and Beckett were still in short supply. Brett Winston was a cheerfully energetic round-faced five-year-old, and—in his mother's opinion—a precocious flirt, which seemed to recall Dugan Beckett's bawdy good humor. But that tenuous link, the next best association available, was of no real value.

Grasping at straws, Jonathan even turned to an astrologer, to have Winston and Beckett's charts drawn and compared. But the results, even spelled out in great detail during an hour-long consultation, did not seem meaningful. A numerologist made much of obvious similarities in the names—five letters in the given, seven in the patronymic, with a double T—and the places of birth—Toledo and Toronto, Ohio and Ontario—but Jonathan was no more impressed.

The best he could do was direct David to map five-hundred-mile circles around the places of death for the volunteers and give the areas where those circles intersected the highest priority. That map became the guide for his and Stephanie's initial efforts to find candidates for testing.

But he was now dealing with the notoriously protective parents of young children, not notoriously cash-poor college students. And it was proving harder to allay the suspicions of parents, even at $250 a session, than it had been to interest students at $10.

New tactics were needed. After a brainstorming session with Stephanie, Jonathan took to visiting maternity wards in person, passing out new-parent gift boxes and coupons for educational savings bonds. Together, they created a "sunrise squad" of students to blanket day-care centers with slick information packets, applications, and Stephanie's phone number. Traffic at the lab nudged up toward 50 percent of capacity.

The only problem with that solution was it meant the money was flowing out even faster.

"Dr. Briggs, this is Arthur Steuben, of Hillerman-Steuben-Welch. I should like to talk to you at the earliest—"

"Cassandra, let me talk to him," said Jonathan, looking up from the plotter charts filling the living room floor in front of him. "Mr. Steuben, this is Jonathan. What can I do for you? Have I broken the bank?"

"Not yet," said Steuben. "But the year is young. I've accelerated the balance of this year's gift to the university on your behalf, but doing so forced me to liquidate some assets on less than wholly favorable terms—sacrificing some of the long-term value of the trust to finance your short-term expenditures. In short, we're snacking on the seed corn. I highly recommend a more prudent strategy."

"Consider your fiduciary duty discharged, Mr. Steuben," said Jonathan. "But the money's all going into the research and the new company, not for thousand-dollar hookers and jaunts to Aruba. I haven't bought as much as a new pair of shoes for myself.

There isn't a lot I can do to hold down the expenses without holding back the work."

"I thought you might say that," said Steuben. "So I'd like to offer some alternatives to the present arrangement."

"I'm listening."

"Arcadia still has substantial income, but rapidly falling expenses. It's a paper company—no one works there anymore. Everything that needs doing is contracted out, from accounting to production and shipping. On the other hand, Vector Systems has no income, and rapidly climbing expenses—my information is that there are now seven full-time employees."

"That's right. Though three of them are being paid mostly with promises."

"Very well. I propose that Arcadia acquire Vector Systems. If Arcadia is to be the milk cow, let Vector suck directly from the teat. It makes no sense for Arcadia profits to be funneled through the trust to the university and then from them to Vector, and taxed every step of the way."

About that time, Archimedes decided that the plotter charts had been laid out for him to burrow under, and pushed his nose under one edge until only the twitching tip of his tail was visible.

"I don't suppose it does," said Jonathan, smiling as he watched the cat. "Except that this way I control the money, and Vector Systems."

"I believe this deal can be constructed in such a way that you'll retain all the control over Vector that you now have, and pick up a voting interest in the operation of Arcadia—something you only have now as a matter of courtesy," Steuben said. "And there'll be more money to control. Arcadia's tax bill takes a third of profits, 13 percent of the gross. And the university takes its cut after that."

"I'm missing something. What's the downside? What do I lose?"

"Potentially, your independence," said Steuben. "Since Arcadia and Vector are both private stock companies, we can escape most regulatory complications. But I am obliged to warn you that other trustees—my successors—may view these arrangements with a more jaundiced eye. Even with me, there will be issues of accountability—I cannot allow this arrangement to harm Arcadia or starve the trust. You still won't have a blank check."

"But I'll have more to work with right now."

"That's the entire reason for doing it. The sale will provide a one-time infusion of capital, and certain ongoing operating expenses will be covered internally by dollars that would otherwise have gone to pay the tax man or the university. But you will have to show progress toward a marketable product for that to continue."

"Then let's do it," said Jonathan.

"Very good," said Steuben. "Then I can talk about my other proposal. Correct me if I'm wrong, but doesn't the Vector start-up depend directly on your research at the university?"

"We're working on some ideas of Alynn's," said Jonathan. "But yes, it feeds off the work we've been doing—work we're still doing."

"Then perhaps there'll be an opportunity for Arcadia to do what Vector could never afford to, which is underwrite the lab work directly, as sponsored research. Same upside, same downside."

As Hypatia cautiously but curiously approached the cat-sized bulge under the scattered charts, Jonathan got up and walked to the desk, where the video portion of the call was playing on one of the small monitors.

"I wonder," he said. "Would there be any chance of Arcadia leasing my lab from the U? Or maybe they'd even be willing to lease me. I need access to that equipment, but teaching is a time sink I'd love to escape."

"Are you talking about resigning?"

"No, no. There are benefits to being there that we can't buy at any price. Prestige and face credibility, for one. Bargain brainpower, for another. But I wonder if just maybe we could make it worth their while to change my appointment—move me from the instructional faculty to the research faculty."

Steuben frowned. "Did I screw up, Jonathan? Is this something we should have planned for from the outset? It never came up in my conversations with the university—"

"No, they wouldn't suggest it. They always want the fewest possible conditions on gifts," Jonathan said. "Besides, most everyone stays in the track they were first appointed to. They start to think of you in a certain way, and it becomes your destiny. But if I could show them that I had the prospect of sponsored research that I could only take on as a full-time researcher—or that they stand to *lose* a substantial gift if I can't give more time to the work the grantor favors—"

"I see. Very well, we can explore that—"

"Great." At that moment, a sudden chorus of crinkling-paper sounds announced that a wrestling match had broken out between Archimedes and Hypatia on, under, and among the charts. "Hey! Enough!" Jonathan called sharply, looking up. "Excuse me, Mr. Steuben, gotta go. The cats are eating my homework."

Jonathan had only been inside a police station once before, to fill out a complaint on a theft from his car—

and that only to satisfy the insurance company. But he had a headful of preconceptions from a lifetime of television, most of which fell away in the first minutes inside the Larcom Municipal Building.

Needs theme music, he thought as he made his way to the Investigative Division offices in the basement. The juxtaposition of suits and sidearms made him think of an accounting department under siege. A hint of that smile was still lingering on his lips when he found Stephen Anderson's desk.

"Detective? Jonathan Briggs. You wanted to see me?"

Anderson pivoted in his chair and looked up toward the doorway of his cubicle. "Dr. Briggs. Thank you for coming in," he said, though he neither smiled nor offered his hand. "Sit down, please. How have you been?"

"Busy. Is there some news about the case?"

"Busy," Anderson repeated. "Yes, I can imagine you must be. I had to call you five times to arrange this meeting. I'm a little surprised you haven't been calling *me*. Open cases usually mean lots of calls from the victim's families. I hear from Alynn's mother a couple of times a week."

"I don't hear from her at all," said Jonathan. "So—is there news?"

"No news. What I have are questions. I'm hoping you could help me with some of them."

"I can try."

"Good. Good. Have a seat, would you?" Anderson sifted through the papers on the cluttered wing of his workspace as though looking for something. There was only one empty chair, directly opposite, and Jonathan settled himself there.

"You don't mind if I record this, do you?" Anderson asked, pausing in his search. "It's department policy, protects everybody, avoids a lot of nuisance lawsuits."

"Go ahead." There was no point in refusing. Jonathan had already noticed the camera module hanging below the shelf above and behind Anderson, its lens tracking Jonathan's movements. It occurred to him that another possible use of the camera was as the one-way mirror, a set piece in every police drama. Anyone could be behind the glass, monitoring the interview.

"Good," Anderson said, and touched a menu pad beside his computer. "You did know that there's a parking lot security camera recording of the attack?"

Jonathan frowned. "No."

"You haven't been keeping up with the news coverage of the case, then."

"No. I haven't."

"Too uncomfortable," Anderson said, nodding. "We released the video to the *CrimeStoppers* program months ago. Would you watch it with me?"

Jonathan flinched at the suggestion. "What good would that do?"

"Memory's a funny thing, Dr. Briggs. But I guess I don't need to tell you that," said Anderson, turning his monitor toward Jonathan.

"I really don't want to do this," Jonathan said sharply.

"I asked you in because I thought you'd want to help. Dr. Briggs, do you want the person responsible for this crime caught and convicted, or not?"

"Of course I do," he said, because it was expected.

But it was a lie. The startling realization was that he no longer cared. It all seemed wholly irrelevant. He had moved beyond thoughts of vengeance, or even of justice. Neither vengeance nor justice was of any use to him. Neither could make him whole again. Only his work could do that.

"Then why not let me do my job?" Anderson was saying. "I'm pretty good at it, you know—we have a 94 percent clearance rate on murder in this division."

Several sharp replies offered themselves to Jonathan, but he quelled the urge to voice one. "Go ahead," he said, turning sideways and hooking an arm on the back of the uncomfortable straight-backed chair. The camera followed every move.

"Thank you, Doctor." Anderson started the video playback, then sat back in his chair with hands folded in his lap. Jonathan watched the video with his face averted, as though it were a light too bright to look at directly. He didn't realize there was an audio track until the first gunshot, which startled him. When Alynn crumpled to the ground, a loud sob tore through his chest and escaped. By the time Alynn's car surged forward from its parking space, tears were streaming down Jonathan's face.

"You see how little we have to work with," Anderson said quietly, offering a box of tissues. "Those images were enhanced to the limits of current technology. There simply isn't enough detail. It shows everything, and nothing. It's frustrating."

"But the killers were in the car—isn't there DNA, fingerprints, fibers? What about the gun?"

"We kind of have to have a suspect before we can try to match them up with that kind of evidence. And these two seem to have disappeared." Anderson sat forward and rested his elbows on his desk. "Do you know where they are, Dr. Briggs?"

Jonathan stared disbelievingly. "What?"

"You're a smart man, Dr. Briggs, so I'm going to put my cards on the table. When this case first hit my desk I was just about certain it was a random initiation killing—"

"What do you mean, do I know where they are? What are you saying?" He gripped the front edge of his chair fiercely, as though that was all that was keeping him from launching himself at Anderson in a blind fury.

"Gang killings make poor secrets," Anderson said calmly. "Someone brags to the wrong person, or thieves fall out, or someone needs money. But this one hasn't played that way. There hasn't even been a whisper. So I started looking at things a different way."

"Looking at me, you mean. This is crazy."

"How much money did you receive as a result of Alynn's murder?"

That question set Jonathan back on his heels. "I'm the beneficiary of a trust she set up."

"And about how much benefit would that be? Ten thousand?"

"I get a hundred thousand dollars a year." Jonathan's voice was suddenly dry.

"And you control another million, isn't that right? How much is the trust worth?"

"Eleven million and change."

"That much," Anderson said. "And there weren't any insurance companies involved, or any probate court, were there? No marriage license. You weren't even registered as a domestic partnership, were you?"

"No."

"But now her money just comes straight to your pocket instead of hers."

Jonathan felt the ground shifting under him. "That's what trusts are for, isn't it? To avoid probate."

"Whose idea was that, Dr. Briggs—hers or yours?"

"Look, I didn't know a thing about it. I didn't know she'd done it. I didn't even think about her money. You can ask Arthur Steuben, at Hillerman-Steuben-Welch."

"We've already talked to Mr. Steuben," said Anderson. "Where are you living now, Dr. Briggs?"

He answered grudgingly. "Huron Towers East."

"In fact, you're living in Alynn's apartment, aren't you?"

"Her former office. Yes." He stared at Anderson with a mixture of amazement and amusement.

"Apartment 801, isn't it? The three-bedroom suite, with the river view?"

"Yes."

"You happy there? Nicer than your old place?"

"No. Maybe more convenient. But that's not why I'm there."

"Why are you there, then?"

"I wanted to be in her spaces, close to her memory. That's not hard to understand, is it?"

"I would have thought you'd choose the place you lived together."

Jonathan loosed an exasperated sigh. "Look, I thought you asked me in because you had some news for me."

"The news is that I don't think we're looking at a random killing. I think we're looking at a hired killing," Anderson said calmly. "Eleven million dollars, you say? And you've moved into Alynn's apartment. I understand you're driving a new vehicle, though—not sentimental about everything, then, were you."

"Would you want that kind of reminder around?"

"And yet you can see the parking lot from your window, can't you? You're down there every day, in fact, aren't you? But I suppose that's different, isn't it." Anderson glanced sideways at his computer display, which was once again angled away from Jonathan.

"You've been making a lot of calls to Toronto, I see—your parents live there, don't they?"

Jonathan saw the trap and sidestepped it. He had scarcely spoken to his parents all summer. "Toronto is a critical link in my research," he said. "A lot of my early subjects live there."

"And a lot of your friends, too, I'm sure. I suppose if I gave you this list, you'd tell me which names were which, wouldn't you? You grew up there, went to school there—you must know a lot of people there. Any of them ever come visit you?"

"Almost never," he said. "It's too much of a nuisance for a weekend trip—two border crossings, and Homeland Security greeting you at the door—"

"But thousands of people from Toronto come into the United States every day. They fly into Detroit and Cleveland and New York, they enter at Sarnia and Windsor and Niagara Falls." He touched his keyboard and peered at his monitor again. "Quite a list, really. Some of them even stay for just a few hours, then turn around and go right home. It's not that difficult getting back into Canada, after all, is it? Not such a nuisance."

"No, not by comparison."

"In fact, I understand you can get from Ann Arbor to Windsor in four hours—even less if you cross in the middle of the night. Have you ever tried that?"

"Detective, why is this conversation about me? I was at the lab when Alynn was murdered—you know that." He sat forward on the very edge of his chair, his voice and body language all earnestness. "I wish to God I'd been with her, so we'd have been in that parking lot together, so she didn't have any reason to be out there in the first place. I love Alynn. I love her more than I've ever loved anyone. She's the woman I was waiting for my whole life and thought would never come. I could never hurt her."

"Oh, I'm sure that wasn't you in the video, Doctor. But you can't deny you've been the principal beneficiary of what happened in that parking lot."

"You're an idiot," Jonathan said tersely. "This is so pathetically laughable I can't even be insulted."

"Dr. Briggs, last week I arrested a sixty-two-year-old woman for poisoning her husband because she couldn't stand his snoring," Anderson said coolly. "The week before that, it was a man who raped his stepdaughter and left her in pieces in County Farm Park. If I didn't ask respectable people any hard questions, half the bad guys would get away."

"Which doesn't mean you're not being an idiot this week."

Anderson was unfazed. "If not you, then who?"

"I haven't the first idea."

"Are you seeing anyone socially?"

Jonathan squinted at Anderson. "No. I don't have the time or the inclination."

"So how would you describe your relationship with Dr. Elizabeth Froelich?"

That was unexpected, and he felt his face betraying him. "A friend. Something of a mentor. She's responsible for my being at the U, thinks my work has merit."

"You see each other outside the department?"

Only Jonathan's determination not to be caught in a lie or an evasion made him answer at all. "Sometimes we have a meal together."

"Visit her at home?"

"Once."

"She visit you at yours?"

"Once or twice."

Anderson nodded slowly. "Do you know what kind of gun your girlfriend was killed with?"

"If you told me, I forgot," said Jonathan. "I don't know diddly about guns. But I don't think you told me."

"It was a .32, probably a .32 H&R Magnum—almost certainly a revolver, since there weren't any cartridges at the scene, and we didn't see the killers pick up their brass."

"None of that means anything to me."

"No? Because it turns out Dr. Elizabeth Froelich owns a Lady Ultra revolver chambered for the .32 H&R—or did, before she reported it 'stolen.' She said that her house was burglarized while she was on vacation."

Jonathan stared. "She didn't say anything about it to me."

"No? Not even when you went to see her on August 5, the day before she made that report? But I guess she wouldn't want to make you suspicious."

Jonathan's answer was a disgusted stare. "You think she had Alynn killed? Why the hell would she?"

"Jealousy. It rivals greed as a time-honored motive. Come on, Doctor—she's a lonely old bookworm. And a drunk."

"You're despicable."

"Me? No, Dr. Briggs, I'm one of the good guys. The person who murdered Alynn is despicable. No matter how many awards and diplomas they can hang on an office wall."

"Liz would never do that," Jonathan said emphatically. "She'd never do that to me."

"Why is that? Because of your special friendship? Or is it more than friendship?"

"Christ—this is so completely absurd." He shook his head. "You can't really think either of us had anything to do with this."

"I think $11 million is a lot of money to an assistant professor with a fringy research project hurting for money," said Anderson, folding his hands on his lap. "Awfully good luck—kind of like finding a winning Lotto ticket on your way to bankruptcy court. I think eleven million's enough to make a lot of people change their life plans. It's certainly more than enough to hire a shooter and buy some kind of silence—"

"It probably is. But that isn't what happened."

"Then tell me what did happen. Why haven't I heard from you, Dr. Briggs? Did you lose interest in who killed your girlfriend, or did you just start feeling safe—"

"That's it exactly. I lost interest. I'm not part of the war you're fighting."

"No? Why is that?"

"Because I'm looking forward, not back. I'm not living in the past. I have somewhere else to be."

"Somewhere else to be," Anderson repeated. "Why didn't you go to your girlfriend's funeral, Dr. Briggs? Did you have somewhere else to be then, too?"

"Mrs. Reed didn't want me there."

"That's not what she says."

"Then she's lying," Jonathan said calmly. "She's a bigot, Detective, and she lost it when she found out Alynn had been living with me. If you've been listening to her, that goes a long way toward explaining this farce. I didn't go to the funeral because I wasn't welcome—because going would have meant an ugly public fight with Mrs. Reed. But I remembered Alynn in my own way."

"By spending her money?"

"What I'm doing now I'm doing for her, and because of her. It's all I have left."

Anderson seemed unimpressed. "Mrs. Reed offered a fifty-thousand dollar reward for information leading to the arrest of her daughter's murderer. How much of your $11 million did you put up to help catch your girlfriend's murderer?"

That stopped Jonathan for a moment. "You're not

going to understand this, but it's just not something I thought of doing," he said finally.

"You're right, I don't understand. Enlighten me, please."

Jonathan sighed impatiently, looking away for a moment. "What happened to Alynn is as impersonal as—as being struck by lightning, or stung to death by hornets, or going into the woods and ending up bear food." Jonathan shook his head. "It doesn't matter who did it. Maybe they're dead already themselves, and that's why you can't find them.

"The point is, anyone can get caught turning the wrong corner, saying the wrong thing to the wrong person. That's the way the world is now. The woods aren't safe. I suppose they never were. You think you're making a difference here, but you're not. And my obsessing about who killed Alynn—that wouldn't make any difference, either. I only have a little piece of my life and sanity left, and I have need of both. I have work to do."

Anderson listened with a stone mask of a face. "Thank you for the philosophical illumination, Dr. Briggs," Anderson said, leaning back in his chair. "But to me, it does matter who did it. I don't like unsolved murders. I don't like it when someone thinks they've gotten away with killing someone. Maybe that makes this more personal to me than it is to you."

"Maybe it does." He regretted the words at once.

Coming to his feet, Anderson leaned across the desk wing in a way that managed to convey a surprising degree of threat. "Dr. Briggs, I'm going to stay on this until I've nailed to a wall anyone and everyone who was involved. And I really don't care if you think I'm being insulting, or you think I'm a crazy son of a bitch bastard with a badge. Because in fifteen years in this job, I've had every kind of lying filth there is sitting across from me, and, you know, some of them didn't look a whole lot different than you. And I learned a long time ago that there's no hard line between the grieving and the guilty.

"I don't know if you had Alynn Reed killed. I don't know if Dr. Froelich did. I don't know if maybe the two of you worked it out together, so you could both have what you wanted. But I'm putting you on notice, Dr. Briggs. I'm gonna find out."

"You do what you think you have to, Detective," Jonathan said, standing to leave. "Just understand that I have my own priorities. And, if you'll excuse me, I'm going to go attend to them."

He felt the eye of the camera on his back as he turned away, and imagined the muttered words behind the closed doors.

As he returned to his car, he wondered if he should talk to a lawyer. But the thought was too absurd to embrace. The guilty needed defense attorneys. He was still free, and he was innocent. Surely, he told Stuart, that was all the protection he would need.

7

The Ghost in the Machine

The first day of Jonathan Briggs's seventh fall on campus found him presenting the syllabus for an unfamiliar course to rows of unfamiliar faces in an unfamiliar lecture hall.

He would have preferred not to teach at all, but when that was denied him, he had expected to at least return to what he knew. But it did not fall out that way. By the time he returned to campus, other instructors, including Dr. Kosslyn, were already slotted for Jonathan's usual class load. And Elizabeth Froelich—who was still keeping her distance—refused to inconvenience them further with a cascade of late changes.

The assigned classroom was halfway across campus from the Neuroscience Building, in Mason Hall, and the assigned course was wholly outside the department—an interdisciplinary survey course, Foundations of Behavior, required for history and anthropology majors. Since receiving the assignment, Jonathan had felt like the department's pariah, and he could not get Elizabeth to say anything to reassure him otherwise.

"This is the course we need taught right now," she said, with no hint of her earlier sympathy for his circumstances. "And bear in mind that your tenure review is under way. You should expect observers in the classroom."

But he had no warning about the cameras of Detroit's Fox affiliate waiting outside. Though the news crew didn't directly confront him, there was no doubt but that he was the subject in focus as he walked across the Diag and up the walk to Mason Hall.

Another surprise was waiting inside the lecture hall, in the person of a uniformed Ann Arbor police officer. The officer contented herself with standing at the back of the room with a digital voice recorder clipped to her uniform's blouse. But when the news crew invaded the room later, they made a point of getting a shot of the uniform. It was a safe prediction that that image would survive the editing process.

Unsettled by these developments, Jonathan struggled through the hour. Though he tried to ignore the intruders, all of the humor and most of the confidence were driven from him by self-consciousness. And though the head count was as expected, even the students seemed to be holding themselves at a distance. Jonathan was struck by the thought that it was like being in front of a grand jury, and from that moment on he could not get the image out of his mind.

When the hour was over, he knew he had failed to connect with them. So it was with puzzlement that he watched fully a third of the class, almost all of them female, make their way forward toward him instead of toward the exits. They formed a ragged line in the left aisle behind a round-hipped young woman whose hard eyes were framed by a tangle of black hair. Jonathan met those eyes and braced himself. Her denunciation was as practiced as it was emphatic, and the news crew caught every word.

"Dr. Jonathan Briggs, we accuse you as an abuser and exploiter and destroyer of women. You are morally unfit to lecture us on human behavior. Your presence in this room betrays the traditions and principles of a fine university. You belong behind bars, not behind a lectern. In protest of your conduct and the regents' refusal to act, we are withdrawing from your class."

Then she presented him with her drop card, followed by each of the others in turn. They trooped out together, disappearing into the corridor with the news crew in pursuit.

The last to leave was the police officer. "Planning to come back?" he called up to her.

"Every day," she said, pocketing the recorder.

"Good," said Jonathan. "It might be just the two of us by Thanksgiving. Think about enrolling. Work on those professional development credits."

She did not smile. When she was gone, he slumped against the projection wall. Anderson, you son of a bitch—you're trying to destroy my life.

Students from the next class were starting to arrive, so Jonathan collected his materials as he tried to collect himself. But there was one more obstacle between him and enough privacy to let loose the feelings he was bottling up—the Fox news crew. This time they homed in on him as soon as they spotted him.

"Dr. Briggs, can you give us a minute?" asked the reporter. Jonathan brushed by them wordlessly, but they followed him out onto the Diag.

"Dr. Briggs, are you aware of Stacey Reed's recent accusations?" the reporter called after him, loudly enough to turn several nearby heads. When Jonathan did not respond, the reporter added, even louder,

"What do you have to say to her allegation that you had her daughter murdered?"

Jonathan stopped short and allowed them to catch him. "What's your name?" he demanded.

"North Barber, WJBK True News—"

"North Barber? Really?" Jonathan said, with a shake of his head. "Some parents—Mr. Barber, don't come into my classroom again unless you're invited, or enrolled."

"We had permission," Barber said quickly.

"What?" Jonathan was rocked back on his heels by the claim.

"We had permission from Chancellor Paton to film in your classroom, so long as our presence wasn't disruptive," said Barber. "Now, how about the question, Doc? Stacey Reed claims—"

Jonathan held up a hand and looked away for a moment, fighting for focus. "Stacey Reed is a grieving mother desperate to find order and justice in a world that has precious little of either," he said. "I can't hold that kind of wild misstatement against her. I know how she feels. We both loved Alynn, and we both miss her terribly."

"But isn't it true that you're raking in millions of dollars from her work—"

"I haven't taken a penny for myself out of Arcadia," Jonathan said. "If I had suddenly come into millions, do you think I'd be back here teaching a sophomore survey class? How much do you think the university pays assistant professors?"

Jonathan walked away pleased with himself, and even more pleased that they didn't follow. He would not realize until that night why they allowed him to go.

Since the morning after Alynn's death, Jonathan had had no use for the media. Those first days that he was unplugged from the world shattered a lifetime habit, his morning news-with-breakfast. When he emerged from his hermitage, he had new priorities, and many things that had mattered to him could no longer command his attention.

The day he returned from Starpath, Jonathan had instructed Cassandra to begin scanning the nets for anything that mentioned Alynn. But he had also asked her to keep it away from his consciousness and archive it sight unseen. The time had not yet come when it was either possible or necessary to look at what the knowbots had found.

Now Detective Stephen Anderson had made it necessary.

Blowing off a meeting with David Helms, Jonathan went home and asked Cassandra to show him what they had been saying about Alynn—and him. He discovered they were saying altogether too much.

In the last month alone, a Cincinnati news service, *Ohio River Journal*, had done two local-interest features on the case, with Stacey Reed starring as the grieving mother.

"I think my daughter was killed by someone who knew her," Mrs. Reed told the reporter earnestly, though she named no names. She taxed the host's system in a follow-up netchat with *ORJ* columnist Marcia Rose Morgan.

By the time the more staid webpaper *Cincinnati Enquirer* got around to interviewing her, Stacey Reed had lost her reticence. "Only one person benefited from my daughter's murder—Dr. Jonathan Briggs. Why the Ann Arbor police are blind to this, you'll have to ask them."

But it did not stop there, not nearly.

Insider, a tabloid channel out of Hong Kong, had picked up a rumor off the chat nets and thrown together a piece suggesting that Alynn had lost the ability to distinguish between VR and real life, and died thinking her attacker was a harmless character she had invented. It followed that story a week later with another "revealing" that Alynn had foretold her own death in her games, and would appear as a phantom in her final creation to accuse her murderer.

Among the less fevered entries, another tabloid, *Real-Life Mysteries*, took a straight true-crime angle, with Stacey Reed's anguish given a featured place and Jonathan himself described as the "mystery man" in Alynn's life. And when *Games Unlimited* previewed High Seas under the slugline "Arcadia's Last Diamond," the editor found it necessary to include a sidebar about the unsolved murder, which quoted both Tommy Ramirez and Stephen Anderson.

Until that night, Jonathan had simply never quite grasped that Alynn's death was a celebrity murder, because Alynn had not been a celebrity to him. By the time he finished viewing a dozen retrievals, he understood what a mistake that had been.

Her murder was becoming a story that would not die. Stacey Reed was providing all the impetus it needed. And the longer it went on, the brighter the spotlight became, the more reason the police had to find an answer to the question that wouldn't go away. Only now, they needed an answer as big as the story had become.

A carjacking gone wrong, a gang initiation, a random, sociopathic street punk—those would no longer suffice. But a contract murder for profit, a love-triangle conspiracy, a spurned and jealous rival—those scenarios would propitiate the media gods, satisfy the public need to nod knowingly, and think *Ah-ha, I thought so—*

He watched North Barber's piece about him with

the sound off, saw the images of himself besieged, furtive, angry, arrogant woven into the tapestry with Stacey Reed's tears and Alynn's smiles, and understood that the words barely mattered.

"That's enough, Cassandra. Resume blackout and continue archiving." He rubbed his eyes and tried to think. *It doesn't matter what Anderson believes. He can't follow me where I'm going. He can only catch me on my way there.* He stopped and considered that. *So I just won't let that happen, eh?*

"Cassandra, call Tommy, secure." He wondered if the police had already started trying to monitor his communications, and what they would think when they discovered he was using an encryption lock that Homeland Security's backdoor key didn't fit. "Tommy? This is Jonathan. Isn't it about time you had some good news for me? I want to know where things stand—"

Weeks flashed by almost unnoticed. The football team got off to an 0–3 start, losing to Georgia Tech, Central Michigan, and, for the fourth year in a row, Notre Dame. There was a double suicide on Fraternity Row, a sixteen-hour blackout on North Campus, and a disc-trashing virus called Quicksand that infected the primary campus network. The law school was sued for ideological discrimination by three conservative white male applicants from the Upper Peninsula, and the student newspaper was sued for refusing an ad from a death-with-dignity clinic in Windsor.

Outside the university cocoon, eleven people were killed when a gunman shot up an overpass restaurant on Chicago's Tri-State Tollway. A phantom air traffic controller directed a taxiing Delta red-eye onto a live Hartsfield runway and into the path of a UPS freighter on final approach. Nine days of riots in Mexico City toppled the government of Ramon Ortiz y Carrera and left the country on the brink of civil war.

Over that span, Jonathan reached an accommodation of sorts with what was left of his class. It was forged the day he arrived to find four of the students trying to scrub a paint-stick graffito off the glass face of the video blackboard. Working under the disapproving gaze of Officer Kimberly Rodriguez, they had managed to reduce the blue M to a pale smear and blur the maize U and the final R, leaving only RDERE readable.

Nothing was said about the gesture, but around their indignation and his gratitude the lecture hall became a place he did not need to fear.

But outside that sanctuary, the harassment by the Ann Arbor police continued. It was intermittent and unpredictable, at times low-key and at others heavy-handed—exactly the schedule guaranteed to make Jonathan hyperconscious of every uniform, every police car, every siren in his vicinity. The heavy-handed episodes were frequent enough to drive a wedge between Jonathan and those who might have remained casual friends, and thorough enough to test the loyalty of those closest to him.

Two or three times a week, a police car openly followed Jonathan wherever he went, with the officer riding shotgun armed with a digital camera. Just being seen talking to or visiting Jonathan meant a knock on the door that evening, or a visit at work the next day by a uniformed officer with "a few questions to ask." The questions asked were damning enough that many of those questioned chose to keep their distance from Jonathan from then on.

Quirky behavior of the netlinks at Huron Towers convinced Jonathan that police technicians were trying

to monitor his communications traffic, and he had
Cassandra adopt a higher level of encryption and
change his keys more often. He also suspected that the
new resident of Apartment 815 was an undercover officer, filming the comings and goings through a key-
hole camera and snooping through the common wall.

His answer to that was a box of soundproofing tile,
heavy drapes for the windows, and the keyboard.
When there had to be conversation, Cassandra could
produce a stream of white noise that masked the vocal
frequencies almost too well. The rest of the time, the
apartment was as quiet as a church on Tuesday.

For all of that, Jonathan tried to tell himself that
the police were little more than a nuisance, their tactics
more amusing than threatening. He relied heavily on
the fact of his innocence to fortify himself against the
intimidation.

If asked, he would have insisted that nothing had
changed since his meeting with Anderson, except perhaps that he was more focused. Those still close
enough to notice might have added that he was more
demanding and impatient, and the laugh light, already
weakened by Alynn's death, came less often to his
eyes.

Jonathan's tenure notification letter arrived unexpect-
edly early, delivered by messenger on the afternoon of
September 15. It was short and coldly formal, and carried a painfully blunt subject line: Notice of Non-
Reappointment.

> *After review and evaluation of your instruc-
> tional and research record during the probation-
> ary period, I regret to inform you that we are
> unable to offer you tenure in the Department of*

*Neuroscience, College of Human Medicine. Your
appointment will end June 15.*

That was all. No polite "We wish you the best in
your future endeavors." No words of appreciation
for past service. No face-saving allusions to "evolving
departmental priorities." No offers to help him find
a "more suitable position," not even a hint that a self-
serving letter of recommendation might be forth-
coming.

Just Elizabeth's signature as department chair.

"No, no, no, this is wrong," he said aloud. "I
haven't even gotten the review committee's report—"

But it was there in the unread mail, dated
September 14. It was a weasel-worded document that
was obviously more the product of sympathy than enthusiasm. Splitting the difference between endorse-
ment and disapproval, the report recommended he
receive an additional year's appointment to address
"certain recognized deficiencies."

The committee had salved its own conscience, and
in doing so justified any decision by the department
chair. And perhaps that had been exactly what
Elizabeth had wanted, since she had moved so deci-
sively after receiving it. She would not have been
obliged to follow any recommendation, but now she
would not even be questioned.

I thought I would have more time.

But he discovered there were no guarantees in the
faculty handbook, only guidelines—all of which had
been honored. There was no appeal for an unfavorable
decision on the merits at this level. And even if there
was, Elizabeth could always point to current circumstances—the police investigation, the ugly publicity,
the student protests.

It was becoming hard to breathe in the apartment. He threw back the sound-deadening drapes and fled to the balcony, where he sucked in the late-afternoon heat in lung-filling gasps.

It was all coming to an end, and a year sooner than his worst imagining had calculated. He was going to lose the lab, his team, his credentials, his identity. There would be no re-appointment, no terminal contract. He had counted on another year beyond this one, but he had only nine more months, and nothing was ready.

Seven stories below, a police car appeared, slowly cruising through the parking lot. The sight of it hardened Jonathan's will and drove him back inside.

"Cassandra—I need to see Elizabeth Froelich as soon as possible. Today."

"I'm sorry, Jonathan. She has no open appointments."

"Tomorrow? This week?"

"I'm afraid not."

"When can I get in?"

"It seems as though there is a problem. The system is refusing to schedule you, all the way into next year."

Pariah, Jonathan thought. "Get me a person."

"No one in the department offices seems to be answering," Cassandra said after a few long seconds. "Shall I leave messages?"

"No," said Jonathan, grabbing up his coat. "Lock up after me."

The police cruiser followed him all the way to the campus gate.

The departmental secretary looked not only surprised to see Jonathan, but uncomfortable being alone with him. He tried to take advantage of it, cornering her behind the counter, then crowding her at her desk.

"Betty, I want to talk to Dr. Froelich."

"She's not here, Dr. Briggs. I don't expect her back today."

"Is she on campus?"

"I—I don't know, Dr. Briggs. She just told me she'd be away from the office."

"But you can reach her, can't you. If her dog was on fire, if the dean wanted a back rub, you could get her. She'll take *your* call."

"Yes, I—Dr. Briggs, you don't want to get me in trouble. I'm sorry. She specifically said she wasn't available to you."

"I know. Tell her I want to talk to her about leasing the lab."

"I'll relay your message," said the secretary. "That's the best I can do."

Sighing resignedly, Jonathan took half a step backward. "No, it isn't. But *you* have a future here to think of, eh?"

He waited fifteen minutes in his car before returning. This time the secretary was nowhere in sight, and the door to Elizabeth's office was ajar. He followed the voices and found them together in the conference area.

"Dr. Froelich," he said. "Thank you for making time for me."

Her tone was every bit as annoyed as his was frosty. "Betty, please tell Dr. Mansfield that I'll be a few minutes late," Froelich said as she walked past him.

He took that as an invitation and followed her into her office.

"Why?" he asked when the door closed.

"There's nothing to say," she said, retreating behind her desk as though it were a castle rampart. "There's no way to unscramble this egg."

"I need more time."

"You needed more results," she said. "And you needed to take better care of your relationships inside the department. I don't think you can claim you didn't have fair warning on both points. Did you think you could *buy* a place with us?"

"I didn't think I had to," he said. "You don't believe I had her killed, do you?"

"No," she said. "No, I don't. But I've stopped stepping up to argue with all the people who do. It's just too much, Jonathan."

"The police are looking at you, too, you know. Because of your missing gun. Because they think—"

"That I'd be stupid enough to hire a killer and provide them with a gun registered to me? They aren't looking at me, Jonathan. No one is looking at me. And I want it to stay that way. Please don't come visiting."

"I've been afraid to come see you, even to call you. Detective Anderson said—"

"Oh, I know, he asked about our relationship. He tried his best to put us in bed together. But he couldn't do it, either. It's laughable, really. It isn't as if I had anything to gain, Jonathan. It isn't as if I ever had any reason to think you'd end up with me." She glanced at the clock. "I think your five minutes are up."

"Wait—wait. You have to give me another option. What if we were to lease the lab, beginning in June? A business partnership."

She shook her head. "There's no one here who wants to be partners with you. Jonathan, this isn't a mistake you recover from. It's time for you to leave Ann Arbor. You'll be paid through June because that's policy, but I'd encourage you to give some thought to pulling out now, before things get any worse for you. You won't be needed for teaching winter semester, and

I'm assigning Eric to take over Foundations of Behavior. You're essentially free to leave at any time."

"Now, hold on—I need Eric in my lab—"

"Jonathan, you're not getting the picture. What you think you need and what you want isn't going to have much to do with what happens now. And I wouldn't necessarily count on your lab privileges continuing until June. I may need to give that space to your replacement."

Fury and frustration squeezed his hands into tight fists. "Why are you doing this?"

"I just can't protect you any longer. I have to protect this department, the med school, the university—and you pose a risk to all of them."

"No—this is vindictiveness. This is personal."

"It really isn't, Jonathan. You've been here on sufferance for at least two years. You just ran out of time."

Mouth dry, he stared at her. "What about my people?" he said finally. "Maybe I deserve this, but you have to give me a chance to do right by them."

"We aren't out to punish anyone. Their current appointments are safe. They have nine months to find new positions. That's going to have to be enough," Elizabeth said, touching her phone. "Betty, let Dr. Mansfield know I'm on my way." She raised her eyes to Jonathan. "You'd better go."

"I want to buy my test rig. I can pay a fair price."

"But it isn't for sale."

"Hell, I'll pay an *unfair* price."

"My hands are tied, Jonathan. It hasn't been declared surplus, and I can't imagine why it would be. But you can probably find one somewhere else."

"Not with our modifications—six years of refinement. Look, it was in a storeroom when I got here."

"I'm sure we can still find space there for it," she

said lightly. "You never know when something you take for granted might become useful."

"Damn it, Liz—this is important. And we are so close—"

"What are you close to?"

"Restoring the balance. Reductionism has us in a stranglehold—"

"That's because the reductionists have been producing all the results."

"But they have a blind spot," he insisted. "They've gotten locked into a digital computing model for cognition, and all they understand is ones and zeroes, on and off. You should understand—you were a functionalist."

"Now I'm an administrator. One who's late for a meeting."

"One more minute, please." He paused, breathing heavily. "You know how unsatisfactory reductionism is for emergent conditions. Why can't consciousness be fundamentally analog? Natural processes aren't digital—the sound of the wind, the course of the planets, the light from the sun. They're cyclical, variable, persistent. I think we can show that consciousness is, too."

"If you'd succeeded in doing so, we wouldn't be having this conversation, Jonathan." She picked up her notepad as though making ready to go.

"We're going to succeed," he said determinedly, moving to block her way. "But, Liz, we're up against a community convinced that the brain is an organic computer that generates the illusion of a mind. Let's say, just for the sake of argument, that we can show that the brain's really a transducer, monitoring something that has an independent existence—"

"Just for the sake of argument."

"If the breakthrough comes while we're still inside these walls, maybe we'll get a decent hearing. We'd have a shot. But if it comes after you throw us out—hell, we'll just look like cranks."

She looked at him with pity. "Jonathan, I'm afraid your credibility problems are already beyond the powers of this department to heal. The cold hard fact is, the university doesn't want its name associated with you or your work any longer. That was made clear to me. Letting you keep your credentials till the end of the year is all the consideration you can hope for." She sighed. "I'm sorry it's ending this way. I really am."

Jonathan collected a speeding ticket and a reckless driving citation during the short, furious trip home.

The next blow—just as predictable, yet just as surprising—came the following week.

Jonathan had been taking a break in a long afternoon of reading, standing shirtless on the apartment balcony and watching brightly colored leaves make their death dives onto the surface of the river. There had been just enough of a chill overnight to condemn the bright yellow sugar maples, and there was just enough of a breeze out of the north to tear the leaves away from the branches. The edge of the slow-moving river was blanketed with yellow.

He had been pointedly ignoring the CrimeSolver trailer below in the Huron Towers lot. It was parked sideways in the two spaces closest to the entrance, its shaded videoscreen facing the walkway. Every time a car passed by or someone came near, the recording began anew: "Your neighborhood police need your help solving the brutal murder of Alynn Reed. The crime scene is close by, and you may have crucial information—" Then the screen would replay the security camera video and the street-level digital reconstruction based on it.

"Excuse me, Jonathan."

Jonathan turned away from the rail. "Yes, Cassie."

"Voice call from Eric Lutton."

Stepping inside the apartment, Jonathan closed the sliding door and the heavy floor-length curtains behind him. "Go ahead."

"Hello, Doc. Say, are you planning to steer by the lab today?"

"No."

"Oh." Jonathan could almost hear Eric's frown. "In that case, maybe you could reshuffle your plans?"

"What's going on?"

"Well—there's a guy from Research Services here taking inventory—"

"I know about that. Let him."

"He's got a lot of questions about what was bought with whose money, wants to see purchase records on the stuff that doesn't have a university inventory tag. Frankly, he's in the way."

"We have records, don't we?"

"We have a box."

"Then give him the box. You don't have to help him any more than that. Was there something else?"

Lutton hesitated. "Maybe you should come over, boss."

"Just tell me, goddamn it."

"Kelly's leaving," Lutton said. "She did a set of twin scans this morning and I noticed it was the last thing she had on the schedule for the month. I asked her about it and she said she's finished."

"Where is she going?"

"Across the hall, it sounds like. She said she's talked to Dr. Kosslyn. And I can't really blame her. The way it looks to her—"

"I don't want to hear this filtered through you. Tell her to call me. I'm going to make her say it to my face."

"I have a better idea," Lutton said stiffly. "Why don't you come in? You've been everywhere but here for the last month. Maybe it would make a difference to her if she thought you were still interested."

"What are you talking about? Have her call me," he demanded. "No, better, have her come here."

"I'll ask her," said Eric. "I don't think this is the best time to be giving her orders."

It was deep in the evening before Kelly and Eric appeared outside Jonathan's door. He had worn himself out with mental rehearsals of the confrontation, his mood changing according to how he imagined her demeanor. But none of those rehearsals had included Eric, and Jonathan was momentarily nonplussed.

Kelly seized the opportunity the silence offered. Standing in the doorway, she handed Jonathan a paper report with a disc clipped to the top. "This is my final report on the twin studies," she said. "I completed thirty-two screenings, all of which have been analyzed. I attached the list of remaining candidates, with a contact history and other annotations. It shouldn't be too difficult for someone to step in and continue."

"You've really made up your mind, then."

"I appreciate the opportunity you gave me, Dr. Briggs. I just need to move on."

"They're closing me down in June. There isn't time to replace you—to train anyone. Please—just see it through to the end."

"I'm sorry," she said, with a tight little shake of her head. "I need to put my energies into something with a future. I have to start thinking about my career. Right now, I don't have anything to show for my time here."

"You're a semester away from a double masters from the University of Michigan, most of it paid for by my lab. You're going to get a letter of recommendation that'll glow right through the envelope."

"I don't mean to be unkind, but that doesn't help me. It's becoming a real liability to be associated with you. I stayed longer than I should have. I didn't expect things to be as they are this fall. And—"

She hesitated, and Jonathan pounced on her. "What? Say it!"

"All right. This project used to be fun. You used to be fun. You've squeezed all the joy out of it. I know something terrible happened, but it isn't a betrayal to her if you survive it, if you pick yourself up and carry on. You've turned yourself into the second victim."

He wanted to stab back at her gut with equally hurtful words, but he was disarmed by too much truth. All he could do was clutch the report and blink.

Eric finally broke the silence. "I'm going to ride down with Kelly and see her to her car," he said to Jonathan. "I'll be back up."

By the time he returned, Jonathan had sunk deep into a couch and a bottle of wine. The wine had deserved better than to be drunk that fast, but he had no sympathy to spare for it. "And what about you, Eric?"

"Too late for me," he said, helping himself to the bottle.

"You're staying on?"

Eric pushed aside a pile of books and perched on the end of the mahogany coffee table. "I didn't say that. I need a few questions answered first."

"All right. Ask them."

"I'm having trouble seeing the direction. This goes all the way back to the anomalous pair. Ever since then, we've been going in too many directions at once. I don't see where they connect."

"Will you be getting to a question soon?"

"If I'm going to keep working, I have to know what we're really working on."

"What do you mean?"

"I know what Kelly was doing. I know what I've been doing. I know what the work-study drones are doing. I even sorta know what Tommy is doing. But I don't know what you've been working on, Dr. Briggs. It's like you're afraid to tell us." He hesitated. "Doc, are you looking for Alynn? Is that what this project has turned into?"

Jonathan took a long draught from the bottle before answering. "We're looking for another anomalous pair."

"And if we find it, what will we know? Will we be able to publish then?"

Jonathan said nothing.

"Are we ever going to publish? Or isn't that part of the plan anymore?"

"It doesn't seem terribly important now."

"What does? Are you going to answer my first question? Are you trying to find Alynn?"

"No," Jonathan said, his eyes focused somewhere far away. "Too soon for that. I'm trying to figure out how to find myself."

"Why?"

"Because I'm thinking about following her."

Eric reached for the bottle. "Following her where?"

"Into the future. Finding her there. That's what would be worth doing."

"How do you know she's going to be there?"

"She knew," he said simply.

"And you're a believer now?"

Jonathan shook his head slowly. "No. That's why it's so hard." He gestured at Kelly Mizimi's report, which was resting on the pillows of the adjacent couch. "Have you looked at the twins results?"

"Sure." As an afterthought, he added, "Kelly needed someone to talk to."

Ignoring the reproach, Jonathan asked, "What do you think?"

"I don't have any problem with how Kelly scored them. I just don't know what it tells us. So identical twins have a 90 percent match on the matrix parameters, more or less. Does that help or hurt our model? Do we still have a model?"

"The only closer match is the anomalous pair."

"Yeah, well, so what? Come on, Doc, unpack this for me. I need a map."

"I hope the twins are teaching us something about how the same mind looks inside different brains."

Skepticism bordering on contempt twisted Eric's features. "Twins only get one soul between them? Mind is immanent in the blastocyte?"

For the first time that night, Eric saw life in Jonathan's eyes. He put the bottle down beside his chair and sat forward, emphasizing his words with his hands. "Identical twins are more like each other than any other two people alive are—but even their brains aren't 90 percent identical in the fine structure. Throw out the sloppy studies, and twins raised apart still show remarkable behavioral and dispositional similarities. Kelly was able to show us exactly where it comes from. So now we can focus on the forty or sixty or hundred parameters that really matter, distill the matrix down to a fingerprint of personality."

"And you had me pulling in the early subjects for longitudinal studies, so we can learn how the same mind looks at different ages. But what doors does it open? Is there anything the matrices can tell us that the subject can't? Or if the subject won't? Can we tell a lie from a truth? A boy from a girl? Can we tell the difference between twins who love each other and those who hate each other? Sometimes I think what we're doing is like taking thermographs of cars so we can tell the owners when the engine's running and the air conditioning's on. If we get really good at it, we might someday be able to tell them the make and model. Where's the depth?"

"There's one thing we might be able to tell them that they didn't already know—who's driving. We might be able to tell them who they are."

"Nineteen-ninety-five at your nearest Psychic Counseling Network sweatshop."

"I think it might be worth more to Dugan Beckett than that."

"You really think Beckett and Winston are the same person—the same mind?"

"I think we're right on the edge of knowing."

"Goodness," Eric said, surprise softening his expression. "That's how you intend to find her."

"That's how I'm going to find her," Jonathan quietly corrected him.

"Oh, Doc—that's not realistic. Even if you're guessing right on all the things we don't know, even if a second anomalous pair shows up tomorrow, the pure chance likelihood of finding any one person is minuscule. We have a few thousand matrices recorded. Most of those people are still alive. Hell, even if we went out and started killing them off, how many people are born each year—"

"Four hundred thousand for Canada," Jonathan said with calm precision. "Four million for the United States. A hundred and fifty million and up worldwide."

"Doesn't that tell you how impossible it is? Minuscule overstates it. We'd need to put a thousand SQUIDs in the field, record every newborn for ten years running just to raise the odds to minuscule."

"You assume that chance is all that's at work."

"Well, actually, I don't, because I think the whole thing is too crazy to care about the details." Shaking his head, Eric stood and walked to the desk, where a matrix trace was playing on the larger of three displays. Resting heavily on the back of the chair, he stared at the swirling colors. "Doc, what you said about following her—"

"Yes?"

"It's crazy talk."

"I want to be able to find her after I die. That doesn't mean I want to die yet."

"So you're not talking about suicide."

"Of course not."

"Does that include working yourself to death?"

"I'm all right, Eric."

Eric turned toward him. "No, you're not. What's the hurry, Doc? What are you lying to me about?" He gestured toward the matrix. "Another twenty years and the library will be huge, the tools will be better. Lay the proper groundwork now and you'd have a real chance of finding someone—if there's anything here."

"I can't wait twenty years."

"Why not?"

The bottle got Jonathan's attention for the next few moments. "Another twenty years and I'll be middle-aged," he said at last. "I don't want to be a creepy old man hanging around school playgrounds watching her grow up. I don't want to be held out of her life because I remember things that happened before she was born. I don't want to come to the door and be taken for one of her father's friends. We aren't supposed to be separated that way."

"Kill yourself, and you give up what slim chance you have of finding her. You'll lose the tools, the knowledge, and most of all the reason."

"How do you know I won't remember? People find each other. Soul mates. Cadre brothers. People who have work to do together. People who have lessons to learn from each other."

"Show me where we've proved that."

"It's there," Jonathan said, stabbing a finger in the direction of the overflowing bookcases. "The experience of thousands of people from dozens of cultures. You can't dismiss it out of hand. She and I have a bond."

"This isn't love. This is obsession."

"If you can say that, you've never been in love."

"What are you talking about? What's love to a neurobiologist, Doc? Pheremones and endorphin highs and neurotransmitter storms in the hindbrain?"

Jonathan gathered himself unsteadily and rose out of the chair. "I'll tell you what love is, Eric. It's knowing you're not alone." His voice had a warning rumble of anger in it as he advanced on Eric. "It's not having to face that moment when the world is quiet and the room is dark and you can't escape the fact that there's no heat in the bed but yours, no voice in the house but yours. You can work yourself to exhaustion all day, and it won't save you from that moment. You can be a hero or a genius or as rich as Gates, and it won't save you from that moment."

"Doc—you knew her half a year. You don't kill yourself over a cold bed—"

Jonathan fought back a blind fury. "You think this is about sex? You think I just got cut off from my drug before my addiction ran its course?"

"I didn't say—"

"There's more to what I felt with Alynn than the heat of her body. There's nothing I want half as much as just to hear her breathing beside me in the dark again, to know that I can reach out to her and she'll take my hand and squeeze it. I lived without that for too many years, and the only way I got through it was by not knowing what was missing.

"But I know now. I had it. I know what's missing. I can stay busy during the days. But I'm not going to face that moment night after night for twenty more years. Or fifty. I can't. And no friend would ask me to."

"If that's what's on your mind, I'm gone," said Eric. "I won't help you talk yourself into suicide—"

"Then go," Jonathan said dismissively, starting toward the balcony. "Cassandra, I want to go outside."

The long drapes opened with a purr as he approached them, and the balcony door unlocked with a metallic snap.

"There's an alternative, though," Eric called quickly after him. "If you'll let yourself take it, I'll be right there with you."

Jonathan stopped short of the door without looking back. "I'm going out for air, not to jump," he said curtly. "You don't need to reel me back from the edge with empty promises."

"Completely self-serving, Doc. I told you an hour ago that it was too late for me to leave and salvage anything."

That was enough to make Jonathan turn halfway and study Eric's expression. "What, then?"

"If you're right—if Alynn was right—Beckett-Winston will only be the first. If we keep building the matrix library, there'll be more. Not just one more, but enough to convince anyone."

"How many nights will that be, Eric? Another thousand? Two thousand?"

"Just one night at a time," he said. "Don't think any more about following Alynn. Think about following her lead, instead. Make us all believers. Change the world." He took a step toward Jonathan. "Let's do this together. Let's find the proof and rub Dr. Clement Harris's face in it."

"That's not important."

"It will be."

Jonathan pushed the balcony door open. "I'll think about it," he said, turning away. "Cassandra, let Eric out, then lock up."

Eric called after him, "The deadline for submitting papers to the Berkeley conference is eleven days off." He glanced sideways at the clock. "Make that ten days."

"Is Harris still on the panel?"

"Taking a year off."

Jonathan stepped away from the open doorway. "You have something in mind?"

"I was thinking maybe the twins data were interesting enough to let us present on the methodology. If we can get some acceptance for the technique—"

"It's not exactly a secret, what we're doing," said Jonathan. "We ran twenty conference participants through the lab last year before Harris lowered the boom."

"All the more reason. Who knows why Harris cut back on his outside obligations? Maybe he's got a pet SQUID of his own now."

"You think we can pull it together in ten days?"

" 'Neural Matrix Visualization and Differentiation in Homologous Structures: A Preliminary Assay.' "

Something which vaguely resembled a smile creased Jonathan's face. "Well—we can keep the colon. The rest we'll work on."

The paper was submitted with six hours to spare.

That mattered less to Eric than the fact that when it was finished, Jonathan didn't retreat back into the her-mit's cave he had made of Alynn's apartment. The portable scanner-recorder was finally ready to come off Tommy Ramirez's workbench, which meant the start of an intense cycle of benchmarking and calibration in the lab. Jonathan was there for all of it, either at the console or in the chair himself. But the first subject was Ramirez, who had never been mapped.

"I can make the next one prettier," he said as Eric fitted the new sensor unit on his head. "The rafting helmet made a convenient substrate. Lightweight, too. But if we're going to be making more of these, we can do a custom mold."

"How long to build the next one?" asked Eric. "Doc's going to want this one on the road as soon as we get it dialed in. Isn't that right, Doc?"

"Exactly so."

"Well—I didn't quite get it down to carry-on luggage size, but a couple of two-suiters is a lot better than what you've got here," said Ramirez. "Give me another two months and the next one will be a couple of overnight bags. I made some trade-offs to get this done quickly."

"We can live with the trade-offs," said Jonathan. "How long?"

"I can start the team on it this afternoon. We can do them in batches of three, I think. Four weeks, if I can stop myself from trying to improve the design. I already gave you 11 percent more sensitivity, by the way—selectable, so you have a compatibility mode. It's mostly in the quality of components, the cryo elements and the stage switches particularly. That dinosaur over there was designed before I got out of diapers. I could do better still—"

"There are other projects that need you first," said Jonathan. "Right now, though, I need you to shut up and devote your attention to the inside of the goggles, so I can start—"

"Aye, shutting up."

They discussed the other projects over a drive-through lunch eaten on the smokers' patio at the back of the Vector building. The bright sun seemed to have no warmth in it, but at least they enjoyed some privacy from the police car that had followed them there, and was now idling at the curb in front.

"The games were Alynn's livelihood, but her private passion was material like Ideation V—the experience of being," Jonathan said between bites. "I want to find a way to bring those programs to the right audience. But I also want to find a way to go further. What I want you to focus on now is closing the loop—getting data to flow in the other direction."

"You want to be able to record a thought out of one person's head and play it back in someone else's?"

"More or less, yes."

"This goes beyond what we'd talked about before."

"Yes. Not game-to-gamer. Mind-to-mind."

Ramirez frowned. "Practicalities aside, aren't we moving into a touchy area, Dr. Briggs? Folks tend to feel really personal about their heads. Protective. I'm surprised more people don't balk at letting you listen inside their skulls. Letting you talk at them from inside—"

"No, you don't understand what the goal is."

"The goal is wireheading, without the wires. Isn't it? Ultimate VR. What did I miss?"

"Something that Alynn and I both believed—both believe—about evil."

"Which is—"

"That it begins with a failure of empathy. I'd go so far as to say that's the definition of evil. Greater and lesser degrees of sociopathy, allowing us to discount the suffering we cause."

"Well—maybe. I don't doubt that Alynn believed that, anyway."

"So what if we could give a person even a few seconds of experience being someone else? What if we could get past the limitations of language, of the senses, and connect two consciousnesses directly? How could you deny the humanity of the other then? That would be an incredible legacy for Alynn."

"Until someone evil figured out how to use it for mind control, or whatever. Anyway, I'm dubious," said Ramirez. "What I did for you the first time is build an antenna for listening to signals we already knew the brain was throwing off. But I can't build one to transmit to the brain unless the brain's already equipped with a receiver."

"Who's to say it isn't? Telepathy, precognition, channeling, twin communication, kin communication—unless you think that everyone who reports extrasensory experiences is a fool or a rogue—"

"I know that Alynn believed in some of that, too," Ramirez said. He gnawed thoughtfully on a steak fry. "I've been thinkng in terms of a crystal radio. But you want global digital wireless broadband."

"Yes, I do. By the way, did you do any shock testing of the portable?"

"Not formally. I knocked it off a stool once."

"Well, I expect to give it a good workout, courtesy of the airline baggage handlers' union," Jonathan said. "Don't be surprised if you get a service call from Tampa, or Tempe."

"I'll put together a parts kit and a scramble bag. How are we doing on money?"

"Don't ask," said Jonathan, crumpling his trash into a ball. "And don't take any calls from Hillerman-Steuben-Welch."

* * *

The Boeing 777 shuddered underneath Jonathan as the Fowler flaps extended and bit into the air. He glanced out the window and saw that the patchwork quilt of fields and pastures beneath them was almost completely obscured by snow. The scene was strangely monochromatic, as though all the color had been stolen from the earth by the overhanging clouds.

As the plane continued its descent into Denver, Jonathan resumed keying. I feel bad about lying to Tommy. In all probability, he could have dealt with the truth and would have worked just as hard on the problem. He's the only one who's never looked at me with that mixture of pity and disapproval that sets my teeth on edge. He would have told me what he thought, but he would have left the choice in my hands.

But, still, I can't forget that I do this in defiance of custom and belief, in defiance of common sense and received wisdom. I would be accused of selfishness at best, insanity at worst. I can afford no confidants. I can count on no allies. I can't change the mind of a skeptic. Nor do I care to be pressed on my own doubts.

That which remains to be done must be done for other reasons, good and sufficient to themselves. Even the urgency must have its own explanation. Let them think I fear arrest, the dismantling of my career. I hold the real reason safe in my heart, and I will never let her go.

David Helms and Stephanie Oroz had done sterling advance work in laying out the itinerary. In Denver, Jonathan packed twenty-two sessions into three days, including two second cousins and a best friend from high school. Portland and Vancouver were similarly intense, with only a single missed appointment.

By the time he left Vancouver, Jonathan had constructed a practiced and polished ritual, down to how his bag was packed and how much he unpacked at each new stop. Every night he uploaded the new matrices, and every morning he reviewed the analysis over breakfast. He fast became a connoisseur of omelets and sausages, and graded restaurants by the size of the orange juice glass.

Winnipeg was only a two-day stop, but while there Jonathan picked up an elderly aunt and the entire roster of residents at her assisted-living center. He was amused to learn that they'd turned down the "sitting fees" Helms was offering, holding out instead for some top-of-the-line VR gear and a library of Arcadia gameworlds.

Crossing back into the United States, Jonathan logged over fifty matrices in four sixteen-hour days in Minneapolis. The focus there was on infants and toddlers, since Subject #041 had drowned in a Mississippi boating accident three years earlier. Stops in St. Louis and Indianapolis tallied more of Jonathan's kin, including a favorite first cousin he hadn't seen for more years than he had realized.

The portable scanner and the schedule broke down in Louisville, Jonathan's jumping-off point for a baby crawl through thinly populated Kentucky cave country near Mammoth. He lost a day waiting for Tommy Ramirez, and most of another day while repairs were made. Banished from the hotel room as a nuisance, he spent the hours walking the 400-million-year-old fossil beds at the Falls of the Ohio, contemplating time and change and the mystery of extinction and survival.

By the time Tommy was done, Helms and Oroz had miraculously managed to reschedule all but three of Jonathan's cave country appointments. The rented Toyota's MapMaster navigator guided him flawlessly up and down winding two-lane asphalt ribbons into half a dozen one-stoplight towns, and onto farms so isolated in the hills that a hard look from the driver of another car could make him hyperaware of the color of his skin. There wasn't time to go into Mammoth Cave itself—that was a casualty of the rescheduling, and Jonathan promised himself and Alynn that he would come back.

He gave up the car in Nashville, his jumping-off point to Texas and the South. There were five former students in Dallas to be brought into the longitudinal studies, plus another first cousin in Fort Worth and a retirement home in Mesquite. Mobile, Jacksonville, and Miami flashed by, ritual devolving into the numbness endemic to touring. He could see the road glaze in his own eyes in the motel mirrors.

The scanner broke down again in Atlanta, and Jonathan looked forward to the break that promised. But just four hours later, he found himself accepting custody of a new portable scanner from Tommy Ramirez at Hartsfield Airport—its polished aluminum case an inch or two smaller, a pound or three lighter, and bearing a smart Vector logo and the sky-blue numerals 03.

"Second of the new batch," he said. "Eric's already put the first one in the field with the drones—I mean, the undergrads. We'll have six more of these finished by the first of the year. You're gonna need to line up some more people, Dr. Briggs."

A wave of unexpected emotion—perhaps it was weariness intersecting with gratitude—made it an effort to say "Thank you" without his voice breaking.

"My pleasure. I've got a return flight to catch," Ramirez said, jerking his thumb toward the gate. "Be sure to watch the tutorial when you start her up—Eric suggested a few changes to the interface, some training wheels for novice operators."

Then he was gone, and Jonathan rode the MARTA South Line back downtown alone, the scanner cradled on his lap. The bustle at the airport had hit him like an assault, and it continued on the train. It was more than the energy and relentless Brownian motion of the crowds and the traffic. It was more than the holiday decorations mocking him with their commercialized cheer. It was doubt slipping past his defenses and attacking his resolve.

So many people, he thought, looking out at the city. How do we ever find each other, even alive? How many chance encounters never quite happen? How many soul mates never meet? How much love and magic do we miss out on just because we're looking the wrong way, or in the wrong place, or at the wrong time, or simply forget what we should be looking for? Even if she does come back, how many years will it take to find her? How do I beat the odds? How the hell do I rig the game?

One of the pleasant surprises during the odyssey from Denver to Atlanta was how few times the subject of Alynn's murder had come up. Even though he was using his own name, by and large Jonathan went unrecognized. Only once was he greeted with such suspicion that a door closed in his face. Only twice—both in Winnipeg—was he called on to defend himself before a session could go forward. Whether it meant that he had overestimated the reach of Stacey Reed's media campaign or the attention span of the audience, he did not know. Jonathan had been happy to credit it to good advance work and not think about it further.

But by the time he finished the Atlanta schedule, it

was clear it was not going to be that way in Columbus. The first warning sign was a trickle of cancellations by the adult subjects, most of whom were relatives or former friends of Alynn's. Then the dam broke, with a one-day flood of cancellations from the parents of the infant subjects.

"We've had some interference," Stephanie Oroz explained apologetically. "Apparently someone on the list got in touch with Mrs. Reed—maybe innocently, I don't know. But she went right to work undermining us. She got on the phone asking people not to cooperate. And she worked her media contacts, and got herself on the local news again yesterday."

"To warn the city that a murderer was coming to town."

"Something like that," said Stephanie. "What do you want me to do? I don't think I can turn this around quickly, if at all. I could get one of the undergrads down there for Saturday, but there really isn't enough of a schedule left to make it worthwhile."

"Skip it," said Jonathan. "I'll go straight to Philadelphia. Or is that buggered, too?"

"Nothing so far."

"Okay. Don't reschedule anything. I'm going to take a couple of personal days there, catch my breath, see a few things."

Philadelphia was a city Jonathan had always felt he should know better. His mother, Ellen Lee Mercer, had grown up there, in a hundred-year-old house in Conshohocken. She had met her husband-to-be, Julian Briggs, there while a student at Drexel.

And her family was still there. The Mercers were throwbacks to the last century, an unusually cohesive family, and several of his mother's closest kin still made their homes in the north suburbs. Half a dozen others were scattered from Allentown to Absecon, still safely within an hour's drive of Jonathan's one living grandparent, Beverly Ann Barnes-Mercer.

It was almost as though they did not dare to roam farther. Formidable as she was traditional, Beverly Ann was the family's gravitational center, the hostess of holiday meals, the organizer of family reunions, the enforcer of etiquette, and the arbiter of disputes.

He had scheduled Philadelphia so he could map those relatives, ostensibly for the kinship study. But they were largely strangers. Aside from one barely re-membered summer visit when he was a preschooler and two weekend reunions as a teen, his family had kept its distance. He was well into his twenties before he understood why. As the only daughter, Ellen Lee's sole defense against being programmed to succeed Beverly Ann was to leave. Only after an heir apparent had emerged from the ranks of the daughters-in-law was it safe to return.

But by that time, Jonathan and Ellen's family were firmly and happily established in Julian's home city of Toronto, which Ellen had often pronounced the most civilized large city on the continent. They welcomed guests, but rarely traveled southward themselves. The maternal relatives Jonathan knew best were the ones he had seen in his own living room, at the family table— Beverly Ann and Grandpa (who died when Jonathan was eleven), bawdy Aunt Ann, funny cousin Carl.

Jonathan spent his days of liberty acquainting him-self with some of the strangely named places that were part of Beverly Ann's stories—the Schuylkill River, Manayunk, Elfreth's Alley, the Main Line. He even braved the cold to visit Grandpa Mercer's favorite landmarks: the ancient battleship *New Jersey* on the Camden side of the river, and the even older cruiser *Olympia* on the Philadelphia side. The name Benjamin

Mercer appeared high on the donor plaques of both ships.

The nostalgia for old battles was largely lost on Jonathan, but the connection across time was not. Did you care enough about this place for it to draw you back, Grandpa? he thought, fingering the bronze casting about the battleship. Have you dragged your parents here, joined the youth volunteers? Can you tell me where Alynn's special places are? Or mine?

His mind was still occupied by questions of what changes, and what endures, when he reached his first appointment the next morning. It was supposed to be with the four assorted cousins of the Thomas Mercer family. He was completely unprepared to have the door opened by his mother, or to see Beverly Ann standing behind her, looking on possessively as though the moment was her creation.

"Jonathan," his mother said, inviting him into a hug. "I'm so sorry about Alynn." Those words were whispered at his ear, where he found he had no defenses at all. Clinging to her, he cried for twenty minutes.

Twenty minutes after that, he was looking for a way to escape.

"Beverly Ann tells me that you're trying to see all of the family while you're here, for this project of yours," his mother said when they'd gained the privacy of a bedroom. "She thinks the sensible thing would be to set you up at the house in Conshohocken, and have the family come to you. Otherwise, you'll be wasting half your time driving."

"I have a schedule to keep to, Mom. People are expecting me."

"People will understand. Beverly Ann will make the arrangements."

"I don't want her to." He moved away. "Why did you come down here?"

"I've been on the verge of coming to Ann Arbor for months," she said. "I'd given up hope of getting you to come to Toronto. Jonathan—when you're hurting, it's all right to lean on family."

"That's the last thing I want right now."

"Why?"

"Because I don't want to feel better. I need—all of it— to get through the things I need to do. I can't afford—" He sighed. "I can't let myself be taken care of. I can't deal with people's—sympathy. With pity. I can't start feeling sorry for myself. I can't start feeling—normal."

"Jonathan," she said, making the single word a tender reproach. "You can't stay in a perpetual state of mourning."

"I can do anything I have to to keep her in sight." His tone was angrier than he had intended, and he hastened to fill the silence. "Is Dad here?"

"No. This is a women's intervention." She smiled tolerantly at him. "Did you think we don't talk about you, just because you wouldn't talk to us?" She hesitated, then added, "Is any of what we see in the news true?"

"Almost nothing after the first week."

"I can't imagine everything you're dealing with," she said. "Do you have anyone there you can talk to?"

"I'm getting help," he said, and flashed what he hoped was a convincing smile to sell the lie. "No shortage of headshrinkers in the building, after all."

"So I suppose you really don't need any well-meaning amateurs meddling and muddling things," she said, and squeezed his hand. "What do you need me to do?"

"Don't crowd me."

"Practical terms, dear."

"Talk to Beverly Ann for me. Tell her this isn't going to fly. Get her to leave me alone. I just want to do my work and go. I'm not about to deal with a houseful of relatives who're trying to distract me and undermine me—"

"No one wants anything but good for you. You have to know that," she said. "Can I offer Beverly Ann one big family dinner? Could you deal with that?"

"At the end," he said. "When the work is done. You could both sit for me today."

"This is something you're doing for her, isn't it?"

"For both of us. It's important."

"All right," she said, standing. "I'll talk to Beverly Ann. Can I say one more mother-thing first?"

"One."

"I know you loved Alynn. But if you're not careful, you're going to have her photo on your desk the rest of your life." She leaned forward and kissed his cheek. "The world is always full of possibilities. Promise you'll call me if you find yourself having trouble seeing them."

"I will."

His mother was as good as her word. By late afternoon, the sittings for Beverly Ann, his mother, and the Thomas Mercers were completed, and dinner was on for the following Saturday.

On Friday, with all the matrices he had come for safely in hand, Jonathan boarded a plane for Ann Arbor. He made his apologies to Beverly Ann by voice mail, blaming a crisis at the lab that demanded his immediate attention.

As though invoking the crisis had invited it, within twelve hours of his plane touching down in Michigan, it was even true.

* * *

The Cottage Inn was less than half-full, which wasn't nearly enough to mask the loud, sharp, and angry voices arising from the conversation at Jonathan and Eric's booth.

"Frozen?" Jonathan stared disbelievingly at Eric. "My discretionary account's frozen? What the hell gives them the right—"

"The Human Subjects Committee does. I tried to make inquiries," he said. "I didn't get many answers. But it seems we've been reported to the committee for irregularities in our recruitment and payment of human subjects, and violations of subjects' privacy. We've been shut down pending a review of our protocol and procedures. You have to appear before the committee at their January 5 meeting."

"Of all the fucking—*what* irregularities?"

"You have to admit you've been doing a certain amount of improvising. And we've gone way outside our original protocol. You ought to pull it up and read it. I'm sure they have. We should have gone back to them this summer."

"No one's been harmed. No one's been coerced—"

"It's Gray Booklet stuff they're worried about. A lot of NIH money comes in here—"

"We're not spending NIH money—we're spending Arcadia money."

"It doesn't matter, Doc, and you know it," Eric said curtly. "Did we run all our recruitment material through the Institutional Review Board for approval? Did we pay everyone the same? *I* don't know. You turned all that over to a goddamned travel agent. Did she know the rules? What about Helms—if there've been patient privacy violations, it has to be him."

"They knew what I asked them to do," said Jonathan.

"Okay—so did *you* know the rules?"

"Why are you taking their side? Why are you angry with me?"

Their plates arrived then, though Eric pushed his away as soon as the waitress had left. "Because it was fucking embarrassing, and it wasn't my fault. Because we can't even wind the project down with some measure of dignity, on account of the sheriff's sale signs and the repo men."

"We're not winding down. And they can't keep our money forever."

"Turns out they can. Because it isn't actually our money, and the provost's promises to the donor only extend so far. Our account manager told me, 'Kiss it good-bye.' Apparently when Human Subjects freezes funding, they're already pretty sure of their facts. She called it a 'death penalty' case."

"Well—I don't know that we had very much left for them to freeze," Jonathan said after a moment's thoughtful chewing. "And we're about to lose the drones anyway—when does the term end?"

"Yesterday."

"Oh. How tough was my final?"

"A gimmee. I thought we owed them."

"I suppose we did. So—we were going to be shorthanded anyway—"

"We've been shorthanded. We're going to be no-handed."

"—and the holidays would make it impossible to get anyone new in. So let's just accept that we're going to be down for a while and not lose any sleep over the games the university is playing. I can defend everything we've done. I'll make this problem go away. Are you going anywhere for Christmas?"

"Actually, the freeze isn't the big problem," Eric said, and handed Jonathan a white envelope. "This was in my box this morning. I thought it was some kind of practical joke—see, it wasn't mailed. But I called and checked. It's real."

Jonathan unfolded the single-page letter. "Goddamn it all. They rejected us again. Without a single word about why."

"Actually, Doc, someone gave us three thousand words about why." He handed Jonathan a thin stapled packet of paper. "This was with the letter. I guess it wouldn't be a complete surprise if Clement Harris has a sycophant somewhere on the staff. Whoever it is didn't know you were back, so they delivered it to me. Makes things pretty clear."

Inside the envelope was a prepublication galley for a guest editorial due to appear, according to the footer, in the next release of the British quarterly *Journal of Neurometric Studies*. The author was Dr. Clement Harris. The title, "Mysterians At The Door."

Jonathan pushed his own plate back and read it.

In essence, it was a three-thousand-word version of Harris's terse dismissal outside the Dow Auditorium. Without ever mentioning any particular target by name, Harris managed to thoroughly savage the matrix research as part of "the creeping infection of egotism and mysticism against which neuroscience must be regularly immunized."

Never one to limit himself to a single metaphor, Harris—writing at his passionate, eloquent, and arrogant best—likened the "soul-hunters" to "gypsy barbarians at science's gate, dressed in the rags of Freudian dogmatism and wearing the blinders of Christian dualism."

They appear unarmed, but they are fully capable of once again poisoning the well of progress, he had written. *Befriended by the philosophers and psychologists whose vocations are threatened by the empire of the empirical, they seek to sell us the shabby old myths of*

*our grandfathers, wrapped in the bright, fragile paper
of a new paradigm.*

*Earnest though they may be, and innocent though
they may be to how they are being used, the price of
kindness is too high—the gates must remain barred to
the mysterians. For should we drop our guard, we
would find ourselves enslaved again, forced to bow
and pray to the graven images of an inscrutable black
box and a transcendent soul. And, so long as we wore
those chains, we would be blinded, like our captors, to
the subtle wonders and secrets of evolution's most elegant creation—the scrutable human brain.*

With a wan smile, Jonathan handed the editorial
back to Eric. "He's good," he said, shrugging. "You
have to give him that."

"Why aren't you upset? This destroys us. Am I
wrong, or am I wrong? Where can we go from here?"

"Why does it destroy us? I don't see that it matters.
I didn't find my name in there, or yours. I'm not important enough to criticize by name, obviously."

"It doesn't matter. No one is going to take us seriously."

"And that changes the status quo how? The people
who matter to us don't read *Journal of Neurometric
Studies.* The people who do read it already know what
they think—even if they don't know how." He smiled
at his own joke.

Eric would not be dismissed that easily. "Look,
maybe the person who delivered that to us wasn't a
friend of Harris's after all. Maybe it was a friend of
ours—someone who wanted to warn us we'd been
chosen to get a pie in the face."

"Contrarily, it could have been someone who
couldn't wait to throw it."

"But either way, Doc, he gave us a chance to get in
a shot or two ourselves."

"Using what for ammunition? Don't you think that one of the reasons Harris did this is he knew we couldn't fight back?" Jonathan shook his head. "I don't know why I let you convince me we had a chance to get a paper accepted. Harris didn't need to be on the review committee to squelch it."

"All the more reason to do something about him."

"Do? There's nothing to do."

"We have to fight back somehow."

"No, we don't," said Jonathan sharply, getting up from his chair. "What we have to do is find another matrix match. Not get caught up in a shouting match with Harris. Which we can't win."

"If we get heard, we win."

"Wrong. Say we write a letter to *JNS* calling Harris a constipated old twit with fossilization of the forebrain, and by some mistake *JNS* actually publishes it. What does that do for us, except identify us as the barbarians he had in mind?"

Eric's frown and glower telegraphed his growing impatience. "That's not what I was talking about—"

"You want something to lift spirits around here?" asked Jonathan, folding his arms across his chest. "Forget Harris. Forget *JNS*. Bring me another match. Nothing else matters. Nothing else can get us where we need to go. Find another match, and we can all have the last laugh."

"How?" Eric demanded, throwing his arms wide in frustration. "I don't get it. What will another match do for us? Whom do you think that will magically convince? How does that put us back in the university's good graces?"

They glared at each other for a long moment, until Jonathan reached for the bill, scanned a payment and a generous tip, then started to climb out of the booth. "In other words, do I know what I'm doing?" he said.

"Well, the answer is yes. I'm just waiting for the right time to do it. No one's going to get there before us."

"Be careful you don't lose me along the way," Eric muttered to Jonathan's back. "And, yeah, I'm going away for the holidays. Cope."

A longer and less emotionally charged conversation with Arthur Steuben the next morning persuaded Jonathan not to fight the Human Subjects Committee's death penalty.

"I'm not obliged to send them another dollar," said Steuben. "We made it a calendar-year gift to get you off to a fast start, and the last installment was paid in November. How much was still unspent?"

"About sixty-two thousand dollars—but there are several thousand dollars in promises against it."

Steuben grunted. "We were planning another gift for the new year, of course, but obviously that won't happen with your status there in question. We can wait on the outcome of your meeting. But perhaps a return to the status quo is not worth the fight?"

"What do you mean?"

"Simply that trying to funnel funds to you through an institution you're at war with is not what Alynn envisioned. Do you need them badly enough to take on what may be a series of running battles?"

"There are certain advantages."

"If I may suggest it, they may not be what they once were."

"Do you have an alternative arrangement in mind?"

"The obvious one, Dr. Briggs—keeping everything in the family. Does Arcadia-Vector have everything you need to become your primary research site? When it does, the foundation can work through them instead."

"All our analysis still goes through the lab. And they're holding our data hostage, too—no one will publish a paper which has Common Rule violations hanging over it."

"What do you think the university really wants most out of this? The sixty-two thousand dollars? To stop you from publishing your research? To reform you?"

"No," said Jonathan. "To remove me."

"Perhaps you can help each other, then."

Jonathan opted to open negotiations with direct action. Early on the morning after Christmas, when the Neuroscience Building was effectively deserted, he appeared at the lab with a small truck and two hired movers. In less than an hour, all the essential components of Molly—data cabinets, digital cables, and display consoles—were being unloaded at the side dock of the Arcadia-Vector building. The SQUID was left behind, rendered redundant by the new portable mappers.

Jonathan then returned to the lab alone to pack up his office and his team's personal effects, a process that consumed most of the day and all of his sense of triumph. Dr. Kosslyn made a brief appearance near the end and wished Jonathan well, which somehow only underlined the ignominy of being forced out of the department.

Eric Lutton returned three days after the new year, just in time for the Human Subjects Committee inquisition. But that meeting took place without Jonathan, for two hours before he was to appear, the dean's office verbally accepted his proposal that he withdraw from all research activity on campus, and that they pay the pending claims against his account and keep the change. All that went on paper, however, was a notation in the complaint report, "Allegations not sustained."

The next day, Eric accepted a job offer from

Arcadia-Vector. By the end of the week he had the analysis system and test databases operational in the back room of the Research Park Drive facility. But there were no new data to process yet, because all twelve portables were lined up neatly along one wall of the conference room, like giant aluminum dominoes. The drones were gone, making Jonathan's first task to rebuild a field staff.

Toward that end, the building now bore a low-key Arcadia logo on the rust-stained front wall, and there was a temp in the front office answering calls as "Arcadia-Vector." Jonathan got a rude education in how little could be had for work-study pay rates, and how much the kind of competence and diligence he had taken for granted cost once you crossed the campus boundary.

But by the end of January all twelve portables were in the field with new surveyors, organized in three operating units. One was dispatched to Columbus, and the other two roamed from city to city at the direction of Helms and Oroz. Nicknamed the "squid squads," they did not know that their itinerary was dictated by the geography of dead subjects, which by then numbered sixteen after a Christmas Eve fire in Benton Harbor.

The recruiting continued into February, for another twelve portables were nearing completion in the assembly room, where Tommy Ramirez supervised a technical team that now numbered five. But Jonathan was far from satisfied with the progress.

"It's not enough," he complained to Ramirez. "We need hundreds of these out there—thousands."

"I don't get it. What could you possibly learn that'd be worth that kind of investment? Arcadia isn't Microsoft, or even Sega. We publish for other people's hardware. We do playtesting. We don't reinvent the VR game interface."

"Why not?" Jonathan demanded. "What if I want the game to respond differently depending on what head it's sitting on? How much of one of these could you build into one of those?" he asked, pointing in turn to a portable mapper and a VR headset.

"At what price point? Gamers won't pay ten thousand dollars to indulge your curiosity. Well, not enough of them will."

"Let's worry about the cost later. Talk to me about the feasibility."

"Without superconduction for the sensors? Without reference alignment?" He picked up the VR headset and turned it over thoughtfully in his hands. "Basically, you want it to be able to sense whose head it's on? To read the same sort of information the silver boxes do, match it against a stored profile, and alter the game play?"

"Or maybe access a hidden message—what do you call them, an Easter egg."

"It'd have to be one hell of an Easter egg to get people to buy thousands of 'em," Ramirez said dubiously.

Would something like, "I can tell you who you were in your previous life" do? "Let me worry about that," said Jonathan. "You figure out what can be done."

"I might have to rent some neurons for this one," Ramirez said. His expression confessed his lingering skepticism.

"Is there any reason to think I'd object?"

"Well—I thought we were in business. Profit and loss, that sort of thing."

"Your paychecks haven't started bouncing, have they?"

"No—"

"All right, then. Hire whatever neurons you need."

"What about the matrix player?"

"Didn't you say you wanted some live heads to test it on?" Jonathan asked. "Give what you have to Eric. He can line up the heads."

Since returning from his expedition with the suitcase scanner, Jonathan had enjoyed a respite from the police's heavy-handed attention.

At first he'd thought it had something to do with the holidays. When it continued into January, he wondered idly if Detective Anderson realized he was back. But, in the main, he tried not to think about it at all. Thinking about it was allowing Anderson to run a game on his head. And that, he realized, was the likeliest explanation for the reprieve—just another attempt to break him down, this time with uncertainty.

If he can get me jumping at shadows, wondering what he's up to, wondering when the knock is coming, he wins, Jonathan told Stuart. *If he can get me to act like a guilty man who has something to fear, he wins. He doesn't understand that my guilt comes from a place he can't touch. He doesn't understand that the pain I feel every day is worse than anything he can threaten me with.*

So he carried on with the work that he could trust to no one else, the preparations no one else could make. The rest of the time, he counted days and dollars, rode Tommy and Eric to the limit of what they would stand for, and studied each day's new matrix maps in long sessions that kept him up past midnight. He adopted Satchel Paige's most famous epigram as his motto, pasting a copy across the top of Cassandra's main screen and endeavoring to keep sight of the underlying humor: Don't look back, somethin' might be gaining on you.

But he never deceived himself with hope that it was over, that Anderson had reconsidered his theory of the crime, much less given up. So it was with weary resignation rather than surprise that Jonathan listened to an angry rant from one of the new surveyors, Darya Tapley.

"I did not take this job to be hassled by the police in front of my neighbors. I did not take this job to be pulled over and interrogated on the highway while my son was waiting to be picked up from day care. No, I will not sit down. I did not take this job to have sniffers watching my every keystroke online. And I certainly did not take this job because I wanted to work for a murder suspect. That woman, Miz Oroz, should have told me who she was fronting for. I had no idea a criminal owned this company. I have a child and a nice home and I am not going to get myself mixed up in something unsavory. Why are you interested in those children, anyway? Mind control? Nondisclosure clause be damned, I have half a mind to go down and tell the police everything I know. I am not going to keep secrets for a criminal enterprise—"

"Two weeks severance, a month's bridge insurance, letter of recommendation with Stephanie's signature on it."

She looked down her nose at him. "Three weeks severance. And you pay my speeding ticket."

"All right. But you turn your kit in now."

"Fine by me," she said haughtily. "I want it out of my car before the police stop me again."

When she started toward the door, he called after her, "Did they look inside the cases?"

"I told them it was none of their business," Darya said with pride. "Just your luck my taillights work and

I had my seat belt buckled and my phone didn't ring. They were very interested in those cases."

By the end of the week, Jonathan had lost two more new surveyors thanks to police harrassment, and that was not the worst of it. Brent Packard was pulled over by Ann Arbor police on the pretext of failing to signal far enough before a turn. Thinking himself in the clear and invited to think cooperation would let him escape a ticket, he agreed to let the police search his RoadStar for "guns, drugs, or contraband." When they found the five-inch double-edged sheath knife in his road emergency box, Packard was promptly arrested for a concealed-weapons violation.

The weapons charge, like the traffic stop itself, was pure pretext, and it was dropped shortly after the bulldog defense lawyer hired by Arcadia descended on the district attorney's office. But for that forty-eight hours, Packard's car and everything in it was in police custody. When the portable was finally returned to their hands, both cases rattled when moved—their contents had been disassembled "with a crowbar," in Tommy Ramirez's words.

"Did they bother to give any kind of explanation?" he demanded indignantly of Jonathan.

"Lawyer says they performed an 'inventory search' for other concealed weapons."

Ramirez held up the optical drive, its cables dangling. "What did they think was hidden in here?"

"Can you tell if the drive was read—copied?"

"I think we should just assume it was. Nothing to prevent it, really, when they can do this. Not that anything that was on the system is of any goddamned use to them. Did you go out of your way to piss them off, Dr. Briggs?"

"I didn't have to," he said, and gestured at the cases. "Get it fixed, will you? Brent quit, but Stephanie will find someone else. And we'll hire them a car and driver, I guess."

By the end of the week, everyone on the payroll at Vector had heard from the Ann Arbor police and from Stacey Reed. Most received two mailings at their personal accounts, one the CrimeStoppers appeal, the other from something called Mothers United for Justice. Together they as much as said, "Do you realize what kind of man you're working for?" But the capper for the week was the video mail Jonathan himself received from Detective Anderson.

"Dr. Briggs, this is Agent Gallin of the Federal Bureau of Investigation's Technical Services Division," Anderson said, indicating the man sitting beside him. "He's been providing us with some assistance on the Alynn Reed case. I wonder if you could help us understand this conversation."

The audio file that followed carried a streaming time stamp as a guarantee it had not been edited. But Jonathan did not have any trouble remembering it, for it came from a recent call between himself and David Helms.

"Got some news for you tonight," said Helms. "Two more of your subjects are dead."

"What was it this time?"

"Light plane crash near Manistee. Went down in a snow squall."

"Fire?"

"No, they survived the crash. Froze before they were found. You'll want the usual profile?"

"Yes, please."

"Getting close to statistical average on your sample now. A little more bad luck and you'll be right there."

"It isn't going to help."

"No? You mind me asking why not?"

"I don't mind you asking. I just can't talk about it."

"All right. I don't need to know to do my job. It's just hard not to wonder, considering."

"What do you think death is, Mr. Helms?"

"I believe dead is dead. Just you and the maggots."

"They say if you die a hard death, your spirit lingers nearby. You believe that, Mr. Helms?"

"Sounds like wishful thinking to me. Are you a ghost-hunter, Dr. Briggs? Is that what this is about?"

"No. But don't you think everyone deserves a second chance?"

"No, sir. I've met too many people who didn't deserve their first one. Should I call off the death watch?"

"No. Maybe I'm wrong about something. We may need them all to die. It may take a potful of bad luck to purchase a little good luck."

The recording ended there.

Jonathan had no intention of explaining anything to Detective Anderson, and he doubted Anderson had expected any different. But the detective's message came through clearly nevertheless. The police were not going away. They were still watching, still listening— listening now with the help of the FBI. And they were curious now about matters where Jonathan could not tolerate curiosity.

I should pack everything up and move it somewhere else. Take it across the border. I'd do that, if I was smart. I'd do that if I could make myself leave the only place I ever knew with her.

Stuart, I'm afraid we're running out of time.

The final schedule for the Berkeley conference was released while Jonathan was in Toronto, mapping or remapping Julian Briggs and his side of the family. Eric wordlessly handed Jonathan the printout on meeting his return flight at Detroit Metro. By the time they got back to Phoenix Drive, Jonathan understood why. Four teams from Clement Harris's lab were listed—two of them presenting unpublished papers on "dynamic neural imaging" and "visualization of personality types."

For the next half hour, Jonathan raged from one end of the building to the other. "The son of a bitch is poaching off us," he thundered. "He's taken everything we're doing and given it to his people—while cutting us off at the knees so they can catch up. And with their resources, they're probably ahead of us now."

"They're not headed in the same direction," Eric suggested.

"The hell they aren't. 'Visualization of personality types'? They're going to come to the podium with our results and tell the world they mean something else. They're going to get it wrong, but they're going to go first, and they're going to be on the big stage with Dr. Clement Walter Harris standing behind them. Damn him! He didn't come down to our lab because he didn't need to. His spies had already been there."

"Spies, Doc?"

By then, they were standing in the conference room, which doubled as a lunchroom. Jonathan riffled impatiently through the depleted honor box of snacks as he answered. "How many conference attendees did we run through? They saw everything. They asked questions. We didn't try to keep any secrets. We didn't worry about who they might talk to. We wanted to win their approval, remember? Son of a bitch—"

"There's nothing to be done about it now."

"No, there isn't, because I had a major outbreak of the stupids back then. I let Elizabeth spook me into worrying about departmental politics. I should have been thinking bigger." Jonathan pounded his clenched fist on the nearest wall. "I handed it all to Harris on a platter."

"It was the best play we had at that point."

Jonathan glowered at Eric. "Don't handle me. I don't want to be placated."

"All right. What do you want? Should I break something? Curse in Reverse Polish Notation? Buy a vowel?"

"How about going back to work? How about finding some way to contribute?"

"I'd love to," said Eric. "But I can only bang my head against the wall so many times. Maybe it's time for us to take a lesson from Harris."

"What lesson can you learn from a claim jumper?"

"Sometimes you can learn where the gold really is. We sure as hell haven't found it."

Jonathan's gaze narrowed. "Did something happen while I was gone?"

"Are you sure you want to know?"

"Why the hell would I ask if I didn't? You're trying to handle me again. Treat me like an adult for once."

"All right. This thing you had Tommy drop on me—the matrix player? It's crap. It's a dead end. I can't make it work."

"Why not? The principle is sound. Energy transfers are reversible," Jonathan said. "Not perfectly, but at least partially. You can wire up a speaker as a microphone. You can use an electric motor as a generator."

"This is more like trying to stuff the electrons back into a television tube. The whole idea is wacky. The brain just isn't listening. There's zero perception on playback."

"At what playback level? What's the measured sensitivity?"

"I told you—zero. I could pump enough power into Tommy's headset to cook a brain and it won't make a bit a difference. Jonathan—I'm sorry. It's useless. I can't hear your recording, and you can't hear mine."

"What about your own? Can you hear your own?"

"What the hell good would that be?"

"What good is a diary?"

Eric squinted at Jonathan quizzically. "You want to use it on Brent Winston? With Dugan Beckett's vector matrix?"

"There's no point in that until Winston's older. A lot older. You really didn't test anyone with their own recording?"

"What Tommy conveyed to me was that the whole point of the project is social uplift by means of ultimate VR—or something like that. So I tested for transmission A-to-B, not A-to-A."

"The whole point is finding out what works. We can figure out what use we can make of it later. Let's go to the lab—you can try it out on my head."

A few minutes later, Jonathan was sitting beside the test console, waiting impatiently while Eric adjusted the straps on the heavy prototype playback headpiece. "I wouldn't get my hopes up," Eric said. "I did bring in two sets of our local twins when the other pairings didn't work out."

"And that wasn't any better?"

"Only because the twins I brought in are better-looking than the rest of the folks around here. Otherwise, same results." Eric straightened and frowned. "That looks good. Try not to move around too much. Which of your mappings do you want me to use?"

"Better that you don't tell me."

"In that case—" Eric turned Jonathan's chair until it faced away from the console.

"Don't tell me when you start, either. I have the thing memorized. I don't want to fool myself."

Jonathan released a long sigh's worth of held breath, and tried to relax into the cushions. He closed his eyes and made a futile effort to clear his mind.

Just a touch. Just a whisper, an echo of memory, a twinge of emotion pressing in out of nowhere. Let me feel what I felt, know what I thought, let go of the present and get lost in the past. Just one little glimmer of hope—

"Doc? I'm going to try a different mapping."

"What's your hurry?"

Eric sighed. "I restarted the replay four times already."

"Let it play to the end next time."

"What makes you think if 'cat' and 'tree' aren't coming through, Verdi and Kierkegaard will?"

"Just do what I say, damn it. Start it again and let it play."

"Fine. Since this isn't science anyway, any objection to me slipping out for a Coke?"

"Go. I don't need you."

What he wanted was silence, and then the dream. He could not remember the last time it had come to him. He could barely remember the dream itself—only that he had believed in it, and that belief had changed the course of his life. But nothing came—neither the silence nor the vision.

After a few minutes, Eric returned. Wordlessly, he settled in a chair across the room and quietly sipped at a plastic bottle. His presence was nevertheless a ticking clock in Jonathan's awareness, counting down to humiliation and recantation.

"Can we try my other maps?"

"Sure," Eric said. He set his bottle aside to come briefly to the control console, then returned to his chair.

But it was the same with each in turn—not a whisper, not an echo, not a touch, not a glimmer of promise. All he heard were his own anxious and restless thoughts, growing darker and more bitterly sorrowful with every passing minute.

There's a little piece of me locked in those swirling vectors, but there's no way to access the moment, the memories—no way to get back to what I was before Alynn was taken, no way to recapture the joy, no way to freshen the memories. How long can I pretend that I can still feel her heat on the sheets, still catch her scent on her clothes—that I can remember any words that weren't recorded, any moment that wasn't photographed—

His mouth was so dry he had to work to summon enough moisture to speak. "Queue up her matrix."

"Alynn's? Oh, hell, Doc, why do you want to beat yourself up?"

"I have to know."

"You already know."

"Queue it up, damn it. Then leave me alone."

Eric rattled the empty bottle into a trash can, then went to the console once more. "Coming up now. Are you sure—"

"Yes. Just go." Jonathan sat forward in his chair, chin resting on folded hands, elbows resting on knees, rocking slightly as his unfocused gaze shifted peripatetically about the room. *Where are you, sweet? Come back to me.*

This time, he could not bear the silence for long. Before five minutes had passed, he ripped the headset off and threw it aside as he stood and turned to the console. Leaning forward, he reached out until his fingertips touched the glass face of the display. The swirls of color danced mockingly just out of reach.

I don't want all your secrets. I only wanted to see that day through your eyes, to know what you were

thinking when we met. I just need to know that I'm
not a fool to still be loving you, still be feeling this unbearable longing to be wherever you are.

Finally, the recording ended, and Jonathan numbly
shut the system down. He found Eric waiting nearby
in the corridor outside, sitting on the floor with a sheet
of digital paper balanced on his knee.

"Go home," Jonathan said hoarsely as he passed
him. "Tell them all to go home. It's over. We're done."

This time, Jonathan did not disappear into hermitage
at Huron Towers. Instead, he threw himself into an
eleven-day orgy of self-amusement as single-minded as
his workaholism. Starting early, finishing late, and
cheating his sleep in between, he looked a lot like a
man who would do anything to avoid being alone at
home.

He wandered the nearly deserted galleries of the
Detroit Institute of Arts to see its ninety-six
Rembrandts, and squeezed into the Soup Kitchen
Saloon to hear gritty blues and drink beer. He spent
two days taking in the Henry Ford Museum and another day watching gorillas at the Detroit Zoo. He fed
a pocketful of two-dollar coins into slot machines at
the MGM Grand casino, but found more entertainment with a pocketful of tokens and the antique arcade
games at Marvin's Marvelous Mechanical Museum.

When he bothered to eat at all, it was with a hedo-
nistic insistence on variety—Greektown, dim sum in
Windsor, fresh kielbasa in Hamtramck. At night, he
restlessly cruised the jazz clubs of Rivertown and
the fleshpits along 8 Mile Road, though he found only
the most superficial pleasure in each. He worked his
way through a checklist of local landmarks—Lili's 21,

the Magic Bag, the Blue Goose Inn, Lionel's—and the money flowed out like water.

But there was scant joy in any of it. It offered little more than distraction, and little enough of that. Still, he could not stop, even when he became aware of how empty it was.

At least he did not have to deal with his own notoriety. Whether it was his new short haircut (which revealed a scalp tattoo he had been concealing since he turned seventeen) or the public's short memories, not once was he confronted. Even the police seemed uninterested—if they were tracking him at all, they were now doing it unobtrusively, by technical means. He had glancing contact with three former students and one university staffer on four separate occasions, but none of those led to as much as a conversation.

The last place Jonathan expected to be accosted was the sterile lobby of the east tower at one in the morning. He was not drunk, but he was exhausted to the point of staggering, and he didn't notice the small woman sitting by the windows until she stood and called across the room to him.

"Johnny?"

Her voice was familiar enough to stop him, but not familiar enough to instantly know as friend or enemy. He was still rummaging his memory as he turned toward her.

"Johnny?" she repeated, advancing toward him.

He fell back a step, squinting at her. "I know you—"

"Quite well, if perhaps not wisely," she said. "Starpath. I suppose I look rather different in my civvies," she added, gesturing at her business suit.

"Eleni. Yes, of course. But what—"

She closed the last few feet between them and went on tiptoes to kiss his cheek. "You smell like a wet-wood campfire. Cigar smoker?"

"Blues club that attracts them. What are you doing here?"

"I was leading a workshop in Royal Oak."

"On witchcraft?"

"Violin pedagogy," she said, smiling brightly. "Though there are witches in Royal Oak. But you meant what am I doing here, didn't you?"

"Not like that—"

"It's all right," she said. "I fly out in the morning. This was my only opportunity. One of your neighbors kindly let me in out of the cold."

"I didn't know I had any kind neighbors."

"Well—I didn't tell them you were the one I was waiting for."

"Oh. Have you been here all night?"

"Only since I gave up on you responding to my messages. A couple of hours."

"I haven't heard your messages—"

"So I chose to assume—kinder to my ego. Why don't you invite me up before either of us gets to the hard questions?"

In the elevator, Eleni took his arm with a light touch, reassuring rather than flirtatious. He remained uncomfortable, nevertheless, and the feeling grew stronger the closer they drew to the apartment. He was on the verge of changing his mind as they stood before the door. Then she said, "This was her place, wasn't it, Johnny."

"Yes."

"It still will be after I've gone. I won't disturb her energy."

"There isn't any of it left," he said sadly.

"Of course there is," she said. "Let's go talk."

They moved enough of the clutter to settle at opposite ends of the couch. Archimedes wounded Jonathan by appearing and making himself comfortable in

Eleni's lap, then nudging her hand with his head until she began to pet him.

"It's not a betrayal," she said, reading Jonathan's eyes. "He's just telling you that you're always in motion, never at rest."

"He's always impersonating other scientists," he said, then had to explain the joke. "But he's right. So—how did you find me?"

Eleni smiled tolerantly. "As tired as you are, you should really start with the question you most want to ask."

He nodded. "Okay. Why?"

"Because your pain stayed with me after Starpath. And because I want to know more about your work. I wanted to know if you succeeded."

"No. The truth is, I've failed completely." It was easier to say than he would have guessed.

"I gathered that much in the course of tracking you down."

"Then why bother to come see me at all? A waste of your time."

"Oh, no—just the contrary. What I heard the last few days made it mandatory. I was prepared to spend the night in the lobby, in the hope of catching you staggering in or out. I would have camped outside your door if the elevators weren't key-controlled."

"Why?"

"Because your failure so far doesn't mean you're wrong. And because the right answer matters."

"Not to the people who matter. They're not interested in even considering the possibility. They're not even listening."

"Are the people who came to your tree 'people who matter'? Because you became one of the stories of last year's gathering. I must have seen a dozen articles in the pagan press. And the dialogue is still going on, in the newsgroups and on the lists."

"I didn't know that," he said, then looked away and sighed. "But the neuroscience community hasn't been so receptive. I'm tired of throwing myself at locked doors."

"When was it any different for a paradigm-smasher? Who ever welcomed a revolution but the revolutionaries?"

"Well—I expect most revolutionaries know enough to lay in some ammunition before they pick a fight. I didn't."

"The other army will provide," she said. "The one essential is passion for the cause. What do you believe, Johnny?"

"I believe the universe doesn't care what we believe. I believe asking what someone believes is asking the wrong question."

"That sounds like the rationalization of someone who doesn't want to risk being wrong."

"It's the only way science works."

"I'm not asking science. I'm asking a man. Do you believe that the woman you love still exists? Or has her spark completely disappeared from the universe?"

He looked away. "You don't understand."

"What do you think I don't understand? You're looking for scientific proof of something you won't let yourself believe in any other way. But underneath that veneer of scientific rationalism, you're still a being of light. You're still connected to the living universe that created you. Why can't you trust what it tells you?"

"It doesn't matter without evidence," he said, feeling the anger rise. "What did you come here to do?"

"I wasn't sure. I think maybe to ask you if you know why you've quit."

"Quit? You don't have a clue what's happened to me—"

"What do you believe, Johnny? Do you even admit it to yourself?"

"I think you should leave."

"I think you should stop lying to yourself," she snapped back. "Because if you failed because you were wrong, and if being wrong didn't cost you something you wanted to believe, you wouldn't be angry at me right now. It would just be a neat idea that didn't pan out."

"Why does any of this matter to you?"

"Because I do believe. And when you admit that you do believe in something, then it becomes time to act." She stopped, as if reflecting on her own words. "Maybe that's it. Maybe it's that you're afraid that you're right. You think you've made your choice, but the choice still lies ahead of you. Being wrong rescues you from having to make it. So does quitting. But if you admit you believe, the decision is upon you— there's no reason to wait for proof."

"Science can't deliver proof. Just theory and evidence."

"You're hiding behind semantics. You already have your theory. Who is the evidence for? Who is it supposed to persuade? What is it supposed to justify?"

"I suppose you think you have answers to those questions."

"I'm not the one who's conflicted," she said, offering a gentle smile. "I already know you're right. I want you to find the evidence because I want it top center in the *New York Times*, instead of *phenomeNEWS* and the tabloids: 'Scientific Proof of Reincarnation: Souls Are Eternal.'"

"That's a lousy headline," Jonathan said. "And I wanted to see it somewhere even harder to ignore."

"To accomplish what?"

He sighed again. "That's a good question. And I don't think I want to answer it."

"You don't need to. It's only important that you know the answer," she said. "Besides, it isn't that difficult to guess. I'm the one entertaining fantasies about weaning the Western world off Christianity. Your goals are much more personal."

"Like seeing a certain apoplectic expression on Dr. Clement Harris's face as he stutters through a feeble rebuttal—"

"I was thinking more along the lines of not feeling foolish for what you believe. Or looking foolish for what you do."

The silence that followed admitted more than words could. "I should let you get to bed," she said finally, gently coaxing Archimedes off her lap.

"No—wait." Her hesitation created an opportunity for Archimedes to possessively return. "I don't really know which prospect worries me more—being right, or being wrong," Jonathan said finally. "If I'm right, I get a chance to be a first-class coward. If I'm wrong, I get a chance to be a first-class fool."

"I'm not sure what's stopping you from being both at once, right here in the present. What do you believe, Johnny? Why won't you let yourself say it?"

He met her challenging gaze with a strength that anticipated his words, and when he had voiced them he felt a calm clarity he had not known for weeks. "I believe I can find her."

"Do you think finding her in this life was an accident? Do you even think it was the first time?"

"That's what my mind tells me. But that isn't how it feels."

"So who is the evidence for?"

"I thought it was for me—the me that won't let

himself believe. To show him the way. But I want to leave the way marked."

"Is that what's keeping you?"

"I think it is. I really think it is." He cocked his head and smiled ruefully at her. "So I suppose I'm not finished after all."

"I'm glad to hear it," she said, answering with a pleased smile. "Can I tell you something about Alynn's energy?"

"I don't know what you could tell me—"

"You're carrying it all inside you. You're so afraid of losing touch with her that you've vacuumed every bit of it up from this place with your grief. That way you can keep it with you wherever you go. The problem is you've bottled it up in sadness and loneliness and loss, where it hurts to touch it. Let her out. Let her be part of you. Let knowing her keep changing you."

The sob that rose in his throat could not be held back. "I don't want to let go of any of it. There's so little as it is—"

"I never saw anyone make a leap forward without letting go of what's behind them," she said gently. "The choice is still in front of you."

She held him a time while he cried, tears that burned as though distilled to pure acid by the months they had been suppressed. Then she held him as he slept. Whether she slept at all herself he did not know; it seemed as though whenever he stirred, she was there with a whispered word or a light, reassuring touch.

Morning found them in a jumble on the floor beside the couch, glued together by damp clothing and weighed down by two coiled cats. The first thing Jonathan did after disentangling himself was throw open the curtains to admit the sunrise. The first words he said to Eleni were, "Thank you."

"I didn't do anything," she said. "But can I ask a favor anyway?"

He waved a hand. "Of course. You need a ride?"

"Make me part of it. Take my matrix."

"How much time do you have before your flight?"

She searched the room for a clock. "Two and a half hours."

"Tight. And the gear is all over at the plant—" he began, then caught himself. "But I was going over there first thing anyway. If we can get out of here in the next ten minutes—"

He was not at all surprised to find that Eleni's matrix was strong, clean, and deep. Neither was he at all sure who had taken whose measure that morning. But he did not dwell on it, for there was work to do. As her cab disappeared from the driveway, Jonathan reached for his phone and began trying to put the pieces back together.

Eric Lutton had left Ann Arbor, and Jonathan could not coax him into returning. In fact, Eric had left the academic environment completely, taking a position with corporate services giant PersonAll in Denver.

"Suspicion is a growth industry, Jonathan," he said in voice mail. "The big multinationals want to know everything the law will allow before they hire, promote, fire, or trust anyone. The psych-testing unit here has grown 30 percent a year three years running. Everything's out of the box new, including my supervisor—he's twenty-six, with a brand-new Ph.D. from Stanford.

"The truth is, Jonathan, I'm lucky to catch on here, and if I didn't know a couple of people here already, I probably wouldn't have gotten a chance. I should have left Ann Arbor in December. Sooner, really. I've got nothing to gain by coming back. I don't blame you, but I don't think I owe you, either. And I need this more than you need me.

"I'm still pulling for you, not least because I've got this big dead spot in the middle of my curriculum vitae. Feel free to rehabilitate your reputation anytime. It'd be nice to be able to be proud of those years.

"Be careful out there, Doc, and good luck."

At the other end of the spectrum, Tommy Ramirez had ignored the shutdown order and continued to work long hours on the augmented headset. "I'm a minority owner, remember? I figured you didn't mean me," he explained without looking up from his workbench. "Besides, it's a good enough idea that someone would want it—if you really intend to close down Arcadia, I can walk it across the street to Sony."

"I don't intend to close down Arcadia," Jonathan said. "I intend to keep it alive for another hundred years. Have you made any progress?"

"I think I've taken it as far as I can with available technology, assuming we're still looking at something simple enough for the consumer market—something you might eventually sell a few million of, instead of ten thousand."

"We're going to give them away, not sell them," said Jonathan. "With Arcadia's next release. With Alynn's Anteriors. How many points of correspondence can the headset map?"

"Twenty. Is it enough?"

"Show me."

Ramirez gestured toward where the prototype was resting near the end of the workbench. "Plug in," he said.

"What're you using for the reference signal?"

"I've got it online to the entire research database. You're going to have to cut it down to fit it into a game module, though. We don't need all the data, and wading through it just slows everything to a crawl."

"In other words, we need a classification system. Categories, not examples."

"Yeah. It'll probably take our system a few minutes to figure out who you are. A standalone V-deck would take half an hour."

The headset crackled to life, carrying Jonathan into V-space. It was a more or less standard design-and-test environment, with static wire-frame objects in a fractal landscape under a neutral sky matte. But the dynamic sprites were a towheaded boy and a tiger three times his height, and when they wandered near to each other snowballs would momentarily fill the air. The only sounds were the wet thumps of snowballs finding their marks.

A few seconds after the third donnybrook, the words THIS SPACE INTENTIONALLY LEFT BLANK appeared in the middle of virtual space. Jonathan read them aloud and asked, "Is that what it's supposed to say?"

"For you and about six hundred other people. Mine says 'Eat a cookie.' You can plug any message you want in there, or have it trigger any event in the playscript."

"And anyone who might be sharing the V-space with you?—"

"They won't see the text. You could have personal audio, too. It's routine, really—just not triggered the way we're doing it. But the playscript is shared."

Jonathan reached up and removed the headset, handling it as though it were fragile as crystal. "This personalization module could be inserted at any point, in any script?"

"Sure. Elementary cut and paste. The only thing hard about this was making the headset sensitive enough. I'd like to try it on a few more heads."

"How long will it take to put this in production?" Jonathan said, gently returning the headset to the workbench.

"There's probably three, four contract production companies on the Asian Rim that could do it in forty-five days. But 'how long' is the wrong question. You should be asking 'how much.' "

"I asked the question that matters to me," said Jonathan. "I don't suppose you know how many copies of Alynn's last game were sold?"

"Grand Hotel? It was a bit of a dog—maybe four hundred thousand legit, half again that many bootleg, twice that many pirated over Freenet. Hey, I just realized—the pirates are going to need headsets. Oh, they're gonna hate that—"

"I need someone to handle getting a manufacturer lined up—bids, contracts, specs, all that. Can you do it?"

"Me? No. But I know whose desk it belongs on, and I can take care of that."

"Thank you. What about production of the game itself?"

"First we have to finish it. Are you going to write all the add-ins yourself?"

"Is there a reason I shouldn't?"

Ramirez shrugged noncommittally. "The payoff has to be special enough to justify the dedicated hardware. If it isn't, it's just going to look like a lame attempt at copy-protection."

"It'll be special enough," said Jonathan.

"It wouldn't hurt to talk to some other designers. Maybe even pick the brains of Alynn's playtest group."

"Give me the name of someone who worked the way she worked—someone who saw things the way she did."

"Well—"

"Exactly. She left us one finished game, pieces of three others, and her high-art experientials. If they aren't special already, just as they are today, we're wasting our time."

"They are special. Because she was special."

"Which is why I'm not letting anyone else touch the scripts. I know what she would want. I've been thinking about this for months. I know what she would do. I know what she was trying to do. If I need help with the mechanics of it, I'll say so. But it's time to get it done. This has to take on a life of its own sometime, if it's to amount to anything. It needs to go on autopilot, and soon."

"You worried they still might arrest you?"

"I'm not worried," said Jonathan. "But they might do it anyway."

The director of Rosehill Memorial Gardens was a round-faced man with thinning blond hair and a dress shirt a half size too small for his stout neck. His handshake was firm but slightly clammy, his smile quick and tired. His hazel eyes had had all the sincere empathy wrung out of them over the years.

This is one of those jobs, Jonathan thought, that no one has written under their yearbook photo. Everyone ends up here by accident, not by design.

"Mr. Anderson," the director said. "How can we be of service?"

"That's what I'm here to find out," Jonathan said. "I would like to create a memorial for someone who was very dear to me. But I don't know if the rules will allow it."

"We allow a very wide variety of stones and markers at Rosehill, in the traditional style," the director said. "We mean to create a cemetery designed for human needs, rather than the needs of lawn mowers. Have you driven through?"

"It's not the marker that I'm concerned about. You see, there's no body to bury."

"Ashes, then?"

"No. No remains at all."

"Oh, that is tragic. How difficult for the family."

"Yes," said Jonathan. "And what we would like, then, is to fill a casket—I suppose it needn't even be a casket—with memorabilia, things which were special to the deceased, and have it interred. If that's even the right word."

"An empty-casket funeral—except rather less empty."

"Yes. Of course, since there are no remains involved, such a memorial could be created almost anywhere," Jonathan said. "It doesn't require a cemetery plot. It could be in my backyard."

"That's very true," the director said, warming to the job of selling. "But at the same time, interment in a well-managed cemetery offers a combination of permanence, atmosphere, tradition, and ritual which many families find extremely comforting. The site is protected, maintenance is provided, and access is guaranteed. Which is unlikely to be the case with a memorial on private land."

"True enough. And how could you ever sell your house, after you'd consecrated it that way?"

"Exactly. So—you want to know if there are any obstacles to creating your memorial here. The answer is, none at all. There are several cenotaphs already in Rosehill. We had two empty-casket interments last year."

"Can I presume that the empty casket is treated with the same respect accorded one with remains?"

"Of course, of course. We fully honor the symbolism of the event."

"Would you need to know the contents of the casket?"

"No, that's private." The director laughed uncomfortably. "As long as you aren't trying to bury the proceeds from a heist. The casket will go into the ground exactly as it reaches us."

"I just want to remember all her love and joy and beauty. She was a princess out of time. She should be laid among flowers and the things that were special to her."

"I can't imagine a finer tribute," said the director. "Shall we go out and look at the spaces available, and see if we can't find just the right setting for it?"

The Denver headquarters of Hillerman-Steuben-Welch were a marriage of old wood and new technology. While the firm had eighty-one employees, the suite had just four rooms—a data center (one corner of which doubled as reception), a teleconferencing room, and two executive offices. Most of the staff had never set foot inside the suite; they were full-time telecommuters.

Two hundred Brandberg existed only because the occasional need for face-to-face meetings had stubbornly outlived the need for ink signatures on paper, over-the-shoulder supervision, hot-breath-in-the-face recrimination, and even office romance. Such were the meetings when one man wished to take the measure of another, when matters of great delicacy needed to be discussed, when the assurance of privacy was more important than convenience. And all those considerations were in play as Jonathan sat down for his meeting with Arthur Steuben.

"I don't imagine I've endeared myself to you in the last year," Jonathan began. "You probably think I've been irresponsible, going so deeply into the principal."

Steuben wrinkled his nose. "It's not my place as trustee to sit in judgment. If Alynn had intended to tie your hands, she could have structured the trust very differently. I wrote it the way she wanted it."

Jonathan nodded slowly. "Do you think I killed her, Mr. Steuben?"

"I think that highly unlikely. But that, too, is outside my responsibilities as trustee."

"It still matters to me," said Jonathan. "But I can live with that answer. I finally got around to reading all the documents you've sent me since that day you showed up at her apartment. Am I right that the trust gives me the power to pick the trustee?"

"Nearly correct. You have removal power. If it's your intention to replace me, I'll do what I can to help you find candidates with an appropriate background."

"It's not my intention—yet," said Jonathan. "What other powers do I have? What exactly can I do as beneficiary?"

"This trust was intended to give you unusually broad powers. You enjoy almost as much control over the assets as if you owned them directly. It's those powers that have allowed me to accommodate your many requests."

"But I don't own Arcadia."

"No. The trust does. The trustee directs the operation of the business."

"They don't have to do what I tell them—they have to do what you tell them."

"Yes."

"But you have to do what I tell you."

"With very few exceptions."

"What are they?"

"A beneficiary can't alter the trust agreement," Steuben said, leaning back in his chair. "A trustee can't violate any of its specific provisions. Other than that—" He shrugged. "You even have special power of appointment—that means you can make gifts of any of the trusts's assets at any time, or arrange to have gifts made at the time of your death."

"Could I give it all away? To another trust, say?"

"Even that. If the receiving trust were properly structured."

"Does a beneficiary always have to be specified by name?"

"Contingent beneficiaries are often defined, not named—'the grandchildren of John Law,' for instance. But one must be careful about the rule against perpetuities."

"I'm quite sure I don't have a clue what that means."

"For which you should feel no shame," Steuben said, raising a hand in warning. "It may be the most complex rule in all of the law, as generations of law students can attest. At the heart of it, though, is the simple fact that the common law abhors uncertainties, and so an uncertain gift—one that cannot be given to a named person at once—is only tolerated for a limited time."

"As long as *you* understand it," said Jonathan. "Speaking of contingencies—what happens to the trust if I walk out of here today and get hit by a bus?"

"Alynn chose not to designate a remainderman. So the trust would be terminated on your death, and the corpus—the assets—would pass to your estate. Do you have a will, Dr. Briggs?"

"No."

"Perhaps we should address that oversight before you do walk out of here."

"Could my estate be used to create a trust, like hers did?"

"Of course."

Jonathan leaned forward and rested his elbows on the finely polished Philippine mahogany. "How good are you, Mr. Steuben? Because I have some very complex arrangements in mind."

"I'm extremely good, Dr. Briggs."

"Are you equally discreet?"

"Always." He turned and retrieved a sheet of digital paper and a stylus from the credenza. "Why don't you tell me what it is you want done and I'll tell you how we'll do it."

Jonathan returned to Ann Arbor and to the two oner-ous tasks that could not be deferred any longer—clas-sifying the matrix database, and scripting the triggers for each variation.

At twenty points of correspondence, there proved to be more than two hundred families of matrices in the database. A dozen or so were represented by a sin-gle example. At the other extreme, Type 20 had nearly a thousand exemplars, and four other types had more than five hundred. Alynn's Type 1 had thirty-eight. Jonathan's Type 2 had nineteen, including his father and, curiously, Eleni.

Jonathan kept the mapping teams in the field with the portables while they waited for the augmented headsets to start arriving from Senegal. There was more than enough for him to do in the meantime, and he allowed almost anything to take him away from the scripting once the crucial Type 1 and Type 2 paths were written.

He subjected himself to the Myers-Briggs personal-ity assessment and a battery of similar profiling tools.

He closed out his affairs with David Helms and gave notice to Stephanie Oroz that the mapping effort was winding down. He met twice more with Arthur Steuben, once in Chicago to review arrangements and then in Windsor to sign documents. He observed the first anniversary of Alynn's death with a quiet visit to Eastlawn Cemetery in Columbus and a bouquet of lilies placed on the hill just above the Huron Towers parking lot.

But his main focus was the upcoming 10th International Neuroscience Symposium hosted by the Helen Wills Neuroscience Institute—the Berkeley conference. Though the organizers would not allow him at their podium, Jonathan had every intention of stealing their spotlight.

After auditioning a dozen public relations firms, he hired Stolla & Renfrew of New York, which had represented several well-known scientists in Nobel campaigns, and whose regular clients included both science popularizers and fringe health gurus. The check he wrote SRI was large enough to put two senior publicists full-time on the task of planning his assault on the general media and his preemptive strike on the scientific press. They in turn assigned him a semester's worth of homework, beginning with writing a summary of the research project for translation into memes and sound bites. That was followed by three intense days with an SRI contract speechwriter and the West Coast event coordinator, shaping not only the announcement in Berkeley but the whispering campaign leading up to it.

The scripting was still not finished when the first carton of augmented headsets hit Vector's doorstep. "They did a good job for you," Ramirez pronounced two hours after he tore open the box and took a handful of headsets to his test bench. "Damned shame we don't have a game to package with them yet—" With Ramirez's help, the balance of the scripting was farmed out to a veteran VR writer, and the work was wrapped up two days later.

Meanwhile, Jonathan continued to dismantle the last pieces of the project. The portables were withdrawn from the field, the mapping technicians dismissed, and the units turned over to Ramirez for maintenance upgrades and final modification. *This must be what it feels like to call off the search after a ship has sunk, or a hiker has disappeared on the mountain,* he told Stuart. *I know it doesn't mean I'm giving up. But it still means letting go of a hope.*

It was time to finalize the database—each of the modified portables would need its own reference copy. But there was a sizable backlog of unprocessed submissions spanning the weeks since Eric Lutton's departure, and Jonathan could not bring himself to discard them unexamined.

With Berkeley less than a fortnight away, Jonathan plunged into a series of marathon sessions in the processing lab. Eric had managed to automate much of the actual importation, integration, and analysis, but there was an irreducible amount of validation and documentation that had to be handled by a human being. And the vector matrices themselves were still seductive as a crystal ball, still tempted Jonathan to stare into their restless chromoluminescent tangles, to scry for pattern and meaning.

He did it without hope, driven by his inner ethic of order and completeness. He did it because he needed to know that it was done, one more piece moved into its place for the endgame.

His great fear continued to be that someone else would take note of the pieces lining up and realize what kind of picture they made. His best defense against that was keeping the people he was relying on isolated from each other. He had already managed to distance himself from the people he considered the greatest threats—Elizabeth, Eric, and Eleni. But it was important to finish before one of them decided to reinvade his life.

The complementary fear that preyed on him was that a piece was missing—something he had forgotten, overlooked, mismeasured, discounted, or refused to consider. He wanted more than a mere leap of faith. He aspired to a leap of knowledge.

Both fears occupied him through the many idle moments in successive fourteen-hour days. The third day, with the end in sight, he slept in late and barely managed to reach Arcadia-Vector before noon.

Even at that hour, coffee took precedence over checking the logs for the processing jobs he had left to run overnight. It was twenty minutes before he noticed that the matrix display had a flashing green bar across the bottom, and had gone into a split-screen mode with two vector maps displayed. Their ID numbers were almost ten thousand apart. But the maps showed more than 170 points of correspondence.

At long last, the second anomalous pair had been found: the late Ruth Treadwell of Hamilton, Ontario, and seven-year-old Kristina Calvin of Sarnia. He held his breath until he saw that the death and birth dates were compatible—he didn't know what he would have done at that point had it turned out that Ruth was still alive when Kristina was born. His theory had survived the new data intact.

There's your experimental falsifiability, Clement Harris, he thought with fierce satisfaction. A correspondence this close between two living subjects would have cut the heart out of my model.

But beyond that brief gleeful moment, the discovery

of the second anomalous pair was strangely inconsequential. It no longer mattered. Anything the new pair could tell him had already been factored into his plans. As Eleni had shown him, it was evidence he did not need. And there was no one to celebrate with in any case.

No, the triumph began and ended there, in one afternoon in the processing center. Jonathan already knew he was not going to drag Kristina Calvin and her family into the spotlight with him. There was no reason to intrude on their lives. Nor could he have properly introduced Kristina to Ruth if he had wanted to. He had little in the way of a personality profile for Ruth—not even a photograph. When she was mapped, he had been pursuing a very different line of inquiry.

He had been very different then, too—the kind of scientist to whom 179 points of correspondence between Subject 208 and Subject 9873 would have been a paradigm-rocking discovery, one to be teased apart with the finest of conceptual tweezers and endlessly examined under the high-powered microscope of theory and intellect.

Can I even call myself a scientist now? he asked Stuart that night. *This feels more like exploring, adventuring—grand schemes married to dubious speculations. Preparing to follow a fragmentary map that points beyond the horizon, because what other way is there to know? Colonel Spofford Herringbone, expounding to the fellows of the Travelers Club concerning what he hopes to find in Aftermatterstan. Why, no, Lord Leaping, cameras would never survive under those conditions. But I vow to return and tell you all that I have seen—*

If my journey means the frontier moves forward, isn't that enough to justify the rest?

I wish it was over.
I wish it would begin.

Stolla & Renfrew had earned their fee in full. Not only were four cameras waiting outside the Alumni House entrance, but SRI had talked up a crowd of more than two hundred curious onlookers with rumors of a controversial breakthrough on the nature of human consciousness. The controversy, with its subtext of scientific censorship and academic infighting, was the key selling point of the lead-up campaign on a campus where the Free Speech Movement was still part of the institutional self-image. Six UC Berkeley police were also in sight, though keeping their distance.

"My name is Dr. Jonathan Briggs. I've just come from a meeting with symposium director Mark Wilkins," Jonathan said, addressing the gathering from the steps. "It was a short meeting. Once again, Dr. Wilkins refused to allow me to present my findings at the conference that opens here today. He refused to examine the evidence himself, or to ask the peer review panel to reconsider their rejection, or to expedite an appeal to the sponsoring body. All doors are closed.

"I won't use the word 'conspiracy.' I won't use the word 'suppression.' It's enough to understand that careers and reputations are threatened whenever there's change. But that isn't science—it's bigotry, and jealousy, and politics. And they have no right to stand between the public and the truth."

He pulled the golden disc from a white envelope and raised it above his head, where it glittered in the California sun.

"I'll make my data available to anyone—to any researcher who wants to challenge my findings, or build on them. This discovery belongs to everyone, even the skeptics. Especially the skeptics.

"But I'm going to remind the skeptics that science is not supposed to be about what they believe, or what's easy to believe, or what's comforting to believe. It isn't supposed to be about what you wrote in your last book, or what you taught for the last ten semesters, or what the company who funded your grant wants to hear. It's supposed to be about the evidence. It's supposed to be about the truth.

"I have a great deal of sympathy for Dr. Mark Wilkins and Dr. Clement Harris and all the other smart, accomplished men and women who're meeting inside this building this week to share their ideas and argue about which ones deserve to be taken seriously. Being taken seriously is the secret need of every scientist. I know. It's the reason why even I wasn't willing to accept what the evidence was plainly saying. They haven't even heard the evidence, so how can they do anything but reject the conclusion?

"But the truth belongs to everyone. No one should be allowed to bottle it up and lock it away. And the truth is that this disc contains extremely strong empirical evidence of human consciousness occupying two different bodies—the second one following the death of the first.

"In other words, this disc contains the first scientific evidence of human reincarnation.

"No, I don't mind the snickers. I expect them. A year ago, I would have joined in. My training and background are absolutely conventional. I've spent the last ten years working as a neuroscientist in traditional university settings.

"My work involved taking pictures of the human mind at work. Like many of my peers, I've found it easier to take the pictures than to understand what they show—what is thinking, what is knowing, what is feeling? What is personality, and what is consciousness? The one thing I thought I knew for certain was that all of the pictures were different—that all of our minds are unique.

"I never expected to end up talking about reincarnation. I never expected to have two pictures of the same mind taken six years apart, and have one of them be a sixty-one-year-old man and the other a four-year-old boy.

"Even now, I can't say that without wanting to add, 'How amazing. How extraordinary.'

"But it might not be extraordinary at all. Because I also find myself with pictures of a forty-two-year-old woman and a seven-year-old girl—just as before, one mind, two bodies.

"These matches are closer than parent and child, closer than siblings, closer than identical twins. They are as close as a photograph of you today and a photograph of you five years from now. Personality persists. Consciousness is continuous. It's the integration of self, child to boy to man—and to child again."

"Metaphysical cant," a gruff voice growled at Jonathan from behind. He whirled to see Clement Harris and three other conferees standing just outside the Alumni House entrance. "You are no scientist, young man, and what you are peddling is not science but fantasy."

There was a smattering of applause from the crowd, but less than Jonathan might have expected. His blood had started pounding at the interruption, but he had not been taken completely by surprise. SRI was also inside Alumni House, making sure that what was happening outside did not go unnoticed. Moreover, he had been rehearsing for this encounter for a year.

"No, Dr. Harris. It's a question. What do the data mean? What's the explanation?"

"Fraud. Incompetence," Harris said curtly. "You've published nothing of consequence. You are uncredentialed. Your last appointment was a teaching position in a department that can barely keep its head above the intellectual waters. You were rejected for tenure. And then there was that ugly business with that girl—"

Someone in the crowd hissed, though Jonathan was uncertain who was being rebuked.

"Deal with the evidence, Dr. Harris," he shot back. "When did dismissing data out of hand become acceptable to you? Is *ad hominem* the best you can do? Questioning authority is even more important when you become one." He took a step toward Harris and held the CD out toward him. "Deal with the evidence. You have forty people on staff in Atlanta. You have the resources to replicate the experiment. You thought enough of what my team was doing to copy the imaging design. You could start work on this tomorrow."

"My lab doesn't do remedial work for failures. Why don't you close up this little sideshow and let the real scientists get back to work?"

Jonathan advanced another step, still offering the disc, still keeping his voice calm. "Dr. Harris, if you weren't afraid I was right, you'd take these data and prove me wrong. Instead, you've done everything you can to keep this from being talked about. Are you a scientist, or a censor?"

The man to Harris's right tugged at his sleeve. "Come on, Clem, this is a waste of time," he said, barely loud enough for Jonathan to hear. "Let's go get ready for the opening session."

But Harris had the fire of righteous indignation in his eye. He jerked his arm free and took a step toward

Jonathan. "You question my integrity? Do you have any idea how many young talents I've mentored, how many grants I've arranged, how many papers I could have put my name on? I'm not afraid of new ideas—"

Jonathan raised the disc higher, to shoulder level. "Here's one."

"Legitimate ideas, Dr. Briggs. Not desperate attempts by unproductive postdocs to salvage their careers at the expense of their betters—"

"Nothing you've said has anything to do with science," Jonathan said, and he was startled to hear some applause behind him. He had forgotten the audience, the cameras, and the plan. "Empirical evidence. Testing hypotheses. Observation and theory. Not personality. Not race. Not politics. Not credentials." He had let his arm fall to his side. Now one more step brought him within arm's length of the older man, and he offered the disc up one last time. "The game is 'What's going on here?' The only rule is 'Can you explain this?' I believe I can. You can't prove me wrong by refusing to play."

The second interruption and Jonathan's rapid-fire elocution derailed Harris. He was clearly not accustomed to being challenged so openly—and for one long moment, Jonathan was afraid that Harris would reach out and take the disc.

But Harris had not forgotten the audience—the one spilling down the steps, or the one watching inside Alumni House. His wounded ego gave SRI everything they were hoping he would, gave them a moment that crystallized the debate in a way that would resonate longer than all the words that had gone before.

His face cut by an ugly scowl, Harris cuffed the disc from Jonathan's hand and sent it spinning into the nearby bushes.

"Ignorant quack," he muttered dismissively, then retreated into the building, still shaking his head.

Jonathan found a bemused smile as he turned back to the crowd. Their faces were noticeably friendlier now—he could no longer pick out the ones who'd turned up on their own. "You see?" he said. "You see how closed a mind can be? But I refuse to believe that everyone in my field is like that."

Someone appeared at his elbow, buffing the rescued disc on a sleeve, and he accepted it back without taking particular notice of the courier. "Don't worry, it's not the only copy," he said, and a ripple of laughter lifted the last of the tension from his shoulders.

"What comes next?" The question came from the middle of the crowd.

"I've created a nonprofit foundation, Virtual Vectors, to manage access to our research database, and to add to it—"

"Will you tell someone who they used to be?" asked a woman in the front rank.

"If we can," Jonathan said. "Eventually, when we can. But we have to be realistic—there won't be many matches for quite a while. The sample isn't terribly large at this point, and 98 percent of those people are not only still alive, they're in no hurry to die. We feel very lucky to have as many as two matches to study."

"Who's 'we'?"

"Well—it keeps changing. But, everyone who's worked on the project. Thirty-one people have had a part in getting us this far—my postdocs, Ph.D. candidates, grad students, field technicians, engineers. And most of all a woman whose generosity gave me a chance to do this, and whose vision and confidence pointed the way for me. She was taken from me, but she is still very much with me."

The SRI rep, who had warned Jonathan not to talk

about Alynn, was grimacing. But her disapproval was belied by the warm, respectful wave of applause.

"So where do we go to get our personality backed up to CD?"

With a little laugh, he said, "There'll be announcements about that in the coming week. But there'll be four regional sites to start. I hope other labs will eventually join in."

"What will it cost?"

Jonathan frowned. "Nothing. This isn't dial-a-scam. This isn't a business."

"So anyone will be able to walk in?"

"My own feeling is there's no point in mapping anyone born in the last ten years until another ten years have gone by. But Virtual Vectors will make the final decision on that. A lot will depend on what they can afford."

"Why are they making the decisions? Where are you going to be?"

"I've got about fifty interviews to do, starting with one on CNN-Science this afternoon. Then I'm going to take a little time off." More and more people were arriving for the conference, and having either to circle around the crowd on the grass, or push through the crowd where it was thinnest. "One more question, and then I think the campus police would appreciate it if we'd get out of the way of progress."

One of the officers raised a hand in acknowledgment, but a man standing near the back shouted loudly, "You're not the one blocking the way."

"Thank you," Jonathan said with a smile.

"I have a question, Dr. Briggs," called a clear contralto voice that settled familiarly in his ear.

Jonathan squinted in that direction and saw, with no small pleasure, that it was Eleni. "Go ahead."

"Have you had breakfast?"

"No."

"I have a table for sixteen reserved at Mortimer's. Can we treat you?"

"Who's 'we'?"

"Anyone who wants to."

Hands went up all through the crowd. "We're going to need a bigger table," Jonathan said with the smile of someone who felt embraced.

A man ten feet away said loudly, "The next time you come here to speak, you're going to need to book the goddamned Greek Theater."

Laughing and applauding, the crowd began to break up at that point. Jonathan started toward Eleni.

"Dr. Briggs," someone called from behind him.

Jonathan turned to see a lanky, curly-haired man of perhaps forty approaching down the sidewalk from Alumni House. "Yes?"

"My name is Tom Weisschurch, Arizona State University. We were in Boston at the same time, if you remember."

He offered his hand, and Jonathan shook it. "Yes," he said. "Working on visual memory storage and recall, wasn't it."

"More or less," said Weisschurch. "Dr. Briggs, I'd like to look at your data."

Jonathan stared blankly for a moment. Then the gold disc changed hands to the loudest applause of the morning, and the quiet whirring of four cameras.

There was never a chance for Jonathan to talk privately with Eleni. She sat near but not next to Jonathan in the restaurant, saying little, and slipped away after breakfast with an oddly shy smile and a wave.

Jonathan had no choice but to let her go—his day

was fully scheduled. He spent it being squired around the Bay Area by SRI's Kinca Utali, who kept him focused and grounded through a series of five interviews and an impromptu meeting with a small group of Buddhist clerics at the Odiyan Monastery in the hills above the Berkeley campus.

"There's nothing at stake here—a private meeting with no cameras, no recorders," said Kinca as their car approached the entrance to the parklike temple grounds. "We get everything we need just by being able to say we were here. If we can get a handshake picture afterward, that's gravy."

"But what do they want?"

"I expect they're just like a lot of people who were listening this morning—they heard something that made them curious. They have questions. The invitation used the phrase 'an exchange of perspectives.'"

"Most American Buddhists don't believe in reincarnation," said Jonathan, looking ahead as the car began to slow. "Only the Tibetan tradition explicitly embraces it."

"Should be interesting, then, don't you think? Relax and enjoy it. When we want to strike real sparks, though, we'll sit you down with some Protestants. But the images from this morning need a few days to sink in before we replace them." She unlocked the car doors. "See you in ninety minutes."

It was an ecumenical gathering, with Shin, Thai, Tibetan, Minh Yuek Jiu Shyu, and Hsi Lai temples represented along with the monastery and the Nyingma Institute. Jonathan spent more time listening than talking, as it turned out that his hosts' primary concern was to see if they could be of assistance to him.

The minister of the Tibetan temple had both the most questions for Jonathan and the most to impart to him, describing in patient detail how the monks carried out their searches for the new Dalai Lama and his predecessor. He, in turn, showed them the matrices of Dugan Beckett and Brett Winston on a portable borrowed from the clerical office.

All seemed intrigued, but Lama Surya Khenpo, a slight and stooped man whose eyes remembered no smile, had words of caution. "Essence is hard to see. The eye craves familiarity, and the mind imposes order. One must learn to search with the eyes closed. Essence is not expressed in physicality. We are not what we think we are."

Then Kinca appeared, and it was time to go. Lama Surya Khenpo was the first to leave the garden. The others also withdrew with little ceremony—all but Reverend Master Hozan Kusada, who came to where Jonathan was standing and touched him gently on the arm.

"Friend—do not be disheartened. Dharma does not come suddenly. Your quest has only begun." His smile became broad and joyful, until Jonathan could not help but smile back. "See everything like a dream."

Dinner was slightly hurried and grandly public—the former because of Jonathan's scheduled return flight, the latter because Kinca Utali insisted on it.

"By the time we're done, you may not be able to take a meal out in peace again for a year," she said as they were being seated at Bernardo's at Ferry Point. The aircraft carrier USS *Hornet* and the Bay Bridge framed the view out the panoramic dining room windows. "You may not get through this one, for that matter—we had very good local penetration today."

Jonathan had little to say. He felt as though he had been talking all day and had used up his supply of words. His dinner companion, though, was suffering no such shortage. Thankfully, she seemed not to mind carrying the conversation by herself.

After the orders had gone to the kitchen, Utali gestured toward the ship with a piece of breadstick. "They say she's haunted—dozens of people have seen the ghost of a sailor. Of course, that could be a ploy to boost attendance. I've been meaning to ask you, do you believe in ghosts, Dr. Briggs? Well, you must, of course, the soul has to be somewhere while it's between bodies."

The breadstick lost another inch. "I have to tell you, Doctor, that I've enjoyed my work today. This has been terribly exciting. And you did very well."

She delivered him to Oakland International Airport with a bare ten minutes to spare, which would have meant disaster in any larger airport. "Check your client clip file when you get airborne," she said, leaning across the car seat toward the open door. "The preliminary report should be available by then. Good luck, Dr. Briggs."

Dutifully, he logged in with the seatback terminal as soon as the ONLINE light began glowing. There was a note from SRI's Brian Fox, who would handle the next two days' events in Michigan. The article in the *Daily Cal* was friendly, even managing to present Alynn's murder as a tragedy rather than a mystery. But the animated "Pot, Kettle" comic in the student humor newspaper *Heuristic Squelch* was twice as gratifying. It turned that morning's encounter into a tableau of a wizard attempting to feed a duck; the duck refused even to taste the offering, stubbornly squawking "Quack" again and again.

But he left the rest unread. All Jonathan really wanted by then was for everything to stop moving. The closest approximation he could manage was to sleep, so he pulled a noise-canceling headset from his carry-on, turned off the seat light, and closed his eyes.

Somewhere over Nebraska he awoke. Still exhausted, yet strangely energized, he amused himself for a time looking out the window at the gibbous moon and the patterns of lights created by the towns and cities below.

Then something he had seized on from the Tibetan's exposition at the monastery burst forth in his head as a full-grown brain weasel. As they passed over Iowa and Illinois he kept himself busy drawing up two lists: one inventory of his own social and behavioral idiosyncrasies, and another of Alynn's. Even though it had been more than a year, he found the latter list much easier to construct—it was hard to see himself with any semblance of anthropological distance, let alone affection.

> *Doesn't like to swim, but is drawn to the water*
> *Never wears socks with sandals*
> *Drinks milk from a chilled glass*
> *Prefers cats to dogs*
> *Bats right, throws left*
> *What is your name? What is your quest? What is your favorite color?*

As they passed over Goshen, Indiana, already descending toward the planned landing in Detroit, he mailed both lists to Cassandra. Then he dozed until the tires squealed against the runway.

Jonathan chose not to rush out before the economy class passengers, nor to fight his way through them. He was one of the last passengers to leave the plane, and it nearly saved him. He was only a few steps past the jetway door when he spotted Detective Stephen Anderson standing near a pillar beyond the last row of passenger lounge seats.

Instantly, Jonathan dropped his bags where he stood and turned back. "Left something on the plane," he said breathlessly to the gate attendant as he ducked past her.

Digging in his pocket for his phone, he broke into a run as he entered the deserted jetway. It seemed an eternity before the handshaking was complete and he could place the call.

"Cassandra, verify Jonathan," he said, slowing to a fast walk.

"Hello, Jonathan."

"Verify security status."

"Status normal, Jonathan. I have a log of attempted penetrations."

"Verify comm status."

"All interfaces active, Jonathan."

"Process the file Rainy Day."

There was a momentary pause, during which Jonathan heard nothing but the blood pounding in his ears—or was it the sound of footsteps pounding down the jetway behind him. "Acknowledged, Jonathan. Closing connection."

In the next instant the phone was ripped from his hand and he was thrown against the wall of the jetway. His arms were seized and twisted behind him, and his wrists were imprisoned by metal handcuffs ratcheted one stop too tight.

"Jonathan Briggs, you are under arrest for conspiracy to commit murder in the first degree in the death of Alynn Reed. Anything you say can and will be used against you in a court of law—"

It required a supreme effort, but Jonathan limited himself to four words. "I want a lawyer."

Anderson seemed disappointed to have elicited no more reaction than that. He grabbed Jonathan roughly by the arm and started back up the jetway with him. "You really should have stayed off TV," he said. "That wasn't smart. I thought you were supposed to be smart."

But Jonathan was barely listening. He was thinking about the tasks in the Rainy Day file, and hoping fiercely that Cassandra could finish before they broke down the door.

Nothing in Jonathan's past had prepared him for the Washtenaw County jail.

Though a new facility had recently been built on Zeeb Road to house sentenced felons, the worn-out Hogback Road Corrections Center was still being used for arrestees awaiting trial or arraignment. It looked and felt a hundred years old, and being on the wrong side of the bars evoked even older and more barbaric nightmares.

Everything about the jail was alien and ugly. There was little color and no beauty. The smell was a cross between stadium men's room and chemical plant, a sour sickness that hung in the air and tainted every breath. The predominant sounds were those of the asylum, the monkey house, and the factory, all reverberating through a warren of claustrophobic spaces shaped in steel and stone.

Everything was taken away from him, even the right to know the time. He sat on the edge of a thin foam mattress in a bright orange uniform, waiting. He could not stop his hands from shaking. He tried to shut it all out with imagination and memory, picturing gardens, the *Pastorale*, sunlight. But he could not make himself close his eyes, even though he was alone in the tiny cell, even though he had not slept.

He tried not to think about Alynn; he did not want to bring her there. He waited, his mind screaming, for the slow-motion nightmare to end.

* * *

"You should have brought me in sooner," said Robert Clark Giddings. The Chicago lawyer had a strong, angular face and a courtroom voice, self-possessed yet powerful. "Did you think that innocent people had nothing to fear from the law?"

"I suppose I did."

"That was damned foolish of you."

"Apparently," said Jonathan. "I plead guilty to not watching enough reruns of *NYPD Blue*. Can you get me out?"

"Ordinarily, I'd say yes. The case is tissue-thin, a ham-sandwich indictment if I ever saw one," said Giddings. "But even if it wasn't, murder suspects routinely get bail—high bail, of course, a million or two. You certainly don't look to be a threat to the general public. You've been out there for a year without stubbing your toe."

"And they've been right there watching in case I did."

"Which helps you now. But they're not going to like this business of your Canadian citizenship with the border forty miles away. Plus, this is a media case. Your little publicity campaign is working against you. Judges don't like to look soft when cameras are pointed in their direction."

"So—"

"No predictions. We've got a shot. I'll do my best, and we'll both know more when the judge tells us so. Now, they're probably going to add charges of resisting arrest and destroying evidence—"

"Walking the other way is resisting arrest?"

"So you call that walking? Yes, it can be. Did the police identify themselves to you at the airport? Ask you to stop?"

"Not that I heard."

"You just saw Detective Anderson, and remembered somewhere else you had to be."

"Yes."

"Why?"

"I had to make a call."

"Which is where the destruction of evidence complaint comes from. You called home. Apparently your home computer was found brain-dead—files missing all over, overwritten with strings of ones."

"Were they?" said Jonathan. "Nothing I destroyed was evidence of anything. Nothing I did was a crime."

"They don't know that. And the destruction will be taken as a guilty act."

Jonathan sighed. "Can you tell, do they really think that I did this?"

"How does it matter? Look, even if they were *framing* you, it wouldn't change anything—you'd still be in here. Their sincerity isn't the issue."

Jonathan held his head in his hands. "Look, you have to get me out. That's all there is to it."

"Number one on my list." He glanced at his watch, then started gathering his papers. "Probably have you in front of the arraignment judge within an hour. Don't be scared, don't be stupid, don't be talkative. You're a learned man, a teacher, a doctor. Hold it together. Control and dignity. Leave the indignation to me. Innocent people get arrested, but when they're my clients they don't get convicted." He stood up and knocked on the door.

"Mr. Giddings—if you do get me out on bail, what happens if I—"

"Don't finish that question, Dr. Briggs," Giddings said as the door to freedom was being opened by a uniformed officer. "Especially not now."

*   *   *

"Emphatically not guilty, Your Honor." Giddings's voice carried to every corner of the courtroom, defying disagreement.

Judge Arden Thompson showed no sign of being impressed. His eyes were well armored with skepticism by fourteen years in the Washtenaw criminal courts. "Does the prosecution wish to be heard on bail, Ms. Monaghan?"

"Yes, Your Honor." A tall, slim, jet-eyed woman who wore the black-and-red tattoos of the Christian Transformation down her right forearm, Monaghan gazed levelly at Jonathan as she spoke. "We ask that the defendant be held without bail. We believe that there is a substantial risk of flight. Moreover, it is our belief that Dr. Briggs represents a threat to any and all of his twelve thousand research subjects—"

"Outrageous," Giddings muttered loudly enough to carry to the judge's ears.

"You'll have your turn, Mr. Giddings," rebuked the judge. "Ms. Monaghan, was there more?"

"Our theory of the crime is that Dr. Briggs had Alynn Reed murdered to advance his discredited research—which claims to prove human beings can be reincarnated." Her voice dripped syrupy ridicule. "Her death not only provided him with the means to pursue his work, but a test subject for his pet theory. We have witnesses who will testify to his continuing obsession with the death of his subjects."

Jonathan's face wrinkled in disbelief, and he looked beseechingly toward his lawyer.

"Mr. Giddings?" asked the judge.

Giddings opened his rebuttal with a contemptuous sideways glance at the prosecutor and an exasperated sigh. "This prosecution is an exercise in face-saving, nothing more. The killing of Alynn Reed was in furtherance of an ordinary carjacking, not a scientific study. My client is accused of conspiracy, but the prosecution cannot even say who he is supposed to have conspired with—the real killer is a Jane Doe. The suggestion that my client is out to kill his subjects is pure fantasy."

Then he turned his intense gaze on Monaghan. "And I take it as a personal affront for you to even suggest that a client of mine would run instead of fighting to restore his reputation. This man has been grievously wronged by the district attorney's baseless charges. We will be here to answer every one of them."

"Please address yourself to the bench, Mr. Giddings," said Judge Thompson. "Rebuttal, Ms. Monaghan?"

"The Michigan Constitution gives no weight to the egos of either defense attorneys or their clients," she said. "This is a murder case, not a case of hurt feelings. The state is explicitly empowered to deny bail to protect the public or guarantee the appearance of the accused. Both considerations clearly apply in this case."

"I am compelled to agree," said Thompson. "Bail is denied. Suspect is remanded to custody."

Giddings positioned himself between Jonathan and the judge before the former could give voice to the dismay and incredulity carved into his face. "Control and dignity," he said warningly. "This is meaningless. I'll get a bail hearing—the prosecution will have to make a case, not just make accusations. I'll get you out, Jonathan. Hang on."

The bailiff was at Jonathan's elbow by then, but he resisted being led. "I need you to get me some information—"

"We'll talk later. Be strong. Believe."

There was no aspect of being jailed that was not difficult for Jonathan, but one of the most unexpected was how hard it was to be unplugged.

It was more than being denied the music that might have helped make the strange familiar, or the books that might have helped hasten time along. He had never known a world without day-and-night access to terabytes of information, to the knowledge and experience and even the company of countless other people around the globe, to every kind of product and service imaginable. He went to the net for answers scores of times a day, as reflexively as breathing.

Now his questions had more weight and urgency than ever, but he was cut off from the answers. Access to a computer, much less a connected one, was not on the list of prisoner rights. His communication with the outside world started and ended with two monitored phone calls a day, and that was not enough.

There had been twenty-eight instructions in rainy-day.cscript.vgp, and knowing that the last had been completed—the purging of Stuart and other personal material from Cassandra's local file storage—did not guarantee that the others had been successfully completed. He needed to know if parcels had been shipped, parcels had been received, files had been transferred, trojans had been activated, messages had been delivered. He needed to know if anything remained undone.

Beyond that, he needed to talk to Brian Fox and Kinca Utali, needed to know if anything was left of the foundation they had been building now that his arrest had blown up under it. He needed to know what was being said about him, not just where they had counted on sympathy and support, but in the mass culture where last impressions counted for more than first impressions. He needed to know what to do.

But he was not yet entitled to visitors, though they had allowed him to fill out a form with the names of the five people who would be permitted to see him when he was.

For the moment, all the questions he had, all the answers he needed, had to be squeezed through the microscopic pipeline of two calls a day and the visits of Robert Giddings.

"Don't you have a friend, an employee, a family member, who can help you with some of this?" Giddings asked in annoyance as he considered the handwritten list Jonathan was pressing on him.

"No. No, not really."

"Your parents would be here on the next train if you'd let them. You didn't even put them on your visitor list."

"Not open for discussion."

"Do you want to at least tell me why any of this is important? Or pretend it has something to do with the case?"

"I have to know what's happening with my work—"

"I have a bulletin for you, Doctor—your work is on hold. Let's focus on Tuesday's bail hearing, shall we? I have a lot of questions for you, a lot of things to go over."

"Will I have to testify at the hearing?"

"The judge may question you. The prosecutor can't. Let's talk about what you might be asked—"

The first night in jail, he did not sleep.

The second, he had the dream again.

This time, the green-black clouds of the storm spanned the sky above a curiously sunlit and silent landscape. He could feel the wind trying to lift him from his feet, but could not hear it, and the surface of the lake before him was still. When he looked into the water at the reflection of the sky, he could see the sinuous energies dancing across the underside of the turbulent clouds. But when he raised his eyes to the sky, he could no longer find them.

"Where are you?" he shouted. "What are you?"

The wind was beginning to break up the overhanging clouds, pushing them away toward the east, across the lake. Through the rents in the fabric Jonathan glimpsed stars like jewels in black velvet, achingly beautiful, seductively distracting. He felt drawn to sit and watch until the entire pattern of night was revealed above him.

But he could not stay. The storm was moving out of reach.

He spread his arms and allowed the wind to lift him. *You have always known how to fly.* As he skipped across the sky in pursuit of the storm, he looked down at his reflection in the lake. He saw only a many-hued lacework of light, cartwheeling and swirling.

But when he looked back from where he had come, he saw a man, naked and bronze of skin, sitting by the shore where he had been standing, looking up at the stars.

By the time he caught the storm he *was* the wind. He reached out and danced with the clouds until he became the clouds. He sensed the deep energy within, and felt the delicate embrace and caress of the energy without. Far above the ground and far below the sky, he was suspended between the real and the infinite, full of longing, full of joy.

"I know you," he cried, his words a rumble that carried to the horizon and beyond.

The dancing energies laughed happily back in a thousand voices.

He awoke to clarity.

Benumbed by five days of imprisonment, Jonathan listened to the arguments before Circuit Judge Marion Miller as though he were watching a stage play.

He knew intellectually that he had a stake in the outcome, but he felt powerless to influence the process. The absurdity of it all reduced him to a mute spectator with a front-row seat to madness. How could he be here? How could accusations so empty of truth receive such earnest consideration? How could any of what he was hearing be real? He had done nothing wrong. How had these people gotten so much power over his life?

No, it was only by distancing himself that he could manage to hold his tongue, to check himself from trying to get up and walk out the door. It was only a play. He graded the performances as they unfolded.

Giddings was a bulldog, strong, stubborn, and passionate. His energy filled the room, and he seemed to have gotten the greater share of the good lines. Monaghan was diligent, precisely spoken, icily dismissive in her rebuttals—and somehow not quite equal to the role. Her words would read well enough in the transcript, but they were delivered by rote, without conviction, and with a hint of defensiveness.

Judge Miller yielded nothing to Giddings, questioning him closely and cutting him short on more than one occasion with a curt, "Very well." But she was equally hard on Monaghan, freezing her with openly skeptical gazes and registering her disagreement with a shake of her head.

It went on for more than an hour, a third of it spent at the sidebar. Finally, Miller asked with weary impatience, "Do you have anything else of substance, Ms. Monaghan?"

"Nothing further unless Your Honor has other questions."

"I've heard enough from the prosecution." She turned her gaze on Jonathan. "Dr. Briggs."

Taken by surprise, Jonathan's mouth went suddenly dry. "Yes, Your Honor."

"You've heard Ms. Monaghan outline the state's case against you, and you've heard your attorney's defense. Is there anything you would care to add before I rule on the motion?"

Jonathan rose unsteadily to his feet, as much to stall as to be respectful. "Yes, I, uh—" He took a deep breath and started again. "Your Honor, I'd like to confess something." He heard Giddings startle beside him at that, but he pressed on, the words coming in a rush once unbound. "I want to confess that I'm afraid. I'm afraid because I don't know what's going to happen. I'm afraid because I've learned that innocence is no defense against arrest—which makes me wonder if it's any better defense against conviction.

"I'm afraid that my work has been irreparably tainted—and listening to the district attorney say the word 'reincarnation,' I wonder if that's not the real reason we're here. I'm afraid that even if I'm cleared, people will never understand, will always wonder. Salvaging my own reputation matters only to the degree that it will allow the work to continue, with me or without me. I'm afraid that the prosecutor wants to put my work on trial along with me.

"But I'm not afraid of the truth. As a scientist, I went where the evidence led me, even when it led me places I wasn't expecting, even when it forced me to conclusions I knew wouldn't be popular.

"If Ms. Monaghan can manage to do the same as a district attorney, I have nothing to fear from the law, either. I didn't hurt Alynn—and whoever did cut the heart out of my life. I will never stop loving her. I'd do anything to still be with her." Tears ran freely down his cheeks, and his throat closed down so tightly he could scarcely swallow.

"Thank you, Dr. Briggs," said Judge Miller. "You may sit down." She glanced at the top of the bench, then leveled a hard gaze in the prosecutor's direction. "Ms. Monaghan, not only am I unimpressed by your arguments against bail, I'm not even convinced that this case won't collapse if any of us sneeze. Mr. Giddings no doubt knows how to write a motion for summary dismissal. Tell the police they need to shore up the timbers. A good start would be tracking down this Jane Doe number one, the shooter, and proving that she and Dr. Briggs actually know each other."

"Yes, Your Honor."

Miller turned her attention to the defense table. "Dr. Briggs. I don't think you're going to run, but in case I'm wrong, I'm not going to let you have a head start. Bail is set at three hundred thousand dollars, cash or bond. Counselor, can your client make bail?"

"Yes, Your Honor."

"Very well. Dr. Briggs, the release I am granting you is a conditional release. When your bail is posted, you will be restricted to your home, your place of work, and the shortest route between them, by means of cellular GPS tether. Do you have any problems with that?"

"No, ma'am."

"Good answer." She rapped the gavel smartly. "This hearing is adjourned."

Robert Giddings settled himself back behind the wheel of his silver BMW and handed the new keycard to

Hudson Towers apartment 801 across the shifter to Jonathan.

"Thank you," Jonathan said, turning it over in his hands as though examining a gemstone. "Did the office give you a hard time?"

"How could they? The rent is current. The trust holds the lease. They don't dare to try to keep you out. And you have a right to change your key."

"I never really read rental contracts," said Jonathan. "I guess I figured they all had a clause in them that amounts to 'We decided we don't like you, go away.'"

Giddings laughed lightly. "Look, Jonathan, no one who knows a man accused of murder stays neutral for very long. I can't really prepare you for that. You find out fast who your real friends are. And the rest of them, frankly, don't matter. It isn't pleasant. Some days it'll get to you. But you can't say anything to change their opinions. You have to learn how to be a duck—just let the rain roll off your back."

"I'll be all right," said Jonathan. "Thank you, Robert. I'll try to be a duck. Thanks for being my three-hundred-pound gorilla. Thanks for getting me out."

"I enjoy it," said Giddings. "This is just the beginning. At the end of this we'll be celebrating a malicious prosecution settlement so big you'll actually be able to ransom your reputation."

"Okay," said Jonathan, his attention focused out the window. The sidewalk was empty and the lobby seemed quiet. "Where are the press?"

Giddings jerked a thumb over his shoulder. "Owner won't let them any closer than the street."

Stealing a glance in that direction, Jonathan said, "I'm going to go up now."

"You're sure you don't want me to come with you?"

"I'm sure," said Jonathan, mustering a reassuring smile. "The cats are going to be spooked enough after a week without seeing anyone but Pet Nanny."

"The cats are fine. We sent a cleaning service in on Friday, because we know from experience the police don't pick up after themselves. But I understand. If you need help with anything else, call Sharon any time," Giddings said.

"Okay."

"And don't forget that just because you have to stay here doesn't mean you have to stay here alone. We can get you any kind of company or assistance you need. Don't turn your home into a slightly larger jail cell. Next week I'll go back at Judge Miller and see if we can't get your travel restrictions loosened. In the meantime, get a massage—throw a party—have the Chess Club up—let your parents come and fuss over you."

"I'll remember." Jonathan cracked open the door, and the late-afternoon heat beat in on him. "I want you to know I am grateful, Robert."

"My pleasure." The men shook hands.

Jonathan reached the doors just as two college-age women were emerging. They took no particular notice of him beyond a friendly smile from the rounder of the two. But the slim thirtysomething man who entered the elevator behind Jonathan carrying a stack of three laundry baskets pushed the button for Five, but left on Two. The woman who had called for the elevator on Two never boarded at all.

His apartment door had been repainted, but the fresh paint bore even fresher graffiti, red letters ten centimeters high slashing across the face at an angle: KILLER.

Inside, he found a handbill that had been shoved under his door. It bore large photographs of both Alynn and himself, each labeled with the single word VICTIM. Smaller print promised "the complete true story" at a NewWeb site. He suspected the hand of SRI, attempting damage control.

Hypatia came to him at once and insisted on being picked up and held. But Archimedes hung back. Later, when he was certain Jonathan was watching, the gray cat defiantly peed on the carpet in a sunny spot in a corner of the living room. It was unmistakably a rebuke. Jonathan could not bring himself to yell at him. When the cleanup was complete, Archimedes softened and came to sit beside Jonathan on the couch. He took the time to clip both cats' front claws, a ritual Alynn had called "counting ten."

There was no mistaking that the police had been in the apartment. Much was missing—the bookshelves in particular were denuded. Much of the rest was displaced. He cataloged the many wrongnesses as he sat with the cats. It felt like when company took it upon itself to helpfully put the kitchen in order, having never seen how its owners preferred it.

Cassandra stood inert in the middle of the room, her drive bays gaping, her media trays empty, her land lines cut. When he finally extricated himself from the cats, Jonathan made one token effort to power her up. The attempt only produced a systems error report too long for him to deal with. None of the answers he needed would come from Cassandra.

But the phone had a rudimentary browser, and it was capable enough to confirm the shipment of a box, visit the directory of a graveyard, and check an FTP site. It was adequate to consult a client file, alter a contract, verify a purchase—to make a request, service a debt, and say a good-bye.

The good-bye was the hardest by far. He had known for a long time that he could not leave without a word to his family—to his parents, at the very least. But there were no words he could say that would protect them from the same kind of wound he still carried a year after Alynn's death.

He had avoided thinking about it, because when he allowed himself to think about it, the guilt was almost enough to paralyze him. His parents were innocent, they loved him—and he was going to devastate them.

Even now, even in the last hour, it was almost too much.

I'm sorry, Jonathan scratched on the touch pad at last. *I have to do this. I love you. I'm not afraid. I believe I will see you again.*

He sat staring at the unsent message for a long time, erased it, rewrote it. He inserted *No one failed me* after *I'm not afraid.* He stared a while longer, erased *I'm not afraid*, then added it back at the end.

It was not enough, but it was all that he knew to do. He signed his name and sent the message on its way.

His hands were suddenly shaky. His chest ached as though the room had been emptied of air. He was committed, and yet all the momentum had left him. Finding his way back to the couch was all that he could manage.

Hypatia wound herself between Jonathan's legs, rubbing her head against his ankles, then looking up and trilling. He heard it as a question.

"I don't know, Patty," he told her guiltily.

The phone had remembered Eleni's UCN for him. She answered on the sixth ring.

"Jonathan?"

A glowing light promised him an encrypted call, but he was still disinclined to say more than the minimum necessary. "Can you take Hypatia and Archimedes?"

"Is it time, then?" Her words were matter-of-fact, but her voice was touched by a tender concern.

"Yes."

"Do you want to talk?"

"No. I just need to know if you can take the cats."

"I can be there late tomorrow. Is that soon enough?"

"I'll tell them," he said. "Thank you—from all of us."

Then he disconnected the phone's base station and carried it and the walkaround to the kitchen. It was not only that he did not want to take any calls, hear any other voices. His final arrangements were fragile improvisations. He didn't know if the phone would remember its recent activity, and he intended to take no chances.

Sixty seconds in the microwave produced several spectacular episodes of sparking, along with enough foul-smelling smoke to trigger the range fan. After contemplating the lightly scorched and partially melted remains, Jonathan taped over the kitchen smoke detector, closed the oven door, and keyed in another five minutes. He was rewarded with open flames, which had to be extinguished with baking soda.

Then he started with Alynn's room, putting things right. All of her herbs and incense were gone, and her library had been plundered. He began by restoring the altar as best he could remember. The meditation candle, red wax filling the bowl of a great geode, had been dropped and cracked. He placed it carefully in the center of the low table and lit the wick. The fire drew him in, and he sat cross-legged before it.

They will see cowardice, not courage. They will see guilt, not injustice. They will think I took the easy way, not understanding how easy it would be to back away.

Eleni knew. *The decision is still ahead of me. What can I live with? What can I live without?*

As it grew dark outside the tower, he moved from one room to the next, putting their world in order—towels folded in the wrong direction, lamps facing the wrong way. Hypatia followed him, talking to him.

"I know, Patty," he said. "She's gone." The cat fell mute, but continued to hover nearby.

When he had done all that he could to erase the invasion, Jonathan returned to the altar room, and sat before the candle. He emptied his mind of thoughts until only one remained. *I can't allow them to take my freedom again. I can't lose the chance to choose.*

He blew out the candle.

Stopping before Cassandra, he scrawled a few words by hand on the back of a printout, and left it by the keyboard. When he stepped to the balcony door, he had to firmly shoo an insistent Hypatia away from the opening.

He stood there in the darkness for a minute, feeling the breeze on his face, looking at the city lights reflected on the surface of the river, squinting to find stars in the nightglow overhead. Then he climbed the railing, folded his arms across his chest, and stepped off into the air.

The air would not hold him.

He counted the floors as he fell, turning lazily head down. He glimpsed a couple tending a hibachi on the third floor, heard their surprised shout a moment before the ground rushed up to him.

There was agony, and ecstatic light. They faded together, more slowly than he had counted on.

Detective Stephen Anderson bent down and peered at the blackened, melted mass inside the microwave.

"What the hell." He straightened up, scowling angrily. "Will someone tell me why this headcase was on the street?"

A uniformed police officer poked his head through the apartment doorway. "The professor's here."

"Let her in."

Elizabeth Froelich entered the apartment timidly. Her gaze darted uncomfortably about, as though fearful of what she might see. Her face was flushed and blotchy, as though she had been crying.

"Detective Anderson? I don't understand why you wanted to see me."

Anderson handed her a piece of paper. "Is this for you? Do you have any idea what this means?"

Jonathan's note was brief.

Liz,
Consciousness is analog.
                    Jonathan
P.S. Please take the cats for Eleni.

She handed the paper back, somewhere finding a smile—a tear-bright smile full of deep sadness and tender hope, a smile that at once loved folly and mocked foolishness.

"Yes, it's for me," she said. "Where are the cats?"

Anderson glowered warningly. "I need more than that, Doctor. What the hell does it mean? 'Consciousness is analog'?"

She changed her mind and reclaimed the paper. "He and I had been having a dialogue on fundamental properties," she said. "Do you know the difference between *adieu* and *au revoir*, Detective?"

"I don't want a goddamned French philosophy lesson, professor. Just unpack it for me."

Her bright, sad, tolerant smile returned. "It means he believed, Detective Anderson. He wanted to tell me he's just gone away for the day."

"So Dr. Briggs *was* nuts, after all."

"I can't say," said Elizabeth. "But ask me again in a hundred years. By that time, all of us should know."

MACHINE, OR MORE: A READING LIST

In the quest to grasp the nature of our reality, the clash between materialism and dualism is arguably the last battleground between experimental science and the beliefs and traditions born of common human experience.

Science has displaced the Earth from the center of the Cosmos and *Homo sapiens* from the center of Nature, but at this point in history the puzzle of consciousness remains one that materialism cannot fully tease apart. For the moment, dualism remains deeply woven into human culture through language, religious belief, moral philosophy, and legal principle. If there is to be a third revolution in our view of ourselves, it still lies somewhere ahead of us—though perhaps only just ahead.

A Sampling of Materialist Thought:

A Materialist Theory of Mind, David M. Armstrong (Routledge)

The Engine of Reason, The Seat of the Soul, Paul Churchland (MIT Press)

Consciousness Explained, Daniel C. Dennett (Little, Brown)

Journey to the Centers of the Mind, Susan A. Greenfield (Freeman)

The Brain Has a Mind of Its Own, Richard Restak (Harmony)

A Sampling of Dualist Thought:

Discourse on Method and *Meditations on First Philosophy*, René Descartes

What Survives?, Gary Doore, ed. (Tarcher)

The Engines of the Soul, W.D. Hart (Cambridge)

The Challenge of Reincarnation, Charles E. Luntz (Luntz)

The Case for Dualism, J.R. Smythies & John Beloff, eds. (University Press of Virginia)

ABOUT THE AUTHOR

Michael P. Kube-McDowell is the pen name of Philadelphia-born novelist Michael Paul McDowell. His prior works include the 1985 Philip K. Dick Award finalist *Emprise* and the 1991 Hugo Award nominee *The Quiet Pools*. His contributions to the extended Star Wars saga, the "Black Fleet Crisis" novels, were *New York Times, USA Today,* and *Publishers Weekly* bestsellers. Most recently, *The Trigger,* a 1998 collaboration with Sir Arthur C. Clark, was praised as "an epic thriller," "solid, intelligent, serious entertainment," and "what near-future SF should be: clever, thoughtful, thrilling, and human."

In addition to his twelve previous novels, Michael has contributed stories to a variety of leading magazines and anthologies including *Analog, Asimov's, Fantasy & Science Fiction, After the Flames,* and *Alternate Presidents.* Three of his stories were adapted as episodes of the George Romero horror-fantasy television series *Tales From the Darkside* (two with Michael's own teleplays). Outside of science fiction, he is the author of more than five hundred nonfiction articles on subjects ranging from "scientific creationism" to the US space program. A former National Merit Scholar and Presidential Scholar Distinguished Teacher,

Michael received an EdPress Achievement Award for his 1999 essay "Divining the Mind."

At various times Michael has called Fairview Village (Camden), NJ; East Lansing, Sturgis, and Lansing, MI; and Goshen, IN home. He currently resides in central Michigan with his wife Gwen, three children, three cats, and "entirely too much stuff." His publicly acknowledged passions include warbirds, following the Spartans and Phillies, making music, and natural philosophy. Further confessions can be found at his Web home: www.sff.net/people/K-Mac

Don't miss the next book
by Michael Kube-McDowell!
Coming out in 2003—

FRAGMENTS

A glittery swirl of snow entered the old cabin with Paula Dennison. It fell to the bare floor of the barren room in silence as the two women faced each other for the first time.

"You're a Monitor," said Shaina, rising slowly from a table covered with nethack gear. "You were in Vermont."

Dennison set the stained aluminum case down beside her and tugged off her gloves. "Yes. And I should have caught you then. It usually doesn't take me this long."

"We could keep it going, if you like," Shaina said lightly. "Tag—you're it."

Dennison did not smile. "Why do you do this? Why risk so much for so little? All those outlaw files, the old VR's—no one would miss them. No one cares."

"I care."

"Do you know what's in them?"

"Beautiful things. Useful things."

Dennison took a step closer. "You *don't* know, do you? You don't have a Reed set."

"Tell me, do most people just confess when you show up?"

"I'm not Monitoring now," she said. "I broke the link to Homeland twenty klicks from here. Check."

Shaina's fingertips danced in the air. "Why?"

"You don't have a Reed," she repeated. "You've never seen the eggs. So—you don't know who you are."

"I'm Pirate Jenny," Shaina said, glancing at her display. When she looked up again, Dennison had opened the case. "Why would you go offlink with me? What do you want?"

The Monitor held out a headset. "I want to find out who you are. Do you?"